Praise for Barbara Wood

"Another winner by Wood . . . A fun, exciting novel for public libraries."

—*Lincoln Journal*

"Wood shows herself a wizard at juggling action and romance, maintaining the momentum and sparkle of both . . . Bright, slick and pleasing."

—*Kirkus Reviews*

"Wood's skill as a writer of well-crafted, impressively researched romances is growing."

—*Publishers Weekly*

"A master storyteller. She never fails to leave the reader enthralled."

—Elizabeth Forsythe Hailey, author of *A Woman of Independent Means*

"Barbara Wood is an entertainer."

—*Washington Post Book World*

"An accomplished storyteller."

—John Jakes, *New York Times* bestselling author

"Wood makes her fiction come alive with authentic detailing and highly memorable characters."

—*Booklist*

CURSE THIS HOUSE

Other Books By

BARBARA WOOD

Virgins of Paradise

The Dreaming

Green City in the Sun

Soul Flame

Vital Signs

Domina

The Watch Gods

Childsong

Night Trains

Yesterday's Child

Hounds and Jackals

The Divining

Books By

KATHRYN HARVEY

Butterfly

Stars

Private Entrance

CURSE THIS HOUSE

BARBARA WOOD

TURNER

Turner Publishing Company

200 4th Avenue North • Suite 950
Nashville, Tennessee 37219

445 Park Avenue • 9th Floor
New York, NY 10022

www.turnerpublishing.com

Curse This House

Cover design by Gina Binkley
Interior design by Mike Penticost

Library of Congress Cataloging-in-Publication Data

Wood, Barbara, 1947-
Curse this house / Barbara Wood.
p. cm.
ISBN 978-1-59652-867-3
I. Title.
PS3573.O5877C87 2012
813'.54--dc23
2012006381

Printed in the United States of America
12 13 14 15 16 17 18—0 9 8 7 6 5 4 3 2 1

This book is lovingly dedicated to my mother, Ruth Reta, a sweet, beautiful, and sensitive person.

Suddenly I felt a chill run down my spine. This was not due to the past but caused by something real and in the present. My shoulders shivered inadvertently. The sudden feeling came over me that I was no longer alone in the coppice. My eyes quickly searched about. This was absurd, for I saw no one, heard no sound. Yet I was certain I was being watched.

Feeling frightened and courageous at the same time, I managed the strength to call out, "Who is there?"

I listened. Only the wind whistled overhead and at the periphery of this tiny wood . . .

CURSE THIS HOUSE

CHAPTER 1

As soon as I saw the place, with the cold wind fighting for possession of my cloak and bonnet, I wondered if I had made a mistake. Standing at last before the house after so many years did not trigger the memories I had hoped it would. Indeed, as I stood in the gathering storm and looked up at that forbidding old mansion, not the slightest glimmer from the past came back to me.

I was having second thoughts. Maybe I should not have come. True, this was the house where I was born and that I was a Pemberton, that my father was born here and his father before him; yet what other claim could I lay upon it, since I could not remember the years I had spent here, or even the people who lived here?

The people . . . I continued to stand in the thrashing wind, listening to the sound of the wheels of the carriage as it disappeared down the drive. I stared with numb face and hands at the old Elizabethan house and wondered: What about the people here? Who were they and why could I not remember them? And, after all these years, how would they receive me?

Then I thought of the letter. Such a surprise it had been to receive in the post an envelope of fine foolscap and bearing a twopenny Victoria "blue." Since it had been addressed only to my mother, I had taken it up to her room while she slept, and laid it at her bedside, thinking to point it out to her after she awoke. That evening, however, when I had gone up to her room, I had found the letter gone and no mention of it from my mother. She must have had her reasons, and as she was very unwell at the time, I decided not to question her about it.

I found the letter a week later while going through her few possessions after the funeral. Why she had kept it I will never know, yet I know now why she had not wanted to tell me of its contents. However, as I alit from the hansom that day to fight the wind for my cloak, I had not the slightest intuition of the bizarre path that letter would lead me down.

For if I had known, I would never have returned to Pemberton Hurst.

It was a bold step I took, coming back this way, and I was armed with little more than a puzzling letter and the memory of my mother having spoken only barely and strangely of this place. As my eyes beheld the mansion now, they also saw again my mother's face as she used to regard me from time to time with a queer expression. It was a cryptic look that came over her and one that I had caught several times—as though she were searching my face for something. As though expecting to find something there. When I finally questioned her about it in my older years, she had merely replied, "You're a Pemberton."

So I knew I was in some important way connected with this house and, indeed, that I had once even lived here; yet my mind was a blank. And my mother, in our 20 years in the slums of London, had spoken despairingly little about this place. But now I had the letter. So I came back.

There was another reason for my hesitation that gloomy day, for as I stood before the Hurst examining my thin courage for coming here, I recalled also the bits and pieces of legends I had overheard about the place. The cloak of evil that supposedly hung over the Hurst. Stories of witchery and haunting. Tales that the local peasants spun on dreary nights and that caused gentlefolk to stay away. And yet, as my eyes scanned that gray old edifice and my mind recalled those stories overheard on the train and at the village inn, all I saw before me was simply a beautiful old Georgian mansion, reliquary of a better age.

Thus did the house appear to me that dying winter day in 1857 as I stood before it in my poke bonnet, crinoline, and unmanageable cloak. The house was grand and impressive, albeit gloomy and the grounds down from it most overgrown. Had I said Georgian? To a degree, yes, but its having been built originally in Tudor days, the Georgian was the latest, most recognizable style, while underneath it remained the Elizabethan and Queen Anne. It was an elegant, staid old house that was an easy match for those noble mansions found along Park Lane in London. But, oddly, the grounds were deplorable. Almost as if untended. The forecourt offered little to impress the eye: a gravel drive, brown-ivied lattices, unruly grass, and barren trees. Although it was merely a neglected bit of landscape, there was something wild and unharnessed in its appearance, and it seemed almost to boast of a dignified freedom that challenged anyone to curb it. The trees encroaching upon the drive's edge were savage things, rustling in the wind and sending down pieces of dead leaf and twig. The decayed flower beds defied the hand of man and had returned to their natural state of clods and weeds. Birds shrieked in the eaves overhead. The sun dropped suddenly behind the horizon. Pemberton Hurst began to take on the character that local legends ascribed to it.

I was becoming more hesitant at this point, and apprehensive. Now that I was here after so many years, face-to-face as it were, something held me back. Somehow, in the warmth of my London flat with my cat and teakettle, the idea of coming to stay at a divine old mansion had been intriguing. And on the train, I had entertained visions of opulent dinners and blazing fireplaces. But then I had received odd looks at the East Wimsley train station. The name Pemberton had evoked uncomfortable reactions. Even the hansom driver had been reluctant to bring me here. And now, standing in awe before the shadowy old edifice, I was beginning to wonder if my expectations weren't to suffer some disappointment.

But my need to go in overcame these small fears. I was full of questions that required answers, and it seemed the Hurst was the only place to find them. Even more than this, however, was my need to belong to a family again.

Twenty years before, in the same year Princess Victoria was crowned Queen of England, I had been suddenly, rudely snatched out of my home, deprived of my family, and taken away to live among strangers.

This was the real reason for my being there that day, mounting each step cautiously, carrying a bag with one hand, and holding my cloak closed with the other. I needed to see my family again, no matter what strangers they would be to me now, and to claim a little of my past before embarking upon the future.

Therefore did I stand at last, 20 years later, on the threshold of the house in which I was born, about to meet the people who were as close to me in blood as brother and sister, and I eagerly anticipated warm welcomes, happy embraces, and long hours of reminiscences.

However, pausing before the ancient, worn oak doors, I was dismayed to find that, so far, not one single shred of memory had returned.

Weren't steps usually a favorite place for children to play? Then why, as I stood poised and ready to slam the great door knocker, could I not recall having played here with my brother Thomas? This environment should have triggered a rush of memory; why did it persist upon being so totally alien that it was almost as if I had never been here before?

I released the knocker for a last moment of thought: I could turn away now from this house of strangers and return to the London I knew and loved and join my friends again; I knew none of the people in this house; not even a shadow of a memory could tell me what they might be like. And how would they receive me, a stranger who bore their name and shared their blood? Would they be strangers, or would they throw out their arms in joyful welcome?

Great-aunt Sylvia's letter came to mind just then, reminding me that it was, in a way, an invitation, that these people were in fact expecting me. Now that my mother was dead—my mother who had lived in this house and had married here—it was my duty both to her and to the Pembertons to answer the letter's call.

Perhaps I should have telegraphed, I belatedly realized, as I stood before the door. Or even sent a simple letter to tell them I should come in my mother's stead. But I had thought it improper to announce the news of her death to the Pembertons by impersonal post. It was the right thing to tell them in person. And Great-aunt Sylvia (whoever she was) deserved at the least a personal acknowledgment of her request.

Swallowing the last self-doubt and straightening my shoulders, I rapped the massive door knocker against the wood and discovered that my palm was perspiring.

Years passed before the door opened, but when it did, a burst of light fell out and caused me to close my eyes for an instant. When I opened them, seeing before me a generous silhouette with a corona about her head, I said, "How do you do? I am Leyla Pemberton. Would you please tell my aunt Sylvia that I am here?"

Such a silence followed that I wondered if I had spoken loudly enough. After all, a terrific wind raged about me, and the trees made quite a noise. But when I was about to repeat my words, the silhouette spoke in a gruff voice, "You're Leyla Pemberton?" almost in an accusing tone.

"Yes, I am. Now if you will please announce me to my family and then allow me to step inside—"

At once, the rotund woman fell back to make way for me. I hurried inside before the wind carried off my bonnet, then made quick gestures with my hands in an effort to make myself a bit more presentable. The fussing ceased, however, when I glanced up at the woman and found that I was being stared at by two pale blue eyes and a gaping, incredulous mouth.

"Is something wrong?" I asked in mild alarm.

"Leyla Pemberton?" the woman replied in a whisper.

"What have I said? Only my name." I wondered if this woman should also be part of the distant memory that was so strangely blank. Had I known this plump Teuton in my early childhood? Had we sung songs together or danced about a tree? "Please announce my arrival to Aunt Sylvia. I believe she is expecting me."

The mouth closed, and the eyes receded into their sockets. With the shock subsiding, the woman was better able to gather herself together. "You say Miss Sylvia is expecting you?" The accent was faintly Prussian. Sylvia sounded like *Sylfia.*

"Yes, she is."

Footsteps into the entrance hall quickly broke the spell and were accompanied by the words, "Who was at the door?" A second woman, not as heavy and not as domestic, obviously a lady of the house, also stopped in a freeze and let her mouth drop open.

"Jenny!" she whispered.

"No, I'm not Jenny. I'm her daughter, Leyla."

This second woman's eyes flittered to the housekeeper, and I saw a brief, unspoken communication pass between them. "Leyla?" she said in a whisper. "You're Leyla?"

I could not discern where her emphasis lay—whether she was saying, "*You're* Leyla?" or "You're *Leyla?*"—but whichever, either way I had never before seen someone in such a state of surprise. Surely Aunt Sylvia had written for the entire family, and they had been expecting me for some time.

But no, it was my mother to whom the letter had been written and therefore my mother whom they were expecting.

"Yes, I'm Leyla, Jenny's daughter. I suppose you hadn't thought I would come in her stead. Forgive me, that was very unthinking of me—"

"In her stead!" The second woman blinked in disbelief. "Dear child, we weren't expecting you *or* your mother. This is such a shock!" And her hand flew theatrically to her breast.

"I'm sorry. I truly am."

"Why, we'd never thought to see you again. Leyla, Leyla. Merciful Heaven, what a surprise!"

With a little more grace and breeding than the housekeeper, who continued to stare with an open mouth, this woman gradually gathered up her gravity and came forward with a hand extended. A thin smile stretched her lips, and the voice came out low and warm. Yet the eyes remained hard. "Please forgive my rudeness."

"Are you Aunt Sylvia?"

Her eyes flicked again to the housekeeper. "No, dear, I am not Sylvia. But look at you, little Leyla after all these years!"

So I had been wrong. Her surprise was not in seeing me instead of my mother but rather in seeing me at all. I wondered why Great-aunt Sylvia had not mentioned her letter to the others.

We two embraced in a perfunctory manner, as though acting a scene in a play. Then I stepped back a little to take another look at this relative of mine, who was beginning to cast a rather ominous feeling over me.

She had a comfortably homely face with slightly exophthalmic eyes, and her middle-aged figure was tastefully dressed in a brown velvet frock with the new fashionable flounces and dome-shaped crinoline and a waistline that tapered down to a V. Her hair was fashionably parted in the center and drawn up behind in a high knot with ringlets over the ears. By the facial wrinkles and sag of her jaw line, and by the profuse gray in her hair, I judged her to be in her 50s, possibly close to 60. As I knew not one member of the Pemberton family, I had no idea just then whom it was I addressed.

As though reading my thoughts, she extended a hand again and said, "I'm Anna Pemberton, your aunt and your mother's sister-in-law. You probably don't remember me . . ." her voice faded but quickly returned, ". . . do you?"

"Not at all. Should I?"

Her little laugh was forced but pleasant. The other woman, tubby behind her apron, continued to stare incredulously at me and probably required a specific order to go away. Yet it was not so much this servant's disquieting attitude toward me as a slight incongruity in Aunt Anna that sent a tiny alarm off in the back of my head. That Cheshire grin, thin lips rubricated by cosmetic paint, was all a disguise to cover her true reaction to my arrival. Despite her smile and handshake and words of welcome, Aunt Anna was clearly not at all pleased to see me.

"Gertrude, some tea at once in the drawing room." She flicked an impatient hand, and the woman obeyed. "Leave your bag here; a man will take it up to your room. In the meantime, you must rest. How it managed to get so chilly out!"

As much as her offer of tea and warmth appealed to me, I felt a pressing need to tend to one thing first. "May I see my aunt Sylvia, please?"

Anna was reticent, to say the least. For the briefest moment did her smile flinch, then she was at a loss for words. And so we stood in the gas-lit entrance hall, two strangers who should otherwise have so much to speak of, so much news to relate, and yet who stood aloof of one another, hesitant to make a move. Clearly, Aunt Anna wanted to know what I was doing here, for she had obviously known nothing of Sylvia's letter. At the same time, it was also evident that the subject of my great-aunt was a trifle delicate.

"Please," she said softly, "let's go into the drawing room. You must be desperate to sit down and take off that bonnet. Tell me, were you on a train?"

I had to acquiesce. "The Greenwich line to Brighton. But I disembarked at East Wimsley and took a hansom."

Aunt Anna shuddered. "Horrible things, trains! I've never been on one myself, never intend to be. I always say, if God had intended for us to travel in that manner, He'd have given us wheels."

I smiled despite myself as I followed her from the entrance hall and into a hallway that was barely lit by small gas lamps overhead. As we passed ornate coatracks and carved umbrella stands, my eyes moved quickly to take in every detail. Aunt Anna walked slowly, her face betraying her effort to decide what to say to me next, and I took the opportunity to find if this high-ceilinged hallway would be at all familiar to me. In our brief passage through, it was not, and all too soon, we came to an elegant room that seemed all fire and light. So typical of our age was this drawing room furnished with the heaviest ornate furniture: dark carved woods and horsehair upholstery. A pianoforte stood against one wall, music opened upon it. Papier-mâché tables littered with flower vases, brass candlesticks, and bijou boxes took up most of the available floor space, so that I had to take care that my full skirt did not cause a disaster. On the mantelpiece, at the center of a mélange of knickknacks, shadow boxes, and Staffordshire figurines, stood a straddle-legged clock that was about to chime five o'clock.

We sat on a sofa after Aunt Anna lifted the cloak from my shoulders, and we exchanged platitudes about the inclement weather. During this time, I saw my aunt's eyes make a rapid appraisal of her niece, taking in my worn leather boots, my practical dress with the old-fashioned tight sleeves, my hair coiled over my ears in two thick plaits. Clearly, I must have seemed a church mouse to her, wearing yesterday's fashions and mending on my stockings. Yet the one feature that seemed to hold her interest above all was my face, for she stared at it intently. Indeed, I felt she was searching my face for something in particular; she studied each aspect as she spoke about the weather: my black and heavily lashed eyes, my slightly too-large nose, my small mouth, and the faint cleft at the tip of my chin. As she studied me, so did I watch her, hoping to see a change of expression that might give away that she had found what she was looking for.

"So, ah, you've come to visit us then, have you?" she said when tea came. "Cream and sugar?" The silver service was magnificent. It was very old, and I wondered if I had ever drunk from these cups before. "Is that what brought you to the Hurst, a visit? You see, we so rarely have guests in the house anymore and therefore keep no rooms in readiness. If only we had known . . . Ah well, possibly you didn't have time to telegraph. There was no need for you to take a cab from the station; we would have been pleased to send a carriage for you. And then we could have received you in a more fitting manner. You must understand what a surprise this is!" The silver spoon clinked loudly around the edges of her cup. "Such memories this house must have for you, Leyla!" As Aunt Anna sipped the tea, she seemed to relax and become more animated. "How exciting it must be for you after all these years!"

"Yes, exciting . . ." I said slowly. There were no portraits on the walls, no daguerreotypes in frames to give me a clue as to what the rest of my family looked like. The fact was, I had not even an idea of just how many people lived within these walls or if they would remember me. Somehow, an intuition not unlike a warning gave me the presence of mind not to let on to this aunt of mine that I was more of a stranger than she suspected. At least for now, until I knew her—and all the others—better.

"You were such a darling child," she prattled on. "And how like your mother you are now! Why, when I saw you there in the entrance hall, I thought you were Jennifer Pemberton."

"Thank you." I was truly flattered. My mother had been quite a beauty in her day.

"Tell me . . ." She stirred her tea thoughtfully. "How *is* your dear mother these days?"

I dropped my head and stared into my teacup. Two months had passed and yet it was as painful as if it had been only yesterday. "My mother is dead."

"Oh. I *am* sorry." Was that a touch of relief in her voice? "Her husband and my husband were brothers, so I always felt like a sister to her. We spent many happy days together, your mother and I." Now I raised my eyes again to this loquacious woman. My mother had never, as far back as I could remember, mentioned my aunt Anna.

"Your uncle Henry will be so thrilled to see you! He and Theo—your cousin Theodore—used to have a nickname for you. Do you remember it? They called you 'Bunny' because you used to hop about and pretend you were a hare. You were five years old then, Leyla. It was a long time ago."

Oddly, no memory of this came back. No memory of anything at all before my sixth birthday, as though I had been born in London and not here. Many years ago, as a questioning child, I had asked my mother why I could not remember my baby days as so many other people seemed to. Her cryptic reply had been simply, "It is because of what happened." Having apparently said too much already, she would say nothing further, and the subject never came up again.

"And Cousin Martha remembers you. She was 12 when you were . . . ah, when you left." Aunt Anna's voice faded away and was replaced by my own questioning thoughts. Was I imagining it, or was this woman's manner terribly guarded? Her speech was stilted and hesitant, as though she were being careful to say the right thing—or, more accurately, not to say the wrong thing. She dropped an extra sugar into her cup and stirred noisily again.

"Grandmother will not be able to receive you yet, so you'll have time to freshen up."

My eyebrows raised. So I had a grandmother, too. In the span of only a few minutes, I had been transformed from an orphan to a woman with a large family of grandmother, great-aunt, uncle, aunt, and two cousins.

Aunt Anna looked away from me now, forcing her eyes to stare disinterestedly into the fire. I recognized this at once to be forced and that, rather than being the relaxed hostess she wished to appear, Aunt Anna was quite involved in how to handle the situation properly. After short consideration to her next words, she fabricated a little smile and said with forced flippancy,

"And if you should happen to encounter your cousin Colin, it would be best if you just politely excused yourself."

So I had *three* cousins. "Why?"

"Well, Colin is—how shall I put it?" She laughed a little. "Rather on the eccentric side. We love him dearly, but he's a bit of a jackanapes, if you know what I mean. The rascal has no manners, and it would hardly be suitable for him to meet you before the others do. You'll meet him later, after Theodore and Martha. That way you'll be . . . ah . . . prepared for him."

I said, "Thank you," without sincerity. Not knowing this woman at all, I could not tell if I were reading her accurately. Was she protecting me from Colin, or Colin from me?

"And Aunt Sylvia?" I persisted.

"In time, dear child. You will meet the entire family, as I am sure you are most anxious to. And of course when they hear who has come to visit, they too will be eager to see you again. After twenty years, Leyla, it will be interesting to hear what has become of you. I see your tea is finished. Please let me take you up to your room. You must be exhausted. Then I shall go look for Theo. He'll be anxious to see you."

Our petticoats rustled as we rose. Firelight glowed warmly on our faces. Beyond the heavily draped windows, the raging wind blew more fiercely than ever. I had the odd sensation that I was detached from my body and watching the scene as if this room were a stage and I, the audience. I saw before me a dozy hearth cluttered with fashionable taste and signs of affluence. I saw two women engaged in a mute confrontation: one dressed in the latest from Paris with grace and refinement, the other garbed in her simplest, with gestures learned among the struggling London middle class. And I wondered, in my brief moment of objectivity, what on earth these two women had to do with each other.

"Tell me, Leyla dear, how is London? Still noisy and sooty? Last time I was there was in '51 for the Great Exhibition. For one breathless week, Mr. Pemberton and Theo and I were jostled hither and thither, keeping up a relentless pace of touring the Abbey, the Tower, and Regent's Park Zoo. We were fed the most abominable oddities from all nations—something called ice cream as I recall. Horrible stuff. And jelly! Fruit-flavored stuff served in jars and put on top of pudding. Have you heard of it?"

"I've heard of jelly, but I've never tasted it."

As I walked at her side and heard only bits of her monologue about "that breathless week in London," I kept my eyes moving about me. The floors were mostly carpeted, which muffled our footsteps, and many walls were hung with tapestries. Huge potted plants lurked in shadowy corners, and oil lamps flickered at intervals. We mounted the stairs toward the bedrooms above, and all about me—though I searched keenly—there was still not a single family portrait.

"We have gas only in a few rooms and in the main hallway. I suppose in London everything is gas now, even the streets, I understand. Theo insisted we have some of it; it's safer, he says, but Grandmother thinks gas is the Devil's work. She is not for anything modern. Likes to live in the past."

Why this scarcity of portraiture? In this age of photogenic drawings (or "photographs," as some people called them), why did I not see the usual gallery of pictures that was present in every home, humble or grand? Not the smallest, simplest portrait of a Pemberton anywhere.

"I'll put you down the hall from us. There's a spare bedroom, but it's quite comfortable. It has a half-tester and a new hip bath from Paris. This was Grandmother's one concession to modernism: taking a bath in the bedroom instead of the kitchen. I find it rather pleasant. Have you ever done it?"

I shook my head.

"We have soap now, too. My, my, how times are changing. Here we are."

My aunt continued her litany as we entered the bedroom, and I wondered if the endless chatter weren't to avoid unpleasant topics . . . as though concealment were primary.

Yes, it was a beautiful bedroom with Tudor ceiling and mullioned windows. Looking glasses were in abundance; a fine old vanity covered almost an entire wall; there was the promised half-tester bed and a roaring fire. Water sat in the porcelain pitcher, and fresh towels hung beside it. My one bag stood by the bed.

Trying to be the gracious hostess and yet apparently in a dreadful hurry, Aunt Anna backed away through the door, rubbing her hands and saying, "I'll send Theo into the library. You can meet him down there when you're ready. If you need anything, there's a pull by your bed. See you in a little while." She started to close the door. "And, oh, you won't forget, will you? Colin? If you should happen to run into him—well, you won't." Her hands fluttered like birds. "Theo will find you first. I'll see to that."

The door closed gently, and I stared at it for some time. Hardly the welcome I had expected, but then, considering that they did not know I was coming, it was certainly a good effort. Aunt Anna's anxiety might have been due to her age, or possibly to my resemblance to my mother. After all, to be suddenly flung back twenty years without notice would unbalance anyone for a moment.

Casting off the odd feeling I had about my talkative aunt, I began to move languidly about the room and to make it as close to home as possible. After my mother's death, I had let go of our London flat, had either sold the furnishings or given them to friends, and had brought with me only my wardrobe, personal effects, and those mementos that I could never part with. Placed now about the room in prominent positions, these "valuables" made the bedroom a little more mine. The daguerreotype of Mother sat atop the fireplace next to a Wardian case of ferns and a seashell box. On the table by my bed, I laid three books: *Persuasion* by Jane Austen, *Tancred* by Benjamin Disraeli, and the Holy Bible. On the vanity table before its huge looking glass, I set a souvenir guidebook to Cremorne Gardens (to remind me of very happy days), and by the washbasin I placed a small decanter of rose-scented cologne.

This last had been a gift from Edward Champion, a man whom I dearly loved and whom I intended to marry.

With the room a little more homelike, my dresses hanging up, my face washed, and my hair brushed out and plaited again, I felt worlds better. Yes, the train ride had been wretched, but not by any means when compared with what the same journey would have been by carriage. And, yes, I was tired and hungry. But more than anything, I was thrilled to be part of a family again, to be back in the house where I had been born, and to be embarking on a whole new future of sharing and belonging.

If only I had known how far from the truth this was.

When I descended the stairs a few moments later, I was struck by the phenomenal silence of the house. It was nearly seven o'clock and pitch black outside, while inside the atmosphere was strangely museum-like. My footsteps were muted by the thick carpeting, and soft halo glows shimmered at each oil lamp. The dark wood paneling of the walls, the tall looming pieces of furniture, the widespread plants in their massive pots all combined to give an air of quiet austerity, of churchlike severity.

The flounces of my skirt brushed along the rug in whispers. My tall shadow followed me down the stairs. I felt that, if I were to speak to anyone now, it would be in whispers.

And again, becoming more and more poignant, there was the fact of the absence of family portraits in the house.

I passed the drawing room, peering in briefly to find it deserted, and wound my way eventually into what must be the library. Here was a mausoleum of books, tiers upon tiers of them, all towering over a small room of easy chairs and the smell of leather. A fire gave off welcome warmth and gas lights forced the gloom into the corners. As I stepped in, I saw at once that I was not alone. The room was occupied.

Seated casually in a *prie-dieu* with his Hessian-booted legs stretched before him and hands clasped over his chest was a man of about 35 staring into the fire. Yet, as I neared, his concentration seemed not to be so intent, for he quickly glanced up at me and was neither startled nor disturbed by my entry. Indeed, his manner was as if he had been expecting me.

Determined to start off on the right foot with this cousin of mine and to avoid the awkwardness that seemed to have sprouted between me and Aunt Anna, I took a deep breath and approached him. "Hello, Theo," I said in my friendliest tone. "I'm Leyla, your long-lost cousin. Aunt Anna told me I was to meet you in here and"—I grinned broadly—"to avoid at all costs running into eccentric Colin. Which I am to assume would be a disaster."

He stood straight and tall, towering above me like the bookcases around us, and said in a dry tone, "How do you do? I'm not Theodore. I'm Colin."

CHAPTER 2

IN MY ACUTE EMBARRASSMENT, I COULD THINK OF NOTHING TO say, not even the required apology. Instead, I stood with flushed cheeks, staring in great dismay at the man I had so rudely offended. His eyes matched mine stare for stare. I noticed they were pale green with gold flecks. The lashes surrounding them, and the eyebrows that had come together, were the same color as the long waves on his head and down his neck—sort of a delicate teakwood. Like most young men of his day—and I judged him to be in his early 30s—Cousin Colin wore his hair moderately long, un-smeared with Macassar oil, with long sideburns. His nose was prominent and straight, his mouth set grimly, his jaw heavy and square.

Curiously, there were no Pemberton traits obvious in him—not the thick lashes or the cleft chin that my mother had once said marked me as one of "that family." And then, reflexively, I went on to compare him to Edward Champion, who was a dashingly handsome man with wild black hair and an aquiline nose and whom I loved more than anything else. He was all I had in this world (except for this strange collection of relatives) and he was ever present in my thoughts. Comparing Colin now with Edward seemed to leave little contest. Although his face might be charming when he smiled and his posture was quite striking, this cousin of mine was no match for Edward.

Somehow, I managed to find my voice. "Oh, I am terribly sorry. How rude of me."

He shrugged. "How were you supposed to know? It's like Aunt Anna to thoroughly muddle things up. Have a seat, won't you? We're frightfully proper in this house, you know: supper at eight o'clock sharp, whether one is totally without appetite or on the brink of starvation. Which, after traveling from London by train, you must be one or the other."

"You seem to know about me already."

"News travels fast in this house. At any rate"—he returned to the *prie-dieu,* stretched his legs before him again, and crossed his feet—"you'll soon find that out. No one keeps a secret here."

"Are you Theo's brother?"

"What!" Colin emitted a humorless laugh. "The blackguard is my cousin, just as he is your cousin, just as I am your cousin."

"I see."

"No, I don't think you do. For a Pemberton, you don't know much about the Pembertons, do you? I dare say your mother wouldn't have spoken much of us, sung our praises and all. You see, it all goes back to Sir John Pemberton, who's been dead ten years now, and his wife, Abigail. Sir John and Abigail had three sons: Henry, Richard, and Robert. Henry is Theo's father. Richard, *my* father. And Robert was *your* father."

"And Martha?"

"Martha is my sister."

"How is Aunt Sylvia related to us all, then?"

"Abigail's unmarried sister. She came to live in this house, oh, I'd guess 50 or 60 years ago, when Abigail married Sir John."

"I see." I folded my hands as I assimilated all the information. "I shall be looking forward to meeting all of them. Henry and Theo and your father—"

Colin's face darkened. "My father is dead. As is my mother. In fact, of the three sons born to Sir John, only one remains. Henry, Theo's father. That leaves Aunt Anna and Aunt Jenny of that generation."

"Yes, well." My voice grew small. "Jenny is gone, too."

"Oh?" He did not seem surprised. "Is that why you came here then, because you're all alone now?" It seemed more an accusation than a question, with something of mockery in the tone, so that I began to grow impatient with Cousin Colin.

"I came here for personal reasons. Among them a desire to see my family again. And the house where I was born."

Now he turned his full attention to me, and I saw gravity in his eyes. All flippancy gone, he said, "Are we at all how you remember us?"

Looking into his pale-green eyes, I knew that he was not asking that exactly. What Colin really wanted to know was: Did I remember them at all?

Evasively, I replied, "Twenty years makes many changes in people."

"Profoundly put, my dear cousin. That day 20 years ago, I was a rascal of 14, and you were only five. How it distresses me to see the love affair did not last."

"Love affair!"

"You adored me then, Leyla, and used to follow me about like a little puppy."

His words made me blush. At the same time, they saddened me, hinting of happy days I had spent but could not remember. It was also distressing that, in the farthest dark reaches of my mind, in all my hours of searching and futile tries to bring back my past, there was not one fragment of memory of Colin Pemberton.

"Behind the house—I don't know if you remember it—lies a rambling field of several acres that Aunt Anna euphemistically calls our lawn. Somewhere past the center of it, as it rolls down away from the Hurst, stands a small coppice of acacias, and it was the favorite spot of all us children when we were small. At its center, there lie the tired remnants of an old feudal castle—oh, eleventh century or so—and we all fancied it to be our private domain. Do you remember?" His eyes were hard upon me.

I shook my head.

"At first, it was only Theo and I who went there to play, he and I being four years apart, but when he outgrew the games, I was still young enough, and Martha joined me, along with your brother Thomas and your little self.

In and amongst the trees and ruins, you used to pretend you were a rabbit or some such creature, bounding about in pure abandon. Tell me, Cousin Leyla, are you still like that?"

But I had not heard. My mind was lost again in imaginary visions of four happy children playing carelessly in the woods as though no such thing as tomorrow existed. Unfortunately, that was all it was, a fabrication of my mind, for I was seeing it as Colin described it and not as I remembered it. I remembered none of it, just as I had no memory of his sister Martha or my brother Thomas.

Then I heard his voice gently say, "You don't remember, do you?"

"I beg your pardon?" His green eyes with their brunnescent lashes seemed to be watching me intently. "Oh, I was very young then. Do *you* recall much of the first five years of your life?"

"Yes, quite a bit."

I looked into the fire and felt sharply uncomfortable in my cousin's presence. Just as with Aunt Anna, the odd notion returned that they were only speaking half-sentences, or not speaking what they were thinking. Somehow, I felt Colin was thinking something other than what his words said and that he was forcing a flippant air.

That made two of them now, Anna and Colin, who put me ill at ease, and three if one counted the German housekeeper, who had stared at me as if I were a ghost from the past.

Impulsively, I rose and walked to the fireplace, where an enormous looking glass hung. Seeing my reflection I could also see the room behind me and Colin in the *prie-dieu,* idly examining his fingernails. Yes, it was a very forced air.

Then I took a long look at myself. I suppose, to these people, I was a ghost from the past. There was a lot of my mother in my face, with black hair accenting the paleness of my skin. Yet my lips were gray and colorless, and my eyes had lost their luster. My mother had been a beauty, and I was really not. Especially not now with grief and strain taking their toll in my face. Had I appeared this way at the train station when Edward had begged, pleaded with me not to go? Had he looked at this blanched face and sworn that my beauty would comfort him on lonely nights? Dear Edward. How unlike him to make public protestations of affection. Dear polite, punctilious Edward, who was so thoroughly the gentleman compared to this boor in the *prie-dieu.*

Colin caught me smiling, and I think he was angry for a second. "Private joke?"

I turned to face him. "Thinking about something pleasant."

"The past?"

"My fiancé."

"Fiancé!" His legs instantly uncrossed.

"Yes, does it surprise you?"

"And he let you come here alone, unescorted?"

I went back to my chair and sat gracefully in it. "Upon my insistence only. Edward dreaded seeing me go. But I had to. Just once, since Mother was now dead and could not be hurt by it, and before I married to become Mrs. Champion, I had to see this house and this family again."

Colin formed a steeple with his index fingers and pressed them against his lips. I seemed to have presented him with an intriguing idea. He surprised me next by asking, "Why did you suppose your mother might be hurt by your visiting here?"

"I don't know . . . just a notion I had—"

"Did she speak of us much?"

"No, not at all."

"As though she wanted to forget we ever existed."

"Pardon me, Cousin, but I believe that is none of your concern. When my mother left here and went to London, she was entirely penniless and entirely on her own. With a five-year-old child and her virtue to protect, my mother struggled for many years as a seamstress for rich women who treated her worse than their own servants. She was a gentlewoman reduced to menial labor. My mother had married a Pemberton, and *I was* a Pemberton, and yet, for eight years, we lived in poverty while the Pembertons had"—I waved my arms about the room—"all this."

"Your bitterness is unwarranted, Cousin Leyla. You must remember that it was your mother who abandoned us; not we, her. Indeed, no one even knew where she went off to that day, leaving behind even her clothes and possessions. All we knew was that you and she had suddenly disappeared, never to be heard from again. Until today."

I sat glowering at my cousin, denying with my eyes the bitterness that I did truly feel. They had not searched; else they would have found us. They had not cared; else, in 20 years, they would have helped us.

Colin must have read all this in my angry gaze, for he asked in that quiet tone, "So, tell me, why did you come back?"

Before I could reply—for indeed my mouth was open and ready to spill out my loneliness, my longing for a birthright, my desire for a blood-family again—the library doors opened, and yet another stranger entered.

"Leyla! Oh, Leyla!" He rushed forward and seized my hands. "I'd recognize you anywhere. The image of Aunt Jenny! Welcome home!"

Cousin Theodore was exquisitely dressed in a wine-colored frock coat, white linen shirt and waistcoat, and black trousers. His hair was the color of mine, inky black, and his slightly exophthalmic eyes were encircled by thick lashes. The nose was a little oversized, and the chin displayed a faint cleft, exactly like mine. That this man was a Pemberton was doubtless.

"How do you do?"

Colin interrupted with, "Yes, Theo. A while ago, Leyla thought I was you and asked for my protection against our daft cousin Colin."

I blushed despite myself. "I really am sorry for that."

He shrugged again in his mannerless way, and with not another word, Cousin Colin strode from the room.

Theodore stared after him for a moment, then turned his attention to me. His mouth smiled, but his eyes did not. Apparently, this was the general order of things I was to expect from now on: my creating an ill ease with everyone I met. Nonetheless, of the four I had so far encountered, Theodore put forth the most effort to disguise his discomfort. He pumped my hands, spoke in a booming voice, and just generally filled the room with his presence.

Still, I did not remember him.

"I hate to ask you to excuse Colin, but I must. He's what you'd call the odd man out, doesn't quite fit into the family, if you know what I mean. More his mother's son than his father's. God knows where he picked up those beastly habits. Now sit down, Cousin, and let me pour you a glass of sherry."

I sat and watched him carefully decant the wine. His manner, under all the easygoing airs, was definitely stilted. Handing me a glass, he leaned a casual elbow on the mantelpiece and regarded me with curiosity as he sipped.

"Pardon me for staring," he said after a moment, "but seeing you has brought back such memories. I used to call you Bunny. Do you remember that? And you used to play in the coppice with the others. My God, how one forgets."

Cousin Theodore appeared to be approaching 40, which meant that, back then, he must have been near 20. Probably 18 or 19 when my mother and I left. It would seem logical that he had figured largely in my life at that time, and yet I could not remember him. His face was in many ways so like mine, and yet the slightly protruding eyes were those of Aunt Anna.

I was glad to be among my own blood relations again and anxious to be accepted as a member of the family. What I did not know at that time, as I shared my wine with Cousin Theo in the library, was that something had occurred before I left the Hurst 20 years ago to prevent this bizarre group from ever wanting me among them again. As far as I knew, my mother and I had left after the deaths of my father and brother and had simply never come back. I never knew why we had left so abruptly or why we had never returned, other than that my mother had been so grief-stricken. And I had never questioned her about it, for I knew she must have had her reasons to wish to eschew this house. Even now, smiling at Theo and relaxing before the fire, it did not occur to me to delve into that dark past that was now gone and buried. All I wanted was a family and a name. Then I could go on with my life, feeling a little more complete.

The time was soon to come, however, when I would start questioning the past and the events leading to my mother's departure from the Hurst.

"Is the House of Commons finished now?"

"Oh quite, but the clock tower is not yet complete. The bell cracked during a test. I believe they've decided on the name of Big Ben for it."

"Big Ben, eh? Very picturesque. I was in London six years ago and vowed never to return. My travels take me as far as Manchester—we've one cotton mill there—but that's about it. We Pembertons are not, ah, travelers."

I looked all about me and thought: With a home like this, who would ever want to go away?

"I suppose you're anxious to meet Grandmother, but that'll have to wait till tomorrow. She's been feeling poorly of late. Bad head cold. By the way, do you ever suffer from headaches?"

"No, not at all. Why?"

"So you'll meet her tomorrow when she's feeling better. News of your arrival quite upset Grandmother."

Grandmother . . . spoken with a certain reverence as though she were some sort of consecrated matriarch. "Well, actually I was more anxious to see Aunt Sylvia."

"What?" He was clearly astonished.

"Yes, well, it was she—" I was about to mention the letter but decided against it, "—who I remember the most." Which was not entirely untrue, since, before the letter, I hadn't known even one Pemberton name.

"How odd that you should want to see Aunt Sylvia."

"Why?"

Before he answered, a third person came into the room, someone who hovered at the threshold as if waiting to be invited in. Seeing Theodore's eyes flicker toward the door, I casually turned in that direction. In an instant, a flash of memory darted across my mind. I saw the face of a girl, a very pretty young girl with scarlet ribbons in her hair, and she wore a stunning lavender dress. My eyes wide in amazement, I slowly rose to my feet, nearly dropping the glass of wine, and heard myself whisper, "Martha." But this was no little girl in lavender satin. The woman who walked toward me with hands extended was older than I, at least 30, and dressed in a smart evening gown of pink brocade with rosebuds bordering the décolletage. Her waist was cinched with a low V, while her crinoline was vast and burgeoning. As she walked, I glimpsed the very stylish satin shoes that were heelless and milky-white stockings. Her hair, as though a model in a Paris magazine, was dressed high in a knot, with ringlets over her ears. In one hand, she carried a medium-sized carpetbag with violets woven against an oyster-white background. Several knitting needles protruded from it. A lovely fragrance wafted from her as she took my hand in hers.

"Hello, Leyla. Welcome home."

Of all my relatives, hers was the first tone of sincerity.

The little-girl vision faded, but I still saw before me a pretty woman and was immediately grateful to her for two things: the first, that she had offered me a sincerely warm greeting, and the second, that she had been the cause of my very first memory of Pemberton Hurst.

"Thank you, Martha."

"I'm sorry about your mother. Recent was it?"

"Two months ago."

"I remember her as being such a dear. How you do resemble her. But then you resemble your father, too. Uncle Robert was such a handsome man. Your face is half his and half Aunt Jenny's."

If I had not controlled myself then, tears would have sprung to my eyes. This was the first concrete bit of information I had about my father. I had never known what he looked like.

"We have so much to talk over, Leyla. So much to reminisce about—"

"Not so hasty, Martha dear," interrupted Theodore. "Sometimes reminiscences are best left unsaid."

For the briefest instant, her face clouded; then the shadow passed, and she was smiling freely again. "Of course. Leyla isn't interested in going over the past. What's gone is gone. We should talk about modern times and the latest fashions. You know, they say, next year, the crinoline will flatten in the front. What do you think of that, Leyla?"

The absurdity of the sudden change of subject put me at a loss to reply. I did not come back to this house of my birth after 20 years' absence, after the death of my mother and a harrowing train journey, to discuss the trend in ladies' skirts!

"Oh, I quite agree with you," she went on after I had said nothing. "It's difficult to imagine a half-crinoline after all these years!"

It was Theo; I could easily see that. His eyes were upon her like a hawk, watching her every word. I guessed that, after all, Martha was going to be another disappointment in a line of four. Five, if one counted Gertrude.

That left Uncle Henry, Grandmother, and Aunt Sylvia. And if Henry Pemberton were anything like his wife and son, I had little to expect there. And as I placed no great hopes in my 80-year-old, possibly senile grandmother, that meant Great-aunt Sylvia was my last hope for a truly warm reception. After all, she was the one who had sent the letter that brought me here.

"It's almost eight o'clock," said Theodore. "May I escort you ladies to the dining room?"

Colin and Aunt Anna were already there, murmuring quietly in front of the fire, while an array of shine and sparkle rose up from the table. That the Pembertons believed in comfort and convenience and coziness was apparent. No expense was spared on even the smallest detail throughout the house. And this grand dining room was no exception.

I say grand not because of size but because of contents. Set upon a massive mahogany table and ancient damask tablecloth were silver and china service fit for, I thought, Victoria and Albert. Amid bowls of fruit and domes of dried flowers, next to Aunt Anna and Martha in their enchanting gowns, I felt such a plain sparrow.

The chair at the head of the table was left vacant, although a setting had been placed before it, while the first two on either side were occupied at once by Uncle Henry and Theodore, as though these were their regular places. Next to them went Aunt Anna, beside her husband, and Martha across. I took a seat at Anna's right, while Colin sat opposite me next to his sister. This left the chair at the other end, between me and Colin, unoccupied and without a place setting. The two chairs at the ends, I surmised, must belong to the elders of the clan—Grandmother Abigail and Great-aunt Sylvia, and I anxiously awaited the arrival of the latter.

Before I took my chair, Uncle Henry came around and encircled me in an embrace. "Bunny," he murmured. "So good to have you back. Don't rush off again so quickly next time." I had wanted a good look at his face, but he gave me no opportunity, scurrying around to take his seat. I know that Uncle Henry's face would be very like my father's, and I had a need to look upon it. Like the others, except Martha, this man stirred no memories.

We all smiled comfortably at one another over the flowers and flickering candles, but as we fluffed out our linen napkins and sipped some wine, I sensed that a great deal of the nonchalance was forced. In my eagerness to explain away this incongruity, I told myself that I was really a stranger to these people and that it would take time for them to accept me as one of the family. The nagging thought that their discomfort might be caused by something else—and I knew not what—I pressed conveniently to the bottom of my mind.

Two maids began bringing in the food—bowls of thick soup, heaps of bread and butter, plates of steaming meat pies and spicy gravies, vegetables grown in our own garden. We ate in silence, all of us, which I supposed to be a regular family practice. Once in a while, I caught Colin's eyes upon me—again that searching look—and I knew he was angry about my first words to him in the library. Occasionally, Martha smiled across at me, but she too was disguising her real feelings. Except, with Martha, it was not the same uneasiness I felt with the others; instead, my quiet cousin looked at me with eyes of sadness and pity. Pity for what? I wondered.

Over a tasty pudding dessert, the constraint lifted a little, and my relatives began to speak.

It was Uncle Henry who broke the silence by saying, "It seems the Americans are having more and more difficulty getting along. Wonder how long it will last before a civil war breaks out."

Theodore replied, "It's the slavery business, Father. Why, an Act of Parliament abolished it in our colonies back in '33. It's terribly uncivilized of them not to match our example. After all."

"Hang it all, man," said Uncle Henry. "It's not the slaves I'm worried about. It's the cotton. If the Americans engage in war, our cotton supply will be threatened."

I listened to this with interest, recalling Theo's mention of a cotton mill in Manchester. Was this how the Pembertons made their great wealth? Such common knowledge it must be, and yet I knew nothing of it.

"It all depends if the Carolinas prefer ethics to profits."

"And who will pick the cotton if the slaves are free? We're not talking morals here, Theo; it's economics. Practically the entire industry of the Southern states is based upon slavery. If they give that up, their economy will decline. Cotton prices will skyrocket. Every businessman knows you can't expect to pay for labor and make decent profits."

"But when the Ten Hours Act was passed 11 years ago—"

While father and son volleyed this back and forth over their pudding, I watched Colin out of the corner of my eye. Once or twice, he opened his mouth to speak, then changed his mind. And while Uncle Henry and Theo discussed the family business—the manufacture of cotton textiles—I wondered where Colin's place was in all this. His face was masked with a blank, yet his gestures were a little abrupt as we listened.

As time went on, however, I too began to grow impatient. It was impossible to tell just how this conversation was intended, this discussion of family affairs in front of me. Was it an indication of accepting me as one of the family? Or was this intense debate simply a way of ignoring my presence, an explanation that I was more inclined to believe.

The dinner had been delicious, the wine superb, and the surroundings most elegant. Yet the company had fallen short of my expectations. But then, just what *had* I expected? Just what was it like to return to one's family after 20 years' estrangement?

There is a saying, "You can't go home again," and I fear I was beginning to see the truth of it. Whatever I had imagined, riding on the train and fantasizing about my "homecoming," this was not it. Could it have been a very naive error on my part?

Then I suddenly remembered what had spurred me to come back to Pemberton Hurst: Aunt Sylvia's letter. Possibly I might never have had the courage to come back here and would have been content to go on and marry Edward without having ever seen my family again, had it not been for that letter. Upon reading her warm and anxious words, saying that they had just found us in London and missed us and very much wanted my mother and me to come back, upon reading all this, I had fancied that the whole family wanted us back.

How wrong I had been! Indeed, it was obvious my relatives knew nothing of the letter at all.

I glanced down at the empty chair with the service before it and was overcome by the need to see my great-aunt. So I cleared my voice and said, "Excuse me, but may I go up and see Aunt Sylvia now?"

Aunt Anna snapped her head about. The others fell suddenly silent And I know by the looks on their faces that I had said something frightfully wrong.

"Oh, Leyla dear," said Martha across the table. There was that pity again, that agonized empathy in her eyes. "Has no one told you?"

A shiver ran down my spine. "Told me what?"

"Aunt Sylvia. She died four weeks ago."

CHAPTER 3

I DON'T KNOW WHY THE NEWS SHOULD HAVE SHAKEN ME AS IT did, for I never knew my great-aunt and had no memories of her, yet all my hopes had rested with her. All along, after meeting each of my relatives, I had placed more and more need in her, a pressing reliance that she would be the one genuinely happy person to see me. And now she was dead.

"I'm sorry, Leyla," said Aunt Anna. "I should have told you sooner. Now I've spoiled your supper."

Across from me, Colin said, "Why so devastated, cousin? You hardly knew her."

"Excuse me." I rose to my feet, sending the chair over backwards.

"Oh dear," said someone.

The three men rose with me, and it was Uncle Henry who rushed around to my side. "It's too much," Anna was saying. "First her mother, now Sylvia. Poor dear needs rest. Take her up, Henry. I'll send Gertrude with tea."

A mist seemed to envelope me as I felt myself being led from the dining room. I had had no idea just how much I had been relying upon Aunt Sylvia until that moment. Then it seemed that her death had taken away not only herself but all my hopes as well.

Uncle Henry had me by the arm and was taking me upstairs. "There, there," he kept saying, patting my hand. The smell of Macassar oil filled my head, and the looming walls seemed to bend in over me. I was not going to faint—I never had before—yet I was losing touch with reality. My mind swam with bitter thoughts. In my disappointment over Sylvia, I was angry with the others. Each one had had the opportunity to tell me the news, yet they had avoided it. Why? She was only a 75-year-old maiden aunt whom I could not remember. Why had they thought it would mean so much to me, and why had they been so reluctant to tell me?

We stopped before my door as I leaned on Uncle Henry. In my fog, I could not see his face. How desperately I wanted to look at him! How I had tried during the meal to peer around plump Aunt Anna to glimpse a face that might have been my father's. And now I could not see it, inches away as I was. Uncle Henry spoke in low, comforting tones. Was this a voice I had heard as a child when my own father had comforted me? Brothers are very often very alike. Was Uncle Henry my father's image?

The bedroom door opened, and I stumbled in. The shock of Sylvia's death and the disappointment of it was taking a heavy toll. Somehow I found my way to the bed and fell on it in a rush of tears. I sensed Uncle Henry's presence as he stood over me. He was near. He was reassuring.

I cried for some time, letting the initial shock pour forth, and finally, containing myself wiped my eyes and struggled back to my feet. Uncle Henry still stood there, inches taller than I, watching in silence.

"Forgive me," I said haltingly. "I hadn't meant to be so rude."

"It's not rude to mourn a death, Bunny."

He persisted in calling me by that name, as though Mother and I had left the Hurst only yesterday. By calling me Bunny, Uncle Henry was closing the 20-year hiatus.

Tears dried, I finally looked up at him. A flash, a vision flicked past my eyes. It was as if a curtain had fleetingly blown open to reveal a scene to me on the other side and then had fallen closed. No, not a scene really, not images that I could focus upon. More like a *feeling.* As I gazed into Uncle Henry's expressionless face, I was overwhelmed with a kind of grief, a deep-felt sorrow, almost anguish that verged upon . . . what?

His thick lashes hung heavily over his eyes. The nose was a bit too large. The chin barely cleft. And the aura I had received in that second was one of . . . of *doom.* Looking into Uncle Henry's face, I felt a great oppression come over me, a feeling of fatality, of defeat, of falling headlong into an abyss that was so inevitable that I must consign myself to it.

But why?

And was this my father's face? In his late 50s, my uncle was not an unhandsome man, although the years had given him lines and wrinkles and gray at the temples. Yet he was still slender and bore himself aristocratically. I imagined that, if my father had lived through that cholera epidemic, this is how he would look.

"You'll feel better in the morning, Bunny. You need a good rest."

"Yes," I whispered. The feeling of depression began to lift and, explaining it away with the news of Aunt Sylvia, I relaxed a little. "I *am* glad to be back." This I said more to convince myself than him.

He was staring intently at me. In the dimness of my bedroom, I saw myself being minutely scrutinized by my uncle's searching eyes. *Searching.* That was the word that had come to me when Aunt Anna had stared at me. Theo and Colin had also stared at me in the same way. As though they were looking for something.

"Tell me, Bunny," Uncle Henry's voice came soft and reassuring against the gloomy night. "Why did you come back here?"

"What?"

"I mean, why did you choose to come now instead of before, long ago?"

I did not know how to reply. Mother's silence about this place had always seemed to me an unspoken commandment that we were to forget the Hurst and our connections with it. But then there had come the unexpected letter. Aunt Sylvia's . . .

"I'm getting married soon, Uncle Henry, and I wanted to see—"

He fell back a step. The gentleness went from his face. "Married!" His reaction matched Colin's exactly.

"Yes. And I wanted to see my family just once before going on to a new life. See the place where I was born and—"

"Bunny, who is the man?"

"You don't know him, Uncle; he's an architect in London. A student of Charles Barry." In my ignorance, I had thought his concern a paternal one, enquiring after the background of the young man who sought my hand. But this was not Uncle Henry's concern at all. Far from it.

"He's quite well-to-do, Uncle, from an upper-class family, and is well educated. I met him—"

"Have you set a date?"

"We plan to marry in the spring. He is working on designs for the new Victoria Station that he hopes will be accepted above the others—"

"We shall have to meet him, Leyla," said my uncle with undue gravity.

"Of course." I fell to staring at this man who had my father's face. Something was wrong.

Seeing my distress, he softened. "Bunny, my dear, you are so young, and there is so much you don't know. When you left this house 20 years ago, we feared never to see you again, such a bright star you were in our lives. We are family, all of us, being of the Pemberton blood. I see it in your face. Some of Jenny is there, but more of my brother Robert is there. You and Theo resemble one another, did you see that? I am only concerned with your welfare. And I want you to feel at home here; we all do."

But you do not act it, cried my mind. How desperately I wanted to pretend that this man was my father and fall into his arms for joy and sadness. Yet I could not. For all he was of my blood, for all he resembled me, he remained a stranger.

"Tomorrow this beastly wind will die, and I can show you about the property. We are not just a hurst, you know, but extend quite far."

"I know. The coppice."

I don't know what had made me say that word, but it had an extraordinary effect on my uncle. Slowly his face changed, the features hardened, the jaw stiffened. "You remember the coppice, do you?"

"No. Colin told me about it."

"I see. And what did he tell you about it?"

"Only that it was there."

"Well, we are a large estate and own most of the land between here and East Wimsley. You'll come to know it all in time. I hope you will stay for a long while, Bunny; I sincerely do."

Again the paradox: speaking words he obviously did not feel.

"Ah, here's Gertrude with your tea. Sleep well, Bunny; all will be better tomorrow."

I watched him go, feeling little better than before. Gertrude scuffled silently in bearing a tray laden with teapot, cup, sugar, and cream bowls. Possibly it was my imagination, but as she set the tray on a small table before the fire and then went to draw back the bedclothes, I had the distinct impression she was watching me out of the corner of her eye. Or, rather, that she wanted very much to look at me but forced her eyes away.

Too tired for niceties, I came out bluntly with, "Do you remember me, Gertrude?"

She stopped what she was doing at once and froze like a statue poised over the bed. "Yes, I do, Miss Leyla."

"I'm sorry, I don't remember you." I circled the half-tester to stand opposite her. "Have you been with the Pembertons long, Gertrude?"

"Almost 30 years."

Still she did not look at me. Still she stood stiff, like a cat about to take flight. It struck me as unusual behavior for a woman who had probably taken care of me as a baby. She seemed almost afraid of me.

"Thank you for the tea. I don't need anything else."

I watched her as she shuffled to the door, her frizzy hair catching the fire's glow. Was there perhaps a hint of familiarity in that odd gait? Had I as a child observed Gertrude walking and wondered about the limp? When she opened the door, a feeling swept over me. A feeling of having known this person before.

"Did you miss me after I left, Gertrude?"

At once, she swung about, and I was astounded to see tears in her eyes. "Yes I did, *liebchen.* You and your dear mother, God rest her soul. I always prayed for your return."

I took a step toward her. "Then I'm back, aren't I?"

"Yes, *liebchen*" Her lips trembled. I could not fathom Gertrude's distress.

"I'd like to talk over old times again. Can we do that sometime, you and I?"

"My memory is poor, Miss Leyla. I think I will disappoint you."

"I think not. You can tell me about my mother and my father—"

"Excuse me, Miss Leyla, but the past is where it belongs. A beautiful young woman should not be concerned with what is over and finished. Forgive me for saying that."

"If that's what you feel . . ." I spread my hands in a gesture of helplessness. "And the others, do they feel this way too?"

She nodded vigorously.

"Does the family ever discuss the past?"

Gertrude shook her head.

"I see . . ." Which of course I did not. "Thank you for the tea. Wake me for breakfast, will you? Good night."

The door closed softly, and I was left alone with the cracking fire and my own dancing shadow. If ever a moment had existed in my life when I had felt lonelier than now, I could not recall it. The bizarre attitude of my relatives (if indeed I were not just imagining it) and the queerness of Gertrude, as well as a newfound longing for my father, all joined to create in me a hollow feeling and new melancholy.

The room was small and strange. Except for the few personal effects I had set out, it was a room I did not know and was a stranger to. The house was also like this, large and empty and alien. The people—even those who faintly resembled me—were strangers whom I did not know and who had not received me in the manner I had so desperately needed.

What was wrong? Or . . . was there really something wrong? Maybe it was just myself, overly sensitive to the magnitude of the situation. I had been born in this house, had lived the first five years of my life here. My father and brother had died in this house. Possibly I had set my expectations too high. After all, how were these people to find me all of a sudden, as much a stranger to them as they were to me? I must be patient. In time they would accept me as one of their own. And after that time, I could go away again a more complete woman. A woman with a past and a family.

The tea worked miracles on me. Delicious and lightly seasoned, it put me in a mild euphoria so that I could don my nightdress and slip between the crisp sheets with some small sense of well-being. Uncle Henry had been right. Tomorrow would be a whole new day.

When I extinguished the candle on my night table, I curled up on my side and expected to fall asleep at once. Yet I did not. For, tired and exhausted though I was, my mind remained awake. Many questions began to plague me. Ones that I had dismissed earlier, having been able to bury them as I had occupied myself with my family, but that surfaced now in the cold darkness of my bedroom.

Yes, some small bit of my relatives' strange attitude towards me could be explained away by our strangeness together, but how did one rationalize their definite avoidance of the subject of the past? They had all done it, purposely keeping that subject away, as though it were painful or embarrassing. But why? What was so terribly upsetting about the past that could not now, 20 years later, be talked about?

That my father and brother had died of cholera in this house had been one of the few replies my mother had ever made to my queries. Understandably tragic, it certainly could not have been an event so devastating as to continue to affect the family today.

Yet they *did* purposefully avoid discussion of the past. Except Colin. He alone had seemed to relish the memories and probably would have gone on all evening if Theo hadn't interrupted.

But then, Aunt Anna had wanted me to avoid Colin . . .

I lay in the darkness wondering about Cousin Colin and why the others felt about him as they did. Bit by bit our conversation returned, the congeniality by the fire, the story about the coppice. Then something he had said came back to me sharply in the night, stabbing my mind with more force than when he had first said it.

Remarking to Colin that my mother had never spoken about the Pembertons, my cousin had then commented: "As though she wanted to forget we ever existed."

Thinking back now, Colin's words made me realize something that I had never before really noticed—that my mother had indeed been very determined in avoiding our past.

Was it not the same here? Had I not encountered the same conviction among my relatives, that the past was best left buried and forgotten? Indeed, that was the one thing she had shared with them all these years, this mutual forgetfulness.

But why?

What was it about my past that had the people in this house, and my mother as well, reluctant to talk about it?

In such a state of mind did I eventually fall asleep. But it was a restless slumber, visited by grotesque dreams and strange visions. One by one, I saw the faces of my relatives as I imagined them to be: Uncle Henry holding me in his arms like a father; Aunt Anna saying lies aloud but whispering truths; Cousin Theodore forward and open, dominating everyone and laughing with falseness; Cousin Colin with his Continental manners and lack of concern for feelings; Cousin Martha becoming impassioned by next year's neckline. And Aunt Sylvia in her grave. The unseen Grandmother Abigail, a conscript mother in a high tower. And lastly Gertrude, who seemed on the verge of telling me everything.

When I awoke, I felt little refreshed but was pleased to see the sun was shining. Beyond my windows stood a winter forest of black and gray and a scattering rainfall of leaves. The wind persisted as gusty as ever, creating havoc with nature but giving us a sky of a vivid blue that is never seen over London.

Changing into a fresh dress, still black for Mother, I smiled at my childishness of the night before. How tired I must have been to have imagined all that! Too many novels, I scolded myself.

Determined to keep my spirits up and make myself as winsome as possible, I descended the stairs toward the smell of breakfast in the rooms below.

My mother and I had seldom eaten a morning meal in London, since we had had to be hard at work as soon as daylight entered our windows. Though not poverty-stricken in my teen years, we were still far from wealthy and had to work hard for our small comfort. Having taught me her arts in dressmaking, Mother gave me such projects each day as would perfect me enough to someday have a clientele of my own. We worked in our flat, did all our cutting and sewing there, and purchased fabrics from wholesalers in central London. Although quite poor, as I said, in my younger days, by the time I was 14, Mother had established a small reputation for herself and had a regular trade.

But that was over now, that quiet life of dress patterns and afternoon walks. I was on my own and without a family until I could establish myself again with the Pembertons and then go on to marry Edward.

Theodore was the only one at the breakfast table. He stood with great flourish and seated me before returning to his meal.

"Did you sleep well, Leyla?"

"Well enough, considering."

"Considering what?" His eyes bugged a little.

"Considering all that country quiet. In London, we fall asleep to the music of horses' hooves, iron wheels on the pavement, street criers, and Arab musicians."

He laughed. "How can anyone live in the city!"

"Oh, it's not so bad." I was thinking of the beautiful townhouses in Grosvenor and Belgravia Squares and wondered why my relatives did not have one.

"You'll like it here. Even in winter the Hurst is a beautiful place to live."

A maid brought me tea and toast. Cousin Theodore, again handsomely dressed, was relaxing over a cup of tea. His eyes, a little fishlike, were once more on my face in that annoying searching manner. And once more saying something other than what he was thinking, he asked, "May I show you about the property today?"

"Yes, I should like that."

I was determined not to let my imagination spoil the day. Aunt Sylvia was dead, all my hopes now rested with these six people, and I made a secret vow not to leave until they finally accepted me as one of themselves.

"So tell me, Leyla," he said as he casually stirred his tea. "What brought you back to the Hurst?"

I gave him a puzzled look. This was trait number two: the need to question my being here. If the Pembertons weren't busy burying their past, then they were busy asking me why I was here.

"For 20 years, my mother was my family. She was all I needed. When she died I felt lost, abandoned. I need a family again, just as I think everyone does."

"What about this fiancé of yours? He'll be your family soon."

"Yes, but not flesh-and-blood relations like the Pembertons. Surely you understand."

"Of course." And he seemed satisfied with that. "By the by, Grandmother will see you today."

Will see me today! Was I being commanded?

"She's been terribly under the weather lately. After all, she is 80 years old."

"I'll go up now then."

"Not yet. This afternoon. I'll have to take you there and introduce you. Grandmother's a bit—how shall I put it?—eccentric?"

"Like Colin?"

Theodore laughed, but there was no mirth in it. His black hair was combed to perfection, and he might have been almost handsome if it weren't for his pale eyes and air of falseness. Somehow, I feared I never knew where I stood with him.

"Where are the others?"

"My mother is with Grandmother. Father has gone into East Wimsley. Martha is embroidering anything she can get her hands on. And Colin—well, who knows where Colin is."

"Tell me, Theo. Those enormous mills outside of East Wimsley, by the train station. Are they ours?"

I think, for an instant, he took umbrage at the word "ours," but I was determined not to cleave myself from the family by such designations as "yours" and "mine." At any rate, he passed over it and said, "Yes, they are. In fact, we own East Wimsley, or at least the outer areas. The Pembertons are the fifth largest cotton manufacturers in England."

"I had no idea!"

His eyes narrowed a bit. Although I could never know what Cousin

Theodore was thinking, I had a suspicion he thought I was here for mercenary motives and that the Pemberton fortune sparkled before me.

"Your mother really did keep you in the dark, didn't she?"

His intimation annoyed me. Guest though I was, I would not be cowed by Theodore Pemberton. "Yes, she did. Would you know why?"

He seized my gaze for an instant, and I felt he was on the verge of a confession. But then he tore himself away and said offhandedly, "Can't imagine."

"Greetings, dear cousins."

I whipped about, startled. Colin stood in the doorway, his feet wide apart, a riding crop in one hand. His fair hair was standing up in tufts as though he had been in the wind, and a churlish grin broadened his face.

"Good morning, Cousin Colin," I said politely. His dress was hardly fitting for the breakfast table, and yet he joined us without ceremony.

"Really, Colin, you're a mannerless lummox."

"Thank you, Theo. You set an excellent example for our new relation here. So anxious to be numbered among the great Pembertons, poor Leyla might be disillusioned by our less than fraternal affection." Colin poured himself some tea and drank noisily. "Tell me, Leyla. Do you ride?"

"A little."

"And I don't mean the pony business on Rotten Row. I mean *do you ride?*"

"Then I suppose I don't."

"See what the city does to a person!"

Looking across the table at the two men, I hardly knew which was worse: Theo with his falseness and politeness or Colin with his brutal honesty.

"Come and look about the Hurst with me, will you?"

"Well, I had promised Theo—"

"Then go with Theo." Colin stood abruptly and grinned down at me, arms akimbo. "I'll wager a guinea you're back in London in less than a fortnight"

"Is that a challenge?"

"Why? Will you suffer this place for a guinea?"

"Pemberton Hurst doesn't seem to me to be a house of suffering."

He threw back his head and laughed. "Did you hear that, Theo! How little she knows of us!"

But the other cousin found no humor in my observation. "You've spoiled our breakfast" was all he said.

"One last chance, Cousin Leyla. You can see the Hurst *my* way, or you can go with Theo. Be careful of your choice."

"She's to go with me, Colin, and that's that. Hadn't you better get back to bullying the stableboy?" Theodore dabbed at his lips with a lace napkin, and for an instant he reminded me of Edward.

Colin ignored what Theo had said and continued to stare at me with his green eyes. They seemed darker today, verging on peridot. "Still following wise counsel and avoiding daft Colin, are you? I suppose since you've received such strong warnings against my company—"

"Theo asked me first, Colin; otherwise, I'd go with you. I've apologized for last night. What can I do to make you see how contrite I am?"

His eyes flashed with adventure. "Come to the coppice with me."

"No!" said Theo suddenly. He jumped to his feet and glared at Colin. "Are you mad?"

"Oh, but I'd love to see it, Theo. Perhaps it will bring back memories."

"No, Leyla. It's dangerous. The ruins aren't safe. I shall have to forbid you to go."

I must have gazed up at him in some amazement, for he averted his eyes. Possibly this aggressive cousin of mine was quite used to giving orders, but I was not accustomed to taking them. With a retort at my lips, I quickly reminded myself that I was still very much a stranger here, that I was a guest, and that it would do me no good to engender this man's enmity. Instead of speaking against him, I said nothing at all.

Colin seemed disappointed. "Well, dear cousin, I suppose what Theo orders is law for you. But it isn't for me. I shall ride where I please. I hope the two of you have a pleasant tour." With that, he turned on his heel and stalked out.

"I'm sorry," I said, although I did not feel it was my fault.

Theo resumed his seat. "You'll get used to Colin. Sometimes I think he was raised by gypsies instead of Pembertons."

My eyes moved in the direction of the door Colin had exited through. "How did his father die?"

"Uncle Richard? It was a carriage accident. Horse got frightened or something, I believe."

"Don't you know? Weren't you here?"

"No, my family was away. It was, oh, I'd say 12 years ago now that it happened. Colin was 22 at the time. Took it very badly. Went into a rage and brooded for months. This is what we were told when we returned."

"And his mother?"

Theo was still stirring his cold tea. "She was killed at the same time. They were in the carriage together."

"My God . . ." I stared at the door for a long time. "Where did it happen?"

"Down the road."

I spun around. "Here at the Hurst? You can't mean it!"

"Why not?"

"But *his* father! And . . . *my* father. It's positively grotesque." For the first time, I felt I had something in common with one of the Pembertons. "I had no idea . . ."

"Well, it's a large family, Leyla, and accidents do happen," he said, as if that explained it.

I stared at my cousin, but he would not look at me. Then another thought crossed my mind. "Where were you when it happened?"

"My father and mother and I were living in Manchester at the time, managing a mill there."

"So you haven't lived at the Hurst continuously all your life."

"No."

His sentences became more and more clipped. I don't know what possessed me to ask, but the question entered my mind, so I voiced it. "When had you left the Hurst?"

There was an imperceptible pause before his reply, as though he were weighing his words. "Let me see, the mill began operation in 1838. Father had to go on ahead to review the plans and fill all the positions under him. It was such a long time ago, but I would guess we left the Hurst the same year you and your mother left. Bit of a coincidence, now that I think of it."

"The same year?"

"Mhm." He made an elaborate gesture of turning to peer at the clock over the fireplace. "Now that it comes back to mind, I'd guess we left for Manchester soon after you and your mother left. Thinking about it now, it seems it can't have been more than a month later."

I continued to stare voicelessly at my cousin.

"Well, have you finished your tea then? You might want a cloak for warmth. That wind is hellish."

"Certainly." We stood together. Although I could not pinpoint it, something nagged at the back of my mind. Just the barest edge of an idea taunted me, would give me no respite until I let the rest of it come to light. Slowly it began to emerge. And when it did, even I was surprised by what I asked next. "Cousin Theo, was anyone else in this house affected by that cholera epidemic?"

"Cholera epidemic?"

"The one that killed my father and brother 20 years ago."

His face went stark blank. "Whatever do you mean, Leyla? Your father and brother didn't die of cholera."

CHAPTER 4

I STOOD MOTIONLESS, HELPLESS. STUNNED AS I WAS BY THESE words, I still had the presence of mind to observe Theo's reaction immediately following this announcement. And he was not pleased with himself. Just as my question had popped out of my mouth before I was aware of it, so had Theo's tongue wagged before he could hear what it was saying. And then he bit it, but was too late. The Pandora's Box was open.

I knew now by the simple words he had uttered and by the sudden regret on his face that there was indeed something afoot at Pemberton Hurst that I had to learn. And in that passage of a few moments I realized also that my mother's silence had been accompanied by a spoken lie.

I sat back down, and, after a moment's hesitation, Theodore joined me. His look was one of regret My cousin rued the words he had uttered, but there was no going back.

I asked simply, "How did they die, Theo?"

"Leyla, what good can come of knowing? You were content in that lie, which I am sure your mother told you for good reason. Trust in her judgment. It was 20 years ago—"

"How did they die?" I persisted softly. My hands were folded calmly in my lap. I was quite composed. It was Theo who became nervous.

He shook his head sadly. "I don't want to tell you."

"Then I shall ask Colin."

"God no! Leyla—" He leaned forward.

"Then tell me, please."

"But why?"

"I have a right to know."

"You'll always hold it against me, Leyla, for having been the one to tell you."

"Why?"

"It will make you unhappy. Can't you just go away from the Hurst . . . No, I suppose you can't. You came here looking for your family and your past. Then I shall give them to you." He rose again but was once more under control. "Come with me."

We exited from the dining room, traversed the gas-lit hall, and went into the library, where we had first met the night before. A fire was burning to keep the chill out. Candles gave the room a cozy air. After I passed Theo and took a seat by the hearth, he closed the door behind him and joined me opposite in the *prie-dieu.* I watched his eyes reflect the firelight, those heavy lashes so like my own. He stared for a long time into the flames before speaking. And then he still did not look at me.

"The past is a tender spot for us all here at the Hurst, Leyla, and that is why we wish not to speak much of it. You lost your father and brother; Colin, both his parents. It is not so much that deaths occurred here, for they are to be expected in large houses inhabited by several generations at once, but rather the *manner* in which they occurred. Carriage accidents do happen, but they are freaks, as this was. It had been pleasant weather, a fresh horse, and a new brougham. No one knows what caused it to tip. But both Uncle Richard and Aunt Jane died instantly. As I say, we only heard of it, but it changed Colin. He has never been the same since."

Having started, it seemed easier for Theo. He relaxed in the chair, his hands resting flat on his knees. I followed his example by staring into the fire and drifting back 20 years.

"There was no cholera epidemic here, Leyla. Not ever. Your father had been ill for a long time, some strange fever that the doctors could not diagnose. It came and went, came and went, until the episodes became longer and more violent and the intervals shorter. We tried everything. Seashore retreats, opium, physical restraints. Nothing seemed to help him. Uncle Robert was doomed. And then one day . . ." His voice caught in his throat. I waited patiently for him to continue. "One day he said he felt well and wanted to take Thomas for a walk. When the two had been gone a long time, around sunset, my father and I went in search of them. We had become concerned because of Uncle Robert's health. We . . . found them in . . . the coppice."

The fire cracked. The wind whistled through the trees. None of this was familiar to me—not my father, nor his illness, nor Thomas, nor . . . the coppice. "Please go on."

Theo's voice came from far away. "He had gotten a knife somehow, Uncle Robert, and had apparently had an attack of the fever while out with Thomas. They were both dead. He had killed your brother and then himself."

Theo and I hung suspended in a timeless zone of neither here nor there. The room closed in on us, and the fire grew increasingly hotter, brighter. I continued to stare into it, feeling my face burn. I searched the flames for two people, for a man I would know as my father and a boy as my brother. But they were not there. They would not come back to me.

"You see, Leyla, you and your mother left under most grievous circumstances, so that, when you returned so suddenly, so unexpectedly, last night, we hardly knew what to say. We didn't know how to treat it. No one knew to what extent you remembered the past or how much your mother had told you. I see now we were right in keeping silent."

Finally I looked at Theo. My face felt singed and red. "Yes, of course," I said distantly. "I quite understand."

"We just knew Colin would let it all out without giving the slightest consideration to whether you already knew or not. He would have ended up telling you anyway. I'm glad I said it first."

"Yes, I am too. And grateful, of course." From far away, I heard the rustle of my petticoats. In another moment, I was standing. So this was why everyone had treated me so strangely. This was the answer to the Big Mystery. My father had committed both a murder and a suicide. No wonder these people felt awkward in my presence. "You know, Theo, I really don't feel like that tour after all, if you don't mind. Perhaps another day."

"I understand."

"I knew you would. It's just that, well, it's like losing them all over again. For 20 years, they had died of cholera. And now they've died . . . another way. It's like having them die twice. This is really most ironical. In two months, I have lost four people. Mother, Father," I drifted toward the door, "Thomas, and Aunt Sylvia. How I wish I had known them. You don't know how difficult it is mourning for someone whose face you can't recall. Excuse me, please."

He opened the door and escorted me down the hall. At the foot of the stairs, I turned to Theo and said, "I shall go up myself, if you don't mind. I'm sure you've other things to do."

"If you're certain you're all right."

I gave a little laugh. "Don't be silly. Of course I'm all right. Explain to the others, won't you? That train ride was more tiring than I had thought. Excuse me."

The stairs glided beneath me as though I flew up them without my feet touching at all. My head was in a mist, my thoughts swirling. The shock of this news was many times more painful than that of Sylvia's death, for this changed so much. It changed the Hurst, it changed my mother, it changed the past 20 years, and— ultimately—it changed me.

I do not know how long I lay upon my bed that day, but when I finally turned my head to glance at the window, the long orange rays of a setting sun were slanting through the panes. I had grieved for hours.

It is one thing to mourn a cholera victim, but for a murderer another thing altogether. I sorrowed for the anguish he must have suffered, for the agonies of his soul to have driven him to commit such a vile act. I cried my heart out for a poor deranged madman, driven to the brink of oblivion and taking his only son with him. Little Thomas, seven years old, stabbed to death by his father, who didn't know what he was doing.

And Papa, cried my soul, my heart, is that why you then turned the knife upon yourself? Did you have one lucid moment in which you saw—too late—what you had done and could not stand the agony of it?

I cried then for my mother and for her grief and for the years of loneliness she spent in the obscene poverty of London's slums, protecting this last child from both the past and the present.

So this is what I came back to the Hurst for. I found what I had come looking for: my family and my past. Now I wish I hadn't. What Mother must have suffered all those years! Never telling me. Looking at my face and seeing *theirs*. Such a burden for one woman to carry. If only I could have shared it with her. If only she could have told me, so that we could have carried it together. But she had not. Instead, in her courage she had taken it all upon herself and had spared me the misery. Only to have me back at the Hurst now, finding out what for 20 years she had tried so hard to conceal!

When I cried my last tear, I realized that it was dark outside, a fierce wind was blowing, and I was hungry. I had spent ten hours in this room, mourning for what was done, grieving for the past. Now it was time to return to the present. I decided this for my mother's sake, since she would not have wanted me to spend my years mourning as she had done. I must spend no more hours dwelling upon what could not be changed. So I donned a fresh dress, replaited my hair, and decided to begin now to carry on with life again as I knew my mother would have wanted.

Yet Fate, it seemed, had other things in store.

I was just applying moist towels to my puffy eyes when a scratching at the door made me stop to listen. Like a small animal trying to get in, the sound persisted until I opened the door to find Martha standing there.

"May I come in?" she asked.

"Of course. Please do. I was about to come down."

"We were quite concerned for you, Leyla. Theo told us about this morning. I'm sorry. We all are."

"Thank you."

She followed me inside and closed the door behind her. "If we seemed aloof from you last night, now you know why. None of us wanted to accidentally say the wrong thing. We had no idea what you knew about your father and brother. As it turned out, we were right."

"That's what Theo said." I sat before the vanity again and resumed arranging my hair. In the reflection, I saw Martha pace slowly about the room, looking first at my mother's picture, then reading the label on my cologne bottle, and stopping to pick up the books on my night table. All of this gave me the distinct impression that she was debating what to say next.

"Uncle Henry told me you're engaged to be married."

"Yes." I smiled into the looking glass.

"Is he handsome?"

"Oh, quite. You will all meet Edward before the wedding. And you will love him, too, I know. He is very smart and very much the gentleman."

"An architect is he?"

"One of the best in London."

"You are very fortunate, Leyla."

I glanced again in the glass and found Martha watching me. Once more, there was that heavy sadness in her eyes, an unshakable pity that I seemed to arouse in her. Yet it was no longer necessary, now that I knew the truth about my father's death. Once accepted, the truth is always easy to bear.

"Is something wrong, Martha?"

"No," she said too quickly. "Not at all. You know we've had supper, but Gertrude kept some aside for you. She thought you would be hungry."

"Yes, I am. Thank you."

My final toilette complete, I felt presentable for the company downstairs. Other than the red rims of my eyes, and the new awareness I felt inside me, I was still the same Leyla Pemberton who had arrived yesterday. Only now everything would be different. My family would no longer have to guard their words or avoid certain subjects or cast each other secretive glances. Now we could all be free with one another. We could be a complete family again.

When we stepped out my door, we were startled by Uncle Henry. He hovered anxiously over me, his eyes paternally concerned. "Forgive me, I thought you heard me coming."

"Not at all." He had made my heart flutter, suddenly appearing there in the shadows.

"Are you quite all right, Leyla? Theo—"

"Yes, yes. All's well now." I closed the door with a decisive click and turned to give my uncle my best smile. But when my eyes lit upon his face, that queer sensation washed over me at once—exactly as it had done last night.

"Is something wrong?"

"No, I . . ." Pressing my palm to my forehead, I tried to force the feeling out of me. Yet when my eyes met his again, it returned, stronger than before, that inescapable *doom.* What was it about Uncle Henry that caused such a reaction? Was it some stirring of a forgotten memory? Surely I was only seeing in him my poor father, using Uncle Henry as a surrogate father as I was. But then . . . I had felt this sensation last night, before learning the true nature of my father's death. How was it, then, that Uncle Henry could make me feel suddenly so utterly helpless? So *hopeless?*

"Perhaps you ought to remain up here."

"No, Uncle Henry, truly . . ."

"She hasn't eaten for a long while, Uncle Henry. That's it, of course. Let's take her down and put some of Gertrude's steak-and-kidney pie into her." Martha's voice was gentle and compelling. The more I was near her, the more I appreciated Colin's sister, for she was kind and patient with me. And, above all, sympathetic. Hadn't she, too, lost her father and mother in a tragic way? "Come on, Leyla. It's warm downstairs. And a hot toddy will put life back into those cheeks."

I took Uncle Henry's arm, and we went to the stairs. As I felt and took comfort in his strong presence at my side, I saw dismayingly that the air of doom still hung over me, though I knew not why.

Aunt Anna and Colin were in the drawing room when we three entered, and when I would have protested having a meal in the best room of the house, Aunt Anna would have none of it.

"At least the parlor then," I begged.

"Nonsense. Now be seated and put your feet on this stool." She fussed over me in a maternal fashion, the diamonds on her neck and wrists sparkling as she did so. The chiffon of her gown made a whooshing sound and her steel-framed crinoline creaked as she stooped for the footstool. "There. Comfortable?"

"Thank you, Aunt Anna." I rested back in the chair in the complaisant knowledge that everything was going to be all right.

Then I caught Colin staring at me.

A half-smile bent his lips as he said drily, "So my cousin Theodore has let the proverbial cat out of the proverbial bag, has he? And they wanted you to keep away from *me* for that very reason. Don't you find that outrageously ironical?"

"Oh, Colin, be still."

He stretched his smile at Martha and nodded obeisance. But when Anna cast him an angry glance, I was reminded of her attitude last night—of trying too hard to conceal something. It was in her manner again this evening, as though Theodore had *not* told me everything. As though there were more to hide.

"It's all right now," I said, only half meaning it "Theo told me everything. I wish I had known long ago. I don't like to think my mother bore it alone."

Colin, ever impulsive, said, "And what makes you think Theo told you everything?"

My eyes flew open in alarm. "Whatever do you mean?"

"Colin!" said Anna sharply.

He shrugged again as if he were a Frenchman and said, "I understand Grandmother's quite angry you didn't keep your appointment with her."

I had forgotten all about it! "Surely one of you told her . . ."

Anna fussed with the yards and yards of material in her skirt. The idea that she was constantly looking for ways to speak anything but what was on her mind was beginning to annoy me. "Grandmother believes in keeping appointments regardless of unexpected circumstances. You know how she is."

"No, I don't. Tell me, please."

Anna's eyes bulged until she looked like Theodore. "You don't remember Grandmother Abigail?" As if I had just told her I had forgotten Jesus Christ. "But I thought you remembered all of us!"

"Cousin Leyla remembers far less than she's willing to admit."

I glared at Colin. It ired me to think that we were back to playing games again, that more secrecy was going on, and that Theo's confession had solved nothing.

Martha came to my aid this time. Walking to her brother's side and shaking an index finger at him, she said, "You are an impudent brute, and you're making our guest very unhappy. Now, I'm going to make you an offer, sir: either you be polite from now on, or you leave the room."

He smiled disarmingly and hoisted his shoulders again. "What can I say? Forgive me, Cousin Leyla. And you can show acceptance of my very humble apologies by doing one thing."

"That is?"

"By letting me take you around the Hurst with me tomorrow."

I was about to give him a flat "No" when I saw Anna and Martha cast glances at each other. The fear in their eyes at the thought of my being alone with Colin forced me to accept his invitation. Impudent though he was, Colin appeared, so far, to be my only definite source of information. If indeed there was more to learn about my father and brother, I was not going to waste time.

Cousin Theodore strode into the room then, beautifully dressed in a dark-green cutaway with matching tie. If Paris were the center of women's fashions, Pemberton Hurst was that of men's. He addressed first his mother, then cousin Martha, and lastly me, lingering a moment before apologizing for his absence. "I've been with Grandmother. You know how difficult she is to mollify. It's the weather, I fear, not ready for winter, I suppose. She'll receive you tomorrow, Leyla, for tea. I explained about today."

"Thank you."

"I say, chilly in here, isn't it?"

"I'm fine, actually," I replied, since I was closest to the fire.

Theo reached for my hand to feel its temperature, mimicking a doctor as he did so, and as I laughed, my eye caught on a bit of glitter on his right hand. Heavy and gold with a large ruby in the center was a ring on Theo's middle finger. Impulsively, I grabbed his hand and would not let go.

"That ring," I said stupidly.

"What about it?"

"Well, I . . ." The recognition did not come close enough to the surface, so I had to let it go, and his hand as well, "Nothing, I guess. I just thought I had recognized it before. It seemed suddenly so familiar, and then, just as suddenly, not at all."

"Common enough type, this." He brought his hand close to his face and squinted. "Not a perfect stone, I'm afraid. You'll see lots like this in London."

"I suppose."

"It was Grandfather's ring," came Colin's voice. "Sir John passed it on to Theo when he died."

"'Then perhaps I do remember it! I must have seen it on my grandfather's hand when I was a child. A small kernel of memory, yet it means so much. Faces and people I cannot recall, but tiny things I do."

"Anything else?" someone asked. It was Uncle Henry, back with us again, and that gloom I was beginning to get used to.

"I must confess that I remember nothing."

"Nothing at all?" Aunt Anna fell incredulously into the chair opposite me. "You remember *nothing?*"

"As far as I am concerned, my life goes back only as far as my sixth birthday. I've known only London all my life."

"But you had such happy times here," said Anna in a strained tone.

"And sad ones, too," added Colin. "Curious she can't remember. Why do you suppose that is?"

"Lots of people can't remember that far back," said Uncle Henry unconvincingly. He dominated the room by standing spread-legged before the fire, his hands clasped behind his back.

I saw no reason to keep it from them any longer. "That was one of my reasons for coming here at last—those blank five years. At one or two, perhaps one would recall nothing, but surely from age three, I would have some recollection. I thought maybe the Hurst would help me to remember."

"Has it?" asked Anna anxiously.

"Not very. None of the house is familiar. None of you are."

"You remembered me."

"Yes, Martha, as soon as you entered the library, my mind saw you as you were 20 years ago."

"Twelve years old and too tall for my age."

"Yes, but you were just as pretty as you are now."

"Anyone else?" prompted Anna.

I avoided looking at Uncle Henry. "No, no one at all. Once in a while, I get a flash, like a curtain blowing open and falling closed too quickly. Nothing remains long enough for me to grasp."

"I'll bet, when you meet Grandmother tomorrow, you'll remember something. You used to be terrified of her."

"Who isn't?" said Colin.

Anna inclined herself a little closer to me. "Didn't you ever ask Jenny about the past?"

"Yes. Very often at first, but as she did not reply or gave me inadequate answers, I soon stopped asking. I'm thankful now I did not press her, else she would have been forced to tell more lies. She wanted to protect me that much."

"What do you suppose she was protecting you from?" asked Colin. His attitude was becoming a little defiant, and I was wearying of him. I was also growing tired of all these questions.

Gertrude chose to enter at the right moment with my supper tray, which Anna helped her spread before me. In an unspoken agreement, the three men left the room while Martha produced a cross-stitch sampler from her carpetbag and was soon absorbed in it. Aunt Anna remained pensively at my side, ruminating, I supposed, over all that I had said.

It was a tranquil evening, one in which I chose to ignore the nagging little doubts that bounced about in the back of my head. After 24 hours of my relatives' company, I was getting used to them and they to me. Acceptance of myself into this esoteric family was not far off, as with each episode we revealed more and more. The fewer walls between us, the closer-knit we become. In my earnestness to recapture the camaraderie we must have enjoyed in my baby days, I purposely ignored the small contradictions that kept trying to surface.

After supper and after hearing Martha at the pianoforte, we all adjourned upstairs to pass the stormy night in secure slumber. Colin reminded me again of my promise to see the Hurst with him, and I regretted having given in. Still, what other choice had I than Uncle Henry, who continued to cast that defeating gloom over me, or Theo, who could be insufferable with his perfect manners?

Carrying into bed with me the Cremorne Gardens guidebook, I let only sweet thoughts of Edward soothe me. I recalled how we had met a year ago, what a charming man he was, and how proud I was to be seen with him on the Serpentine. Edward was everything a woman looked for in a man, and I was so fortunate to have him.

Yet, while I slept deeply and soundly, it was bizarre dreams of Colin Pemberton that plagued me.

The next morning showed a frightful wind whipping about the Hurst, crashing trees together and stirring up whirlwinds of dead leaves. All of us were at breakfast today, eating heartily against the biting air and warming ourselves through and through with Gertrude's spiced tea. The congeniality of the atmosphere cheered me a great deal, although thinking about my father and brother now and again tended to tone me down.

Martha and Aunt Anna planned a trip to East Wimsley, riding in the brougham with Uncle Henry, who was going to visit the mills. They usually went twice a month to pay their respects to the vicar and donate old clothes to the poor. In East Wimsley, I gathered from their conversation, there was a great deal of poverty and a large laboring class.

"If it weren't for the Pembertons," boasted Uncle Henry over toast and jam, "those blighters wouldn't even have jobs. They'd follow the rest of the exodus into the big cities and overcrowd the slums even more. We've got to keep the peasants in the country where they belong."

"It's the trains, Father," voiced Theo, who seemed ever anxious to say just the right thing. "Before the steam engine, a peasant could go nowhere. Now, for a penny a mile, he can pack up his family and move wherever, whenever he likes. It's what's ruined London."

"London's not so bad," I ventured to intercede. "Certainly we have overcrowding and noise, but we also have the best hospitals in the world."

"Poppycock! We wouldn't need them if the cities were cleaner." Uncle Henry waved my opinion aside. That he was a firm believer in the worthlessness of women's thoughts was obvious. We were not to have opinions, and we certainly were not to voice them.

"Leyla dear," said Aunt Anna, "have you brought adequate attire for this beastly weather? You appear Martha's size, and I'm sure—"

"Thank you, Aunt Anna, I've a sufficient wardrobe. I was always taught to be pragmatic about clothing, to look for value in a dress rather than style."

"One can have both." She was eyeing my morning frock, and I could see she thought I should have better.

"I shall do fine, thank you."

Colin spoke for the first time. "I suppose, now that you're one of the family again, you'll be able to dress like a Pemberton. I think that's what Aunt Anna is implying."

"Do let us make some dresses for you, Leyla!" said Martha. "It would be such fun."

Colin was watching me carefully, and I had a good idea what he was thinking. Cousin Leyla has come back to the family to enjoy its riches and live like a Pemberton. As much as I would have liked to shatter this vain notion of his that it was the Pemberton fortune I was after, I would not come down to his level.

"It's kind of you, really, and I appreciate it. But I shall have new ones made when I marry."

"Of course!" Martha became even more animated. "And the wedding will be here at the Hurst!"

Uncle Henry snapped his head up. "What!"

"Oh no," I protested. "I hadn't expected to. Just a small church and a few of our friends—"

"Oh, you mustn't. Aunt Anna, don't you agree? We haven't had a wedding at the Hurst in years! Decades! Uncle Henry?"

"I am certain Leyla and her young man have plans already; it would be impudent to offer changes." There was a heaviness in his tone that sounded ominous. He looked away from me when he spoke, and I received the impression that Uncle Henry preferred to avoid the subject of my marriage.

It was just as well. I intended to leave the Hurst long before that event.

"Shall we go?" said Colin, rising abruptly. Acting always on an impulse with little thought for others, my capricious cousin knew nothing of etiquette and good manners.

"Colin, really!" corrected his aunt.

"Leyla's teacup has been empty for ten minutes. For an Englishwoman, that means she is quite finished. We've a lot to see today."

"Certainly. Let me run up for my cloak."

"I shall wait for you here."

Uncle Henry and Theo stood when I left the room, and then I did exactly as I had promised. I ran up the stairs, seized my cloak, bonnet, and gloves, and fairly danced back down, for I was anxious to be shown about. However, my absence was not long enough, I discovered as I neared the dining room, for I overheard my family in heated debate.

"I shall take her where I please," came Colin's voice. "Or where *she* pleases, for that matter."

"And I say you will not!" It was Uncle Henry. He sounded furious. "You are to avoid that place, or I will not allow you to take her around."

"Leyla has a mind of her own, Uncle," Colin answered smoothly. "And I imagine she'll go there on her own before long. No doubt it's better one of us goes with her."

"Not today, Colin. I forbid you."

Realizing that I was the cause of such dissension and feeling awkward at listening, I made a noise outside the door and entered the room in a rush. "I'm ready!" I said breathlessly.

Before me stood Cousin Colin and Uncle Henry, glowering at one another across the table like two stags about to lock antlers. There was a fierceness in both their eyes, a battle of dominance and supremacy that appeared at the moment to be a tie.

"Cousin Colin?" He swung his head round to regard me, and I saw depths of passion in his eyes. Where could it be that Uncle Henry so vehemently wished me to avoid? "I'm ready now."

"Very well." He thrust back his chair and strode toward me. Taking my cloak from my arm, he cast one last angry glance at the others, then defiantly left the room. I hurried after him, catching him in the entrance hall, and asked, "Is something wrong, Colin?"

He did not reply. Holding out my cloak for me, he rested it on my shoulders and tied it under my chin without a word. While I carefully seated my bonnet snugly on my head and then pulled on my gloves, Colin stood lost in thought with a terrible frown on his face. Seeing that I was ready, he pulled open the front door, indicated that I pass through, then brought it closed behind us with a slam. An icy wind blew in our faces, raising Colin's hair on end and whipping my cloak out of control. We stood thus on the threshold for a very long time, my cousin scowling to himself and I waiting patiently for him to remember me. As much as I would have wanted to inquire after Uncle Henry's forbidden area, I did not, for it would have made me appear an eavesdropper. The opportunity would come, I assured myself, when I could learn from Colin what part of the Hurst was to be denied me.

"Where shall we go first?" he asked suddenly. "Have you a preference?"

"Not at all."

"Then we'll begin with the stables." He started down the steps, and I had to walk quickly to keep up with him. Buffeted and thrashed about in the wind, I had a strong fear that this tour of the Hurst was not going to be as pleasant as anticipated. Colin was saturnine as we hurried along, continuing, no doubt, the argument in his mind. Of course he had to obey Uncle Henry, who was the head of the house, but it was becoming more and more apparent that Colin did not care for his uncle's prominent position.

The stables were around the house and to the left, with a private road for carriages. Four horses and a stableboy were the entire population, and that smell peculiar to husbandry pervaded the air. As we fell inside, forcing the door closed with our bodies, I had to catch my breath and straighten my bonnet, while Colin ran ten fingers through his wild hair.

It was quiet in the stable, dim and warm with occasional sounds from the animals. Startled mice scattered away from our feet. The horses rolled their eyes back at us. In the darkness, I could see the black shapes of the carriages and then wondered where the stableboy had got to.

"This is it," said Colin flatly. "Not terribly impressive, but serviceable."

I took a step forward, but my cousin held back, still leaning against the door. "Colin," I said impulsively, watching his expression in the half-light "Please take me to the coppice."

"The coppice?" His eyebrows arched. "Whatever for?"

"You said we used to play there as children. I should so love to see it. Perhaps I will remember something."

Cousin Colin seemed about to laugh. "You don't know what you're asking."

"Why?"

"Uncle Henry doesn't want you down there."

So I had hit upon it. My eyes still watching Colin, I went on, "Why not? The wind can be managed."

"It's not the wind, Leyla. I think you know why he doesn't want you there."

"It's because of my father and brother, isn't it? I do appreciate his concern for my welfare, but it won't upset me. It will only be a small wood of trees to me, even knowing that it is where they died. Please take me."

But he slowly shook his head. "You really don't know, do you, why you should stay away?"

"Haven't I said it?"

"Oh yes, your father and brother. But that's not the entire reason."

"Then tell me."

"I cannot."

"I have a right to know!"

Because I had shouted, Colin suddenly seized me by the shoulders and gave me such a look that I shivered despite the warmth of the stable. "Why did you have to come back, Leyla! It's for no good, can't you see that? You think you know everything, but you don't know the half of it! Leave the Hurst today—"

"No!"

"—and go back to your handsome architect. Forget the Pembertons; we can bring you no good."

"Colin, tell me please what everyone is keeping from me! I can feel it in their presence; I know you and Theo and my aunt and uncle are keeping secrets. I want to know. I have a right!"

"You have no right!"

"As much as you do, so do I, for I am a Pemberton, too. I was born in this house! Your father and my father were brothers. Whatever there is here, no matter how shameful, I have a right to know it. That's why I came back. Not for money or fancy dresses, but for a heritage I can call mine!"

"Even if that heritage is full of madness and murder?"

"All the more so. Tell me, Colin, please!"

His green eyes scanned my face in that search I was becoming accustomed to. "All right," he murmured. "I'll tell you. But when you've heard, when I am finished, promise me one thing."

"What is that?"

"That you will not despise me for it and hate me for having been the one to tell you."

"Colin—"

The darkness closed in about us while that evil wind created voices in the trees. Colin set his jaw grimly and began in a monotone. "Your mother left this house 20 years ago not only because she was stricken with grief: she also left to take you away. *To take you away,* Leyla, from something that had occurred here. I know you have wondered why you cannot remember what went on before your sixth birthday, but I know the reason . . . as do the others. We all share the memory that you were so mercifully spared. Yes, it has to do with the coppice, and your father and brother dying there. But it has to do with something else, too."

Colin took a deep breath. His hands were still firmly on my shoulders. "We were all here that day; no one was away from the Hurst. Sir John and Grandmother Abigail, Great-aunt Sylvia, my own father and mother, Uncle Henry and Aunt Anna, Theodore and Martha. And, of course, you and your mother. We were all home that day. Oh, Leyla . . ." He stopped to search my face again. "Leyla, it's difficult for me to say the words because I know what they are going to do to you. If you had never come back, you would have gone on with your happy life, marrying Edward Champion and never looking back to Pemberton Hurst. But because you did come back and because I must now tell you the truth, your life can never be the same again."

He took another deep breath and his fingers went deeper into my flesh. "It's about your father and brother and the way they died. What Theo told you is all true, about the knife and the murder and the suicide, but he left one fact out. The fact that there was *another person* in the coppice that day."

I stiffened.

"A third person who stood hidden in the trees and watched the bloody crimes committed. Who watched as Robert Pemberton slit little Thomas's throat and then plunged the knife into his own breast. And that third person . . . Leyla . . . was you."

CHAPTER 5

I TURNED AWAY FROM COLIN AND COVERED MY FACE WITH MY hands. I heard his voice continue, "We three found you there, standing over their bodies with the most bewildered expression on your face. You didn't cry, Leyla, or utter a sound. You were just a little five-year-old child staring in wonder at the two people on the ground. Uncle Henry lifted you up and carried you back to the house while I rode into East Wimsley for the doctor. Theo found your mother in the garden and brought her inside where the news would have to be broken."

Colin's hands were on my shoulders again, but this time gently. "You didn't make a single sound that day, Leyla, or the next day. And you wouldn't eat. You just sat in your room with a dazed expression on your face. But your mother cried. She cried so loudly as to be heard all over the house. It was terrible. I've never known such a black day."

I managed to find my voice and say, "What happened next?"

"You both disappeared. Early the morning of the third day, we heard wheels on the drive and discovered the dogcart missing. You and your mother had gone off in it, but you left all your belongings behind. She had packed not even one case."

"Did no one follow us?"

He was silent.

I spun around. "A grieving widow and a five-year-old child out on their own, and no one went after us?"

"Leyla, please listen—"

"So we had to live in the stink and misery of Seven Dials, my poor mother thin as a skeleton and me with no memory, while you lived on in your fat opulence as though we didn't exist!" My voice rose to the rafters. "How were you able to sleep at night!" I cried shrilly. "You monsters! All of you!"

With small fists, I feebly pounded Colin's chest until my knees gave way and I fell against him, sobbing. At once, his arms were tight around me, comforting, giving me the care I had needed 20 years ago. It was yesterday all over again, crying my soul out for my wretched father and brother, for the suffering my mother had endured. But this time I was crying for someone else, too. For a five-year-old child whose mind had been erased by tragedy.

We stood this way for a long time, Colin and I, while I poured my heart onto his tear-soaked lapel. After a while, I was able to manage words between sobs, saying, "I don't remember it. I don't remember it."

"God has been merciful to you, Leyla," he whispered against my hair. "It's best that you don't remember."

With this, I pulled away from my cousin and gave him a long, hard look. His eyes were sad and forlorn, his face heavy with sorrow. Yet there was something else there, too, something vague and imperceptible . . .

"You haven't told me everything, have you?"

He averted his eyes. "I've left nothing out."

"Don't lie to me, Colin; I don't deserve that. With each hour, I become more and more deeply enmeshed in the Pemberton tragedy. I was a part of it. More so than any of the rest of you. I have a right, Colin, to the *entire truth*."

When his eyes met mine, I knew I had won. Painful though it all may be, I had to know. For my mother's sake, since she had borne the burden for 20 years, it was now my turn to take it up. I owed that much to her.

"The whole truth," he went on gravely, "is your father. Or rather more precisely, the Pemberton line. Let's sit down, Leyla."

We moved to a bench, where, after Colin brushed it off, we sank down and leaned back against the slatted wall. The smell of hay and leather mingled with the soft whinnying of the horses gave an unreal atmosphere to the place, as though we were miles and years away from anyone else.

His voice came back to me again, speaking in a monotone close to my ear. As he spoke, pictures appeared before my eyes. "What you were witness to on that day and that you do not remember was a scene that has been enacted here before. There is a trait in the Pemberton blood—where it came from no one knows—but it appears in the form of a horrifying madness. Your father had no mysterious fever, no strange illness; he had merely become a victim of the Pemberton madness. The stories go back generations about bizarre killings and freakish deaths. Some of the legends you hear about the Hurst have foundations of truth in our history, and it is for this reason the local folk avoid us. We are known to be cursed—cursed by a bad strain of blood that condemns each and every Pemberton to a fate too macabre to imagine."

I looked up at him with great weariness. I was tired and weak, drained as if I had run many miles. "Each and every Pemberton?"

He nodded gravely. "According to the story Sir John told me, no Pemberton in the history of the Hurst has been spared. One way or another, at any time, the madness can strike."

"But that's absurd! Even if insanity is hereditary, it rarely strikes all offspring and usually skips a generation or two."

"Not so with us. We are a doomed line."

Doomed. Defeated. Inevitable. So this was what had caused the air of gloom I sensed about Uncle Henry. Possibly due to some faint memory as a child, perhaps after having overheard the adults speak of this inescapable fate, the sight of my uncle reminded me that he was a doomed man.

"It's too farfetched, Colin. I can't believe it."

"Why do you suppose your mother took you away? So that you wouldn't remember what you witnessed in the coppice? Perhaps. But I think she did it to take you away from this place in hopes it would free you of the destiny that awaits you."

"No, no, no," I said many times over. "It makes no sense. I refuse to believe it."

"Sir John killed himself by throwing himself off the east tower. His own brother Michael poisoned their mother and then himself. It goes back, far back. My own father was spared the fate by being killed in an accident. Otherwise, he too would have gone the way of all Pembertons."

"I feel ill, Colin. Take me back to the house."

We both stood shakily while I leaned on him for support. What he had said earlier, about my holding it against him for telling me the truth, was coming to pass. Colin was the bearer of very bad tidings; he had turned my life into a nightmare, and for the moment, I focused all my resentment upon him.

He must have sensed this, possibly in my altered tone or the way I would not look at him, for he said unhappily, "I had not wanted to tell you all this. It can achieve nothing. Yet you had to know. You persisted. My only hope now, Leyla, is that you will leave the Hurst at once, go back to London, and start a bright new life with your Edward. Forget us. Never think of us again."

We journeyed out of the stable, through the wind, and back into the house in silence. Colin's arm kept me upright as we mounted the stairs, the house silent and foreboding. When we paused before my door, I pushed him away in an effort to prove I could stand alone, and I said in a bitter tone, "I will not leave the Hurst."

"It can do no good for you to stay."

I shook my head violently. Although I could not delineate it myself or put the concept into words, a force other than my own was compelling me to remain in this house for a while longer. I didn't know what I was to do or why, yet I knew deep in my conscience that I had to stay.

When he turned to go, I said thickly, "And you can tell Grandmother I shall join her for tea."

As I stood before my vanity looking glass, I straightened my back and squared my shoulders as if part of a regiment being inspected by an officer.

What lay ahead of me was perhaps going to be one of the most important moments of my life. Obviously, Grandmother was a very important person, and I suspected it was she—not Uncle Henry—who manipulated the Pemberton household and fortune. If this were true, that Abigail Pemberton was a small-scale Empress Victoria, then she also had the answers to the many questions I intended to ask. Questions concerning my ancestry, my bloodline, my own past, my father and mother, and my standing with the family. Before becoming Mrs. Champion and relegating myself to an outermost branch of the Pemberton tree, I had to know everything.

My hours since seeing Colin had been fatiguing, spent in a mental battle of trying to keep a hold on reality. In less than 48 hours, I had come upon such startling revelations that my mind was having difficulty adjusting. What had started out to be a pleasant sojourn among long-lost relatives had turned out to be quite the opposite. My unexpected presence at the Hurst had upset the quotidian tranquillity of my relatives' lives; this to such an extent that they were uneasy with me and possibly resentful of my intrusion. And those blissful reminiscences I had looked forward to had turned out to be grisly nightmares that everyone wished to leave buried.

My mother's fortitude amazed me more and more. Before coming here, I had always known she had endured many torments to give me a comfortable life. It is never easy for a single woman, especially with a child. Yet through strength and courage, she had done it. But now that I knew the real truth behind her suffering silence—the true manner of her husband's and son's deaths—the fact that her daughter had witnessed them and that this tainted Pemberton blood supposedly doomed her child to a similar fate—now that I knew all this, I was even more in awe of her.

I was also now ready to meet Grandmother Abigail.

I rapped sharply on her door, strongly and with boldness. It was necessary to let her know from the start that, whatever mysterious power she wielded over her family, I was my own mistress and not at all like the others.

When I entered the room, I found that my estimations had not been overstated, for the very imperiousness of this woman was felt at once as I closed the door behind me. It was not unlike entering the private cloister of some great tyrannical ruler. The air was quiet and commanding, the furniture strong and imposing; the walls and hangings and plants seemed imbued with a sense of authority.

"Come forward where I can see you," came a voice made of stone.

She was seated high in a straight-backed chair, her face hidden in the darkness. Abigail Vauxhall Pemberton sat rigidly in black, from the collar clasping her thin throat to the broad skirt spread over her legs to the floor. I approached her warily, my self-confidence now being greatly on guard, and stood where I supposed she wished me.

"Step closer, child." It was a cold order: a disembodied voice suspended in the shadows. "I am 80 years old and my eyes are poor. How am I to look at you if you stand so far away?"

Moving closer, I felt annoyed with her critical words and tone, for they intimated she had already—within seconds—made a complete appraisal and judgment of me. And as I stood before her, trying to glimpse the face that sat behind a wall of darkness, the memory of a minor recollection stirred: that of a news item I had read not long before, telling the strange tale of an American seaman named Perry who was breaching the isolationistic policies of Japan, that mysterious country no Caucasian had ever seen. And out of his efforts had come bizarre tales that were printed regularly in the London *Times,* one of which now came to mind—that the Emperor of Japan never uncovered his face to anyone but sat always shielded because it was said he was too lofty to be looked upon. This was how I felt now, standing before this enthroned matriarch who seemed disinclined to expose her face.

"You approach timidly. Afraid of me, are you?"

"My approach is one of respect, not fear."

"Another step closer, Leyla. The light is poor, and I have not been well lately. That's better. Do you see the lamp on the table at your right? Turn it up now to illuminate your face."

I did as told, adjusting the flame from the bit of glimmer it was to a full glare, and when I turned round again, found that the light had revealed not only me but my grandmother as well. And as a consequence the two of us remained stiffly poised, regarding one another across the decades that separated us.

Grandmother Abigail was a phenomenally old woman. With a pale visage that might be found in Tussaud's, she was a preserved old dowager with fleece-white hair, dressed entirely in black with no jewelry or cosmetic to break the austerity. And yet, even though her skin hung in folds and was blanched of color, even though her hands were long and skeletal with bulging blue veins and brown spots, and even though she appeared emaciated to an alarming degree, it was her eyes that dominated her portrait. Hard and brilliant like those of a badger, they bespoke a youth and vitality not evident anywhere else in her body. By the sheer force of her indomitable eyes, Grandmother Abigail had full command of any situation, even to the extent of wielding some primeval power over those in her presence.

"How like your mother you are . . ." she whispered, almost as if she were seeing a ghost. "Jennifer . . ."

"I am told—"

"Do you know me?" asked the trembly voice.

"No, I don't know you, Grandmother; you are a total stranger to me, and yet you are my father's mother. I have your blood in me, but we are strangers."

"Your mother never spoke of me?"

I shook my head.

"That is a rude gesture. I might expect it of Colin, but not of you. If you have a reply, then you should make it with your voice and not your body. It is very unbecoming for a young lady to draw attention to her body."

"Yes, Grandmother," I said, a little nonplussed. That dilemma again: this woman was a stranger to me, and yet she was my closest living relative.

"I understand you know very little of us here. If that is so, then why did you come back?"

Not curiosity but more a command to explain my presence. That was her way of questioning. And those eyes remained fast upon me, hard little bullets that were deepest black and glistened like jet.

I thought of the letter. Had Aunt Sylvia, her sister, spoken in confidence of it before she died? For some reason, I had not yet been able to fathom, a tiny warning at the back of my head prompted me once again not to divulge the letter's existence.

We fell to staring at one another, myself unwilling to answer her question, she sensing my reticence. Staring from under heavy lids, those black orbs pierced me through and through, revealing nothing of the thoughts going on behind them, telling me nothing of how Grandmother regarded my sudden appearance. And as we stared like competitors for a laurel, the wind outside howled uncannily and sent branches flailing against the mullioned windows.

When she spoke, she startled me. "Two days ago, it was calm and still here at the Hurst. And then *you* came. Along with those winds from Hell. Did you bring them with you, Leyla?"

"I came from London, not Hell."

She raised an eyebrow to indicate they were one and the same to her. "So now my daughter-in-law is dead, and her daughter has returned to claim the family fortune."

Abigail was baiting me, but I would not rise to it. Such an innuendo, that I was here only for my share of the Pemberton wealth, had already been made by my other relatives so that by now I was inured to it and not so quickly angered.

"I came here for a family and a background, Grandmother. I was not free before this because my mother had been ill for a long time. Now I am free, and I also plan to marry, but before I do, I want to see my family again."

"And this . . . background? What are you looking for?"

"My past. Five blank years of my life that I want filled in."

She remained rigid. Whether or not my words had moved her I could not tell, although she must have discerned the bitterness in my voice as I had spoken of Mother's sickness.

There was a knock at the door then, and, upon a command, Grandmother's personal maid entered with a tray of tea and cakes. Without a word, she placed it between us on a low table and left the room.

As though nothing had changed, my grandmother went on, "I suspect Pemberton Hurst and its inhabitants are not how you imagined them. No one had ever expected to see you again, Leyla, so you must understand their slowness to accept you."

For an invalid who never left her room, Abigail was aware of a great deal that went on in her realm. There was obviously a chain of command in this house, and I suspected that my uncle Henry, her eldest son, headed the hierarchy.

"It will take time, I know."

Stiffly and with fingers impeded by arthritis, my grandmother started to pour the tea. "Cream and sugar?"

"Please." I stood gazing down at her, watching those ringless fingers and wondering how she must have appeared 50 years ago when her sons were little boys. I wondered also what the great Sir John had been like and the mysterious manner in which he had died. What did Grandmother think of Colin's fanciful Pemberton madness? Surely she was too pragmatic a woman to give credence to such fiction!

Another thought was also beginning to jell just now at the back of my mind: a vague, nebulous idea that had had its beginnings at the moment of Colin's startling news. And as the notion grew, it seemed I might soon voice it.

A teacup and saucer were set before me on the little table, although I was still standing. Then she rested back in her chair and brought her own cup close to her chin.

"Darjeeling tea has been served in this house for generations. Did your mother carry on the tradition in London?"

I was becoming indignant. Venerated matriarch or not, the old woman was purposely toying with me, asking me trivial questions when she should have shown more concern about those vacant 20 years. And still she did not invite me to take a seat.

"We couldn't afford it," I said flatly.

"Pity." She sipped it now and pursed her hard lips. "Tell me, Leyla. Do you ever suffer from headaches?"

"Headaches?" Someone else—who?—had also asked me that. "No. Only rarely."

"If ever you should have one, I've an old remedy that works wonders." She sipped again, observing me over the rim of her cup. "If you should ever have a bad headache."

"Thank you, I shall remember that." I stared down at my cup. It steamed invitingly.

"You know, Leyla, there is little to keep you here at the Hurst. You have seen what you came to see. There can hardly be any further reason—"

"Just one," I said softly, containing myself. "Those five years."

"Nonsense. Many people do not recall their infancy. Some people are slow and not terribly quick-witted. They forget easily."

"But I *should* remember. At least . . . one particular day of those five years."

Grandmother Abigail perused the cakes on the silver platter. "How so?"

"The day I saw my father kill Thomas and then himself."

It was imperceptible. Indeed, if I had not been purposely studying my grandmother for a reaction, I would have missed it. But I did not, and therefore glimpsed the briefest breakdown in composure, the most fleeting slip of her carriage. Then, quickly gathering herself together, the old woman straightened and raised those black currant eyes to mine.

So, she had not known that someone had told me about That Day.

"There is very possibly good reason for not remembering such an event. It can be a protective mechanism of the mind, enabling you to carry on a normal life without the onus of a horrid memory."

"Or, possibly, Grandmother, I had lost that memory due to the fear of something *else* happening. Of it possibly happening *to me.*"

Her lower lip trembled. "If you saw your father die, then you could not be afraid of his killing you."

"Quite right. Unless, of course, it was not my father that did the killing . . . but *someone else.*" There, it was out. The nagging thought that had been slowly growing at the back of my mind. It was a wild stab I took, a gesture that had no careful thought behind it or rational consideration. Yet, for some reason, I had to voice it, to let her know what I was thinking.

My heart began to pound. "Perhaps the five-year-old child that stood hidden in the bushes saw a *third person* enter the coppice and kill the father and brother. That would certainly be enough to instill such fear into the child that she might forget what she had seen. Is that possible?"

Grandmother was glowering angrily. "A moot point, Leyla. We know your father committed the acts. He was sick, deranged—"

"Yes, I know. The Pemberton madness."

Her eyes flew open. "Who told you? And who told you that you had been there that day? Was it Colin?"

"I don't know why there is such a ban on knowledge in this house, Grandmother. Obviously, up until yesterday you were assured that I knew nothing of my last day here. And obviously, you didn't want me to know."

"That's a great assumption."

"Why should you want me kept ignorant of that event? It occurred 20 years ago. Surely its telling cannot be so painful. Are you afraid I might remember something? Do you fear that, with Colin telling me about the incident, I will suddenly remember it all? I will suddenly *see* what it was I witnessed?"

"This is absurd. Why should I fear that?"

"Only for one reason. That there was a third party—"

"There was no one!" Her voice grew shrill. "It was your father! He went mad with the Curse as do all the Pembertons. No one escapes it, Leyla, and neither did your father."

"I don't believe that!" Something was coming back to me. Vaguely, like a mist, it stalked the exterior of my mind. Something about Grandmother's hands.

"You should leave this house at once. There is nothing for you here. If it is money you want—"

"I want no money."

"Go back to your fine architect—"

"You're a knowledgeable woman, Grandmother. Who is it that sneaks to you in the night like a spy and whispers in your ear? Who is it that acts as your eyes and ears while you're confined to this room? Uncle Henry? Aunt Anna? Theodore? Martha?"

"Your impudence is most displeasing to me, Leyla. I wish to be left alone. You are too much like your mother, always tiring me. And you are your father, too. It's in your eyes and your chin."

"Are you warning me of the madness, Grandmother? That query about headaches was no idle concern, was it? Is that how it starts?"

"You'll find out as the others did."

Our eyes became locked in combat again. How terribly distraught I had become during this interview, how distressing it was to find that my own grandmother had not offered me the family welcome I so desperately needed. Then I was overcome by a paroxysm of contrition. The woman before me was my father's mother—she had given birth to him, had nursed him as a baby, and had seen him grow tall and handsome. She had also presided over my own birth and had probably dandled me upon her knee in maternal love. How desperately now I wanted to go back 20 years, become a child again, and feel once more the affection and security of a closely knit family.

But it was gone. Whatever had happened these past 20 years—from that disastrous day to this—these people had metamorphosed into antagonists who made it quite clear I was unwelcome among them.

"I don't believe in such a foolish curse, and I am surprised that you do. If you know so much about me, Grandmother, and can see how like my mother I am, then you must also know that I am a stubborn and unrelenting person and that I will not leave this house until I have found what I came for."

This I said in a low, calm voice, and yet the words made a great impact. Her hard little eyes flashed at me in anger. "I see your mind is made up. Since you are a Pemberton and a direct descendent of Sir John, I cannot forbid you residence in this house. For as long as you are here, you may live as one of us; that much is your birthright. However, I cannot guarantee you will find this . . . this quest you so mindlessly seek. Obviously, you will not be satisfied until you think you have found it. But let me warn you . . ."

Her ancient voice rang across the shadows like that of a prescient sorceress. "One thing you cannot ignore, and that is your Pemberton blood—the Pemberton 'inheritance.' I warn you to leave this house at once, *tonight,* and go marry your architect while you yet have time to enjoy him. But I know you will not heed me. And so . . . in the interim—"

"In the interim, dear Grandmother, you will pass along an edict forbidding the others to make me too comfortable and to insist they not speak of my past."

"You're very imaginative, Leyla." She leaned over the cakes again and picked one up. A picture of her hands flashed in my head. Slightly different from these, less bony and veined, but definitely her hands. And then a ring on one of them. A red-stone ring.

"It is impolite not to taste your hostess's tea."

The memory vanished. I looked down at the cup, thinking what a treat it would be to taste a rich, imported tea. But I had no chair and could not eat while standing. I knew Grandmother's game and refused to play it.

"I have had a lot of tea already today, Grandmother, and I'm very tired. I think I shall go back to my room."

"It is also impolite not to ask permission to leave. Your education in social etiquette, it would seem, was sadly lacking in your youth."

"That would be due, I suppose, to the long and strenuous hours my mother had had to work, laboring in crowded, lightless rooms until the bad fevers eventually rotted her lungs. When one doesn't know where tonight's supper will come from, it is difficult to keep one's social etiquette in mind."

With this, I turned on my heel and swept gracefully to the door. As I started to open it, a crone's voice said behind me, "You are a rude child, Leyla, and in an unforgivable state of impertinence. If your stay here is for long, your manners will have to improve."

I walked out and closed the door softly behind me. Tears stung my eyes. A sob caught in my throat How desperately I had wanted to be accepted by her, to share an embrace and enjoy the warm relationship of grandmother and granddaughter. But this obviously was not to be.

I hurried to my room lest I encounter one of the others of my "family" and latched the door once inside. A cozy room with a fire, it was not my room. It was not the flat in London where so many of my cherished memories dwelt: Mother's final payment of our last debt; my first gentleman caller; bringing Edward home for supper; his proposal of marriage in the parlor. The only happiness I had ever known in my life I had known in that modest flat. But here in this regal old bedroom of noble furnishings I was not content.

I roamed the chamber restlessly. The episode with Grandmother had unnerved me far more than any with the other relatives. Her acceptance of me had been important. But now that was gone. I had handled the situation terribly. I had walked into her trap, had fallen for her cheap ploys, and had let myself show anger and haughtiness. Whatever little hope there might have been of salvaging Grandmother's affection was all lost now. And with it, all hope of ever befriending the other members of this household. I was on my own.

CHAPTER 6

THE WIND CONTINUED TO HOWL DEVILISHLY FOR THE REST OF the afternoon and into early evening. My body and mind were spent from the two days of startling revelations and mental travails, so that I sat now in a window seat staring out at the turmoil of the forest.

A similar tumult was swirling in my mind as a myriad of questions plagued me. That Grandmother had unsettled me was to say the least. Her warnings that I leave . . . Her obvious awareness of everything that went on . . . Who was her special confidant? It could not be Colin, for his talk with me in the stable had come as a surprise to her.

And what about that talk? Had he really told me such a bizarre tale of killings and bloodshed? Was it true I had really been the only one to witness it?

And this brazen new idea I had blurted out to Grandmother—about a "third party" at the coppice—where had I got it from? And did I truly believe it?

And the Curse, this madness that everyone seemed to believe in. What was its basis? Where were the foundations behind this legend that doomed every Pemberton to such a wretched end?

While I sat and pondered this, a new and fresh quandary found room in my beleaguered mind: Aunt Sylvia. Why had she, out of an entire family that purposely eschewed me, been the only one to want me to come back? Why had she been different? What had gone through her mind at the writing of her letter? What had been her motive, her intention to write me in secret to bring me back to the Hurst?

It was a puzzle with no solution. Nothing made sense, nothing fit.

Without purpose, I moved aimlessly to the vanity table and idly picked up the guidebook to Cremorne Gardens. The romantic footpaths, the fragrance of acacias in bloom, the glittering lanterns against a summer sky all came back to me. This had been Edward's favorite place to take me, where we would drink lemonade, walk arm in arm through the flowers, dance the quadrille or possibly—daringly—the polka. How I loved Edward. Such a dear man with handsome face and bearing. So formal and so polite. A gentleman that made any girl proud to be on his arm.

And next spring I would be his wife. The wife of a man who had helped design Trafalgar Square and the new Houses of Parliament. A man who was impeccable in dress and carriage, who wore beaver top hats and carried an ebony cane. My handsome Edward, whom other women espied out of the corners of their eyes. I would be his wife, his envied wife, and I would be free of Pemberton Hurst forever.

Then I thought of Colin, my 34-year-old cousin who had the manners of a gin-house keeper and whose wavy hair was never quite in place. Why wasn't he married? I wondered.

A knock at the door brought me out of my reverie. It was Martha, dressed as usual in a beautiful gown and smelling of imported perfume. I remembered Martha more and more, a quiet little girl who played simple tunes on the pianoforte and worked endless hours of needlepoint. She had the alluring Pemberton lashes, the slightly large nose, and the faint cleft in her chin. Cousin Martha with her charm and taste and domestic qualities would be a fine catch for any man.

Then I wondered: Why isn't *she* married?

"It's almost suppertime, Leyla," she said, searching my face. I supposed the whole family knew by now that Colin had told me what they had been forbidden to speak of. And now Cousin Martha, in her typical empathetic manner, was searching my face for signs of sorrow, of defeat.

"Leyla." She approached me with hands extended. "I am truly sorry you had to find out the truth. I had hoped, we had all desperately hoped, that at least one Pemberton could lead a happy, normal life, without the obsession of the madness. I will be a victim, too, Leyla, just as you will be, because our fathers were brothers. My fate will be the same as yours. I'm sorry you know. If only Colin weren't such a—"

"No, Martha, it's not his fault. I forced him to tell me. It was apparent from the start that you were all keeping something from me. I would have had to know sooner or later."

"And now that you know," she squeezed my hands, "you *will* go away at once, won't you, and have a happy life?"

I stared at my cousin Martha.

Everyone was at supper except for Colin. No one explained his absence, and I did not ask. An air hung over us all that was as thick as the soup we ate, and I suspected its cause was Grandmother Abigail. So now I knew what it was these people had wanted me never to know. Yet surely this was not cause for such a taciturn mood. Granted, they would have preferred I never know the truth of my father's death, and this was kind of them, but now that I did know the facts, surely no cause existed for such gloom.

Unless, of course, I did *not* know all the facts.

The mutton was excellent and the potatoes boiled just right. Our country air did something to the appetite that London's sooty fog could not. Feeling the whalebone stays of my corset dig deeper and deeper, I put away as much of Gertrude's treats as possible.

Yet despite the excellence of the food and the congeniality of our setting, no one seemed inclined to speak.

Aunt Anna sat solemnly before her plate with a purposeful avoidance of my eyes. One hand in her generous lap, she ate as automatically as if she were a machine. Uncle Henry, continuing to affect me with an aura of doom, seemed preoccupied with something and hardly ate at all. Cousin Martha was her usual sweet self, sympathetic and apologetic and anxious about my feelings. Cousin Theo, on the other hand, savoring the meal as much as did I, appeared many times on the verge of speaking but instead only acknowledged me now and then with his eyes.

I knew what they were all thinking, and I was prepared to answer them. The conclusion I had reached was this: When I had first come to the Hurst—was it only two days ago?—the least of my intentions had been to recall those lost five years, since my main objective had been to rediscover my family again. However, in the course of my short stay here, many things had occurred to change my mind, to alter priorities. Where my infancy had once only been a secondary consideration, it now became my prime concern. The need to remember was growing within me.

I recalled Colin's words of this morning as we had left the stable: "Leave the Hurst at once. Go back to London and forget us." And I recalled also my inner reaction to that: that a strange and compelling force seemed to be telling me that I must stay. The ensuing hours of great mental struggle and the ludicrous "interview" with my grandmother had all strengthened a vague intuition deep within me. It was the nebulous idea—perhaps having germinated from a forgotten memory of the past that I still could not recall—that somehow, for some reason, my father was innocent.

I could not pinpoint such a notion, or really even put it into words; yet so strong a feeling it was that I knew I must let it govern my future actions. Just as I had learned that my sensation of defeat and fatalism around Uncle Henry was in fact based upon the truth of his supposed doom from the Pemberton madness, so did I now believe that my impalpable intuition of Father's innocence of crime lay in a forgotten truth.

Because of this, because of a new conviction that somehow my father could not have done what everyone said he did, I knew that I had to remain at the Hurst and remember that last day.

So this was to be my answer to the queries I knew my relatives entertained. I somehow suspected my father of being not guilty of a horrible murder, and I knew, therefore, that the answer would lie in my memory. If I were suddenly to remember what it was I had witnessed in the coppice that day, then it followed I would also remember who the real murderer was. If the killer was a Pemberton who supped with me now, then their present mood would suddenly make sense. They did not want me to remember; they were protecting someone.

It was not until trifle was served that Uncle Henry opened conversation. As usual, I tried to imagine it was my father I watched and listened to. As usual, Aunt Anna came up with trite banalities that I knew to be cover-ups of what she really felt. And as usual, Cousin Martha remained aloof from discussion, anxious, I supposed, to find a pillow to embroider.

"So tell me, Cousin Leyla," said Theo in forced idleness, "are the streets any quieter now that London is replacing stone paving with wood?"

"The experiment did not last, Cousin Theo, since it was found that wood was too slippery in the rain. Unfortunately, London will always be afflicted with noise, which I suppose is what keeps you away."

"Not really, my dear. Pembertons aren't travelers, you know." He echoed his own words of two nights before. The Pembertons did not travel. The Pembertons rarely left their house. Why?

"You miss so much by staying at home," I ventured.

Uncle Henry rejoined with, "We have all we need right here at the Hurst. Pembertons are not Society people, for we are industrious enough to entertain ourselves within our own walls and with our own resources. Gentry who require townhouses cannot be terribly imaginative."

I stared at my relatives. They were *proud* of their sedentary existence, even boasted of it. At once, I was reminded of a cloistered clan of monastic brothers, sworn to secrecy and to eternal fraternity. By the hour, this house was becoming more and more bizarre.

A brief silence passed, with each of my relations, I was certain, thinking of what to say next. It was—oddly—Aunt Anna, unfolding and refolding her table napkin with downcast eyes, who asked, "When will you be leaving the Hurst?"

"Aunt Anna!" said Martha impulsively. "That's not polite."

"Seriously," followed Theo, staring at me directly. "What are your plans, now that you know."

"Now that I know what?" This was what I had been waiting for, preparing for.

"Well, surely now you'll be leaving the Hurst, now that you've found what you weren't able to remember from the past," said Martha.

I looked at her. She, too, wanted me to leave. "You mean about my father?"

She nodded tacitly.

"That might be true, that I would leave the Hurst tomorrow, were I to believe the story. However, I do not. And as it happens, I've decided to remain until I *can* remember just exactly what did happen that day."

"Whatever do you mean?" Aunt Anna's pudgy hand fluttered to her breast. "Are you saying we are lying?"

"No, not you. It is possible you are all laboring under a falsehood and not aware of it. But I have a feeling, a strong intuition, Aunt Anna, that my father did not do what you all think. He was blameless, I can *feel* it."

"But that's absurd," began Theo.

"How do you know?" I turned on him. Now I was defending not only my father but my mother and myself as well. "Did any of you see it? Were any of you—other than myself—there that day to witness the actual murder? Then how can you be so sure? When I first came to the Hurst three nights ago, I was content to let bits of memory dribble back to me. And I would have been content with whatever memory returned, no matter how slight. But that has all changed now. Now it is important that I remember. Rather than sit back and let the memories happen into my mind, I will *fight* to bring them back. Do you understand, Uncle Henry?"

"You will only do yourself injury, Bunny. You will remember a horrifying event that will haunt you for the rest of your life. Spare yourself that, Leyla."

"It would seem I am now saddled with the Pemberton doom to which we must all succumb. Why not add a little more to make the burden complete?"

Not catching my sarcasm, Uncle Henry leaned far across the table and seemed to plead with his eyes. "Leave well enough alone, Bunny."

"But it's not well enough. Don't you see? I don't believe my father was a murderer. I don't believe my mother ran away from here because of a bad memory. I think she took me away to protect me from something or *someone.* And, furthermore, I don't believe in the Pemberton Curse. This is 1857, an age of enlightenment and scientific progress. Ghosts and curses no longer exist."

"But it caused your father to do what he did."

"I won't have it!" Forgetting myself, I stood abruptly so that I towered above these people who would condemn a man without a fair trial. "I think the Pemberton curse was a fabrication, a spurious tale to lay the blame upon my father and conceal the true murderer."

"Stop it, Leyla!" said my uncle.

"Henry!" cried Anna. There was fright in her eyes.

"Every one of you is anxious for me to leave here. Why? I was only five when I left you. I should have been received with open arms and friendship, a time for reuniting and reminiscing. Yet you did not. You treat me as a plague. What happened, tell me, what happened 20 years ago to cause all this?"

"You're just bringing back bad memories, that's all."

Everyone whipped about as Colin strolled into the dining room. His hands were swaggishly thrust into his pockets, and his smile was as sloppy as his hair. He had been listening at the door, and I wondered for how long.

"And you're spoiling their trifle as well. See? No one's had more than a bite. Your presence makes them remember things they don't want to remember."

"Colin—" began Uncle Henry.

"Have you noticed we have no paintings about the house? It's because no one wants to be reminded."

"Of what?"

Colin shrugged, and it annoyed me. "Am I too late for the mutton? Ah well, I'll have two helpings of dessert, then. Pass the bowl, will you, dear Sister?"

As he sat opposite me and accepted the trifle from Martha, I felt my anger increase by degrees. So different from the man he was that morning in the stable, my cousin Colin was once again the flippant boor. I thought of Edward in that moment, my dear predictable Edward, who was always even and never capricious, and I resented the vagaries of my cousin. Not only was he impolite, he was also uncaring of the effect his manner had upon others.

"Colin," said Martha quietly. "Leyla has decided to stay with us."

He did not look up. "Indeed? Gertrude has left the sliced almonds out of the trifle again. You really must speak to her about it, Uncle."

Uncle Henry and his wife and Theodore exchanged glances while Martha withdrew diffidently into herself. I was beyond caring now what these people thought; I owed them nothing, just as they seemed to owe me nothing. Angry and confused, I sped from their presence and out into the hall.

Darkness met me everywhere; the giant plants that stood in their corners like soldiers awaiting an order, the gloomy tapestries covering the paneled walls, the immense furniture that towered above me as my grandmother would wish to do. Her presence was all about me, omnipotent and omniscient. This house *was* her.

I found my way into the library after a few moments and sank down wearily before the fire. Nothing made sense. Nothing was happening the way it should.

I was staring morosely into the fire when Martha entered. She crept catlike to the stuffed chair opposite me, hovered over it for a moment, then sat very quietly with sorrowful eyes upon me. She had been 12 when I left; now she was 32: a spinster as chaste and untouched as if she had taken the veil.

"Oh, Leyla, I am so, so sorry." Her little white hands wrung themselves bloodless. "How I wish I could change it all for you. How deeply I feel what you must be going through."

I raised my eyes to her. Of all the Pembertons, I liked Martha best. Yet that really was not saying much. "Martha," I said tiredly, "why are there no portraits of the family?"

"It's Grandmother's wish. She does not like to be reminded of the madness."

"I don't believe in the madness."

"But it's true! Sir John—our grandfather—succumbed ten years ago when he went mad and threw himself off the east tower. Such a history it has had!"

"How far back?"

"Pardon?"

"How far back does the Curse go? Can you tell me?"

"Why . . ." Her pretty eyes squinted in a frown. "Let me see. I've been told it goes back for many generations, but the oldest story I know any details of is Sir John's brother Michael, who, in the delirium of the madness, poisoned himself and then his mother. Beyond that, Sir John's father and so on back, I've never heard the real stories."

"And who told you all this?"

"Grandmother, of course."

"I see." My eyes wandered back to the fire, perceiving there the withered face of Empress Abigail, who wielded some mysterious force over her tiny realm.

"Are there any family Bibles or genealogies I might be able to read?"

Martha scanned the tiers and tiers of books surrounding us. I could see she was not a reader. "Not that I know of."

"It's all right, Martha. I have plenty of time." Listening to the crackle of the fire, I weighed my next words. "What can you tell me about Aunt Sylvia?"

"Aunt Sylvia? Oh, she was very old, though not as old as Grandmother. And she never married, but came with her sister Abigail to live here many years ago."

"Did she die of the madness, too?"

"Oh no. Aunt Sylvia was a Vauxhall, not a Pemberton. Only those of Pemberton blood have the sickness. Like you and me and Uncle Henry and Theodore and Colin. Grandmother Abigail and Aunt Anna are not Pembertons and so are free from it."

"When I was five years old, Martha," I said carefully, "who were the people dwelling in this house?"

She hesitated before replying. "Well, there were Sir John and Abigail. Then Aunt Sylvia. Next there were Uncle Henry and Aunt Anna and Theo. There were my father and mother and Colin and me. And there were your father and mother and you."

"And Thomas."

"And your brother Thomas."

"So on that day, then, there were 14 people in residence here. And now, 20 years later, there remain but seven."

"Yes, but 20 years is a long time, and some of them were old. Aunt Sylvia had to die soon; she was 75. And Sir John was 70."

"And your father and mother?"

Martha looked down at her clasped hands. The knuckles were white. "They died in a carriage accident."

"Martha." I leaned forward with a spark of hope. If I were clever, if I were cautious enough, I could win my cousin to my cause. "Martha dear, forgive me for exhuming such bad memories, but I have 20 years to fill in. Please be patient with me. Martha, you have lost your father and mother; I have lost mine and a brother. It would appear to me"—I spoke slowly now—"that the sharing of the fortune is being narrowed down a great deal . . ."

She gazed wistfully into my eyes for a moment, then, "Leyla Pemberton!" She stood so fast that she nearly lost her balance. "How dare you insinuate such a thing!"

"Please, Martha—" I glanced toward the door.

"How can you say such a horrid thing? My parents were killed in an accident like hundreds of people are. Your father committed suicide, and your mother died in London of an illness. How can you link any of these to a sordid plot to gain all the Pemberton money!"

Martha's voice rose higher and higher. I had not thought her capable of such a show. "It's beastly what you're thinking! We are a loving family. It is you who are the stranger here! We had quite forgotten you until you showed up unexpectedly like a mendicant for a handout. Grandmother was right. If anyone is after the Pemberton fortune, it is you!"

"Martha, that's not true!" I also flew to my feet and sought frantically to mollify her.

"I don't like what you said, Leyla. Now you've upset me, and it's hard to be your friend."

When she started toward the door, I seized her wrist and tried to say a word, but another voice intervened. "Let her go, Cousin. You've done enough."

I glared angrily at Colin. "Don't you ever knock?"

"I said, let go of my sister."

Martha dashed out of the room between us and could be heard pounding up the stairs. To where? To tell Grandmother?

"This is none of your affair," I said furiously.

"Come now, dear Cousin." He shrugged like a Frenchman, kicked the door closed with his boot, and sauntered to a chair before the fire. "Anything that concerns the Pembertons concerns me. I warned you we were a tight family."

"But why?"

He shrugged again.

"Colin, for the love of God"—I placed myself before him—"why won't anyone answer my questions?"

"Sit down, you're blocking the fire."

Like a petulant child, I fell into a chair, chastising myself for having blundered again.

"Is it so important to you to remember the past?"

"Yes, dearly yes."

"Why? What good can it do?"

"I don't know. Somehow I feel if I can alter the past, I can alter the present, too."

"Aren't you happy in the present?"

I met his bold gaze. "Right now I am not. Before I came to the Hurst, I had an entirely different past—thinking my father and brother died of cholera. But now that past has changed, and in so doing has reached out to change the present."

"What is it that makes you so certain your father was innocent?"

"Deep inside me, Colin, is a memory I cannot grasp. Yet a shade of it, a mere vapor of it, has risen to my conscious to tell me that what I hear of that day in the coppice doesn't ring true. Although I cannot remember what did happen, there is a strong feeling all the same within me that what has been told me is not the truth. Do you understand this?"

When I looked at him again, my face hot from the fire and my cheeks flushed, I saw Colin once again as he had been that morning—serious, compassionate, and strong.

But in an instant, the character vanished as a skittish smile broadened his face. "Bit melodramatic, don't you think?"

My shoulders slumped forward. "I cannot believe this nightmare. Something is terribly wrong somewhere, and it's up to me to find out what it is. Tell me, Colin, did Aunt Sylvia ever speak of me?"

"Aunt Sylvia?" He gave this brief consideration. "No, not that I had ever heard. None of us in this family ever spoke of you or your mother. Least of all Aunt Sylvia. Why do you ask?"

I shook my head.

"What is so special about Aunt Sylvia?"

"I will not answer your questions, Colin, if you don't answer mine."

"Hang it all, Leyla, be fair with me!"

"And I'll ask you, sir, to mind your language. This isn't Billingsgate!"

"I suppose your proper Edward never offends you."

"Surely not! Edward is a gentleman."

"Then go back to him. Get out of this house where you don't belong and marry the poor blighter before he comes breaking down the door after you."

Such an amusing suggestion brought me to smile despite myself, for Edward would never be so lunatic as to storm a door for possession of me. An idea like that might come from Colin, who obviously wouldn't give a second thought to committing such a social effrontery.

"What is so amusing?"

"You sound like a domineering brother."

"Isn't that what I almost am? Our fathers were brothers. That makes us quite close in the bloodline."

I offered Colin a smile of friendship, as much as he irritated me, and was surprised to receive one in return.

"Now what do you mean to be fair with you?"

"Already you have forced me to tell you more than we thought you should know." He held up a hand. "Please hear me out. All the others and I agreed with Grandmother that, for your own good, we were not to let slip any words about the past, for we wanted you to be free of it, as we are not but wish we were. Instead I weakened, sensing what it must be like to wonder and have no one tell you. So I told you about your father, and then—out of fairness to your memory of him—I told you about the madness so you would at least know he was not responsible for what he did. But I regret that moment of weakness, Leyla. Look at the anguish it is causing you—trying to remember something that will only hurt you."

I sighed restlessly before my cousin. His eyes were sincere, his words fetching. Could it be so simple? That the story of the madness and my father's delirium had been true? That these people had only been trying to protect me?

My eyes wandered over Colin's face. Not as handsome as Edward's, nor as well bred nor refined; there were, however, lines of character and candor and other special qualities.

No. It was all wrong. My intuition was stronger than ever, and I refused to relent. My father had been innocent, and the Curse only a myth. And the proof of this lay in the frightened mind of a five-year-old child.

"Answer my questions, Colin, please. Why doesn't anyone ever leave this house? Why is Martha the youngest one here, and she 32? Why do I still harbor the feeling that you are all keeping some knowledge from me? What had you meant that first night when you said my mother would not have sung praises about this family? Why does Grandmother—"

"Leyla, Leyla! Stop, please." He performed a bit of histrionics to move me, then said as if exasperated, "Your questions are as outlandish as your imaginings. You are creating puzzles, not trying to solve them."

"I want to exonerate my father."

"By asking me why my sister is 32."

"You devil!" I cried, infuriated once more. "Now it is you who are being unfair to me. Well, Colin Pemberton"—I stood with arms akimbo—"if you want me to leave the Hurst, then you will first have to answer my questions."

With that, I stormed out of the room, a habit I was quickly forming, and climbed the stairs in a most unladylike way. Once in my room, I fumed before my looking glass, enraged that my churlish cousin should be able to manipulate me so. It ired me that he was so changeable and unpredictable. And his ungentlemanly frankness was most annoying.

My eyes fell upon the Cremorne Gardens book, and I decided at once to write a letter to Edward. I wanted to tell him the entire story, ask his advice—indeed, his protection, if necessary. The reputation of my poor father was relying upon me, and if I were in any way bringing danger upon myself for it, then Edward's knowledge of the situation would be my insurance.

I had been writing for an hour when there came a knock at my door. Several attempts at starting the letter had caused a mound of crumpled stationery by my feet; my hair had come unbound from its knot and was brushing my face. The exact words to say to Edward, the words that would describe exactly the situation I had encountered here, had still not come easily after an hour.

"Come in," I said wearily.

Uncle Henry poked his head round the door. "Are you asleep, Bunny?"

"Not at all. Please come in."

He entered with a secretive attitude, as though not wanting anyone to know what he was up to. He tread softly across my carpet, looking first left, then right, and spoke in whispers. "I've disturbed you."

I glanced down at the letter and slid my hands over it. "Not at all. You're welcome anytime, Uncle Henry. Shall we sit by the fire?"

"Yes, oh yes."

I followed him to the horsehair sofa that glowed yellow in the ember light, and puzzled over his arcane attitude. The familiar air of doom still hung about him, but I was becoming used to this and gave it no notice. There was something else, something odd about his person that I could not define but that was there all the same. He hesitated, seemed to pick over his thoughts, and kept looking about the room in small, furtive glances.

"What is it, Uncle Henry?"

He finally turned his full face to me, and then I saw it. The small pupils, the glassy eyes. My uncle was under the influence of opium.

"You quite distressed your cousin Martha tonight. Indeed, your words have worried us all. You are being irrational, Leyla, and I must warn you."

"Warn me?"

"Not to venture into areas that do not concern you."

"Do not concern me! My father's and brother's deaths? You think they do not concern me?"

"They occurred 20 years ago, Bunny!"

"Whether only yesterday or 20 years ago, it is all the same to me. My duty to them is to clear their names."

"But it's futile, Leyla! What you are trying to remember is only a ghastly nightmare. Believe me, if you do one day recall what you saw in the coppice, then you will see we have told you the truth."

"If that is so, Uncle, then why do you all care so much that I remember? Why do you all seem to *fear* that I will remember?"

"For your sake alone, Bunny."

"And all you wish for me is to return to London and marry Edward. Is that right?"

Uncle Henry did not answer. Instead, his eyes darted about the room, restless, searching. I wondered why he had taken the laudanum.

"Or"—I dropped my voice—"don't you want me to marry after all?"

He swung round and seized my hands. His palms were moist and clammy. "If you marry anyone, Leyla, you will be passing on the Pemberton taint!"

"There exists no such thing, Uncle Henry. How can you believe a myth that has no basis in fact?"

"Because it does exist!"

"I refuse to believe it."

Uncle Henry's face clouded. "You should never have come back here, Leyla—"

"Well, I have and there is no turning back. I intend to go forward with my plan and recover the memory—ghastly as it may be—that is rightfully mine."

"It might never come, Leyla."

"It will. I know it will."

"None of us will help you."

How well I knew that. Aunt Anna had never helped in the first place. Colin was now against my knowing. Martha was angry with me. And Theo—what was *his* position? The memory was to be brought back through my own willpower alone.

"How do you propose to recover a memory that is locked fast in your mind and is unwilling to come forth?"

I gazed at Uncle Henry with all the composure I could manage, for I was tired and full of anxiety. In my best voice, I said to him, "I will do it by going tomorrow to the coppice."

CHAPTER 7

He sat for a long time staring dazedly at me, and I wondered if he had heard. Finally Uncle Henry licked his lips and murmured, "You must not go to the coppice, Leyla. Not ever."

How like my father he must be—in the face, in his posture, in the sound of his voice. Under normal circumstances, I would love this man who had my eyes and chin, with the striking gray hair and handsome coat. Yet I did not, could not for as long as I feared him. Not fear in the usual sense of fright, but a terrible wariness of how far he would go to protect the family secret. Uncle Henry would never harm me, I was certain of that, but his opposition could make me very unhappy.

"I will go because I must go."

"And why!" he burst suddenly. "To what end!"

"So that I will remember."

"I know what your plan is, Leyla; I know what you are after. By claiming your father's innocence, you are shifting the guilt to another member of this house. You are accusing a Pemberton of murder!"

"My father was a Pemberton, and you all nicely accuse him."

"That was different. He was driven by the fever and delirium."

"How very convenient for you all. But I don't believe it."

"And motive? What could be the motive? Your insinuation to Martha was beastly, that we have internecine rivalry for the money. How base and common of you."

This hurt me to the quick. For them to accuse my defenseless father of murder was noble and compassionate. But for me to accuse one of them of the same reduced me to vulgarity.

"There can be no other way. I will go to the coppice tomorrow."

After this, Uncle Henry seemed to recede into a world of his own. I cannot imagine how much laudanum he had ingested or why he had taken it, but I knew it to be a potent analgesia.

My curiosity was satisfied when he next said, placing a palm to his forehead, "This one is worse than any before."

"What is worse, Uncle?"

"The headache. Oh, these headaches, Leyla, how tedious they can be."

I gazed at my uncle in mild alarm. "How much laudanum did you take, Uncle?"

"Hm?" His eyes missed mine by an inch. He was not able to focus. "Anna gave it to me in my tea. I need more this time, though. That dreadful wind is blowing bad drafts all through the house. That's what causes the headaches."

"I see . . . Tell me, Uncle Henry, did my father ever suffer from them?"

"What? Oh, I've got to be getting back. Mother always expects me to see her before she retires."

"Grandmother can wait a moment—"

Then he laughed loudly, sickly. "How little you know, Bunny. No one makes Abigail Pemberton wait for anything!" He rose on unsteady legs and blindly laid a hand upon my shoulder. "Leyla, go back to London while you can."

"I don't think so, Uncle. Not now . . ."

As he found his balance, his eyes swept the room again, and I saw them light upon my unfinished letter to Edward. "Writing to someone?"

"No," I lied. "Just jotting down some thoughts for a diary entry. The wind inspires me—"

"It gives me blasted headaches!" Uncle Henry fell at once sheepish. "Forgive my language, Bunny, but my head is bursting apart. We can talk more in the morning when you feel better."

"But I feel fine."

"Guide me to the door, will you? I'm a bit unsteady."

I led him as if he were a cripple, which caused me to suspect he had taken the medicine just before coming to me, for now its effect seemed to be increasing. At the door, he paused and let his eyes rove my face. How badly I had wanted to be loved by this man who could be my father but who made it impossible—just as with Grandmother Abigail, whom I had so wanted to endear but who had rejected me.

"Sleep well, Bunny."

"Good night, Uncle Henry." I kissed him on the cheek, but he seemed not to notice. Watching him stagger down the candle-lit hall until he reached his own door, I felt a great wave of despair come over me. Uncle Henry cut a tragic figure indeed. For whatever reason—his domineering mother, his impotence as head of the house, or his debilitating headaches—my uncle was not to be my source of strength.

Turning back into my room and leaning heavily upon the door, I wondered in the darkness how I was to endure all this. Grandmother Abigail had abandoned me, Uncle Henry had let me down, Martha was angry with me, and Colin was not to be counted on for anything. Who then? Aunt Anna? No, she would sway with Grandmother's will even more easily than did her husband. Theo? No, for he was most likely to join the ranks of his parents.

Who then?

I dreamed my way across the carpet, seeing the last dying embers out of the corner of my eye, and let myself be drawn to the windows. These windows that kept the *sane* world out and kept *us* locked in. These windows through which one could view the violence of nature, yet not have to suffer it. How wise it would have been of me to return to London at once and take up my place with Edward! But then, love and hate and sorrow are not lent to wisdom. There is no explaining the logic of the heart.

I turned away to peer into the blackened fireplace. If I could get Edward to join me here, it might satisfy both alternatives at once. But in the meantime, I would need someone to talk to. Someone to answer my questions.

Then I thought of Gertrude, the Germanic housekeeper whose face upon seeing me I would never forget. Shock? Fear? Or simply surprise? How did *she* regard my homecoming? As improper as it might be to discuss family affairs with a servant, I knew that Gertrude must have figured largely in my baby days, perhaps even to having been my nursemaid on occasion. And if that were so, if she looked back on those times with a sweet sadness, then possibly she would be more given to talk.

But it would have to be in secret. I knew that for certain.

Edward's letter came easily this time, for my uncle's visit had reinforced my resolve to find the absolute truth, no matter what the cost. I let my thoughts and pen run freely together, writing exactly what I felt—from my heart. There was no other way to tell him. With my closing words, I prayed he would recognize my desperation and come at once, dropping his floor plans without a thought.

I sealed the letter with care and decided that a maid could carry it by coach in the early morning to East Wimsley. From there, it would be two days going to London. If Edward left immediately, I could hope to see him in a minimum of four days—at the most, six.

Feeling far better for having made this bold step, I relaxed into preparing for bed. The room was chill and dark but not as alien as before. The thought of Edward's soon being here was my comfort; I used it as security.

As the down mattress sighed beneath my weight, I felt both complaisant and excited at the thought of what tomorrow would bring. Surely a visit to the coppice would restore all memory. Then the answers would be out in the open. And besides the coppice, I decided before drifting off, I must also explore the rest of this magnificent old house to see what other recollections of my infancy it could produce. There were other floors, two sealed wings, countless locked rooms . . .

Just before dawn, I rose, quite refreshed, performed a hasty toilette, and tiptoed down into the house while everyone yet slept. I wore a woolen morning frock with a fringed shawl about my shoulders to keep out the chill and carried a candle against the darkness.

It was icy cold all throughout. The little flame was a feeble weapon against the shadows that encompassed me, yet I was determined. I had slept well for the first time, albeit plagued with dreams of Colin and Edward, and now I had the fortitude to face my hidden past.

The servants were all gathered in the kitchen, warming themselves before a sea-coal fire in the stove. They dipped their heads courteously as I entered. I gave my letter and a few shillings to one maid who was familiar to me—a girl who did the upstairs bedrooms—and emphasized the urgency of her task. Without a word but gawking at the money, she hastily seized a mantle cloak and left the kitchen for the stable. The others watched me mutely, all of them too new or too young to have been here 20 years ago.

"Where is Gertrude?" I asked.

"Not down yet, mum," answered one. "Not afore six, mum."

"Thank you."

"Want me t'send 'er up, mum?"

"No, no, it's all right. Thank you."

So I had an hour yet before my private interview with Gertrude, and possibly two before the family awakened. Surely there could be no better time than now to begin the exploration of my childhood home, for I was sharp and alert and full of optimism.

The corridors were dark and chill, haunted by icy drafts and shadows that danced upon the walls. The opposite wings of the original Tudor design were quite locked now, being never used, and I imagined that there must have been a time—long ago—when the Pemberton family was large and had frequent guests and therefore required all the space the old mansion could offer. But now, with only seven inhabitants and infrequent visitors, only the central part of the house was used at all.

I encountered many locked doors, particularly on the third floor, where more empty bedrooms stood. As I swept along the dusty carpet smelling the mustiness of disuse, I tried to open my mind to any flashes of memory that might come back. Yet none did.

On the second floor, where we all had rooms, were two long corridors that appeared to have been closed more recently than the rest of the house. Here and there, a plant still thrived, and oil could be seen in some of the lamps. Cautiously, I tried each door, not really knowing what to expect on the other side but found them equally as locked.

Except for one.

This room, nearest our own corridor, must have been used very recently, for the table by the door was well polished and dusted and the fern recently watered. Very slowly, I pushed the door in, thrusting my candle through first, then poking my head in until I could see something of the interior. It was a bedroom and, judging by first glance, belonging to a woman. I entered all the way until I stood clear of the door, leaving it open, and could see all round me fairly well.

That it was no longer used was fairly evident in the clean fireplace and absence of candles or lamps. Yet the furnishings remained—the Staffordshire figurines, the shell boxes, the heavy draperies, and smooth bedspread, I wondered whose room this had been.

Moving closer to the bed, I felt the sudden sensation of having been here before. It was a room I knew, or had known in the past, and its feeling was a good one, a friendly one to me. Whoever the occupant had been, I must have loved her even though I did not now remember who she was.

A book stood on the night table. It was a leather-bound volume with no title, and I was compelled to place my candle on the table and open the book.

Sylvia Vauxhall's diary of 1856 lay open in my hands, clearly legible and written in a lovely feminine hand. As I read her private words—some sweet nonsense about getting a recipe from the vicar's wife—I felt new emotions sweep over me. A paroxysm of love and sentiment caused tears to flood my eyes as I suddenly felt near to Aunt Sylvia. The woman whom I could not remember yet whom I knew I had adored as a child. Reading her floral script made me think of gingerbread, then of lavender, and I knew that, as an infant, I must have associated her with these two scents. Although not good at faces, any five-year-old child will remember hot gingerbread baked by a kindly old aunt who lavished herself in lavender cologne.

Dear Aunt Sylvia. How sorry I was now to have missed her, that she had beckoned to me but had not lived long enough to see me again. Dear God, what a wonderful reunion it would have been! None of the other Pembertons would have mattered then because Aunt Sylvia would have been here to love me.

As I wiped a happy tear from my cheek, I suddenly froze. My eyes remained glued to the diary, my hand still upon my face. In an instant, all the sweet sadness of her memory blew away with an icy horror—even my heart seemed to stop. Those words on that page—they shouted belligerently out to me, as if boasting. The delicate florid swirls and little circles that dotted the *i*'s—this gentle handwriting was not the same as that in Aunt Sylvia's letter.

My mind swam in confusion. I did not understand. This was her diary, written right up to the end of the year in a hand so different from that in the letter that it did not seem possible she could have altered it in so short a time. Even if she had grown increasingly weak and arthritic in her last days, the handwriting would not have evolved from this to what I found in her letter. Those words that I read in London had been written in a firm, strong hand—a hand other than this. Yet whose?

In my bewilderment, I did not notice that I was no longer alone in the room, that someone had joined me and now stood quietly behind me. It was only when I heard the door click softly shut that I gasped and spun about.

"Dear God, you startled me!" I said breathlessly to the silhouette before me.

A soft, low chuckle was heard across the darkness.

"Is that you, Theo?" I fumbled behind myself for the candle and brought it quickly about. Colin's face became brightly illuminated in a sardonic way, his mouth twisted in a grin, his hair askew.

"What are you doing in Aunt Sylvia's room?" he asked in an accusing tone.

"I—I was looking about the house for places I might know. This door was unlocked—"

"Bit rude, isn't it, reading a woman's personal diary?"

I looked down at the book. My eyes felt as if they stood out of their sockets. "It made me feel so close to her. I almost remember her."

"What else did it tell you?"

I brought my head up sharply. "What do you mean?"

"Are you mentioned in there, is that why you read it? I'll wager you were disappointed, Leyla. Aunt Sylvia never spoke of you; none of us did."

"No . . . I'm not mentioned in here." My thoughts flew wildly about. *Who* had sent that letter!

"You know, Cousin," he said quietly, taking a step closer to me. "It's not safe to roam this old house alone. You should have a guide. Some of the unused stairs are in bad repair, and you might injure yourself."

"I was anxious, and no one was up yet."

"Well, I'm up, and I can take you round. Theo's up, too, but they've gone into East Wimsley."

"They?"

"He and Uncle Henry. They go together once a week to check on the mills."

"Don't you ever go?"

"I have nothing to do with the mills. Neither my uncle nor my cousin thinks I'm competent to manage them, so I was never let in. There was a time, however, when I was quite involved in the management of the mills, but that was a while ago, and then only briefly."

"Why?"

His eyes clouded over, and his voice grew distant. "It was after you and your mother left. Uncle Henry gathered up Anna and Theo and went off to Manchester to manage one of our mills there. So I remained here with my father, running the mills for Sir John. But then my father—" his voice caught, "—and mother died in that road accident, so Henry and Theo and Anna came home. They took over and have been doing it ever since. I suppose I'm not capable."

"Are you?"

He gave a short but unconvincing laugh. "1 don't care a jot or a tittle about those mills. I'm not a businessman, I'm a man of leisure. And besides"—his voice grew hard—"it's not to my taste to oversee a bunch of noisy, smelly cotton mills that spew fevers into the air and breed pestilence among the poor beggars that labor in them. I'm no Reformist, but I do deplore the conditions those damned laborers must suffer."

Colin did not excuse his language, but for once I did not mind. I was marveling at the sudden passion in his voice. And his words intrigued me, for I agreed with them. Anyone who had seen London factories would.

"And my magnanimous uncle Henry was actually opposed, *opposed*, dear Leyla, to the Ten Hours Act! He claimed that it would create idleness for the laborers, more hours to spend in the gin houses. Well, I say bully for them! The day will come when an Eight Hour Act is passed and children will be banned from factory work altogether. And when that day comes—" Colin stopped short. He fell into an awkward silence.

"Yes, please go on."

In a slightly incredulous voice, he said, "You actually agree with me, don't you?"

"Of course I do. And you said you would be incompetent. What a pity you can't have a hand in those mills. Think of the improvements you—"

But he waved a hand at me. The mood was gone, the fire dispelled. My old flippant cousin came back. "Let's leave this room, Leyla. There's nothing more for you here."

I replaced the book as I had found it, shelving the mystery of her handwriting for a later time, then departed with Colin to the hall. Once there, he turned to me, took my candle, and held it close to my face. "You look so like your mother," he said softly. "So very much."

"And my father?"

His eyes narrowed. "Yes, your father is there, too. You have the Pemberton features that make you definitely one of us. That makes you doomed like the rest of us."

"I will not speak of doom, Colin."

"How right you are! Oh, Leyla, if you only knew how seeing you brings back the past. I may have been only 14 at the time, but I was old enough to recognize beauty and grace. Many's the time, as a romantic adolescent, I lived in hopes of catching a glimpse of your mother's ankle. She may have been my aunt, but she had the ability to make my brow feverish."

"Oh, Colin!" I laughed.

"And you, Leyla, oh, you fickle female! How easily women turn their hearts from men. You followed me about like a little pest. But that's all gone now." His eyes swept over my face. "Isn't it?"

"You must have been mistaken, Colin. Surely I looked upon you as an older, wiser brother, as I might do now. It would have been most unseemly of me to fall in love with my first cousin."

"Do you remember that I read to you a lot?"

I felt my face frown. "No . . . I don't . . ."

"And I once made you a zoetrope for your birthday. I had labored over it many weeks—"

Suddenly, a flash. "Colin!" My hand darted out and seized his wrist. Not just a vague remembrance or intangible mist, but a solid memory with detail and life. "I think I remember it. Was there a picture of a rabbit on it?"

"Yes, there was."

"And you had put a dress on it just like mine. The rabbit was supposed to be me, hopping up and down as I spun the drum. Oh, Colin, I do remember!"

"It took me positively forever to make it for you, Leyla, but it was worth it to see your face light up when you spun it. I'm glad you remember it."

"Yes, I do." Unknowingly, my fingers dug deep into his arm. Other bits of memory were coming back, like pieces of a mosaic. I saw the birthday party in the dining room, cakes and sweets decked out upon that table that, in my memory, seemed monstrous and insurmountable. I saw a rainbow of ladies' skirts swirl about me, pink satins and blue brocades. They were hooped skirts of that decade, not the crinoline of today. I remembered the zoetrope and kissing Colin for it.

"Dear Cousin, I believe you're blushing."

I looked up at Colin, snapping out of my reverie.

"And my hand is numb."

"Oh, forgive me!" I released his arm. "I was remembering. I can almost see everyone at the party! They were all there, weren't they? But to me and my five-year-old eye level, it was all a forest of gentlemen's legs and ladies' skirts. I can't see the faces."

"In time you will."

Our eyes met again and held for a long time. Why I do not know, but just then, as I was locked in Colin's gaze, I tried to conjure Edward's face. And could not. "I thought you didn't want me to remember."

"The good times, Leyla, for they belong to you. But not the evil ones. I wouldn't want you to be hurt."

"Thank you, Cousin, but all the same I must go."

"Go? Go where?"

"Why, to the coppice, of course. I'm going today to see—"

Now it was my cousin's turn to seize my wrist, and with such strength that I winced. "You can't mean it, Leyla! *Don't go down there!*"

"But I must. Colin, you're hurting me."

"It's insanity if you do! You might not remember a thing yet feel the horror of it all the same."

"Please let me go!"

He threw my hand down angrily, and I saw depths of passion in his eyes. How quickly this man could change himself, how easily he could go from mood to mood like an actor changing disguises. And his sudden outbursts, his unpredictability frightened me.

"Leyla, please—"

"I'm going, Colin."

"Then let me go with you."

"Why?"

"Don't ask. Just let me accompany you to the coppice. You might need me there if . . . if . . . you should remember."

I softened toward him. Colin's brotherly concern sometimes eclipsed his less redeeming qualities. "Very well. I shan't go without you. I plan to visit it this afternoon."

"I'll be about, Leyla. Now, if you wish to see more of the house, let me take you."

I suddenly remembered Gertrude. "No, thank you, Colin, I'm tired now and could do with a rest. I shall see you later, if that is all right."

He escorted me back to my room, waited till I closed the door, then went off down the hall and eventually down the stairs. I had not altogether spoken an untruth when I had said how tired I was, for the revelations of this morning had been monumental indeed. The birthday party, obviously a landmark hour in the life of a child, had come rushing back with one word from Colin, and now the memory was mine to keep forever.

But then there was also the question of Aunt Sylvia's letter. Sitting upon the sofa before the fireplace, I read that letter for the 100th time.

"Dearest Jenny," it said. "Please forgive this sudden communication after so many silent years, but I am gripped with a longing to see you. I know how you must feel about the Hurst, and I do not blame you. However, all that was long ago, and so much has changed since then. I wish to see you but cannot come to London, for I am an old woman and want to be among my family when the angels call. Won't you please come back for a little time, and bring Leyla with you? It would bring peace to my heart. Lovingly, Aunt Sylvia."

An innocuous and simple enough letter, yet definitely not my great-aunt's handwriting. But who in this house wanted me and my mother here? And why, whoever they were, did they not write under their true identity but chose Aunt Sylvia, who must have been about to die?

Of all the riddles, this seemed the most unfathomable.

So now I was back, answering the call of this letter, and yet everyone in this house had appeared surprised to see me. And everyone appeared also to want me to leave. That could mean only one thing.

That someone was lying.

CHAPTER 8

Gertrude came as soon as I called for her, appearing reluctantly at my door and with worry in her eyes. We had said little to each other so far, she and I, yet I maintained the hope that something might be gotten from her. To accomplish this, however, I was experienced enough now to know that I must use wiles and coyness to manipulate her into playing into my hands, for if that anxiety in her eyes was any indication, Gertrude was not a willing subject.

"You know, Gertrude," I said as we crossed my room together. "I'm sorry we haven't sat down for a chat before now. After all, we have so much to talk over. Those good old days and all that."

"Yah, Miss Leyla, but you know my memory is not so good anymore."

"Neither is mine, which I suppose you've already heard. But I'm anxious to rediscover those memories, if you can help me."

"I'd like to help, Miss Leyla, but I doubt I can."

"At least we can try. We must have been good friends 20 years ago. I have that feeling."

"Oh, we were, we were!"

She and I sat on the sofa before a small table set with tea and biscuits. The first hints of a crisp morning were shining through my window and casting bright rays upon the carpet. A fierce wind continued to howl, but the sky was a delectable blue and the air quite exhilarating.

I served for the two of us in an attempt to put her at ease, for she sat on the edge of the sofa until her bustle was touching her elbows. The years had been kind to our Prussian housekeeper, for despite the decades of serving others, Gertrude's face was nearly free of lines and her blonde hair only sparsely interrupted with gray. She was my aunt Anna's age, between 55 and 60, but plumper and shorter. Like any overseer of the pantry, this rotund woman had the hips and bosom of one who liked to taste her recipes. Gertrude was a good housekeeper, loved by those who employed her and respected by those who worked under her. She had come to this house many years ago. She had supervised my mother's childbed. "Do you take cream and sugar? Please take a biscuit, Gertrude; I took care to bring them from London."

"Packaged in a tin."

"Yes, but baked with love, I assure you. Won't you please sit back, Gertrude?"

"I've a lot to do, Miss Leyla, before the family rises."

"But there's time yet, and we never seem to have an opportunity to be alone together. And we've so much to talk about."

"If you think so, Miss Leyla."

"But I don't just think so, I know so. After all, you must have known me very well as a child. Didn't you bake for me, for all us children, then?"

She paused, weighing her answer. "Yah. Of course I did."

"Gingerbread was your specialty, wasn't it?"

"*Nein,* Miss Leyla. Your Aunt Sylvia was the one who baked the best ginger. You children always liked my hot apple strudel."

"Oh yes, of course." There was no memory there.

"And hot chocolate that I made the German way. It's better than English. You children always liked mine best."

"Did we?"

Gertrude remained stiff and unrelenting. Whoever had instructed her had done an excellent job. Yet housekeepers were notoriously sentimental—it was this fact I counted so heavily upon.

"Was it my brother's favorite, too, Gertrude?"

Her back straightened even more. Here was a tender spot. "He was like the others, little Thomas. He loved everything I baked."

"I don't remember him, Gertrude; can you tell me a little about him?"

"My memory is poor, Miss Leyla. I think I have only disappointed you. There is nothing I can say."

The wind whistled against my windows and down the chimney flue. Its voice seemed to prognosticate bad omens.

Putting my teacup down, I rested my hand on her arm. So far she had not looked my way but had kept a rigid vigil over the empty fireplace. "Gertrude, please, you must understand what it is I'm after. I've lost all memory of my baby days, and I desperately want them back. I was hoping you could help me."

Her profile remained sharply unmoved. Obviously, I had overestimated the sentimentality of this woman or underestimated her devotion to duty. Wherever the command had come from—Grandmother or Uncle Henry—this woman was going to remain true to her vow.

"Oh well," I said with a sigh. This time the disappointment was easier to bear. First my aunt and uncle, then my three cousins, then my grandmother, and now Gertrude. I had tried them all. "I'm sorry I've kept you from your work, Gertrude. I had only hoped you could give me a little of my past. Something to remember, to take with me through life and tell my children about as they grow. You may leave if you wish."

"The family will want breakfast—"

"I understand."

We rose together, and as we did, I decided to resort to one last trick. Very undramatically, I placed my hand upon my forehead, moaned a little, and murmured, "Oh, my head."

It worked. Gertrude stopped on the spot and swung about to look at me. There was sadness, wells of sadness in her eyes. So she was not all that unmoved. "Your head bothers you, Miss Leyla?"

"Only a little." It did not, of course, but I had resorted to this form of bait as a last effort to reach Gertrude. And I had not been wrong.

"Have you had this before?"

"Why yes, now that you mention it. On and off for the last few months. How did you know?"

"Poor little Leyla." Her eyes could not express more sympathy. "It is what your father had, God preserve his soul. He suffered from terrible headaches in those last weeks."

A memory came back to me. Sounds of a man crying on the other side of a locked door.

"He suffered terribly, *liebchen,* and no doctor could help him. We gave him the medicine, but each time it was more and more until it could not help. Then the fever came over him and the insanity. Oh, *liebchen,* you should not wish such memories! They are sad. They are *evil.*"

But I was only half listening to her words now. As much as I had wanted my little ploy to loosen Gertrude's tongue, I now paid scant attention to what she said, for another idea was suddenly in my mind. Something I could not quite put my finger on . . .

"You are so young, *liebchen,* to have the headaches now. Your father was a man in his prime, and your grandfather quite elderly. I pray to God that these are caused by something else. Tension, perhaps. Or because of your mother's death . . ."

Gertrude's voice faded from my ears, because I now realized what new idea she had put in my mind. The headaches, the pattern, the increased dosage of opium brought Uncle Henry to my mind. He was suffering now exactly the same way my father had 20 years ago.

I returned my attention to Gertrude's face, searching it for some evidence of theatrics. Yet her tears were too real to be forced. In Gertrude's opinion, my father *really had* suffered from excruciating headaches and delirium. This part of the story was true, such did I glean from her terrified eyes and trembling hands. My father had indeed been the victim of some unknown fever.

Gertrude left me now, on the verge of breaking down, so I waited patiently until she could no longer be heard on the stairs. Possibly it was unkind what I had done to her, yet it had accomplished a great deal. My father, it seemed, really had suffered from a peculiar illness, for Gertrude's grief had been genuine and I had had a fleeting memory of it myself as well. There was something about a forbidden room and a man on the other side of it. I seemed to sense my father as that man and a childlike desperation to reach him. If this were so, if what I saw in Gertrude's eyes and a vague memory were all true, then possibly my father *had* been very ill before his death.

Yet the nagging thought remained that, sick or not, he had *not* committed two killings. Something was missing from the picture, and since Gertrude, my last hope, had proven bound to silence, I knew where the final answer lay.

It was late afternoon when I felt the time ripe to go down to the coppice. Aunt Anna was napping from a big lunch. Cousin Martha was engrossed in a new pillow for the drawing room. Uncle Henry and Theo were still in East Wimsley. And the rest of the house was ominously silent. Seizing a mantle cloak and bonnet, I left my room quietly, going softly past my relatives' rooms so as not to draw attention to myself.

This visit to the coppice would most likely be the paramount moment of my life, returning to me all the memories that were rightfully mine and answering the many questions that robbed me of rest. At the coppice I would regain my childhood again, for the releasing of one bad memory—the one that blocked all the others—would reunite me with the pleasant ones as well. The coppice would also tell me who had murdered my father and brother, who had sent that letter in Sylvia's name, who had started this insane Pemberton madness tale, and who was my enemy in the Hurst.

The house was so still and silent that I could find no servants anywhere. Not the maids, or valet, or Gertrude. And neither, after a few minutes' search, could I find Colin.

Either he had forgotten or changed his mind; whichever, it was apparent I was to go to the coppice alone. There was no harm in this since, after all, that had been my intention in the first place.

The wind had gotten worse, blowing icily through the skeletal trees and freezing the tip of my nose. Gray clouds began rolling overhead, and in the distance was the sound of giant wagon wheels thundering across the sky. We would have a storm tonight, replete with thunder and lightning and sheets of rain, so I knew I had to hurry with my appointment at the coppice.

Around the house I ran, using both hands to manage my cloak and skirt, until I was on the drive that serviced the stables. From here, I could see the expansive green lawn that rolled away down from the hurst and ended at the bottom in a border of dense forest. The trees were gray and brittle, beating against one another in the wind. Immense shadows glided over the lawn as the clouds obliterated the sun in their speedy passage. More and more of them came in the gathering storm, building into an army of malevolence that was threatening to break loose. Their shadows covered the lawn entirely now, allowing only occasional leaks of sunlight, so that it seemed today's outing might be very short-lived.

I followed the drive to its end until I stood upon the crest of the hurst and could see all the way down the gentle hill to the foliated bottom. And from my vantage point I saw, sprouting up from the center of the clearing, about halfway down, a dense growth of trees that grew tightly, like an oasis in the desert.

Knowing it for what it was, I held back, stood apprehensively staring down at it as if appraising an opponent in battle, for surely I was fighting for my right to know the past. The bare acacias stood grouped against the wild wind as if desperately trying to protect the pathetic secret they had guarded all these years, and now I had come back to wrench it from them. Yes, there would be a fight if need be, for if the memories did not return easily to me, then I would persist until they did. I would come continually to the coppice until every shred of the past was mine again, regardless of how horrifying it might be.

And so here I stood, as if I were five years old again, gazing down at the coppice where I had seen my father and brother go. The others were all back in the house or, in the case of my mother, working in the garden. I was young and curious and wanted to be with my father and Thomas.

So I started down. Had it been cold that day? Had gray clouds filled the sky with the threat of storm? Or had I hopped down in warm sunlight, pretending to be a rabbit on her way to a warren?

As the coppice drew nearer, I felt my tension mount. No memories returned yet, nothing to let me know that I had ever been here before. The wind sliced my face. The grass crunched underfoot. I was a stranger visiting a strange land. Whatever memories I had here would have to come at the actual scene of the "incident." After all, it was the witnessing of the murder that had walled up all the rest of my memory. In an effort to save me from the remembrance of a terrifying moment, my mind had also succeeded in blocking away all other memories—pleasant as well as bad. In order to recover all of it, I must break down the barrier of this one. And to do that I had to go back to the original spot.

I grew fearful, apprehensive. What would my mind's eye see? What terror would I have to relive in order to accomplish my goal? As I trod heavily toward the coppice, I argued with myself that I could still turn around and go back, return to London, and forget all that I had found here. Yet that was not possible, I argued back, for I was set upon a path on which there was no turning around. My father had been innocent—of that I was certain—and I owed it to his poor memory, to myself, and most of all to my mother, who had suffered 20 years on his account, to prove his innocence.

Suddenly I was at the coppice. Turning, I stared up the hill and saw the old house sitting atop the hurst like something out of a novel. It was all so bizarre, so preposterous what was happening to me. Had I really been in London only a few days before? Had I really once known nothing about the two murders in this small wood or a ridiculous curse that conveniently explained them away? Had there really been a time, only a few days before, when the names Colin, Anna, Henry, and Theo had meant nothing to me?

I had to face the coppice. No more procrastination, for I had come with a purpose and it was not in my nature to put things off. In the midst of a wide, flat lawn stood this acre of closely knit trees and weedy shrubs. There was an inky darkness at its center; one could not see through to the other side. I squinted and gaped, trying desperately to see four children playing happily among the bit of medieval ruins that stood at the heart of the coppice. But I could not see them: five-year-old Leyla, seven-year-old Thomas, 12-year-old Martha, and 14-year-old Colin.

All that beckoned to me now was a formidable forest of darkness and wind and barren trees.

The first, bold step was the hardest; the rest came easier. As I pressed forth, with my cloak and skirts hugged close to my body, I felt as if I were stepping through a door into the past. All about me, slight changes occurred: the wind seemed to die and grow distant; the air became clearer, sharper; there was the rich smell of damp earth. My mind strained and wrestled with itself, trying in desperation to seize upon the smallest flash of memory. Were these sensations a part of the past? Were they here with me today? Or were they products of my imagination?

Without knowing why, I came to a spot at the center and stopped. My eyes ached with strain, wide and bulging, trying to take in all they could to feed my desperate mind. My ears seized upon every sound, my nose filled with all the scents. Every sense that was at my command worked to its limit to fill my mind with the coppice in hopes that it would pick up one tiny clue that could bring all the past suddenly back to me.

That jumble of stones. That smooth boulder. That moss-covered wall of gray stone. That rotting log. The deserted beehive. Would one of these items trigger off a chain reaction in my mind that would eventually tear down the barrier over my past? How anxious I was! How desperate for it all to return!

And had it happened here, that "incident"? Had I as a five-year-old stood upon this spot and seen the deed committed over there by the ruined wall?

I looked up suddenly at the patch of blue sky between the treetops. A picture flashed in my head. It was a gold ring. A ring with a red stone.

My eyes fell again upon the castle ruins. My mind seized upon the ring. On a man's hand. No . . . perhaps not a man's hand. A thin, bony hand. The ruby ring flashed in the sunlight. It was familiar to me somehow. I had seen it somewhere before.

Then, just as quickly, the picture left, and I stood alone and empty again in the coppice. What had it meant, that ruby ring in the sunlight? How does one explain the workings of a five-year-old mind? There was no way I could make a connection between that ring (it was the one Theo now wore) and what had happened in the coppice 20 years ago. Possibly the murderer had worn it. But surely that would not be all I would remember. And then, if I remembered the ring, other memories would surely follow. Had that ring been on the hand that had wielded the knife? Or did it belong to some other memory of the coppice? Possibly, as a child, I had come here with my grandfather Sir John and had been fascinated by his ring then. Maybe it was the remnant of a *happy* memory and did not belong at all to the events of the murders.

How on earth was I to find out?

Suddenly I felt a chill down my spine. This was not due to the past but caused by something real and in the present. My shoulders shivered inadvertently. The sudden feeling came over me that I *was no longer alone in the coppice.* My eyes quickly searched about. This was absurd, for I saw no one, heard no sound. *Yet I was certain I was being watched.*

Feeling frightened and courageous at the same time, I managed the strength to call out, "Who is there?"

I listened. Only the wind whistled overhead and at the periphery of this tiny wood.

"Come now. I know you're there, and I don't appreciate your spying on me!"

I was surprised next when, unexpectedly, someone did move in the trees nearby. Heavy feet crunched the dead brush, and arms pushed branches out of the way.

"You'll have the good manners to identify yourself!" I called out, trying to sound unshaken. "And stop this charade!"

Yet no one spoke. Clearly, the footsteps were coming closer. The intruder remained without identity, staying hidden in the trees but not bothering to tread lightly upon the brittle ground.

I felt the back of my neck prickle. This was ludicrous. Why did the intruder not speak up? Yet I held my ground, determined not to show fear in the face of a prowler who was possibly watching for any sign of weakness.

The footsteps ceased very nearby. I stood completely still, not breathing, hearing my heart pound inside my head.

"Hello," he said suddenly.

I gasped and spun around. "Colin! That's not funny!"

"Who said it was?" A sloppy smile accompanied his shrug.

"Why didn't you answer me when I called out?"

"I didn't want to disturb you."

"Well, you did!" I put my hand on my chest to symbolically calm my racing heart "I think that was very rude of you."

"I'm sorry."

"And you were spying on me! Why?"

"Because I thought it would be better if you were left alone. After you agreed I should come along with you to the coppice, I had second thoughts and decided it would be best, after all, if you were to come alone. You might not have been relaxed with me here. Or perhaps my presence might have spoiled the mood necessary for bringing back the past. Whatever, although I decided you should ostensibly be alone on your visit to the coppice, I did not want you to be *really* alone."

"So you accompanied me from a distance. An admirable attempt, dear Cousin, but you scared ten years off the end of my life."

"Come now, what's a clump of trees compared with London streets after dark? Surely you've encountered worse beasties in your experience!"

Despite myself, I had to smile, and I was in the end glad to have someone with me. There was something strangely unwholesome about the coppice, and it left me feeling hollow and morose. This was due, unfortunately, not to any memory of the past about the place but due to what others had told me about it. After all, this was the spot where my father and brother had been so monstrously killed. This was the place responsible for my having gone to London 20 years ago.

"Did anything come back to you?" he asked.

I searched the area again, roaming over the broken wall and dead trees. "No, Colin, nothing at all." I decided to keep the ruby ring to myself. "It wasn't quite right today. Something was wrong. Perhaps the weather. Had it been warm that . . . that day?"

"Yes, as a matter of fact, it had been. At least a little, not stormy like this."

"Then maybe the weather hampered me. I shall have to return alone again on a better day. The atmosphere must be just right. I shall come back as many times as are necessary."

"It is that important to you?"

I looked at Colin. His eyes held concern. But for whom I could not guess. "It's very important to me."

"And if it takes a long time?"

"Then you must pay me a guinea."

"Pay you a—?" Suddenly, he threw his head back and laughed to the sky. It was a good laugh, deep and hearty, and it brought me to smiling with him. How extraordinary it might have been growing up with Colin. He would have been a brother to me, guiding me possibly, entertaining me certainly. I would have learned to know him in that time, as I imagined Martha knew him now, instead of puzzling over his complex behavior as I did.

How different he would be next to Edward, for the day would soon arrive when Edward would be at the dinner table, making mute appraisals of my eccentric relatives. There would be my divinely polite and predictable Edward next to my boorish cousin and probably disliking every minute of it.

The imaginary scene made my smile even broader. Seeing this, Colin said, "So you are not such a dimly serious girl after all. Come on, Leyla, let's get you out of this inclement climate."

We turned and walked a few steps toward the edge of the wood. "Don't come back too soon," he said guardedly. "Give it time. Rest your mind and come back after you've, say, read a good book. I think you're trying too hard."

"Perhaps I shall do that."

"And besides, next time you should come in from another direction."

I stopped short. "Why do you say that?"

Colin's face was again a mask as he replied, "Well, if you truly want to re-create the atmosphere of that day in order to remember what you saw, then you should at least stand in the proper spot."

I glanced over my shoulder. "Proper spot?"

"Yes. Where you stood today is not at all where you were 20 years ago. When you sat hidden in the trees as you watched your father and brother, you were in an entirely different place altogether."

CHAPTER 9

When we returned to the house, we were met with two items of news. One, that Uncle Henry was ill in his room, and, two, that Grandmother had summoned me to her presence. Yet neither of these affected me with much impact, for, after I left Colin and mounted the stairs to my room, a question was screaming loudly in my mind: How had Colin known where I had stood hidden that day 20 years ago?

As if in a dream, I closed my door behind me, carelessly dropped my cloak and bonnet on the bed, and sank with a sigh on the bench before my looking glass. No pallor here, no colorless lips or dull eyes as of a few days before. Instead, my cheeks were radiantly pink and my lips a bright rose. My eyes were bright and alive, as though my whole body had suddenly come to life.

It was seeing the coppice again, I told myself. Or it was the weather—that wind and the cold. It was the long walk uphill. Perhaps it was the memory of the ruby ring. In my desire to deny that Cousin Colin was beginning to have an effect on me, I manufactured all sorts of excuses to explain away the sudden vitality in my face.

While I brushed and plaited my hair, I heard voices and footsteps in the hall. They belonged to Gertrude and Aunt Anna and Theo, each one performing a task for the better comfort of Uncle Henry, who, I was told, was suffering again from his headaches. Yet I ignored the activity beyond my door, having enough on my mind to keep me occupied for a while.

Just as with every other day since coming to Pemberton Hurst, today had been full of revelations and new questions. Among them was the problem of Aunt Sylvia's letter, which, although I had put it out of my mind for the afternoon, I had not forgotten. And now there was the puzzle of Colin's words at the coppice. How had he known where my hiding place had been? If I had been the only one there and if they had later found me standing over the bodies, then how could anyone but myself know where I had hidden in the trees?

There was a sharp rap at my door. "Leyla?" came Theo's anxious voice.

"Come in." I half turned on the bench.

"Leyla—" He thrust his head in the door, his eyes popping like those of a fish. "What on earth are you up to? Grandmother is waiting."

"Grandmother! I'm brushing my hair, you can see that, and I intend to finish. Grandmother can continue to wait a little longer."

Forgetting himself, Theodore strode all the way in. "Really, Leyla, you are going to have to learn. We understand your circumstances and how you were raised, but all that must change now. If you are to be part of this family, then you must live by our rules. And Number One is never to keep Grandmother waiting."

"I beg your pardon," I said a little coolly. When I stood abruptly, my hairbrush fell to the floor. "And is it also one of your rules to enter a young lady's bedroom when she is unchaperoned? Oh, Theo, I have had an exhausting afternoon. I intend to rest a little, to have some tea, and to make repairs upon myself before rushing to see Grandmother."

He opened his mouth to speak.

"And furthermore, Cousin Theodore, Grandmother waited 20 years to see me; she can wait a little longer."

"Good God, what's gotten into you?"

"Nothing!" I bent and retrieved the brush.

"And where have you been? You look the devil, Leyla. Where did you go to today?"

I sat on the bench again with a resounding thump and snapped the brush through my hair. "I went to the coppice."

"You what!" he whispered coarsely.

"I said I went to the coppice."

In the reflection in the looking glass, my cousin went positively white. "Leyla, I don't—" His hand went to his forehead.

Now I turned to him again, gravely. "Why? What's wrong?"

He searched for a chair, sat in it, and continued to shake his head in dismay. It was so unlike Theo to lose even the slightest control.

"Please tell me, what's wrong?"

When his eyes finally met mine I was startled, for they seemed to hold great fear and worry. For an instant, I thought this might be for me and a concern for my welfare, but then second thoughts prompted me to believe Theodore was worried for other reasons.

"You shouldn't have gone there," he said in a tight voice. "You really shouldn't have."

"Why not? Oh, Theo, what's wrong?"

"Tell me, Leyla. Did you . . . did you remember anything?"

I looked long at the ruby ring on his finger, the ring that had glinted in the sun and was in some way connected to the coppice and the past. I considered it for a moment, then said, "No, I remember nothing at all."

Relief was visible all over his body, yet his voice remained strained. "It could have been . . . disastrous for you, remembering and all. God is being merciful to you by keeping the memory hidden. You'll only upset yourself to see it all over again. My God, it was ghastly."

I stared for a long time at my cousin, studying his anxious gestures, watching the worry work in his face. I had been right to believe that Theodore was concerned more about something else than my welfare, and I guessed that he must be fearful of what I might remember.

"I assure you it won't be as catastrophic as you anticipate," I said calmly.

"In my lifetime, I have been witness to some dreadful sights in London—death is not new to me, and neither is the sight of blood. I once happened to see a man lose his legs under a vegetable cart—"

"It's not the same, Leyla." Theodore's eyes popped right out; his hands spread as if beseeching. "In accidents, there is the physical horror, but in murder, there is the emotional horror. And to see one's own father and brother murdered would be all the more terrifying. I can't imagine this desire of yours to relive the memory, Leyla. I just don't understand it."

Now I rose smoothly and started toward the door. "I think you do, Theo."

"What is that supposed to mean?"

"You know very well why I want to remember what I saw that day, and I think you're very anxious to keep me from remembering."

He flew to his feet. "Really now! You've upset Martha with such talk, but I won't stand for it. And besides, your rendezvous at the coppice proved fruitless anyway."

"This time, yes, but there will be other opportunities." I glanced down at his ring. "Perhaps each visit will break the barrier down more and more. Or possibly one day, the weather will be right, the mood just perfect; even the lighting in the coppice will be exactly as it had been 20 years ago. And then, dear Cousin, I shall remember everything."

With that, I turned smoothly on my heel and glided out. I would have wished to change my frock before confronting Grandmother, but Theo's presence had unnerved me, and I had been anxious to be away from him. He had his mother's exophthalmic eyes, her nervous gestures, and her manner of speaking anything but what he thought. Cousin Theodore also had an annoying habit of trying to dominate me as he did his mother and Martha, but I had too long been my own free agent to allow just any man to be my master.

With such a headstrong humor did I make my way to Grandmother Abigail's room. A concoction of anger, peevishness, and sadness brought me before her door in an unsettled state, wholly unprepared for any encounter with her. Yet rather than delay any longer, I ran my hands down my bodice, fluffed my skirt a little, and tapped lightly upon the door.

"Come in," she said flatly.

Everything was the same as it had been the night before. Her room was generally dark and illuminated only by low oil flames or flickering candles, which altogether gave one the impression of entering a sacred shrine. She sat again upon her favorite straight-backed chair, her small feet propped up on a stool, her hands resting on each arm of the chair. Again a diagonal shadow fell across her face, so that, while one could not see her, she could watch the face of her visitor. Yet this time I was not to play into my grandmother's trap, for I knew her better and had more of an idea of what she was up to; so, instead of standing as I had done before— directly in front of her with the oil lamp shining on my face—I sidestepped to the fireplace where I would be seen as a silhouette. This caused her to turn her head to the right, a gesture that I am certain she did not appreciate having to make.

"Why are you over there? I cannot see you."

"I'm cold, Grandmother."

"Step closer, child. My eyes are not like yours."

"I prefer the fire, Grandmother, if you don't mind. It's really dreadfully cold in here."

There was a barely perceptible pause before she said, "Then you shouldn't have been out in this weather. We had sunshine before you presented yourself on our doorstep, but since then, we've had nothing but the winds of Hell. Satan's on your heels, child. Be careful."

"A walk in the cold air is good for a body, Grandmother."

"And visits to the coppice?"

So she knew. Should that surprise me? In light of the fact that Theo had not known, yes. And who had told her? Who else but Colin knew I had been there? Although we could have been seen by someone, I supposed . . .

"And you remember nothing," she went on grimly, almost smugly.

Dear God, *had* Colin told her?

"You're quite wrong, Grandmother, I remembered something indeed."

Although one could not see it, Grandmother altered quite suddenly. She made no move, she uttered no sound, yet the very atmosphere of the room changed instantly. It became charged with hostility: the shadows darkened, the wind sounded louder beyond the windows.

"What could you have possibly remembered? Certainly nothing of worth."

"I don't know, Grandmother; that remains to be seen. It was only a small memory, just a flash really, but it occurred only at the coppice, and I believe it will lead me to further discoveries." As I spoke, my eyes unwittingly went down to her hands. Like shoots of bamboo, they were hard and knobby and had great brown spots on the pallid skin. Then I imagined how they must have been 20 years ago—strong and bony and probably heavily ringed.

"Will you tell me what it was, Leyla?"

My eyes snapped back to the unseen face, sitting concealed atop a high-necked throat with a bit of black lace touching the edge of the shadow. This was a new tack, and it caught me off guard. Instead of commanding me, she had asked. And instead of the imperious use of such words as "child" to indicate my subservience, she had spoken my name. It all made me very suspicious and wonder what she was up to.

"I can understand your reluctance, my dear, and I wish there were some way I could put you at ease. We must not be enemies, you and I, for we are of the same flesh and blood. I am your father's mother. We should be friends."

"I tried that last night."

"You are a very narrow-minded child, Leyla, only a little of which can be excused by youth. You have a mind only for your own private condition, but never bother to try to see another person's. You came here full of expectations, full of naive hopes, and were sadly disappointed by what you got. Instead of tears of joy and a ready-made family full of love, you found only a house of strangers, who were knocked off their equilibrium by your sudden appearance. Then, like the spoiled child you are, you proceeded to pout about the situation and imagine all sorts of idiotic and melodramatic fantasies about us that are wholly untrue. You have done us a great disservice, Leyla, with your accusations. We feel you are treating us most unfairly."

I remained by the fire for a moment to digest her words, then, feeling the small bite of truth in them, suddenly rushed to her side and fell to my knees by her chair. "And what about me! Have you bothered to see *my* side of it all? Can you at all imagine what it must be like for me to come back again, almost *begging* you to love me, only to be treated aloofly and with suspicion? I made those accusations because the same ones were made against my father. Yes, I came full of hopes and expectations because I felt I deserved something of a homecoming. For years, Grandmother, while my mother and I dressed in rags and ate gruel and fought the drafts of Seven Dials, *for years* I lived with the dream of seeing this house again and the beautiful people that must live inside. I should be treated as a sheep returning to the fold, not as an intruder. I *was born here,* Grandmother, I *belong here.* It is not my fault that I went away 20 years ago. I was *taken away.* I would never have left. And it was not my fault that I stayed away, for I had no choice. And when the very first opportunity presented itself—with my mother's death—my first step was to come at once to Pemberton Hurst and my family. Tell me, please, what have I done that is such a terrible disservice!"

I was surprised to see my grandmother's eyes suddenly fill with tears. She was not looking down at me but kept her gaze fixed straight ahead. My words had moved her deeply; this was obvious.

"It was the work of the Devil that drove you away from us, Leyla," she said in a distant voice. "Your poor father—my favorite son—had become possessed by demons and had committed atrocious acts. Our family is a doomed one; every Pemberton will follow his example."

"But it's not true, Grandmother! My father was innocent. And Satan had nothing to do with it. There is no Pemberton Curse, no madness that we are all doomed to. I don't know why you all choose to believe it, but I can somehow *feel* that it's a lie. And I want to prove it. If I can remember what I saw that day—"

"No, Leyla!" The strength of her voice startled me. "Leave it alone. You should never have come back; it is all wrong. Let the dead lie as they are, and go back to London." Suddenly one of her bony hands gripped mine in a remarkably strong hold. "Leyla, dear Leyla. Get out of this house at once! You are putting yourself in the gravest danger! Go away from here and never come back! I *beseech you!*"

Tears rolled down my cheeks as I watched her thin, trembling lips beg me to go away. I imagined what grief she must have known to have had her son and grandson killed in such a heinous manner. I imagined what horrible memories the coppice must daily bring back to her. And I imagined how my presence exhumed all this.

"Please forgive me," I whispered. "But I have no choice. I owe it to my father—"

"Your father is dead!"

"To his poor memory then, and to the 20 years of suffering my mother endured because of what she thought he had done. Now I must prove everyone wrong so that I can go on with my own life. I cannot leave this house now and marry Edward thinking that I had somehow let my father and mother down. I had hoped you would understand, Grandmother." I let the tears drop onto her hand. "To have your son's memory made pure again."

"It's too painful . . ." she groaned. "I cannot bear it . . ."

I remained at her side long enough to let my tears subside. Then, rising unsteadily to my feet and drying my eyes, I said, "I suppose in a way it is all my fault. If I had chosen never to come back, all of this anguish would have been spared. Uncle Henry and Theo would continue managing the mills. Aunt Anna would run the house unperturbed. Martha would be happily creweling a pillow. And Colin . . . well, Colin would just continue to be the nuisance he is. Forgive me. But I've done it and I shall continue to the end what I have started."

I managed to walk to the door with a great deal more composure than I had expected, but hesitated before opening it. Behind me, my grandmother's voice asked, "And what will the end be?"

A great black wall stood inches from my face. I knew it to be the bedroom door that led to the hallway, which in turn led to the outside and beyond. Yet it also seemed to be my future standing before me, as blank and forbidding as my unknown past. It seemed—in that brief pause before going out—that I was a woman who knew neither where she was going nor whence she came. My past and future were unknowns, and at that moment, it seemed my present was none too reliable.

"The end will be the joining of the past with the present, Grandmother."

"For what good? We all know what the future holds."

I turned to regard her, seated behind those protective shadows like a hermit dwelling in a bygone age and refusing to take a step into the future. Had she lived like this since that awful day 20 years ago? Or had she become reclusive with Colin's father's death eight years later? Or had the final straw been her husband's suicide off the east tower ten years ago?

"I don't believe in that future. There is no curse. The Pembertons are not doomed."

"You think not?" came the frail voice from the shadowy past. "Then keep telling yourself that as you visit your uncle Henry, because it is happening again."

By "it" I supposed she was referring to the syndrome that was supposedly associated with the madness: headaches, fever, delirium, and lastly death. This was how Sir John's brother Michael had reportedly died 45 years ago. This was how I was told my father died. Sir John then later succumbed to the same fate. And now, it appeared, Uncle Henry was another victim.

Aunt Anna was beside herself with emotion when I finally stepped out of Grandmother's room. It took little for me to snap out of the mood she had put me in and become at once aware of the turmoil in the hallway. Gertrude was running past me with two maids at her heels: one carrying a pillow, the other a tray of tea. Aunt Anna stood outside their bedroom door wringing her hands until they were white, her ringlets hanging like vines down to her shoulders.

"Oh dear, oh dear," she said over and over again. Her eyes were out of their sockets, her face puckered into a terrible frown.

When I went to her side and laid a hand upon her arm, she looked at me with a dazed expression. "Oh, Jenny, I'm at sixes and sevens. I don't know what to do."

"Uncle Henry?"

Her head bobbed up and down. "Dr. Young's been fetched. He'd have come earlier, but there's been an accident at one of the mills. The boy said he should be here some time tonight. I don't know what to do till he gets here."

I started to go into the chamber, but her pudgy hand held me back. "It's worse, Jenny, worse than it's ever been. Last night and the night before. It's Robert all over again. You remember how he had an occasional headache, then they got closer together, then they got so terribly strong."

A cry from inside the room made me jump. I recognized Uncle Henry's strangled voice in agony.

"He hasn't the fever yet," she went on rapidly. "But it will come, Jenny, you'll see. His time's come. Oh God, my poor Henry!" Aunt Anna's hands flew to her face as she burst out crying.

That Aunt Anna was hysterical was doubtless, but the degree of her hysteria was evident in her use of my mother's name. I could see that she was crumbling beneath the strain and that her total acceptance of "the inevitable" was to be her undoing. Able to offer little more than a comforting embrace, I parted from my aunt's tears and stole softly into the dimly lit chamber where my uncle lay writhing among the bedclothes. His hair was all a tangle and matted to his forehead. His face was a shocking gray, his lips totally without color. I approached him cautiously, unsure of what to say or to do, only vaguely aware of Gertrude standing hidden in the shadows like a forgotten suit of armor.

Uncle Henry released intermittent moans and screwed his eyes tightly against the pain. To see the jumbled bed, his blanched complexion, and to hear the groans of agony made my heart go out to him. Adversary or not, he was still my father's brother and a man suffering terribly.

"Uncle Henry," I whispered, falling to my knees at his side. "Uncle Henry."

After a moment, his poor tortured head rolled to one side, and I was met by glazed eyes with pinpoint pupils. "God," he barely said. His lips were dry, cracked "Jenny. I'm dying."

"Nonsense, Uncle Henry." I put a hand gently upon his forehead and was shocked at its coolness. "This will pass. You will be all right."

"No, no!" he whispered. "My uncle Michael, then my own father Sir John, and then my brother Robert, and now me. Next it will be Theo and Colin. Then Martha. And Leyla, too. Little Leyla. We're all Pembertons. Oh God!" His eyes shut tightly again, and his entire body moved in a quick spasm. "My head is going to explode! God help me!" Uncle Henry's voice rose to a shriek. *"God help me!"*

"Please quiet yourself," I tried consolingly. "You will get better, Uncle Henry. I know you will." These words were more to bolster myself than him, for his curse of doom upon me and the rest of us had sent my heart sinking, and as well I suspected he heard nothing I said anyway. In his pain and torment, Uncle Henry was living in a twilight between the past and the present—somewhere between my father's death and my arrival—for he thought I was my mother.

His eyes next became wild, searching. My uncle was rapidly losing a rational hold upon reality. "Dear God, don't let me commit the acts my brother was forced to. Please spare me that abomination. Don't let me be another instrument of sorrow among this family!"

I stared in horror at Uncle Henry. With prehensile fingers clawing the bedclothes and his wild eyes insanely searching the air above him, my uncle had one shred of reason, one remnant of sanity left to warn him of what might unfold during his delirium. Twenty years before, he had seen his brother suffer the same symptoms, culminating in the grisly acts of murder and suicide.

"No, Uncle Henry," I cried. "It won't happen. That's not what my father did. He was the *victim,* not the killer!"

"You don't know, Jenny. You weren't there."

"But Leyla was! *I* was there!" I pounded my forehead with a fist "*If only I could remember!* Uncle Henry, if I could remember what I saw that day in the coppice, I could ease your mind, for my father was not the murderer, and neither will you be. Don't you see? You've got yourself convinced that—"

"My God!" he bellowed, both hands tearing at his hair. "This pain! It's like a burning poker stabbing my brain!" And he began to writhe so violently that I became alarmed.

In the next instant, Aunt Anna was at his side and laying soothing arms across his body. "Hush, my darling." she said with tears streaking down her face. "Quiet yourself now; it's going to be all right. Dr. Young is on his way."

When my uncle had calmed considerably, Aunt Anna turned to me and said with such vehemence that it startled me, "You! You've upset him! Get out and don't come back while he's ill!"

"But I wish to help—"

"You've done enough! Get out now!"

I backed away from my aunt as if she were an inmate at St. Mary's and found my way to the door. All about me was a scene from nightmares—

deep shadows, oblique angles—so that I felt the hairs on my arms prickle. It had devastated me to see my uncle, my strong uncle whom I had regarded as a father figure, so reduced to raving and delirium. I was at a loss for words, for coherent thoughts. All I could do was dash from that bedroom and race down the hall toward my own room.

Death seemed to surround me all about. The ghosts of my father and brother hovered near; my suicidal grandfather; my accidentally killed uncle Richard and aunt Jane; my suicidal great-uncle Michael; the unexpectedly dead great-aunt Sylvia; and my own mother, whose lingering illness had taken part of me with her.

As I flung myself down the corridor, blind and confused, I slammed right into Cousin Colin, nearly toppling the two of us off our feet. But he caught me quickly in his arms and held me until we caught our breath. Then he released me and asked, "Where to in such a rush, Cousin?"

"Not *to,* Colin, but away from."

"From what are you running then?"

I glanced over my shoulder, the vision of Uncle Henry still stamped upon my mind—his pallor, his mad eyes, his groping fingers. This was not a house at all, it was a necropolis.

"Leyla?"

I looked up at Colin. His eyes were heavy with concern. "I've been to see Uncle Henry."

"Oh . . . I see . . ."

"Oh God, he's so wretched. Why can't they do something for him? Laudanum—"

"He's already receiving the maximum dose, Leyla. Dr. Young dare not give him any more, or else . . ." Colin spread out his hands.

Yes, I was familiar with laudanum. A mixture of morphine and alcohol, it was a great panacea for pain, but it also had its lethal limits.

"There's nothing more we can do."

"But he's suffering so!"

Colin's expression held more than any words could convey. He was telling me about my tragic father, about Sir John flinging himself off the turret, about Michael, who had poisoned himself and his mother.

"I won't accept it," I whispered bitterly. "'It can't be true. There is no Pemberton sickness."

"And you don't think we're all doomed?"

"Not at all! It's a coincidence, or a local illness that strikes periodically. There's an explanation for it, and you are a fool not to see that! Colin, *how can you be so ignorant!*"

While I screamed at him, I was releasing all my anguish for Uncle Henry's suffering, for Aunt Anna's despair, for my own mother's years of poverty. In the words I shouted at Colin I was letting out the stored-up tension of the entire day—from finding Aunt Sylvia's diary, to visiting the coppice, to pleading with Grandmother, to seeing my wretched uncle. It was getting to be more than I could take.

In the next moment, I forced myself to calm a little, creating an exterior of sobriety while inside I continued to rant and rave. The green eyes of my cousin were hard upon me, masking—in the true Pemberton fashion—what he was really thinking. He stood silent, staring, as if waiting.

"I've also had a visit with Grandmother," I managed in the steadiest voice possible.

"Oh?"

"Yes, and it seems she knew I had been to the coppice today."

"You hardly kept your intentions a secret, Leyla."

"She also knew that I remembered nothing by going there. That the visit had been futile. Somehow"—I squared my shoulders and tipped my chin—"in the few minutes between my return from the coppice and going to her room, Grandmother was informed of what had happened."

"Indeed?" His face betrayed nothing.

"Oh, Colin, I suppose I shouldn't be surprised, and I suppose I have no right to be angry, but must you run to Grandmother each time and tell her everything? Must you be her personal spy?"

Curiously, Colin remained unmoved. His guarded expression neither denied nor admitted guilt, so that I was frustrated even further.

"What is the matter with you! With all of you!" I suddenly cried out. "In the brief glimpses of memory that I do have, I remember laughter and happiness in this house." Tears brimmed my eyes, threatening to fall. "What has happened to all of you? What have you done to turn this house into a mausoleum?"

With unexpected sympathy, Colin took one of my hands between his and said, "Come with me, Leyla. There is something I want to tell you."

Like a child, I let him lead me along the hall, down the stairs, and into the library below. The house was still and quiet despite the violent rainstorm that crashed all about us, and in the womb of the library, with its roaring fire and softly ticking clock, I felt myself relax by degrees. Upstairs, in the atmosphere of gloom and death, I had felt desperate, trapped. But down here, enveloped by towers of books and a hot fire, I grew calm and sank wearily into one of the easy chairs that faced the hearth.

Colin stood before me, his back to the fire. "Leyla, you've been nothing but unhappy here. Ever since you came, nothing has been right, and my simple-minded aunt would have you believe it's all your fault. But of course it isn't. Nothing's gone right in this house for decades, and I doubt it ever will. Even in the next century, if the family survives that long, the Hurst will stand as it does now, housing the doomed Pembertons like a secret order of monks."

I snapped my eyes to Colin. It surprised me that he would use the same analogy that had come to my own mind in describing the family. We were a reclusive group, sequestered and arcane as if sworn to a mysterious canon of ethics that bound us together as if we were Trappists.

"You once asked me, Leyla, why Theo and Martha and I were not married. You once noted that Martha was the youngest here, and she 32. You have also noticed, though you've never outright remarked on it, that there are no children here. There have been no children at the Hurst since Thomas died and you were taken away. Surely you must wonder why."

"The Curse," I said flatly.

"Precisely. You see, Leyla, we cannot let the taint continue any further; it has to be stopped. If our ancestors had realized this long ago, then you and I would not be sitting here today facing the same fate that now has Uncle Henry in its grasp. No, wait, Leyla, let me finish. I know you don't agree, but you will in time. I saw what it did to your father, what it did to Sir John, and what it is now doing to Uncle Henry. Theo and Martha and you and I will all follow the same path, each in our own time. Sir John's brother Michael, I understand, was young when it struck him. In his 30s."

"No, Colin. I won't go along with it."

"Nevertheless, the other Pembertons do, and as a consequence, we decided long ago to put an end to this misery. To spare future generations from this suffering."

I stared long and hard at my cousin. "I see . . . Sort of a self-imposed celibacy. Is that why none of you ever married?"

He nodded gravely.

"How villainous! It is unnatural and against God's Law not to marry and have children. You have no right to make such a judgment."

"Do you think so? Do you think it is part of God's Law and nature to propagate children who will become monsters like ourselves? Have we that right? And you, Leyla, can you give birth to a child that you know will be doomed to a ghastly fate like that of your father?"

"There is no curse!"

"I wouldn't expect you to agree now, but in time you will."

I fell to staring into the fire, suddenly very unappreciative of my cousin Colin. His words greatly unsettled me. I did not know what to think. "So that's why Uncle Henry opposed my marriage to Edward."

"And rightfully so."

"Not rightfully! I shall marry whom I please and when I please. Oh, Colin!" I glowered at him fiercely. "And you, do you go along with them?"

His eyes carried such a look of sadness that I had to turn away.

"There must be an answer somewhere," I said with grim determination. "And I am going to find it. Colin . . . Colin, you are as pathetic as the others and a grave disappointment. But the fighting spirit has not been killed in me, so I intend to prove you all wrong. And I intend to have children by Edward that are going to be strong and healthy and long-lived."

He stared at me but—curiously—did not rise to my challenge. Instead of trying to discourage me as I had thought he would, Colin only continued to gaze at me with his jade-green eyes.

"I will find the answer," I whispered with a little less heart.

"And God help you in your search."

CHAPTER 10

I HAD SLEPT BADLY THAT NIGHT, HAVING BEEN AROUSED BY THE late arrival of Dr. Young and footsteps past my door, so that when I awoke to an ice-cold bedroom and a blue dawn coming through my windows, it was no wonder I had a mild headache. Before I had retired, Gertrude had tacitly brought me a small supper and a mug of hot chocolate. Yet none of this had helped, for my mind had been too electric with the day's events. Lying under the blankets and listening to the storm, I had tried to recapture my feelings of that afternoon in the coppice, yet it was as distant a memory as if it had happened months before. It was Colin's words that had obsessed me for most of the night, his calm acceptance of an insidious fate, and the decision to remain forever without an heir. It was all too grotesque to believe.

And then there had been Aunt Sylvia's diary, which had proven to me that someone other than she had written the letter to bring me to the Hurst. But who had done it? And why had that person used Aunt Sylvia's name rather than his or her own? And now, if one of them had lured me here, why did they all seem anxious for me to leave?

I pulled the curtains apart and looked out at a gray, miserable day. Great pools made a moat of the gravel drive, and the trees hung heavy with soaked branches. Drops of dew glistened upon the leaves of hedge-parsley and campion. Boughs of ash and acacia twinkled as if festooned with strings of diamonds. It was a wet, cold world. And inside, life was little better.

A maid came up to help me dress, brushing off my velvet morning frock, cinching in my whalebone corset, and arranging the petticoats on my crinoline. She worked quietly, never looking at me, her mobcap set neatly upon her copper curls, and I wondered in passing what the servants thought of our eccentric family.

When I went downstairs to the breakfast room, I was surprised to find that not one of my relatives was around. Gertrude informed me that Aunt Anna and Theodore were keeping vigil over Uncle Henry (who was much worse), while Martha chose to remain in her room and knit. Cousin Colin had left the house early for a ride upon his favorite mare.

After tea and biscuits and a drop of brandy for my headache, I decided to walk about the house. Back in London, whenever I had had a problem to work out, I had always gone for a walk by the Serpentine rather than remain caged in my flat. Fresh air and exercise always helped me to think better, but since the weather was so beastly today, I decided to cover the miles of stairs and hallways that made up this vast mansion.

My first stop was the parlor, expecting to sit at the pianoforte and play a few tunes, yet so unsettled had I become that I could not sit for even a moment at the keyboard. I gave cursory exploration to lesser-used rooms on the first floor: another parlor, a study, a musty solarium, and a ballroom with dust covers on the chandeliers. Everywhere I walked, my footsteps either echoed upon polished wooden floors or whispered softly over heavy carpets. I encountered many plants, massive furniture, Gothic statuary, and the same severe silence that prevailed everywhere. It was Grandmother Abigail's stern presence that I felt, her unswerving dominance over a secret society, her tenacious hold upon the past, and her ability to staunch the onrush of the future in an effort to make time stand still.

After a long tour of the ground floor and having run into no one but mutely polite servants, I wandered back to the library, a room that was rapidly becoming my favorite. Here I roamed among the many titles that had accumulated over the years and wondered if it would be possible to find a good novel in which to immerse myself for a while.

Yet as I casually read the spines, I shivered with the chill of the drafts and dampness that were inherent in big old houses, so I moved to the fireplace where, standing at a judiciously safe distance, I warmed myself. My eyes fell to the flames as they often did, and stared hypnotically for several minutes. My mind became a pleasant blank and drifted into a sort of netherworld, not thinking of anything in particular, until my eyes happened quite by accident to focus upon a very small object at the fire's edge. I stared at this bit of refuse for a long moment before my mind joined my eyes in their idle curiosity. Drawing myself back to the present, I wondered what it was I so intently stared at until, focusing a little more carefully, it suddenly came clear to me that the object was a small piece of paper: stationery.

Not knowing why, I inclined myself a little closer to it and, seeing the remnants of handwriting there, bent all the way down and picked it up. Blackened along all its edges, the scrap of paper was doubtless the last of a deposit of trash that one of the maids had delivered into the fire, and this scrap had most likely been blown free of the flames by a draft and thereby saved from total incineration.

I flipped it over between my fingers and read the few legible words. In an instant, I froze, and a cold terror gripped me harder than if someone had plunged a knife into me. For what I held in my hand was all that remained of my letter to Edward.

Words escaped my lips. "Oh no," I whispered. "Dear God, no!"

My legs suddenly went weak, and I had to stumble to a chair before I fell to the floor. At once, perspiration sprung to my brow, and my headache returned.

Edward's letter had been intercepted, read by someone, and then thrown in this fire for destruction.

But by whom? Which of my family had done this thing? To whom had the maid gone directly with this letter, probably under orders?

I rubbed my temples with ice-cold fingertips. Only Grandmother Abigail would have that sort of power over my silver coins. But no, Uncle Henry could have done it. Or Aunt Anna. Possibly Theo had enough influence over the servants to have ordered them to bring him any communication I might write.

This was nightmarish! There in the fire burned my letter to Edward, my plea to him to come and help me. My one link with the outside world. And one of my diabolic relatives had intercepted the letter, read what I had written (Oh God, the things I had written!), and then had destroyed it. Why?

Obviously, he or she, whoever it was, did not want Edward to know what was happening, did not want him here, did not want me to have help in this.

Did this also mean I was a prisoner in this house? I wondered if the same person who had done this horrible deed had also been the one to write me that letter in Sylvia's name bringing me here. Obviously, one of my relatives—or possibly all of them collectively—had wanted me here, lured me here, and wanted to keep me from ever leaving. From returning to Edward.

Of course . . . that was it. I slowly rose and put a steadying hand on the mantelpiece. Uncle Henry was opposed to my marriage to Edward. He wanted me to remain here like the others, unwed and childless for the rest of my life.

But did that explain Sylvia's letter? Why would Uncle Henry have also wanted to bring my mother back?

It made no sense. My head ached terribly from the shock, and I saw I would have to go upstairs and think this all out. My letter to Edward . . . there in the fire . . .

A fresh lot of rain lay siege upon my windows, muted now by the heavy draperies, and the smell of dampness hung in the air. My fire did little to ward off the chill as icy breaths found entrance between faults in the old Tudor construction. It was not a cozy chamber, this, but at least it was quiet and private and totally mine.

More than anything I needed to be alone. I needed to sort things out, go back over the last four days—had it only been four?—and determine where everything had begun to go wrong. But this was futile, for it had obviously all begun with my knocking on the door that first evening and with Gertrude's look of shock at seeing me. It was all so confused. Their reluctance to welcome me warmly, their secretiveness, learning the truth about Father's death, learning that I had witnessed it, being told about the inevitable sickness that would claim us all, Grandmother's abominable reaction to my return, those blank five years, Uncle Henry's illness, Aunt Sylvia's unexplainable letter, and now my letter to Edward. They all culminated in one ghastly nightmare that I desperately wanted to be free of. But I needed help. These people had the answers, but they would not share them with me.

The solution to the conundrum lay in my memory. Buried somewhere at the depths of my mind lay the vision of a scene at the coppice that I had witnessed as a child and that had since been driven farther and farther from my grasp. What was I to do to retrieve it once again? Obviously, my own defenses had built a wall over the memory for my own protection, yet now, for my own protection, I must exhume that memory and relive it again.

When my headache had gone and my shock subsided, I lay upon the bed with a new determination to find the answers. I would go once again to the coppice, I would do everything in my power to remember what happened that day, and then I would prove to them all that my father had been murdered. This then would have to prove the Curse a hoax, simply a story invented to cover up the true details of the crime.

I lunched in my room before a fire after a maid had brought a tray and placed it on a small table before me. Due to my mood, however, the tea tasted bitter and the soup flat, so I ate little and followed it with a nap.

It was around four o'clock in the afternoon that I was awakened by a knocking at my door. Opening it, I found Martha, quite obviously upset, wringing her hands. The ever present carpetbag was by her feet.

"Grandmother wants to see you, Leyla."

"Now? Is she all right?"

"She wants to see us all. At once. You had better come with me."

The gravity in her tone put me on my guard. "Very well," I said, and I dipped back into the room to retrieve a shawl, then closed the door behind us. "She's not ill, is she?" I ventured.

"Grandmother is never ill."

So we walked in silence down the hall until we reached Abigail's suite of rooms. As always before an audience with this imperious old woman, I felt a cold apprehension rise within me. I detested the effect she had upon me, a feeling of power over me that I liked to think did not truly exist.

The door stood open, so we entered. Inside the cloistered room, my other relatives were already gathered. Grandmother sat unchanged upon her throne behind a protective veil of shadow, while Aunt Anna sat in a chair before her with Theodore on one side and Colin on the other. Uncle Henry must have been in his sickbed. No one turned to us as we came in; all of them kept their eyes obsequiously upon our matriarch. The air, though dim and gloomy, was charged with emotion. I wondered what had happened.

Martha took her brother's arm, and I remained a little apart as Grandmother suddenly spoke. "You all know why you're here; therefore I shan't procrastinate. A foul deed has been committed among us, and I want the perpetrator found. You can decide among yourselves what is to be done."

Confused, I looked at the others, their faces blank. "What foul deed?" I asked innocently.

"Leyla Pemberton," came Grandmother's intrepid voice, "you above all should know what I speak of."

"But I don't."

"It's Theo's ring," I heard Martha say softly. "It's missing."

"His ring?"

Grandmother said, "Not missing, child, stolen! And I want the thief known."

Then it dawned on me. The ruby ring Theodore had inherited from his grandfather Sir John. The ring that had flashed in my mind as a memory of the coppice. Somehow it was related to what happened at the coppice, yet I had not so far figured out how.

"But who would take it?" I asked.

Silence met me as everyone in the room remained unmoving. The bit of jet at Abigail's throat glinted now and then with the rising and falling of her chest—the only clue that she was alive—and the others all found something upon which to focus their gaze.

Then it struck me. "What do you mean that I above all should know what you speak of? Are you accusing me of stealing the ring?"

"Those are your words," said Grandmother.

"But that is preposterous!"

Now Aunt Anna spoke up. "But you admired it just the other night in the drawing room. We all saw you."

"I did not admire it. I only remembered it, that's all."

"From where did you remember it?" asked Grandmother.

"I . . . I don't know. It was just a flash."

"Well, who else would take it!" said my aunt in a sudden outburst.

"Aunt Anna! How dare you! I will not stand here and be accused like a common thief!"

Finally Cousin Theodore spoke up. "Leyla's right, Grandmother; this is really most unfair. Other jewelry has been missing before this, and recently too. I think we ought to examine the servants."

While he spoke on my behalf, I looked across the gloom at my cousin Theodore and for the first time saw a humanitarian side of him. Tall and erect and in his usual striking attire, my cousin cut quite a handsome figure among these others. Colin, whose hair was untidy and necktie crooked, stood with his arms boorishly folded and left me quite alone to fend for myself. He said not one word in my defense, and I was angry with him for it.

After he had spoken, Theo offered me a conciliatory smile, and I showed my gratitude in return. Behind Colin's and Martha's backs and over Aunt Anna's head, Theo and I exchanged unspoken communication.

"We will examine the servants," decreed Grandmother. "And we will make a thorough search for that ring. I will stand for no petty thievery among my family."

What sort of thievery do you want? I thought in sarcasm, but held my tongue.

With a wave of the hand, she dismissed us, and I became overcome with impatience. This entire scene had been solely for my humiliation because, upon a whim, she had judged me guilty. For all this, I was enraged, yet I did not show it. I was fighting for my rights and for the purification of my father's memory. One of these people had read my letter to Edward and then had destroyed it. One of these people did not want me to have help. Yet I was going to continue to fight to remember the past, and these petty scenes of threats and accusations did not frighten me off but only lent fuel to the fire of my crusade.

Out in the hall, I stepped to one side to allow Aunt Anna to pass. She cast me a sideways glance, and in the gaslight, I saw how taut and haggard her face had become. She must have been up all night with Uncle Henry, who I assumed was no better, and I felt a little more charitable toward her. After 24 hours without sleep and food, my aunt was bound to be a little irrational.

Yet when Colin passed me, I glared at him sharply, but he seemed not to notice. The notion I harbored about his special confidence with Grandmother was beginning to irritate me, as though he weren't his own man after all but a swaggering popinjay that clung to the skirts of an old woman.

As Theo passed by, he paused to give me a special smile. It bespoke sympathy and possibly a little contrition for the way I had been treated. In that moment, when our eyes met beneath the glow of the gaslight, I felt the hope that we might try again to be friends.

Martha and I walked back toward our own rooms together, myself deep in agitated thought, she with a worried frown on her face while her fingers worked nervously at the handles of her carpetbag. When we reached my door, I was not surprised that she hesitated with me, for I had sensed for some minutes that there was something she wanted to say.

"Leyla, Grandmother really thinks you stole the ring out of Theo's room. I have never seen her so angry."

"She is senile, Martha. Why should I possibly want the ring?"

"Well, because . . ." She would not raise her eyes to mine. "Grandmother says it is because you are penniless. She said you came to Pemberton Hurst only for money, and when it wasn't readily offered to you, you resorted to stealing."

"That isn't logical, Martha," I said dryly. "After all, the man I am going to marry is quite well off. Once I am Mrs. Champion, I will have no need of the Pemberton fortune. You can all keep your cotton mills and your vast acreage and your petty squabbles. I want only one thing from this house, and that is my past. Once I have regained it, once my memory has returned, I will leave forever."

Now she looked up at me, her eyes glistening. Although 32 years old, Martha's face was still smooth and young, her eyes heavily lashed and her delicate chin barely cleft as was my own. We vaguely resembled one another, this quiet creature and I, but only physically, for emotionally we were quite different. Cousin Martha had a retiring personality. She shrank in the presence of men and seemed to lead a life entirely inside of herself.

"I envy you," she whispered unexpectedly.

"You envy me? Whatever for?"

"You can leave this house and go off and marry and have children."

"You can do the same, Martha."

She shook her head, and the ringlets framing her face danced. "Grandmother Abigail will disinherit anyone who leaves the family. She has forbidden us to marry ever and will leave us without a penny if we defy her. You have Edward waiting for you, and you say he is well-to-do. I would have nowhere to go were I to leave. I am a prisoner here. We all are."

She had spoken dispassionately, yet there had been a longing in her eyes.

"I don't really mind," quaked her tiny voice. "It's just that I wonder once in a while what it must be like to . . . to know a man." Suddenly her face flushed crimson. "Oh forgive me. That was an improper thing to say."

"Nonsense. Every woman dreams of love. Every woman wants to marry the right man and have his children. You are no different."

"Yes, I am. I must be because I am a Pemberton. It would be loathsome of me to wish to give birth to children who would one day have to face what you and I must now face. Grandmother is right; the line must end." A tear tumbled down Martha's cheek, and I almost cried with her. "Still, though . . . once in a while, in East Wimsley, I spy a handsome fellow and I wonder . . ."

"There, there, Martha."

"I don't even know what it is like to be kissed by a man."

I thought just then of Edward and his cold kisses on the cheek. "You will someday, when you marry." Martha ran her hands over her eyes to dry them. "You probably didn't take the ring," she sniffed, "but you'll have to convince Grandmother of it."

I stiffened again. "My word should be sufficient. If you will excuse me, Martha."

I slipped into my bedroom with a mingling of sadness and anger. To have been so rudely accused in front of everyone with no defense except from Theo had been humiliating. But now I also wondered about the truth behind the ring.

What a coincidence that I should only yesterday afternoon have a flash of memory of it, and then it be stolen the very same night. Did it play a greater part in that day at the coppice than I knew, and did someone know this? But why steal the ring? Somehow I had a strong feeling that Theo's ruby ring was directly connected with the morbid events that took place in the coppice 20 years ago and that its sudden disappearance now was no idle coincidence. If someone were afraid of my linking the ring to my father's murder, then possibly that had removed any further chance of that ring causing a sudden jog of the memory.

This was one explanation, yes, but it was inadequate. Somehow I had the feeling that there was more to it, yet I could not fathom what. Between Edward's letter and Theo's ring, I was thoroughly perplexed.

After that travesty in Grandmother's room, I refused to join my family for supper, but took my meal once again in my own room and before a comforting fire. Afterwards, I sat curled in the chair and flipped through the pages of my Cremorne Gardens guidebook and escaped for a while in reminiscences of happy days with Edward. It would be no use to attempt another letter to him. And it was not really necessary. I felt certain that, with good concentrated effort, I could unravel the mystery of this house and then return to my Edward's arms a more total woman.

When the hour was late, I changed into my nightdress, brushed out my long hair, and retired to the bed for some desperately needed rest.

It was as I was about to extinguish my candle that I first noticed the book. Atop *Tancred* and *Persuasion*, two books I had earnestly planned to read during my stay at Pemberton Hurst, lay a third volume, which was not one of my own.

After staring at it curiously for a moment, I reached for it and, frowning over it, brought my candle closer to the edge of the table. In the improved light, I examined the strange book with a mingling of surprise and hesitation.

It was an old book, at least 30 years or so, and was bound handsomely in black leather. The title, imprinted on the spine in faded gold, read: *The Collected Works of Thomas Willis.*

Totally bewildered, I stared for some time at it, not immediately opening it, far more curious as to the reason for its being here than what it might contain.

My candle flame flickered in the occasional drafts blowing through my bedroom. The clock over the cold fireplace gently ticked in a soft reminder that time was passing, passing, passing . . . And I stared incredulously at *The Collected Works of Thomas Willis.*

Finally, I opened the book and was confronted at once by the gravely solemn gaze of Mr. Willis himself. Peering out from behind an oval frame that bore the words, "Thomas Willis, Medic Professor Collegü Med, London et Societ Reg Socius" was a seventeenth-century face full of wisdom and noble character. His eyes looked down somewhat from under heavy brows and sat over protruding cheekbones and a magnificent nose. His mouth, beneath a slight moustache, was thin-lipped and half-smiling, as though guarding a secret. An archaic costume reminiscent of Cromwell covered the man and bespoke the prominence and affluence he must have known in his life. Beneath the oval portrait were the words, "Thomas Willis (1621-1675) Copper engraving at age 45 by Isabella Piccini. Frontispiece taken from *Opera omnia* 1694."

The title page informed me that this compendium of Willis's books had been put together by Sir Anthony Cadwallader, Regius Professor at Oxford, and published by Mortimer and Sons in London in 1822. From here, I flipped to the table of contents, still totally bemused and without the slightest clue as to who had made this gift to me or to why he or she had thought I might be interested in the works of a man almost 200 years dead. In the next minute, my questions were answered.

The table of contents listed all the works within the volume and a brief description of each. It read like this:

Pharmaceutice rationalis or an Excercitation of the Operations of Medicines in Humane Bodies (in which he first describes myasthenia gravis; the Diabetes or Pissing Evil; Asthma; Cardiospasm; and Pleurisie)

De febribus (in which we have his early accounts of epidemics of typhus fever and typhoid fevers)

Anatomy of the Brain (including his accurate descriptions of the Anatomy of the nervous system and arterial circle at the base of the brain called the "circle of Willis")

Practice of Physick (in which he describes pestilent, malignant, and epidemical fevers)

One would not have to be overly bright to guess that the book's purpose was to enlighten me on the point of the hereditary Pemberton sickness. Why else would it have been put here? I was certainly not a medical student or the slightest bit interested in anatomy, or a collector of odd books. Indeed, I was not even a reader of works other than those that were fiction, and then I generally read the popular novels of the day. Obviously, whoever had secretly entered my room and placed this book where I would find it had hoped I would peruse the contents (as I was now doing) and fall by chance upon a particular passage. And what else could that passage contain, what else would be of any interest, but some small information about a sickness that resembled the supposed Pemberton Curse?

I regarded the book with something less than patience, for I was by now extremely bitter and quite angry with my family. As if Edward's letter had not been enough, the accusation of stealing Theo's ring had quite set me against everyone. And so now, for some reason I could not fathom, one of my relatives had chosen to give me this book surreptitiously—possibly afraid to give it to me in person for fear of my reaction—and was probably counting very heavily upon my finding the right passage. And for what reason? To engender my goodwill by proving to me what a pathetic lot they were? By trying to make me rue my anger with them by showing me the truth of their sickness?

Whatever, I was in no humor to be softened. This book was a ruse, and I did not appreciate it. No matter what this Thomas Willis had to say, my heart could not be warmed to the Pembertons. They had hurt me and they were a selfish lot. If the historical physician had written about a disease similar to the one supposedly afflicting the Pembertons, then I was still not interested. It was a tactic of which I did not approve, and I was not to be taken in by it. I would not play into their hands.

Angrily I dropped the book to the floor, puffed out my candle, and slid under the bedcovers. After such a tiring day, I was desperately in need of sleep, of escape for a while, before facing another day of wrestling with my memory and my tenacious relatives.

Yet sleep would not come. Apprehensively, I lay staring at the ceiling, the hooded eyes of Thomas Willis gazing sagely at me through the centuries. A forgotten scientist after whom a network of arteries had been named, what on earth could he possibly have written that someone in this insane household wanted me to read?

I rolled over in an attempt to become more comfortable. With my eyes tightly closed and the winds swishing the trees outside, I heard my mind whisper again the itinerary of Cadwallader's book: myasthenia gravis; diabetes; asthma; cardiospasm; pleurisy; typhus and typhoid fevers; the anatomy of the brain . . . "in which he describes pestilent, malignant, and epidemical fevers." I opened my eyes.

No rest would ever come to me, I knew now, until I had discovered the words in Willis's book that were in some way cogent to the Pembertons. Whoever had placed it on my night table—Aunt Anna or Theo or Colin or Martha—had known that my curiosity would drive me to reading through the book until I came upon the salient point that would strike a cord familiar with the Pemberton plight. And since I was a slave to my curiosity (had it not been one of the reasons for my coming back here in the first place?), I conceded once more and gave in to its power.

Knowing that sleep was to be a long way off, I got out of bed, drew on a dressing gown, lit a small fire in the fireplace, and curled up in my easy chair next to an oil lamp with *The Collected Works of Thomas Willis.*

The biography of the man was mildly interesting. Born in 1621 at Great Bedwyn in Wiltshire and receiving his master's degree in 1642, Thomas Willis had gone on to join the army of King Charles I in the Civil War and had become a soldier in the garrison of Oxford. In 1646, Willis took his bachelor of medicine degree and began practice at Oxford, during which time he remained faithful to the Royalist Cause and to the Church of England. Also during this period, he published dissertations on Fermentations, Fever, and Urines.

After the Restoration, Willis became Sedleian Professor of Natural Philosophy at Oxford and in the same year was granted the degree of Doctor and became a member of the Royal Society. In 1667, he set up practice in London, where he became immensely popular and wealthy, which led him to become a Fellow of the Royal College of Physicians and was appointed Physician to the King. After a laudable career of astute clinical observations and noteworthy publications, Thomas Willis died in 1675 and was buried in Westminster Abbey.

Thomas Willis, I gathered, had been a man of great learning whose word could certainly be trusted.

The first "book" I leafed through was the longest and most tedious—the "Pharmaceutice rationalis"—and I found little of pertinent interest. Among the chapters on respiratory distress, muscular atrophy, sugared urine, and chronic vomiting, I saw nothing that might have any connection with the Pemberton family. The detailed accounts of typhus and typhoid fevers in "De febribus" seemed also to have little to do with the problem at hand, and the "Anatomy of the Brain" was so complex with terminology and diagrams that I skipped over it altogether. It was the last chapter, "Practice of Physick," that seemed to hold the most promise, for it was described as being a treatise on fevers of many varieties, both specific and general, and, judging from the accounts of my father's death (as well as observing poor Uncle Henry's febrile state), it would seem that fevers were of the greatest concern to us.

And so, with the clock gently ticking off the 2 a.m. hour and with the wind assailing my windows, I began wading through the awkward and archaic literary style of Dr. Willis.

CHAPTER XIV—Of Pestilential and Malignant Feavers in Specie, and of others Epidemical

> After having unfolded the Nature of the Plague, by the order of our Tract, we ought to proceed to the Diseases, which seem to be nearest like its Nature; which chiefly are Feavers, called Pestilent and Malignant, for tis commonly noted, that Feavers sometimes reign popularly, which for the vehemency of symptoms, the great slaughter of the sick, and the great force of contagion, scarce give place to the Pestilence, which, however, because they imitate the type of Putrid Feavers, and do not so certainly kill the sick as the Plague, or so certainly infect others, they deserve the name not of the Plague, but by a more minute appellation of a Pestilential Feaver: Besides these, there are Feavers of another kind, the perniciousness and Contagion of which appear more remiss, yet because they are infectious . . .

I flipped on to further pages. Obviously, the Bubonic Plague and other pestilent fevers were not of interest to me. I would have to move more slowly, studiously, in order to discover the hidden "treasure" of this book.

Dr. Willis went on to describe lesser plagues, "Camp Feavers, and other virulent Contagions," while at the same time citing examples among such notables as the Earl of Essex and the Countess of Kent. I read on:

> That Diaphoretick was only the pouder of Toads, purged thoroughly with Salt, and then washed in the best Wine, and lightly calcined in an earthened Pot. The Autumn coming on, this Disease by degrees remitted its wonted fierceness that fewer grew sick of it and many of them grew well . . .

Still he spoke only of epidemical diseases that took countless victims in one swoop. So far, after pages of laborious reading, nothing seemed pertinent.

I was about to close the book once and for all, deciding its sudden appearance in my bedroom to have been a mistake or practical joke, when my eye caught these words:

> There exists, however, another Feaver by whose very symptoms we can observe a divergence of Nature from the Pest, in that it is not epidemical.

My eyes drove down upon those words "it is not epidemical." Rearranging myself in the chair, I drew the page closer to my eyes and read more slowly.

> When this Feaver first began, it was something like the figure of a putrid Synochus; but it was impossible to be cured, and was found to be always fatal. This Feaver which we call the Brain Sickness, and is wont to reappear most insidiously with an onset of most wicked Symptoms, has a History of being reclusive to certain maligned Families. One observation which I made in particular, about the Summer Solstace, was of the son of Sir Geoffrey of Pember Town in a Parish which is south of London. The story was told that the esteemed Sir Geoffrey had suffered the same Fate as the son which was now troubled by the Symptoms of the Fever; those being Delirium, Madness, Phrensie, Stupefaction, Sleepiness, Vertigo, Tremblings, Convulsive Motions and divers other distempers of the Head, and these shewed the great hurt of the Brain and nervous stock. After the deaths of Father and Son I occasioned to look into the Brains of them both, having the permission of the House to see into the nature of the Pember Town Sickness, and found a Poyson egg which I gave the appellation of Tumor that grew in the flesh of the Brain and corrupted the arteries, so that no apothecaries could help, and the victims could not be free from the virulency of the Disease. In the Hyrst where Sir Geoffrey and his Son suffered the Brain Sickness, there are others of the stricken Family who will have the same Fate, for it is in the Hands of God that the Tumor is born, and that the prescripts of Physicians will go for naught, and the

Brain Sickness (or Pember Town Fever) will not bow to Empirical Remedies.

I sat for a long time staring at those last words, the book lying agape in my lap while outside an ominous morning was struggling through the trees. Beyond this small reference, written in 1674, nothing more was mentioned by Thomas Willis. The next page started out with, "No less frequent a symptom of Feavers is a Diarrhea, or Flux of the Belly . . ." and had nothing to do with the sickness of the Pembertons. His one small case history, like the ones before it, had been terse and effective, having made its point and requiring no further deliberation. Dr. Thomas Willis of Cromwellian England had been an authority on fevers and the brain and had been called to treat the suffering family at this Hurst. Not epidemical or pestilential like plagues and infections, the Pemberton sickness was peculiar to this family and caused by a specific trait in the bloodline.

With a sigh, I lay my head back on the chair and gazed at the ceiling, tears stinging my eyes. So . . . it was true . . . For 200 years or more we had always been the doomed victims of a brain tumor, as hereditary as hemophilia and about as curable. Just like the Romanovs, the Pembertons were doomed.

I do not know at what time I finally extricated myself from the chair, stretched my limbs, and walked stiffly to the bed, but a gray light was poking between the curtains, and that special chill peculiar to early morning was shivering my flesh. I had been reading all night.

With a hollowness I had never before known, I climbed between the sheets of my bed, moving like a mindless automaton, and lay trancelike for a very long time. Before my eyes swam the prescient face of Thomas Willis, the man who had discovered and described the Pemberton sickness, and I knew not whether to curse him or bless him for what he had found. At least, through his archaic words, I knew the basis for the hysteria in this family. I now knew the reasons and the answers I had been seeking. *There was indeed a Pemberton madness,* seated in a tumor of the brain, and a biologic quirk of nature that promised to drive every descendant of Sir Geoffrey of Pember Town to an insidious fate.

So my father must have been such a victim then, and in his helpless delirium had killed my brother Thomas and then himself. The tumor had killed my great-uncle Michael, my grandfather Sir John, and was currently taking Uncle Henry. It would also have claimed Colin's father had it not been for the untimely carriage accident.

Well, I had wanted proof and now I had it. Scientific facts that had been observed and set down by a worthy man. The autopsies had shown the Pemberton tumor, just as we all must have the bare beginnings of one in our brains.

Was it there now in my head, a small seed of death lying dormant until the time it would begin to grow and blossom into an instrument of evil? Was my own brain tumor getting close to its maturation period, or would it wait many years before striking me?

And Martha, too, and Cousin Theodore. How long did they have? Would they follow Sir John's brother Michael by succumbing in their 30s, or would they be nearly 60, as Uncle Henry was?

And Colin . . . Tears rolled down from my eyes and stained my pillow. Dear God, Colin was doomed also. His own brain, boorish and mannerless though it was, also harbored the germ of a tumor that would sooner or later have him in the grips of fever and delirium.

Colin . . .

CHAPTER 11

GERTRUDE WAS THE ONE TO ROUSE ME FROM MY DEEP, DREAMLESS sleep. Sunk into the blackest abyss, I did not awaken to her door knock but only floated up to consciousness when she gently shook my shoulders.

"Miss Leyla," she murmured gently. "The family is asking after you. They missed you at breakfast and wonder if you will be coming to luncheon."

I blinked up at her. "Luncheon? What time is it?"

"Half past noon, Miss Leyla. Are you ill?"

By now fully awake, I rose up in bed and surveyed the bedclothes. They had barely been disturbed, as though I had slept the entire time in one position. "No, I'm not ill." My body ached, and my neck was stiff. Where an appetite should have been was only a gray void, as though some spark in me had been quenched. "I'll be down, Gertrude. Thank you."

She hesitated, hovering over me in maternal worry. There was an anxiety in her eyes that told me this plump housekeeper was more a member of the family than a servant.

"I'm all right, truly I am. So please inform my family that I shall be down shortly."

"Yes, miss."

As she turned to go, her old-fashioned hoopskirt making a swishing sound, my eyes fell upon Sir Anthony Cadwallader's book, and I trembled involuntarily. "Gertrude."

"Yes, Miss Leyla?"

"How is Uncle Henry this morning?"

Her hands went to her generous bosom in an attitude of concern. "*Er ist sehr krank, liebchen.* Very sick, very sick."

"I see. Thank you for waking me."

I waited until the door was closed and the housekeeper a good distance down the hall before I slipped out of bed and tiptoed across the cold room to my washstand. As I freshened myself in the icy water and patted my face dry, I happened to notice the delicate decanter of rose cologne that Edward had given me my last birthday. A desperate pang gripped me then, thinking of poor Edward and what I had almost done to him. But he would understand, would have to be made to understand that I could no longer be his wife.

"*. . . we call the Brain Sickness . . . reclusive to certain maligned Families . . . found to be always fatal . . .*"

I brought the cologne to my nostrils and filled my head with the dainty scent. I was a Pemberton, one of these special people, and must therefore guard against the possibility of ever continuing the line. I would not bear a son whose fate might be the same as my poor father's, or a daughter who would suffer as I did now. What I had to do was find a way to tell him, to explain about the hereditary illness and how cruel it would be to inflict it upon innocent children.

"*. . . the victims could not be free from the virulency of the Disease . . .*"

I could see how he would take the news—gravely, with concern, but without a great deal of emotion. Edward prided himself on his thorough Englishness, his genteel breeding that had taught him moderation in all things, and I knew he would regard me with an unmoved expression and nod knowingly as if approving a new floor plan.

Once I had loved Edward for these traits. I had admired his total objectivity, his cool airs, and lack of passion. I had thought him so refined and well bred, so polite and mannered. But now, sniffing the cologne and recalling the matter-of-fact way he had asked my hand in marriage, I saw Edward for what he really was—stiff, boring, and snobbish.

I put the cologne down and finished washing. Then I gave my hair a good brush through, parted it in the center, and plaited it at the nape of my neck. It was all over now, my entire past up until last night, for this morning was the dawning of a new era for me. Now I realized that I was one of these people, that I belonged in this house and had no right to be part of the real world. Now I knew what it meant to be a Pemberton.

". . . *In the Hyrst where Sir Geoffrey and his Son suffered the Brain Sickness, there are others of the stricken Family who will have the same Fate . . .*"

Before I left my room in a maroon wool morning frock and my usual shawl, I paused again over Thomas Willis's words, as if to reassure myself that they had been real last night and not just a dream.

". . . *for it is in the Hands of God that the Tumor is born, and that the prescripts of Physicians will go for naught, and the Brain Sickness (or Pember Town Fever) will not bow to Empirical Remedies . . .*"

Everyone was in the dining room except for Uncle Henry. At once, I recognized the saturnine mood of the small group and could easily match it with my own. My soul, upon learning the truth of our family, had been drained of all its life and force, leaving me empty and without energy. I was not sad or depressed; neither was I in a state of shock. Instead, I was simply numb overall, existing in a state that modern doctors might call "anesthesia."

Only Colin looked up at me when I sat at the table. He watched me carefully, his guarded expression revealing nothing of his mood. I avoided his eyes, pretending instead to be hungry and desirous of some tea. Theo and Aunt Anna were in a deplorable state with stringy hair and dark circles under their slightly popping eyes. The two must have sat up all night with Uncle Henry, being absolutely useless and helpless in the face of his suffering. Martha sat glumly with that carpetbag sitting in her lap like a sleeping cat, and I envied my cousin the small escape she found in her handiwork.

"Are you all right?" asked Colin finally.

"I am fine, thank you. Can you pass the jam to me, please?"

His air was one of forced flippancy, manufactured for I knew not what purpose. After all, Anna and Theo were lost in their own dreary melancholy, while Martha pouted childlike for unknown reasons. If Colin were pretending a careless manner, then it could only be for my benefit, and I could not imagine why.

"I went out riding before dawn," he went on as he refilled his teacup, "and saw a light on in your room. Either you went to bed awfully late or rose indecently early."

"I was reading," came my terse reply.

"Oh?" One pale brown eyebrow went up. "You seem disgruntled today."

"I am not disgruntled."

"Yet not altogether gruntled, I expect."

I would not smile at this. I felt gray and lifeless inside. Beyond the windows stood a flat sky, and that is how I felt—no black and white, no bright colors, and no sharp contrasts. Everything blended into a nondescript grayness, and I was content to remain that way.

"Were you reading anything interesting?"

"Only mildly." I finally met his eyes to see if something could be read there. But he wore the Pemberton mask. There was no telling what was going on behind that handsome face.

The bread and jam tasted of nothingness. The tea, although it steamed and had been spiced with orange, tasted bland and lukewarm to me, so unfeeling had I become. Here I sat, like one of my fatalistic relatives, totally surrendered to the inevitability of my fate. Yet how else could I react?

Yesterday, I had been alive with anger and love and passions that drove me to fighting tooth and nail for the past that rightfully belonged to me. This morning, I no longer cared. What was past was past; there was no need to bring it back. I no longer felt the urge to battle these people, and the desire to visit the coppice again was gone. Indeed, I did not even care to find out who had placed the book on my night table, for the purpose had been accomplished, and that was sufficient.

"You don't look yourself, Leyla dear," I heard Colin say.

"Indeed? And how am I supposed to look?"

"Still brooding over the ring, are you?"

"Ring? Oh that. Nothing could be farther from my mind. It was one of the maids, I'll wager."

He regarded me a while longer. "Are you angry with me then?"

My eyes flew open, "Angry with you? Whatever for!"

He made a boorish shrug. "Your manner this morning. You seem so distant, so aloof, that I thought—"

I gave a mirthless laugh. "How terribly vain of you, Cousin, to expect my mood to be caused by you. It has nothing whatever to do with you."

"Oh." He appeared disappointed. "Then what is it, pray?"

Finally, I placed my cup in my saucer, put down the barely eaten toast, and dropped my hands in my lap. I had lost my appetite anyway, and food had no taste. While I stared ahead of myself, vaguely in Colin's direction, I thought again about the passage in Thomas Willis's book—that one innocuous page written on the front and back, no more than 300 words, yet more powerful than the sting of a snake. Such a blow it had been to find actual mention of the Pemberton name! Where I had only been expecting to find words on a disease that might, with some stretch of the imagination, vaguely resemble the supposed curse, I discovered instead substantial, irrevocable proof that the Pemberton affliction did indeed exist. The written record of Dr. Thomas Willis was not something I could refute.

"Twopence for your thoughts, Leyla."

I shook my head and looked at Colin. Was that a brief reflection of sympathy I glimpsed crossing his face, a sudden tide of affection? But then the mask went up again all too quickly.

"I was thinking how, as a child, I often used to catch my mother staring at me, as if waiting for something to happen. Perhaps that's what it was; she was watching me for early signs of the madness."

"Leyla—" He leaned across the table.

"And all of you here, how rudely you all stared at me the first day I was here, studying my face for a sign of something, asking me oblique questions about headaches. Now I understand it all."

"What are you saying, Leyla?"

"I am saying that you were right about the illness. It does exist."

Theodore's face suddenly snapped my way. Had it been an act, his morose engrossment within himself, while all the time he had sat listening to us? It did not matter and I did not care.

Colin appeared genuinely taken aback. "But what in God's world caused you to change your mind? Last night, you were like a soldier on the eve of battle; you had the wild look of a savage animal. And now, after one night, you are quiet and deflated and say that you've finally been convinced of the truth. How did it happen?"

I looked from Colin to Theo back to Colin again. At my side, Martha had taken a cross-stitch out of her bag and was quietly engrossed in a sampler. Aunt Anna, thus far taciturn, continued to stir an empty cup with distance in her gaze.

"Suffice it to say it has happened."

"And then?" prompted Theo.

"And then, what? I have come to full realization of what it means to be a Pemberton. The need to recapture the past is gone. You must be right about my father. And as well I cannot go back to Edward. Not now, not ever."

Both my cousins appeared relieved, although each in a different way. Theodore was suddenly pleased I had abandoned my project with the coppice, whereas a smile escaped Colin's lips at my mention of Edward.

"You know about the tumor, then," said Theodore.

"Yes, I do. Why did none of you tell me about it before this?"

"Because we wanted you to leave this house and go on with your life as though we did not exist." Theodore's voice was gentle, compelling. His taut face softened into empathy as he took my hands across the table and enveloped me in brotherly concern. "You came to us so innocent, Leyla, so naive and ignorant of the history of this house. Indeed, when you first arrived, you had no inkling of your true past, having believed your father and brother had died of cholera. We had hoped to send you away from us in your original purity, untainted by the scandals of this doomed house. Yet bit by bit, we invariably had to reveal the truth to you, still hoping that you would tenaciously cling to the ideal of goodness and justice in this world. Even last night, when it was suggested you might have stolen my ring—which I did not for a moment believe—we hoped you would become angry enough to leave this house once and for all and return to your waiting fiancé."

I nodded slowly, seeing the reasoning behind what he said. The fact that someone had lured me to this house with Sylvia's letter and had tried to keep me here by burning Edward's letter no longer entered my mind. If one of this family had wanted me to stay, I gave no more thought to it.

"If we had shown you the proof behind the illness, you would have stayed, just as I suspect you have seen it and have—as I said—made the decision to stay. I am truly sorry, dear Leyla, that your homecoming had to turn out this way. It is not what we had planned."

"It's all right, Theo. The truth is better known."

"Then you've read the book?"

"I have."

"Where did you find it?"

"Someone put it in my room."

Both of my cousins looked surprised. "Do you mean on purpose?" said Colin. "Someone deliberately set that book before you?"

"It doesn't matter now. I'd rather know the truth."

"But it's unfair, Leyla. You might still have gone away from us never believing the story of the cursed sickness, and you would have had a happy life."

"Is that what you would have wanted? My continuing on the line when you and Theo and Martha could not? Tell me, Colin, would you call that fair? Whoever put it there, and I don't hold it against him or her, did it for a good reason. To make me see the justice of your ways and the truth of my family's illness." My throat grew dry and narrow as I spoke. "Would you, Colin, have thought it right that I go and be happy and bear children while you and Theo and Martha must lead fruitless lives?"

His green eyes stared at me without answer, but Theodore quickly said, "We are not so miserable in our existence, Leyla; we are not to be pitied. The Pembertons are profoundly wealthy and have more than enough in comforts and luxuries."

"You still have not answered my questions, Cousin, yet it does not matter. One of you or possibly Aunt Anna or Gertrude or even Grandmother Abigail put that book in my room. And for a very good reason." The corner of my eye picked up Martha's busy hands, recalling to my mind her words of the night before—her envy of my being able to go off and marry the man I love. "I don't really care to find out who it was, for that is irrelevant. What matters is that I have learned the truth." My eyes fell to my lifeless hands. "And for that I'm grateful."

The next minutes were long ones, bloated with a heavy silence that blanketed even the ticking of the clock over the fireplace. All our emotions had run cold, as gray as the day and without life.

Eventually, I pushed myself away from the table and surveyed my family one more time before saying, "I shall go out for a walk now. Oh, don't fear, Cousin Theo. I do not intend to go near the coppice but in the opposite direction instead. In London, I often found that a walk in the afternoon air helped me to think and sort myself out. That's what I shall do now. Won't you please excuse me?"

Theodore and Colin rose with me, their eyes steadily upon my face, their expressions guarded. For one moment, it appeared Theo was going to speak, but he changed his mind and remained silent.

As I was up in my room collecting my bonnet and gloves and cloak, I heard a carriage come up the drive and, looking out the window, saw a stately gentleman carrying a black leather bag disembark and approach the front door. When I was suitably attired for the cold wind outside and about to leave my room, I heard footsteps pass my door—just as I had during the night—and Aunt Anna's anxious whisperings offset by staid murmurings. It was Dr. Young again seeing Uncle Henry. Promising myself that I would visit my poor uncle later on, I descended the stairs and went out the front door.

The hurst was a turmoil of wind and ice and whistling trees. It was all I could do to manage my wide skirt and flapping cloak, yet the biting air felt good on my cheeks and in my lungs. I faced it head on, that wintry gale, and breathed deeply of it before embarking upon the gravel drive that eventually met the road to East Wimsley.

I suppose that I must have walked for hours along that lane, my fingers numb with cold, my cheeks prickling and red, but it did me good and offered me the opportunity needed for a good, long search into myself. There was so much to meditate upon, so much to sort out, that the barren trees and muddy ground and cloudy sky were quite conducive to inner reflection. Nothing disturbed my train of thought; I was left entirely alone among this wild nature to reexamine myself and set a new course for myself.

And what I discovered while walking was this: that I had indeed begun a new phase in my life. All of a sudden, with the reading of Thomas Willis's book, everything that had been important to me yesterday no longer seemed so. Aunt Sylvia's bogus letter, my own burnt letter to Edward, Theo's stolen ring, and every other "mystery" surrounding my relatives quite suddenly lost all importance. And above all, the driving need to remember the past had also fallen by the wayside.

I knew now that what they said of my father was true, that he had been the victim of the Pemberton brain tumor and had committed those unspeakable crimes in a delirium of insanity. It was recorded in history by a scientific observer; it had happened to previous Pembertons; it was now happening to Uncle Henry; and in time it would also strike me.

I could never return to London now; I was resigned to that, for Edward no longer seemed to matter. Looking back, it seemed I had not really loved him—not deeply and passionately as one must—but I had only been fond of him and had looked to him for comfort in a time of grief.

These people were my family now, and this house was my home. For as long as I should live.

Dr. Young had been invited to sup with us, and so his carriage still stood by our stables. I entered the house through the rear, not wishing to encounter anyone yet, and crept quietly up the stairs and into my own room. Here the fire was roaring in readiness, and my oil lamps were brightly burning. The heavy drapes blocked out the chilly twilight, and I was pleased to find the bedroom quite warm.

Thomas Willis's book still lay where I had left it by my bed, its worn binding and gold-printed title a symbol of the abrupt change in my life. Yet, oddly, I felt no bitterness, no resentment. All my soul was filled with a sort of gentle resignation, an acceptance of a fate that could no longer be fought.

My cheeks were still brightly flushed when a knock at the door interrupted the arrangement of my coiffure. For an instant, I hoped it was Colin and was amazed at my disappointment to see Theo standing there. But he was dressed handsomely, strikingly, as all the Pemberton men were, and gazed down at me with something close to admiration in his eyes.

"How you do resemble your mother!" he said quietly, a faint smile playing at his mouth.

"Why, thank you, Theo."

"Her cheeks were always flushed like that when she came in from outside. Your mother loved to be outside, always gardening or walking or riding her favorite mare."

"She did . . ." I pictured her in our cramped slum flat, her thin body bent over a needle and thread, her skin white from never seeing sunlight.

"You're like her in so many ways," he said more slowly, speaking almost in a whisper. "She always wore her hair like this." He reached out and barely touched his fingertips to the long waves falling over my shoulders. "Grandmother never approved, always saying that hair worn free was the sign of a Jezebel. Even after she married your father, Jenny remained wild and childlike."

I continued to stare at Theo in a most incredulous way, for I had never before heard him speak like this, nor ever seen his face so gently molded.

"I missed her terribly when she went away with you, Leyla. I was positively stricken."

I stepped back from my cousin, for he was standing unusually close to me. "Then why didn't you follow us?"

His eyes misted over. "I couldn't, Leyla. I just couldn't."

I swung away from him and returned to my vanity where I finished plaiting my hair. Looking again as I had before going on my walk, with hair neat and cheeks less bright, I turned back to Theodore and said coolly, "I wish you had followed us. There were years in London I would have preferred not to experience."

Then a strange manner came over him, one I could not exactly define. It was a mingling of anger and remorse, as though I had evoked some long-buried emotion that now broke to the surface and disrupted Theo's usually well collected mien.

"I wanted to, Leyla! I truly did!"

Then who stopped you? Grandmother? Oh, Theo, it doesn't matter now, not anymore. I am as willing as everyone else to leave the past buried, for it can come to no good to remember old sorrows. We all share the same future now, and the same fate. Nothing can ever be the same again."

Theodore continued to stare at me for a moment longer with an expression in his eyes that made me think for an instant that he was looking at someone else. But then the disturbance passed from his face like a cloud leaving the sun, and Cousin Theo was once more self-assured and poised. He kept up a small conversation as we went down the stairs together, yet I did not listen, for I found myself looking for Colin and a little anxious to see him.

We went first into the drawing room for a small glass of wine before dinner, and as I preceded Theo into the room, I found Martha, busily engrossed in her cross-stitch sampler by the fire, in the company of someone I had never met before.

Behind me, Theodore's voice said quietly, "Leyla, I don't believe you've ever met our family physician. This is Dr. Young."

His face looked to have been created for the profile alone, so exquisitely chiseled it was, so handsome the nose and firm the chin. I marveled at the youth of his appearance, he having such a vitality in his bearing that it was hard to imagine him Uncle Henry's age—nearly 60. Dr. Young wore his immaculately white hair in gentle waves combed away from his attractive face but not slicked with Macassar oil, and his sideburns were long and white, but not the muttonchops so popular among older men. When he smiled, it was with genuine warmth and good cheer, and his small blue eyes lit up like one of Prince Albert's "Christmas trees." Below the striking face was an aristocratic body that walked with uncommon vigor and seemed the strength of a man half his age. Dressed in a maroon cutaway coat over black trousers with linen waistcoat and shirt, Dr. Young was the quintessence of impeccable dress and gentility.

Yet more than all this was I struck by Dr. Young's voice. When I entered the room and saw how quickly he rose to greet me with his boundless smile and sparkling eyes, I warmed to him at once. But when he said in his soft, personable voice, "How do you do, Miss Pemberton?" I knew, somehow, in that instant that he was a man I could trust. It was a voice that was quiet and yet filled the room. A voice that was gentle and yet carried the power of command. It was a voice that was sure of itself, that somehow magically directed itself to the person it addressed and made that listener feel that Dr. Young spoke to no one else in the room.

"How do you do, Doctor," I said quietly. Aunt Anna entered the room as I spoke and glided to the doctor's side. She waited politely, albeit anxiously, and hung in his shadow, wringing those poor hands of hers and worrying at his back like a rejected lover.

"Dr. Young," came her tremulous voice finally. "You must go to Henry, please."

His smile broadened, a smile full of all the patience in the world, unhurried and unselfish. "Yes, of course, Anna. I've never met your lovely niece before. Been living in London, have you?"

Again he had spoken directly to me in a familiar tone, with a smile that was mine alone and with a gaze meant only for me. "Yes, Doctor. Have you ever been there?"

He laughed softly, patiently. Not at me but within himself, as though I had reminded him of some sweetly private joke. "Yes, Miss Pemberton, I've been to London."

"Dr. Young—" Aunt Anna's voice was shrill.

"I'm here, my dear. You'll work yourself into a state." He turned his full attention to her, intending his handsome smile for her alone, as though we others in the room ceased to exist. And I marveled at how easily he mollified her with this gesture, how quickly my aunt relaxed beneath Dr. Young's personal attention.

Here was a physician of the spirit, I told myself then, as well as of the body.

"He's awake now, Dr. Young, but he won't eat a bite of his supper," said my aunt.

"Very well then, I shall come and have a word with him." Dr. Young returned his attention to me, at once focusing himself entirely upon me, and said in that smoothly nasal resonance, "Excuse me please, Miss Pemberton, I have to see to your uncle. But I will return shortly and have the pleasure of dining in your company."

I watched the doctor leave the library and felt all his magical personality go with him. Whether such a commanding bearing was innate with the man or practiced over many years, I could not guess, but that Dr. Young had a most remarkable quality of engendering trust and confidence was beyond a doubt.

In the next instant, the tranquillity of the library was rudely jolted by the sudden intrusion of my third cousin, who at once filled the room with his volatile personality.

"Wretched night out," he complained with a smile, still brushing brambles and nettles off his trousers. As he decanted himself a glass of sherry, Colin tossed me a mischievous glance, then gave a quick look at Theo and Martha. "In a partying mood, are we?"

I laughed a little and tried to hide it, but Theo was not amused. "You really are a boor, Cousin, entering a room as if you were performing at the Hippodrome. And weren't you taught to dress for supper?"

Colin looked down at himself. "What am I then, naked?"

Martha's head snapped up. "Colin Pemberton!" Her face was crimson.

"Forgive me, Sister. A poor jest on my part. Well, Cousin Leyla." He strode away from the buffet and approached me with something of an air of belligerence. "Did you enjoy your walk?"

"I did indeed, thank you."

"Now you will have to let me teach you to ride."

"I'm sure I should love it."

His eyes fell to staring at me, matching the boldness of my own gaze. "Would you really?" he said more quietly.

As I stared back at him, standing only inches away, I felt my heart race slightly with his nearness. Of course it was impossible, I chided myself, that this lout should excite me so, and attributed the flutter to the wine I had just drunk.

"Then may I escort you into the dining room?" He extended his arm, and I lay my hand upon it, while behind us followed Theo and Martha.

As we were the only four present, the seating arrangement was altered to allow for more congeniality, with Theodore and Colin across from Martha and me, and when the servants entered with a tureen of thick soup accompanied by hot loaves of bread and slabs of butter, conversation was abandoned for the usual etiquette of silence.

Dr. Young and Aunt Anna joined us shortly after, Uncle Henry having quietly been put out of his misery again with a sleeping powder, and took places next to Colin and myself. While Dr. Young helped himself to a modest amount of soup, I could not help but watch him, finding his manners most polished and his face pleasantly handsome. The candlelight danced off his wavy white hair, and every now and then his mouth drew back in that special smile.

It was not until after the mutton and potatoes were eaten and a course of steamed vegetables appeared that conversation opened up. It must have been for Aunt Anna's benefit, so crestfallen and battle weary did she appear. In an effort to bring some mirth to those black-circled eyes and that sagging mouth, Dr. Young told a witty anecdote about the new fashion of taking holidays at the seashore. We all laughed, but my aunt could not even force a polite smile, so morose had she become. Indeed, I was not even certain she had heard the doctor's tale, for she appeared sullenly preoccupied and most neglectful of her plate.

"I've never been to the seashore, Dr. Young, but I understand the experience is good for one's health."

He nodded thoughtfully. "The air is therapeutic and the waters most rejuvenating. I recommend it to all my patients, the healthy ones as well as the sick."

"I myself should hate it," said Martha, as she gave the doctor one of her prettiest smiles. "All that sand and wind must be horrid to contend with. Not to mention the filthy water."

While they carried on the topic, I watched Dr. Young in an earnest attempt at remembering him. If he had been as prevalent during my father's illness as he was now with Uncle Henry, then surely some shred of remembrance would come back to me. However, just as with Colin and Theo and the others—except Martha—Dr. Young remained hidden behind the curtain of my past.

Finally, catching me staring unreservedly at him, Dr. Young drew his face into the most golden of his smiles and said in that wonderfully resonant voice, "Twopence for your thoughts, mistress."

"I was wondering, sir," I said haltingly, "if there is nothing else can be done for my suffering uncle."

"If there were, dear lady, I assure you it would be done, but unfortunately, the brain is a mysterious organ about which mankind knows sadly little. Few anatomists have charted it; few diagnosticians have described its aberrant syndromes. Illnesses of the brain are in the hands of God as are, ultimately, all afflictions of the human body. Physicians are agents of the Lord, and what God prefers to keep a mystery to us—such as the brain—we are helpless to cure."

I sighed and laid the fork by my plate. It seemed such a shame, so unfair that of all the hereditary diseases people suffer, the Pembertons should have the one that is the most unreachable by doctors.

"Still," said Cousin Theodore, as he dabbed a napkin at his lips, "great discoveries are made all the time. That young scientist in Paris—what is his name?—has finally disproven the theory of spontaneous generation. And after that great British discovery, anesthesia, there is no telling how far medicine will go."

Dr. Young smiled politely, his eyes twinkling. "I believe anesthesia was an American innovation, but you are quite right about Monsieur Pasteur in Paris and his laudable experiments. Possibly if science and medicine could be joined in some way instead of working independently of one another, we would make even more rapid progress."

"How do you mean, sir?"

Dr. Young looked at me as he answered Theo. "It is my belief that more physicians should learn to be their own researchers, turn to the microscope, as it were, and not be so singly devoted to bedside care; for while science is making progress, it is doing so in the fields of chemistry, zoology, and geology but sadly not in medicine, where it would be of benefit to mankind. But surely such a topic is a dull one for the ladies at our table, and we can choose a more universal dinner subject."

"Not at all, sir!" I protested eagerly. "I should be very interested in your opinion of what progress medicine might make. You see, I have been touched rather closely by death and—"

"Your father, I believe."

"Did you know him?"

Dr. Young shook his head. "I came to East Wimsley barely six years ago after deciding to retire from practice, or at least semiretire from the frenetic pace of the city. It was Dr. Smythe who ministered to him."

A flash in my mind. A familiar name triggered off a vague countenance and a sort of dreamlike sensation. The name of Smythe spoken in whispers. A stout little man who had been ushered into my father's room in the midst of swishing hooped skirts and hurried footsteps. From inside, a young woman sobbing.

So much did the mere mention of the name reveal. This, then, was why Dr. Young had not sparked a memory: he did not belong there, he was not part of that elusive past.

"—so of course I read the histories."

His warm voice broke into my thoughts. I had been busy remembering, and Dr. Young had been talking.

"I beg your pardon? Forgive me, sir, I was not listening."

He laughed comfortingly. "I only said that, when I came to East Wimsley to retire, I took the time to read the records of Dr. Smythe's patients. When he died, he left behind quite a file of histories. Since the Pembertons were so prominent and seemed to have suffered more than their share of losses, I read the histories. In so doing, I familiarized myself with the tumor."

My eyes fell to my lap. Those two words "the tumor" had a phenomenal effect upon me. That tumor was also *my* tumor and was also my death sentence.

Colin chose at this time to speak, having polished off his plate and emptied his cup. "Tell me, Dr. Young, from what you know about my family's plight, have you ever before in all your experience encountered a similar problem?"

The doctor paused to think a moment, his handsome face set in thought. "There are hereditary afflictions that exist elsewhere in medicine—color blindness for one, or hemophilia, club feet, insanity, and even the heart attack. Yet I have never before encountered one with so long a history, for I believe yours dates back centuries, nor one so encompassing as to strike every family member. Yet it does not surprise me. In my lifetime, I have witnessed many strange things in medicine, some stranger than what the Pembertons have, so that I have learned never to be surprised."

Now I asked, "Excuse me, Dr. Young, but what is the heart attack? I have never heard of it."

"It is a new name for an old affliction, miss, and one that is still in the research stages. Here is an excellent example of why I believe doctors should pay more attention to scientific research than they do, for out of it comes valuable information that can aid in the future saving of lives. An attack of the heart, as it is being called more and more, is the name given a syndrome characterized by pains in the chest and left arm, shortness of breath, nausea, and diaphoresis. There is strong debate among my colleagues as to the cause of this attack, but autopsies—forgive the mention, ladies—have disclosed clots of blood in the arteries that feed the heart wall itself. It is a mysterious ailment, yet one that, we are learning, runs in families. Say, for example, a man whose father died of such a heart failing. He, too, has a great chance of falling to the same fate."

"I've never heard of such a thing!" said Theo, visibly impressed. "And is there no medicine for it?"

"Only such that is palliative but not curative. For some unknown reason, the extract of the foxglove plant, which we call digitalis, given at the time of an attack can often remove the pain and restore the patient's health. Why this is, no one knows."

I glanced at Theo and saw that his expression matched mine. I knew he was thinking the same thing as I. "Then do you believe, sir, that someday a medicine can be found for our brain tumor?"

Dr. Young's eyes were gentle, his mouth sadly compelling. "There is always hope in medicine, mistress, but the brain is a long way off from being researched. Today, physicians are trying to combat infection in the operating theater; they are searching for a cure for tuberculosis, which is such a widespread killer, or how to fight gallstones or appendicitis. These diseases are killers at higher rates than tumors; they claim far more lives, and we continue to be helpless in their presence. We need the researchers . . ." He shook his head.

"Tell me, sir," said Theo, "did you not mention once that you came to East Wimsley to conduct private research of your own?"

"As a matter of fact, yes, and that is why I chose to live outside the town in semiseclusion. The old Ivy farm was up for sale at the time, and since it was far enough out of town to be private—a good two miles—yet near enough the road for emergencies, I took it. I have a small laboratory and even my own microscope. My specialty is diabetes, for which I would like one day to see a cure. Right now, it is a monumental killer."

Diabetes. I pictured Thomas Willis's book and recalled the chapter devoted to that disease. Then I wondered if Dr. Young had ever read Willis's works, which he surely must have, and if he found that archaic physician's conclusions accurate.

While Theodore and Colin, hungry for conversation that did not revolve around cotton mills or British foreign policy, engaged Dr. Young in debate, I watched them silently with my own thoughts tumbling over in my mind. If only I could see Dr. Young alone for a few minutes and ask him his professional opinion of Thomas Willis's findings. I would have liked to question him then, delve more deeply into the problem of this tumor, but I did not feel free to speak in front of my cousins. Surely, I would be able to confer privately with him at some later time.

A heavy pudding with dollops of whipped cream was served next, and I ate in silence. Aunt Anna, who had spoken not a word, now excused herself to go up to Uncle Henry's room, and I felt compassion for her as her tired and drooped form wearily left the room. Or possibly I was feeling compassion for all the Pembertons, and myself as well.

After this, we adjourned as a group to the parlor, for the men insisted upon remaining with me and Martha instead of their habit of separating themselves for a cheroot and glass of port. This divergence from the norm was due, I supposed, to the uniqueness of the evening—the uniting of the family in a stressful time, for we were all feeling the effects of Uncle Henry's suffering above us. After all, his torture was in a way ours, a prelude to what must inevitably come to all of us later, and I supposed we each in our own way commiserated with Uncle Henry and with ourselves.

Reservedly and without mirth, we arranged ourselves among the sedate furniture of the family parlor, ensconcing ourselves against the frigid night with a blazing fire, dancing candles, some red wine, and turns at the pianoforte. I joined Dr. Young on a horsehair love seat that was populated with beaded pillows and lace doilies, while Colin claimed the *prie-dieu* before the fire and Theo sank into a leather easy chair with his feet on a footstool. Martha glided automatically to the pianoforte, daintily arranged her billowy skirt upon the seat, and proceeded to charm us with a few light pieces by Chopin.

It was easy, in this atmosphere, to relax by many degrees and lose myself in a world of unreality. After all, for the past few months, since burying my mother, I had had little opportunity to give myself up to even a few moments of serenity and idle reflection. While Martha played softly, her ringlets twinkling in the candlelight and that ever-present carpetbag by her feet, I sat contentedly at Dr. Young's side.

The hour passed almost delightfully with no one speaking and my cousin keeping up an endless repertoire of piano pieces, all of which were chosen for their lightness and benign melodies. At the end of the hour, when Martha sat back at last to give herself a rest and with Dr. Young's voice gently praising her talent, I found to my alarm and mild dismay that I had spent the entire time staring at Colin.

His profile, so sharp against the fire's glow, had not been at all at ease, with his chin taut and his mouth set rigidly. He had sat with a scowl engraved on his face, his pale eyebrows meeting over his nose in a frown. The Chopin had done nothing to mollify him, whatever it was that disturbed my cousin, and when the music stopped, his restlessness seemed at a breaking point.

How odd, I thought, comparing the turbulence of Colin with the placid exterior of Theodore, for, in the present circumstances, it should be the latter and not the former who should be troubled and unable to relax. Yet it was not. While Theodore's father lay upon a probable deathbed awaiting the fate of his brother Robert of 20 years before, Theodore appeared very detached and not the slightest bit disturbed. Colin, on the other hand, his face glaring angrily into the fire, seemed on the brink of bursting.

When he next turned unexpectedly to look at me, I felt my face flush in an instant. His green eyes, the color of summer moss, now studied me intently as though he were returning my own stare of the previous hour, as though he had known all along my eyes had been fast upon him, and I suddenly did not know what to say.

"Who will play next?" asked Theo.

"Cousin Leyla, of course," said Colin.

"Oh, I haven't for so long . . . truly. Compared with Martha—"

"Go on, miss," came Dr. Young's nasal voice dose to my ear. Seeing his broad smile and kind eyes, I could not deny him, so I rose and reluctantly went to Martha's side.

"I fear you will quite eclipse me," I said to her as I bent and picked up her carpetbag. Heavy with needles and hooks and yarns and embroidery hoops, this bag was Martha's entire life; it was her sole escape, and in a way I envied her for it.

Martha said, "My brother tells me my playing is quite mechanical, that I put none of my soul into it. Possibly, you can please Colin, Leyla, for Heaven knows I cannot."

Trying to ignore Colin's rude stare, I arranged myself upon the seat and felt a small nervousness come over me. It had been quite a while since I had played the pianoforte, and I was certain, as I held my hands poised above the keys, that I should remember nothing of what I once knew.

I began awkwardly enough indeed, partly from being out of practice and partly for being aware of Colin watching me. It was disconcerting, this new effect he had upon me, and I attempted through music to drive him out of my mind. Yet I could not, for although it required great concentration to bring the Beethoven piece back, I could not help but be acutely aware that I was playing for Colin and Colin alone, that no one else in the room—in the world—existed, and that in that moment I was coming more and more under a spell over which I had no control.

When I finished "Fur Elise," there was polite praise from everyone, but I knew Colin had expected more of me.

"You play excellently," said Martha. "Much better than I."

"Thank you, Cousin, but I disagree. Theo, won't you please rescue me?"

"I never had a talent for the instrument. It is a social grace I always left to my more talented relatives. Colin, show Leyla what an artist you are."

The internecine rivalry between Colin and Theo, which they generally kept at bay and which I had seen flare only twice before, was now patently apparent. They regarded one another like gamecocks, their eyes locked.

"Please play for us," said Martha energetically. "Colin's better than all of us, and he's written his own music as well."

So I rose from the bench and waited for him to take my place. When Colin did stride arrogantly forward, I tried to avoid his belligerent gaze, but I could not and again felt my heart race with his nearness. As he sat, I quickly regained my seat next to Dr. Young and fixed my eyes into the heart of the fire.

It was indeed a new experience listening to Colin play, for there was more to it than the music; there was the fervor in his soul as it poured from his fingertips and onto the ivory keys. I was astonished at the fierceness with which he attacked the pianoforte. As if a sorcerer weaving a magic spell, my cousin captured us at once and carried us from the most abysmal depths up to towering heights, forcing us to feel the passions of his own heart, entangling us in a web of emotion and spirit. I had never before heard such inflamed music nor witnessed the bare soul of a man, as Colin did indeed expose himself to us through the artistry of his playing. Bent over the keys as if trying to tame a wild beast, my cousin had us all at the mercy of his witchcraft, making us laugh when he would laugh, weep when he would weep, and feel the very depths of our own souls stir in turmoil as his must.

And while I watched and listened and fell under that magical spell, I knew with certainty that I was falling in love with Colin and that no power on earth was going to stop it.

CHAPTER 12

IT WAS CLOSE TO DAWN WHEN I FINALLY FELL ASLEEP, FOR I HAD spent a restless night of tossing and turning, haunted by strange new feelings and apprehensions. Gone was the security of London and its familiar surroundings; gone was the comfort of Edward's love and protection; and gone forever was the bright tomorrow of a family and children. In exchange for these, I had received membership into a bizarre family, a decaying old mansion rife with ghosts, and the beginning of a futile love for a man who no doubt regarded me with scorn.

I had known Edward 11 months, seeing him socially every other week after having met him at Mudie's Library, when I finally fell in love with him. And even then it was a lukewarm affection, more of a need of him than a passion for him, and it had been because Edward was genteel, comfortable, and proper. Yet I had known Colin only six days before falling in love with him, and the end feeling was something totally different from anything I had known before. It reached down into corners of my soul I never knew to exist, awakened passions I had never known to have, and stirred my heart with a rare, electric emotion that made me want to laugh and cry at the same time.

When I did finally fall asleep, it was to take part in wild, uncanny dreams, for Colin had set my imagination free and had caused the birth of a whole new creativity in my mind. Seeing with my sleeping eye wondrous visions and brilliant colors and feeling in my dreams fresh new emotions that had before lain dormant, I became aware that Colin had not actually created a new person of me but only set free another side of myself that had heretofore been hidden under my more pragmatic side. If Colin never gave me anything else in life, he had given me this: a new and beautiful way in which to view life.

I was troubled by this dichotomy when I awoke late and breakfasted alone: that I was at one time happy in my newfound love and at the same time sad about the Pemberton legacy I had to accept. There could be no future for me and Colin, even if by some queer twist of fate he should some day come to love me, for there was the sickness that hung over us like an evil spell and prohibited us from ever having normal lives. And so, while I was pleased to feel my new love for Colin growing ever by the hour, I was also sad about it, for it was a doomed love and one that should not be allowed to exist.

At least it would be my secret alone, for no one would ever know how I felt. I would carry it with me, rejoice in it when I could, but never reveal to a single person what was in my heart. This is what I promised myself that gray, blustery morning as I prepared to take another long walk along the lane. Another headache had come over me, caused by the struggle in my soul, so I hoped the crisp air would be therapeutic. But as I left my bedroom and closed the door behind me, I found that the day was not to be as pleasant as hoped at all.

Martha, looking petulant and out of sorts, was hurrying down the hall toward Uncle Henry's room. "It's Theo's ring!" she cried in answer to my morning greeting. "Grandmother searched the servants' quarters and questioned them herself but got nothing out of them. Now she's threatening to search our rooms."

"That can't be!"

"It's true, and I don't appreciate such treatment. I truly wish whoever took the ring would give it back."

"Why is it so important to her?" I asked, ignoring the insinuation of her remark.

"Oh, she doesn't give a hang about the ring itself; it's the principle of it. To have a thief in the house is abominable to Grandmother. She's positively furious."

"How is Uncle Henry this morning?"

Martha shrugged atypically. "Dr. Young stayed the night last night, and he is there now. I'm going to give Aunt Anna a rest. I don't think she's slept for nights. Oh, Leyla, this is all so upsetting!"

Martha shuffled off with her knitting like a child who's been denied a picnic. My 32-year-old cousin could be so puerile in many ways, pouty and spoiled like a little girl, and yet in other ways like an old maid so set in her ways that the slightest ripple was resented. I watched her scuffle down the hall, her crinoline swaying to reveal ruffled drawers of lace under yards of petticoat, and wondered if I might be like Martha after seven years under this roof.

The walk was healthful and exhilarating, allowing me to be alone with my thoughts, yet it did not cure my headache, so that, when I returned shortly before sunset, I had Gertrude bring me a small dose of laudanum with my supper. None of the family ate downstairs tonight, for Uncle Henry's condition required that his wife and son hold a vigil at his bedside. Martha withdrew into her room and engaged in one of her many handiworks, while Colin disappeared to I knew not where. I fell asleep early in the warmth of a bright fire and an unread book open upon my chest.

I awoke the next morning to yet another headache, and although I should have been alarmed, I was not. That it was due to anything other than the oppressive tension hanging over this house did not occur to me, so I dismissed it and took a little more laudanum before embarking upon another day of solitude.

I passed the daylight hours in exploring the woods surrounding the house and delighting in the freedom of nature and being away from the city, and after a light afternoon tea in my room, I curled up in a chair to read a book of poetry by Edgar Allen Poe that I had taken from the library downstairs.

All about me was that weighty silence, heavy and hollow as if waiting for something to happen, as if the very house itself were holding its breath in anticipation of what was to come. Time had come to a standstill. The servants whispered softly about, speaking in hushes, taking care not to disturb the brittle air. No sound came from poor Uncle Henry's room, and there was no traffic in the halls. It was as if we were all suspended in time, waiting . . .

When the headache returned halfway through "The Raven," I asked Gertrude to bring Dr. Young to my room.

The gentle knock at the door was characteristic of the doctor himself, soft and considerate. I drew my feet under the many yards of velvet that made up my lounging frock, slid a bookmark between the pages I was reading, and said, "Come in."

Gertrude entered first as if to inspect the way before allowing this man to come in. Her buxom form filled the room as she appraised me with her square shoulders, long bombazine gown, and stiff white collar. Her eyes made a quick, meticulous search of the chamber and then more carefully of myself to be certain there was nothing untoward about my appearance and that everything was suitably proper before stepping aside for my gentleman visitor.

"Thank you for coming, sir," I said to Dr. Young, who hovered patiently behind her.

Now Gertrude, satisfied that I was decent and respectable, stepped to one side to allow Dr. Young to pass, after which she closed the door behind him and stood before it with her arms crossed like a sentinel.

"How are you this evening, Miss Pemberton?" His warm personality expanded at once to fill my bedchamber and dispel every shadow, and his smile, so brilliant and charming, swelled my heart with a sense of well-being. Dr. Young's presence had the remarkable quality of being able to set everything upright, to smooth any discord, and to appease the most grievous soul.

"Almost in excellent health, sir," I replied demurely, unused to anyone but a member of the family in my room.

Bending without the slightest effort, Dr. Young drew a tapestried straight-backed chair before me so that we sat facing one another at eye level. His gaze was direct and penetrating. "What is bothering you then?"

"A slight headache, but it is really nothing."

"Wouldn't it be better if I were the judge of that?" As he sat yet a little nearer me, he snapped open his black leather bag. At once, Gertrude glided noiselessly to my side, her cue to be on hand during the examination. I had never before been looked at by a physician, but during my mother's declining days, I had been enough in attendance to know what to expect.

The first thing he did was to measure the rate of my heartbeat as it is felt at the wrist, and I sat quietly while he went on to examine my eyelids, the color of my earlobes, and the tip of my tongue. When he next drew a stethoscope out of his bag, I was both pleased and impressed, for I had hoped Dr. Young would be a man to keep himself apprised of the most modern methods. In London, only one of my mother's doctors had owned a stethoscope. Dr. Young situated the foot-long cylinder of polished wood upon my breast and then, placing an ear at the other end, he said, "Please take in a breath. Thank you. Now let it out. Thank you."

We did this six times, each time with the end of the instrument at a different site on my chest, and all the while with faithful Gertrude ever watchful at my side. Then he replaced the stethoscope inside the bag and snapped it shut. After this, Dr. Young proceeded, in that comfortingly deep-toned voice, to ask me a series of questions.

"Have you ever suffered from blurred vision?"

"Blurred vision?" For some reason, this question put me at once on my guard, causing me to become tense. "My eyesight is quite normal," I said rigidly.

"Have you had any nausea in the past few days?"

"None at all, sir." Gertrude's hand, which had been resting upon my shoulder for the entire time, now seemed to become unbearably heavy.

"Have you noticed any impairment of motion, any loss of activity in one or all of your limbs, or any sudden pain in them?"

"None, sir."

"Has your speech been suddenly altered at any time, as in slurring or stuttering?"

"My speech is perfect, Dr. Young."

"Yes, I am sure it is." For an instant, those brilliant eyes glanced up at Gertrude, as if a thought flashed behind them, and then returned to my face. "You are not relaxed now, Miss Pemberton. Have I said something to offend you?"

His acuity caught me off guard. I fumbled for a reply. "The questions you ask me, sir, seem to be leading in a definite direction, as if you had an idea . . ." Gertrude was leaning close to me, her hand heavy upon my shoulder.

"Yes, they were, and your answers have satisfied me that my suspicion was wrong. Your headache, Miss Pemberton, is the result of tension and nothing more."

His voice was suddenly warm and assuring again, and Gertrude's weight, as if also relieved, raised off my shoulder.

"Did you think I suspected you had a brain tumor? Forgive me, but how can I diagnose the ailment if I do not ask questions? And questions from a doctor must sometimes be alarming. Now, if you had answered yes to any one of my questions . . ." His voice died and his blue eyes said the rest.

"Thank you, Dr. Young," I said with a sigh. "Uncle Henry had headaches often, and my father before him."

"I understand the history. The first time I saw your uncle was a year ago; indeed, that was my first visit to Pemberton Hurst." He grinned to the edges of his face. "In East Wimsley, the townsfolk shudder at the very name of the place. They say it's haunted. That madmen live here. That you're all a family of poisoners."

"There's some truth to that." I was thinking of my great-uncle Michael, Sir John's brother.

"I also visited this house twice to treat your cousin Martha for an attack of the vapors." His eyes twinkled knowingly. "As for yourself, young lady, I can only prescribe lots of rest and any diversion that will take your mind off your unfortunate uncle."

"I've been taking laudanum."

Dr. Young frowned at this. "That is a drug that is taken in excess in this country, for people think of it as a cure-all. Particularly among the idle classes, who have nothing more to do than ingest an opiate to take their minds off their boredom. The wealthy condemn the poor for their gin houses while themselves sipping down quantities of laudanum. Morphine is a dangerous drug, Miss Pemberton, and is too easily available."

"I shall be careful."

"Good," he said with a slight smile and glimmer in his eyes. The way he stared at me, I had the notion Dr. Young enjoyed my company. "Good."

With a sudden thought, I threw back my head and looked up at Gertrude. She stood tall and stern and protective over me. "You can go now, Gertrude, Dr. Young is finished."

"But, *liebchen*," she began, hesitating.

I laughed and gave her a gentle push. "It's all right, Gertrude, I promise you."

She went unwillingly to the door, uncertain as to what to do, and it amused me to see her stiff sense of proprieties so upset. When she had been my age, a physician could not have even touched her, let alone be allowed to listen to her breast and ask personal questions. Now, to leave him alone in my bedroom with me, unchaperoned, must have been the height of indecorum. "I will be nearby if you need me, Miss Leyla." She threw a sharp look at Dr. Young. "Very nearby."

"Thank you, Gertrude."

When I returned my attention to the doctor, I found he had picked up my volume of Edgar Allen Poe and was reading from it:

"'Once upon a midnight dreary, while I pondered weak and weary,

"'Over many a quaint and curious volume of forgotten lore—'"

His sonorous voice, like that of a great actor on the stage, suddenly stopped and left the room frightfully empty.

"Please go on, sir," I urged. "You read so well." Dr. Young bent his noble head and proceeded to read the rest of the poem, and did so with such feeling of heart, such sensibility that I sank back in my chair with my eyes closed and tried to picture the "lost Lenore."

When he was finished, I heard the book close and Dr. Young asking me, "How is your headache, Miss Pemberton?"

He made me smile. "I had forgotten it." Now I sat all the way up and inclined myself a little toward him. "I would like to talk with you a moment, if you aren't busy. May I detain you?"

His eyes held all the patience and timelessness in the world. "It would be my pleasure."

"I am very much afraid, sir, of what is happening to my family. Why can nothing be done?"

"Medicine is full of mysteries, Leyla."

"I know, and yet . . ." I stared past him and into the glowing embers of the fireplace. "It does seem so unfair, so terribly beastly that we should know about it and yet be unable to prevent it."

He said nothing, speaking his mind rather with those vigorous blue eyes.

"It is not so much for myself that I am afraid"—my fingers intertwined and began to twist themselves—"as for the others. I'm the youngest and probably have the longest to go. But my cousins . . . Theodore is almost 40! And Martha is 32. I feel so helpless."

"And your cousin Colin?"

I brought my eyes sharply back from the fireplace. "Colin?"

"He's 34."

"I'm worried for him, too." I studied Dr. Young's face, tried to delve into his eyes to discern what he knew. Had his astute perception noted my feelings for Colin?

"I can't bear the thought that we're all doomed. Dr. Young, you read the book, did you not, by Thomas Willis?"

"Thomas Willis?" His lips pursed. "He lived many years ago. I read his works, yes, but when I was a medical student."

"We have a certain book that contains all his writings, compiled by someone named Cadwallader. Do you recall his mention of the Pemberton tumor?"

Dr. Young laughed. "Thomas Willis, I recall, wrote tedious sentences, drew baffling anatomical diagrams, and used abominable spelling! And that is all I remember. Does he indeed mention the Pembertons? I had wondered where the roots of the family history lay."

"I have the book if you care—" and I started to rise.

But Dr. Young stopped me with a gentle hand, saying, "Please do not disturb yourself. My own humble cottage is stuffed to the eaves with books, among which I am sure is a copy of Cadwallader's book. I shall look for it at my leisure and see what the illustrious Mr. Willis had to say about the matter." Then he fell silent again and regarded me for a long time. "Is there anything else you wish to discuss, Leyla?"

I wrung my hands even tighter. All I had wanted from him was further insight into the family sickness and possibly even a little hope for the future. But this was beyond his ken—I saw that now—and Dr. Young was after all as fallible as any other man. There was one more thing, however, that I had to know.

"Tell me, sir, when the symptoms begin, what must I expect?"

"My dear Miss Pemberton, I fear you dwell upon this overmuch, to the point of preoccupation. You are very young and have, I am sure, a long life ahead of you. Don't waste yourself on an obsession that can come to no good. Forget it for now. Possibly you will be lucky and escape the illness."

"I appreciate your sentiment, sir, but if it's all the same to you, I should like to know what I might expect."

A heavy silence followed this, broken only by the sound of coals dropping in the fireplace. Dr. Young's lips were pursed thoughtfully, his long fingers spread upon his knees. "This is not a classic brain tumor, Leyla, for its symptoms do not conform to textbook cases. This is due, I suppose, to the area of the brain where it inherently grows. The traditional cerebral lesion exhibits such symptoms as aphasia, that is to say, a loss of coordination or understanding in speech; motor dysfunction of the arms and legs; vision impairment in some way; nausea; headache; sensual loss in any part of the body. In short, Leyla, any part of the body that is governed by that part of the brain containing the tumor will show an aberration. In the case of Pembertons, however, I do not know the physiologic structure or site of the tumor, as no autopsies were written in Dr. Smythe's records, and so the symptoms are atypical. I will say this, however, that, in comparing your uncle's course in the past year until now, it matches exactly with the history of your father and Sir John."

"I see." My shoulders slumped forward a little. "And what symptoms are those, sir?"

"Your uncle Henry and your father and Sir John, according to Dr. Smythe, all followed the same course of headaches, nausea, vomiting, abdominal pain, muscular weakness, delirium, convulsions, and sudden death. Each was visited by these afflictions for a period of less than two months prior to death."

"But you said you came to see Uncle Henry a year ago!"

"He had a headache, to be sure, but only such a one as was caused by a congestion of the sinuses and in no way connected with his present illness. I was called because he had been alarmed by it; otherwise, I understand from my predecessor's notes that few visitors—including doctors—ever enter this house."

"I fear my family has no wish to be sociable. Our history is a sordid one, and we do not wish to be stared at as circus freaks."

"I hardly believe guests would come with that intention."

"There are those horrid stories among the peasants!"

"Yes, there are."

"Oh, Dr. Young, I am so confused. I arrived here over a week ago with such bright ideas, and now they have all been dashed. It seems I've not smiled much since my mother's death and—"

"Your mother? Forgive me, but at supper the other night when you mentioned you'd been close to death, I had assumed you meant your father. Did your mother die recently?"

"Two months ago. Actually, it was not sudden, for she had been ailing a long time. Dr. Harrad had prepared me for the—"

"Dr. Harrad!" His eyebrows shot up. "Forgive me for persistently interrupting you, Miss Pemberton, but your disclosures are a surprise to me. Was your mother attended by Dr. Oliver Harrad?"

"Yes, that was his name."

"Of Guy's Hospital?"

"Yes. Why?"

I had not thought Dr. Young could be so animated, so different from his usual staid self. His blue eyes, normally settled and comforting, now suddenly grew brilliant and alive. "I knew Oliver Harrad in medical school. We joined the staff of Guy's Hospital together at the same time and shared a practice for many years.

"When I went up to Edinburgh to join the staff of the Royal Hospital there and engage in some research, Oliver and I promised to maintain communication by writing often. But as is the case when two friends part for a great distance and are each involved in demanding enterprises, our correspondence eventually fell to the wayside until, after a time had passed, we lost contact altogether. That would be over ten years ago now." Dr. Young stared vacuously ahead of himself, his eyes fixed upon something only he could see. "Oliver Harrad, that old rascal. So . . . he's still at Guy's . . ."

"And a well-loved man he is," I murmured.

Now Dr. Young focused his gaze upon me again, his eyes misted with the sweetness of nostalgia, and said, "Such memories you have suddenly brought back to me. It has been so long, and I have been so busy . . ."

"He did his best for my mother, for her comfort, and I shall always be grateful."

If Dr. Young had previously given me the illusion of being a close and trusted friend, of treating me with a singularity of having known me for years, he did even more so now. With that unique quality of his of looking directly at a person with the intimacy of knowing their very thoughts, Dr. Young looked at me now, and I guessed that, by mentioning Dr. Harrad's name, I had further engendered his friendship.

"How strange it is," he said philosophically, "that, just when we've left the past buried and forgotten, one word suddenly brings it all back with the freshness of having happened only yesterday. Oliver Harrad and I were fast friends in our younger days, being radical upstarts in medicine who thought we could change the universe with our bravado. We've mellowed since then, Oliver and I, and are content now to make small steps for progress rather than bounds. Such a coincidence that you knew my dear old friend Harrad."

"I am glad, sir," I said, recalling with a pang how, only a few days before, I had fought for that same sudden rush of the past to come back.

As Dr. Young opened his mouth to speak again, there came a tapping at my door. "Come in," I called and saw Gertrude, her eyes darting from me to the doctor and back to me again, enter with caution. “Excuse me, Miss Leyla. I was sent by Madame Pemberton.”

“Does Aunt Anna wish to see Dr. Young?”

“No, Miss Leyla, it is not Madame Anna who sent for him, but Madame Abigail. She is with Mr. Pemberton now and requests the doctor be present.”

My eyebrows arched at this. For Grandmother Abigail to leave her suite after so many years of seclusion was a monumental event. It could only mean one thing.

“Uncle Henry!” I sprang to my feet.

In an instant, Dr. Young was at my side, his voice gentle and reassuring. “I shall tend to him; you are not to fret. I will do everything I can for him.”

Gratefully, I pressed Dr. Young’s hand. “Thank you,” I whispered and watched through a brim of tears as he left with Gertrude.

I ate supper alone again, having been denied entrance to my uncle’s sickroom by Grandmother Abigail. Only once had I glimpsed her, as I opened my door late in the evening to the sound of footsteps in the hall, and she glided past my view with a queenly grace I had not expected of her arthritic body. Cousin Martha visited me briefly, her eyes red-rimmed and puffy, to announce the worsening of our uncle’s condition, and I not once saw Anna or Theo. Nor did I see Colin.

Uncle Henry was gravely ill.

The next day, as if all nature commiserated with us, was gray and chill, the wind rising to new force and the sky a threatening turbulence of storm clouds. In the morning, I wandered the house out of restlessness and anxiety but encountered no one. The only sign of activity I found, as I strolled the dreary halls of this house unable to stay for long in any one place, was when I happened to wander past Grandmother Abigail’s suite. Hearing her sharp voice suddenly pierce the heavy door, I stopped short, for I had thought she was in Uncle Henry’s room. Although her voice was loud, the words were incomprehensible, so that, although I could gather from the tone that she was angry, I could not discern why. In the next moment, I heard soft, faint sobbing also come from her room, a penitent sort of crying that seemed to indicate Grandmother Abigail was severely censuring someone. Again, due to the door between us, although I could distinguish the other person as a woman, I could not tell who it was or what her age might be. The weeping victim of Grandmother's chastising could be Aunt Anna, Cousin Martha, Gertrude, or one of the maids. Embarrassed by my brief eavesdropping, I hurried away before the woman's identity could be learned.

In the afternoon, I took my usual walk, which my relatives had no doubt accepted by now as my custom. When I returned to the house to find it still and quiet, I hurried up to my room for the comfort of a fire and hot tea. A maid served me my supper at eight, and by nine, out of the sheer exhaustion of waiting for something to happen, I fell asleep.

It must have been around midnight when the screams woke me.

I sat bolt upright, having been startled out of a deep sleep, and strained my eyes in the darkness. Beyond my door was the thudding of running feet, some hurried voices, and the swishing of dressing gowns. By the time the second shriek tore through the house, I was on my feet and dashing to the door.

Not bothering about my appearance or the fact that my feet were bare, I darted into the hallway in time to see Martha emerge sleepily from her room. With a dopey gaze she looked up and down, rubbed her eyes, and made an inarticulate sound. I was poised on my own threshold when a third shrill scream pierced the night and this time rang familiarly. It was Aunt Anna.

I wasted no time. Stopping only to seize my dressing gown, I dashed down the hall thrusting my arms into the sleeves. Martha followed sluggishly behind.

The door to Aunt Anna's and Uncle Henry's chamber stood ajar, and there was no one inside. More screams now led me away from our wing of the house and toward the unused floors where previous generations of Pembertons had lived. Although I had no time to think, my heart responded by racing with an intuition of what was happening. I only blindly ran, following the direction of the screams, and hearing up ahead other heavy footsteps on the dusty carpet.

Aunt Anna's cries led me to the next floor above, the third story of the house, and into a wing where no light had shown for years. Up ahead, I saw what appeared to be glowing moths or fireflies flitting in the darkness, small haloes of light dancing in midair, but as I drew nearer, I saw that they were the lights of candles carried by those who preceded me down the hall.

Hurrying to catch up with them, I noticed the horrible musty smell of this area, the stale air and cobwebby unpleasantness. It was a dead, foul odor that made my throat close up and cough. These rooms had not been used in decades.

As Anna's cries grew louder, I drew nearer the others ahead of me and in time heard Colin's voice call out, "Aunt Anna! Where are you?"

She replied, but her words were unintelligible. We pressed on, and by now I was part of the group. Instinctively, I moved close to Colin and walked in the flicker of his candlelight. I was surprised to see him fully dressed while the others of us—Dr. Young and Gertrude and I—were all swaddled in hasty dressing gowns. There was patent fear in all of our eyes, not for ourselves but for the ominous foreboding of dangers ahead.

Colin did not look at me but maintained a relentless search in each chamber and recess with a fierce determination in his eyes that surprised me. At once angry and alarmed, Colin was obviously the leader of the group.

Eventually, we came to the narrow corridor that led to the steps that climbed into the east turret, the place where my grandfather Sir John had fallen to his death ten years ago. It was from up there the screams were coming. As there was not enough room for us all to ascend, Colin ordered Gertrude to remain below with the candles. Then, to my great surprise, he seized me by the hand, requested Dr. Young to also remain behind, and mounted the stone steps with me close by.

Up ahead, there came the muffled sobs of Aunt Anna, halting and intermittent as if she were on the verge of collapse. As we rounded the curve, my hand tightly squeezing Colin's, we heard a new voice, a calmer one, an intelligible one.

"Please stay back, Mother. Don't come near. Stay back." It was Theo, his voice gently commanding.

Now Colin slowed his pace, looking down at me with an expression of great caution. We did not know what was taking place in the turret, so we had to move with care lest our sudden intrusion create disaster. Slowly, we mounted each step, our eyes bulging in the darkness, and heard Theo's voice clearer and clearer.

"Now stay just as you are, Mother; it's going to be all right. Don't move. Don't speak. I shall handle this."

At last we were at the top and were able to look into the small tower room that served no more than an architecturally ornamental purpose. There was an oil lamp in the center of the floor, its wick all the way up to full brightness, and so illuminating the inhabitants of the turret.

Aunt Anna was the first one seen, as she was nearest the stairs. Her face blanched and frightened, she wore a flannel nightgown and hair that hung past her waist in strings. With the light from the lamp casting a glow upwards from the floor, her face took on such a bizarre configuration—her eyes were enormously protruded, her mouth thin and lipless, her cheeks dark caverns—that it at first startled me. Then, seeing past Colin and Aunt Anna, my eyes fell upon the two central players of the scene: Uncle Henry and Theo.

The only recognizable one was the son, for in his madness and in this distorted light, Uncle Henry was a horrifying stranger I did not know. With wild eyes aglow like burning coals and an angry slash of a mouth, this poor tormented man stood at the edge of the room brandishing a butcher's knife in his two hands. Sweat streamed down his face while the blade flashed menacingly. With the movements of a cornered rat, Uncle Henry's eyes darted back and forth between his wife and son.

Cousin Theodore, also pale and taut and in his nightclothes, looked at Colin and me with no change of expression. Our entrance went unnoticed by his father, and it was better, if we could help it, that we did not intervene.

"Now listen to me, Father," came Theo's steady voice. He caught breaths between words, and he, too, sweated in the cold night air. "You must put that knife down. Put it down, Father."

Uncle Henry made an animal sound, baring his teeth and hunching his back as if ready to spring. There was nothing familiar in his face, none of the refined handsomeness of the Pemberton men, none of that noble grace

I had admired. He was reduced to a raving, delirious madman on the brink of going berserk.

Aunt Anna let out a sob and at once flung her hands over her mouth. The fear in her popping eyes made my heart go out to her. Twenty years ago, my mother must have suffered the very same way.

"Father, put that knife down," said Theodore firmly, quietly.

But Uncle Henry only stretched his mouth in a kind of leer. So this is how it happened, how my great-uncle Michael had ended, and my own father, and Grandmother Abigail's husband Sir John. Was this also how the Pemberton women were going to die—Martha and I?

Now Colin stepped forward and I with him. Theo straightened a little, heaved a great sigh, and said out of the corner of his mouth, "He attacked me with that knife but fortunately missed. He ran from me and eluded me to this point. I'm afraid I'm at a loss, Colin. It's Uncle Robert all over again. And we were powerless back then to stop him, too."

Colin did not reply. He stood on his guard, his eyes upon Uncle Henry.

"Is Dr. Young down there?" asked Theo. "He has one of those new needles made for pushing medicine through the skin. Now might be a good time to test its worth."

"No," I whispered involuntarily. I could not bear to see my uncle assailed by three men and tied and bound like a wild animal. Dangerous as he was, demented as he was, Uncle Henry was still a man and deserved to be treated with humanity.

The sound of my voice caused him to suddenly look at me, and in that moment, that fleeting second when his madman's eyes stared at me, I feared for my life. The knife would be fast, and Colin and Theo might not be able to stop him in time . . .

But then, in the next instant, a curious thing happened. While we gaped at one another, our eyes locked across the room, my uncle's face began to alter in appearance, almost imperceptibly melt from one expression to another until after a moment, although still wild and terrifying, his face seemed somehow gentler, subtler.

"Bunny?" he said in a strangled voice.

"Yes, Uncle Henry." With my heart pounding madly and the breath held in my throat, I mindlessly mounted the last stair and took a few steps toward my uncle.

"Bunny, you shouldn't be here. You know . . . you shouldn't . . . be here."

Uncle Henry, at the sound of my voice, was experiencing a brief interval of rationality. For this moment, he was sane and clearheaded, and he knew exactly what he was doing. "I can't help it," he sobbed pathetically, "It's the pain. Oh, Bunny, I cannot bear the pain. My head is on fire. And it drives me to committing insane acts. I cannot stop myself. Dear God, help me! Don't let me do what my brother did!"

Cautiously, I moved again closer to him. I was aware of all eyes on me, of how stiff my body was, how painfully my heart was beating. And then, through some unknown tap of strength, I managed to reach out my hand to him.

"You won't do anything wrong, Uncle Henry," I murmured. "Give me the knife."

His eyes flashed. "I must kill!" he cried suddenly. "It's the only thing that stops the pain! Oh God, the pain!" His voice filled the room, filled the entire house and was carried out to the forest and into the night. *"I cannot stop myself!"*

"Give me the knife . . ." I repeated.

He glared at me, and we held one another with our eyes for another fleeting instant. Then, with a quick movement that almost made me cry out, Uncle Henry thrust the knife's handle into my hand and whispered, "Take it away quickly!"

At once, I fell back as Colin and Theo rushed forward to take my uncle by each arm. My knees began to give way as I turned to go down the stairs, and thankfully, Dr. Young was suddenly behind me, his arm around my waist, helping me down.

We all moved back to our own wing like a funeral cortege, Dr. Young and I leading the way with myself leaning heavily upon him, followed by Uncle Henry, who staggered blindly between Colin and Theo, and at the rear was Aunt Anna, crying uncontrollably, with Gertrude managing the candles.

When we reached my aunt and uncle's bedchamber, Colin exchanged places with Dr. Young, putting his arm about my waist, for I still could not stand alone, while the doctor helped Theo guide Uncle Henry to his bed. As we lingered in the doorway to watch, Colin wrenched the knife out of my white fingers and gave it to Gertrude. He said not one word; indeed, no one spoke as my uncle was laid to rest on the bed.

As Anna was pulling off his boots and as Dr. Young was preparing his new "hypodermic" syringe, my Uncle Henry suddenly gave out one last pathetic cry and sank deep into the covers. We all froze; the only one who moved was Dr. Young as he quickly seized my uncle's wrist and stood over him for one suspended minute. Then I heard his sonorous voice say softly into the night, "Henry Pemberton is dead."

Aunt Anna was the only one who reacted, falling to her knees at the bedside and flinging her arms across Uncle Henry's chest. Dr. Young stood at her side with a hand resting gently on her head while Theo, numb and dazed, dropped into an easy chair.

Colin quietly drew the door closed and led me away. "He is out of his misery now, poor beggar."

Yes, I thought, in a stupor, Uncle Henry's misery is over, but ours is yet to begin.

When we reached my door, Colin turned to regard me, a hand on each shoulder, and looked intensely into my eyes a long moment before speaking. "It was a brave thing you did tonight."

"Was it," I said flatly. So stupefied, I could not even react to Colin's nearness, to his touch or gentle voice. The cold numbness I had felt since first reading Thomas Willis's book four nights ago was all the more manifold now in light of seeing the Pemberton curse actually come true. What I witnessed tonight must have been similar to what my five-year-old eyes had watched in the coppice 20 years before. Only tonight I had been able to stop it.

"I'm sure you saved someone from a great deal of harm," Colin was saying. "We have a lot to thank you for."

In my bemused state, it did not occur to me to wonder why, at midnight, Colin should still be fully dressed. Nor had I noticed Martha's disappearance. Nor did I wonder how Uncle Henry got hold of that knife. All I cared about was the inevitable doom that hung over us all like the blade of a guillotine, and that no power on earth could stop it.

"Good night, Colin." I tried to turn away from him, but he held me fast.

"Leyla," he said quietly. "You must tell me something."

"Very well."

"Have you completely given up trying to remember your past?"

"There is no need now."

"Then you believe your father and brother died the way we told you?"

"Yes. After tonight . . . what I saw with Uncle Henry, I know it must be true. Please let me go, Colin."

He released me without another word and waited until I locked my door. After his footsteps faded down the hall, I paced my room in profound anxiety. It was all so wretched, all so terribly unfair. This hideous curse that had already marked me, marked all of us for the same fate as Uncle Henry's.

When I finally collapsed on the floor to cry, it was for a very long time, and it was to sob and weep until no more tears would come. Then, dragging myself over to the half-tester, I cast off my dressing gown and burrowed into the bedclothes. Thomas Willis's collection of writings still lay upon my night table. I reached for it and read, with swollen eyes and by poor candlelight, that accursed page once more.

CHAPTER 13

My tenth day at Pemberton Hurst began with a throbbing headache. Before falling asleep the night before, I had managed to get a maid to bring me some tea. Awakening now well after sunrise, I found that the tea had not helped me to sleep well at all and had only induced incredible dreams and nightmares.

After freshening myself at the washstand and donning my mourning gown of black wool, I sat before the looking glass in a futile attempt at putting some semblance of order to my face. The ordeal of the night before was etched in bold print around my eyes, mouth, and chin. Puffy and creased, my poor face looked to have been besieged by a hundred fists, so that no amount of cool cloths and facial creams would help. My hair, a bird's nest of tangles, required half an hour to be combed out and plaited at the nape of my neck, and in the end did little to improve my appearance.

I glowered petulantly at myself. The incident in the turret had been nightmarish, and my head now throbbed until the laudanum took effect. Yet what annoyed me above all, this rainy morning, was the fact that I could not remember a particular dream I had had. The others, so vivid and lifelike, had all been the usual nonsensical sort peopled with faceless spectres and cryptic settings. But one of them had stood out, had seemed terribly important to me at the time, as though it were a message from the deeper levels of my mind, and yet, try now though I might, I could not recall the dream. I vaguely remembered it as having something to do with the tumor, and it seemed to have been something to require my immediate attention. But it was gone now, on this horribly dreary morning, and my headache would allow me no probing thoughts.

The vicar was with Aunt Anna in the drawing room, while Cousin Theo held her hand in some small reassurance. To my surprise, Martha was calmly engrossed in crocheting a shawl with her carpetbag ever familiarly in her lap, her face pale and drawn but not exceptionally so. My fortunate cousin had the remarkable ability to withdraw from unpleasantness and entertain herself with that carpetbag. Colin, I heard down the hall, was seeking escape at the pianoforte, pouring out his frustrated soul over the ivory keys as if he were the world's last angry man. I did not join him, although I would have wished to, for my place at the moment was with Aunt Anna and her son.

"Such a terrible way to die!" wailed my poor aunt, her face buried in her hands. "It isn't fair! It isn't fair!"

I gazed at Theo, knowing a little of how he must feel. He and I had now lost our fathers in nearly the same manner, and he and I also shared the same fate. We had a great deal in common.

Seeing me, Theodore left his mother's side and joined me on the horsehair sofa. After some deliberation, he said, "I didn't have the opportunity to thank you last night. I suppose you saved my life."

I thought of my father slashing Thomas's throat. I imagined myself, five years old and hiding in the brush, witnessing it. "I acted blindly, Theo, not courageously."

"Still . . ."

We sat and listened a while to the violent strains of music coming from the parlor. I pictured Colin, his hair flying and his eyes wild. I envied him the mechanism of relief.

"Father will be buried tomorrow at East Wimsley in the family vault. He'll be with his father and Uncle Michael. And his two brothers."

So went the Pemberton men. "You'll be there, too, someday, Theodore. And Colin. And Martha and me."

"Leyla, everyone must die."

"Yes, but not so horribly. At least your father had you to help him. Sir John had a son and grandchildren to mourn him. We cannot afford the luxury of children. Who will mourn us, Theo? When you and I are old and insane and burning with the Pemberton fever, who will be there to comfort us?"

My words stopped short. The Pemberton fever. Thomas Willis had written about it. What was it that eluded me . . .? Something in that dream . . .

Dr. Young entered at that moment, and having come from outside, he wore a cape, beaver top hat, and gloves. He informed the vicar that Henry's body was now ready to lie in state at the church and that the funeral arrangements had been made. I watched him execute his duties with efficiency and diplomacy, having removed the body during the night and making everything as smooth as possible for the grieving family. "I also wired Mr. Horton in East Wimsley. He'll be here tonight."

"Thank you, sir," said Theodore. "You've been more than kind."

Dr. Young paused to regard me across the room. I don't know what he was thinking, but he seemed on the verge of saying something.

"Mr. Horton will settle with you," said Theodore, referring to the family solicitor.

But Dr. Young ignored him. His blue eyes sparkled in an odd way, and he said, almost in a murmur, "If you should need me at all for anything, I shall be at my home."

"Thank you, sir," said Theodore, although I had the odd notion that Dr. Young had been speaking only to me.

"It is wise not to have your father lying in state in the house," he went on. "The people of East Wimsley can pay their respects at the church as well as here."

"That was my thought. And there will be so many. The mill workers and their families, the few affluent people of the community, the officials . . ." He shook his head. "I can't imagine them all traipsing through our house."

I stared ahead of myself. No, we mustn't have strangers intrude upon our privacy. Like monks in a monastery . . .

All of a sudden I stood. The drawing room, despite its overall chill, was closing in on me, becoming tight. "I shall go out for my walk now," I announced to no one in particular.

"Take care," said Theodore.

The lightest rain fell on me as I trudged along the lane, but I paid it no attention, for my mind was deeply troubled by something else. It was the dream of the night before, a nocturnal revelation that I had experienced but then had forgotten upon awakening. In my sleep, the dream had seemed frightfully important, and even now, although it was forgotten, that pressing urgency remained. It had something to do with Thomas Willis's book.

I let the rain drip off my bonnet and trickle down my cheeks. It weighted down my lashes, blurring my vision now and again, while the occasional puddles splashed beneath my boots. The wind was not so harsh now nor the air so biting, but perhaps this was because I was oblivious of it, being so wrapped up in my meditation that I was scarcely aware of my environment.

I had dreamt about Thomas Willis's book, and it had come to me as a startling revelation. Now that it was forgotten, it seemed only logical to let it remain forgotten, and yet some small portion of my mind remained puzzled by it, one nagging little problem that would not let me rest . . .

The walk proved fruitless as, after two hours in the rain, I could not remember the dream. Finally feeling the dampness soaking through my cloak, I hurried home and decided for the first time to try a bath in front of my bedroom fire. Afterward, a little more refreshed and my face coming close to normal again, I donned a dark brown velvet dress that covered my throat and came to my wrists in old-fashioned tight cuffs, rearranged my hair into a knot at my neck with waves over my ears, and decided to eat supper with the family.

When I entered the dining room, a little apprehensive about the mood my relatives would be in, I was pleased to see Colin look up at me and smile. He, too, seemed to have made some small attempts at improving his appearance, for his dark-green coat and black trousers were new and stylish, his boots highly polished, and his light brown hair, for the first time, I thought, was combed.

"How do you feel, Leyla?" he asked as he stood when I came through the door.

"As well as can be. And yourself?"

His eyes were on me as I crossed over and sat opposite him in my usual chair next to Martha. She seemed not to notice me, a needlepoint sampler in her hands.

"You look much better," said Colin, "after last night."

Remembering how I had been dressed in his presence, that my hair had hung freely to my waist and that only a dressing grown had covered my nightdress as he had had his arm about my waist, I blushed a little and looked away.

Theo sat quietly before his place setting, his dark-circled eyes staring at the chair that had been his father's. Aunt Anna was not present.

We ate in our customary silence, finding the mutton stew a bit too heavy for our slim appetites, but we helped ourselves to the wine quite freely—even Martha drank two glasses until her cheeks were flushed. When we were finished, Gertrude announced that Mr. Horton, the solicitor, had arrived and was ready for us in the study.

Colin accompanied his sister while I went with Theo into a room I had never visited before. Not unlike the library, it was a cozy, leathery room with many books and dark-wooded furniture. The only difference was the addition of an enormous mahogany desk replete with pigeonholes and countless drawers that was no doubt the place where the vast financial affairs of the Pembertons were handled.

Behind it sat an extraordinarily little man, a mouse almost, with a shiny pate and the tiniest eyes. He was all the more dwarfed by the desk and the great leather chair he sat in, but I soon found that his stature was more than compensated for by his keenness of mind.

Aunt Anna was already there, so startlingly pale in her black silk frock and black veil over her hair. She sat stiffly upon her chair and at its edge as if ready to spring. We four arranged ourselves about the room so that we could face the solicitor and easily hear his voice.

Mr. Horton, not a man for pleasantries, went straightaway into the matter at hand, that is to say, my uncle's will. Not looking at any of us, but keeping his beady eyes upon the papers before him, Mr. Horton spoke evenly and most matter-of-factly.

His first words were, "Mister Theodore Pemberton and Mister Colin Pemberton, sirs, it is my duty to report to you that Henry Pemberton died intestate."

He waited for his words to be absorbed and, when he had allowed what he thought sufficient time to pass, went on, "Under such circumstances there are—within the law—usually several steps that might be taken. However, in this instance—"

"What do you mean, sir," said Theo all of a sudden, startling us, "that my father died intestate?"

"It means, sir, that he left no will."

"Hang it all, man, I know what the word means! But how did he happen not to leave a will? He did write one; I know he did."

"He made no arrangements with me about it, sir, and I have handled the family business for 12 years."

"In the safe then. That must be where he put it."

"We have searched, Mr. Pemberton, and there is no will. Under the law, your father died intestate."

Theodore, who had half risen out of his seat, slowly sat back down and composed himself. "Then what are these steps to be taken?"

"The law has quite provided for such instances, protecting all parties concerned. However, the case at hand is an exceptional one in that, while your father died intestate, his predecessor, your grandfather, took care to foresee such an occurrence. As it is, then, your grandfather's will contained a clause providing for the disbursement of the estate should your father leave no will."

"And have you a copy?"

"I have, sir." Mr. Horton rattled the papers ceremoniously, although I am sure he could have recited them by heart. As we waited for him to finish shuffling and clear his throat, I took a last look around at my relatives.

Aunt Anna's bloodshot eyes were fixed on the carpet, her hands wringing mindlessly. I doubt she had heard a word thus far. Cousin Martha was engaged in her knitting, the clicking of the needles counterpointing the ticking of the clock. Only Colin and Theo were attentive to Mr. Horton, and Theodore, with his florid expression and clenched fists, much more so than Colin. Colin, on the other hand, his tawny hair bright in the fire glow, appeared almost casual, relaxed.

"The codicil to your grandfather's will stipulates that, in the event your father Henry Pemberton were to die intestate, then all the lands, income, buildings, and contents therein are to go in whole to his grandson—"

Theodore leaned forward.

"—Colin Pemberton."

There was only the barest moment, and then, "What the devil!" Theodore flew to his feet and snatched the will out of the solicitor's hand. Colin's face at once blanched; his eyes grew wide.

"That cannot be!" cried Theodore. He towered over Mr. Horton as a hawk over a sparrow. "We knew nothing of this!"

"It is all very legal, Mr. Pemberton," said the unperturbed Mr. Horton. At the readings of wills, he had witnessed such outbursts before. "If you did not know of it, it is only because no one thought it of any importance to read to you. After all, no one suspected your father would die without a will."

"Sir John seemed to think so," growled Theo, as he keenly scrutinized the paper.

"You may examine it all you wish, sir, but I assure you it is quite in order. There is the date and my own seal affixed to it."

Theodore read a little more, than slowly put the paper back on the desk. The look he next turned to Colin was so foul and full of hate that it startled me. "You, you bastard," he said through clenched teeth. "You knew all along! You had done this, twisting my grandfather's mind against us while we were away. Well, it won't work!"

Colin rose to his full height, standing straight and erect and a bit taller than Theo. With forced calmness he said, "I assure you, sir, I had no knowledge of this."

"You knew!" shouted Theodore. "You with your sneaking and conniving—"

"That's enough!" came another voice suddenly from out of nowhere. We all turned toward the fireplace and saw, for the first time, that there was a sixth person in the room. Hidden in a *prie-dieu* with her back to us, Grandmother Abigail had listened to every word.

Now, with the sheer force of her presence, she was able to stop the fight between Colin and Theodore. With those fleshless, bony fingers, she seized the arms of her chair and brought herself to her unsteady feet. Grandmother was tall and lean with not an ounce of flesh on her body anywhere. Her black silk gown hung from her as from a skeleton, and her skirt was wide atop an old-fashioned hoop. That fleecy white hair sharply contrasted with her hard black eyes, which glinted with an imperiousness that cowed us all with one sweeping glance.

"Mr. Horton speaks the truth," she said in a deep, stentorian voice. "I was present when my husband John made that change. At the reading of his will ten years ago, you all learned that he had left everything to his only surviving son, Henry. But he had also added a codicil that would cover the possibility of Henry's not leaving a will . . . considering the abrupt manner in which Pembertons die . . . Well, such has happened. All along it was Sir John's wish that control of the estate go to Richard's son, not Henry's. All along he wanted Colin his heir. Now it has come to pass."

Her voice was cold and impersonal, betraying none of her own opinion. Whether Grandmother approved of Sir John's choice of heir or not, she did not show it. "This is a cursed family. It never should have been allowed to continue. My husband died of it. All three of my sons died of it. Now my two remaining grandsons will die of it." If she had attempted to engender our sympathy, she failed, for her voice was without warmth, her manner without emotion so that no one could feel pity. Instead, we marveled at her stoicism, her cool bearing after the recent loss of her last son. If she were a grieving mother, it did not show.

"We are going to respect Sir John's wishes," she decreed peremptorily.

Then her small black eyes flashed at Colin. Was it anger? Hatred? Or possibly triumph . . . ?

Grandmother next looked at the solicitor. "Mr. Horton?"

The little ferret cleared his throat. "For one reason or another, Henry Pemberton saw fit to write no will. Or possibly it was an error, an oversight. Whichever, it is not uncommon for a man to leave such matters to the last minute when, in many circumstances, Fate steps in as a most untimely intruder. As I said, generally such cases are then taken into the courts, but in our particular instance, it will not be necessary. What has happened is perfectly legal. Now then"—he cleared his throat again—"Sir John Pemberton has also provided for the female members of the Pemberton family, which is to say they will be taken care of in the comfort they so desire for as long as they reside under this roof. In the event that any woman of the Pemberton name should desire to leave the Hurst, then her allowance and support will be ceased at once." Martha's clicking needles froze for an instant in the air, leaving the room suddenly, uncomfortably silent. Then, without a change of expression or posture, she resumed knitting again. "That is all there is, gentlemen. A copy of the will is here for your scrutiny. If Mr. Colin Pemberton will set aside a day next week and come to my office, I will apprise him of the business and financial holdings of the family. Are there any questions?"

"There are none," said Grandmother in a voice of slate. She passed her hard eyes over us all once again, her jaw and mouth set grimly. Then she turned to leave the room.

I rose from my chair as she swept past me, and Martha also managed to gather everything in her arms and stand. Only Anna remained seated—Anna, who seemed not to have heard a single word.

When the great oak doors closed behind Gertrude, who had been on hand to attend my grandmother, I felt the atmosphere become charged at once with electricity. Colin and Theo regarded one another angrily, Theo with hatred and Colin with indignation.

"I tell you, sir, there was a will," said Theodore evenly.

"Perhaps there was. I had nothing to do with it. Mr. Horton does not know about it—"

"I am cognizant of no will written by Henry Pemberton," said the weasel behind the desk.

"Then there are ways!" shouted Theodore. He alarmed me; I had not expected such a display of wrath. "I will secure my own solicitor, sir, and go to the law with this. There is a matter of primogeniture, Cousin—"

"Excuse me, Mr. Pemberton, but in this instance I think you will find—"

"I think, Mr. Horton, that your duty tonight has been executed. We are no longer in need of your services."

Mr. Horton now stood and did not come very tall, but his eyes were narrow and shrewd. "As new master of Pemberton Hurst, sir, that will be for Mr. Colin to decide."

Theo's eyes flared like balls of fire, his neck veins bulging until his face was a bright crimson. "He is not yet the master of Pemberton Hurst! Not while I can prevent it!"

If it had been my place to speak up, I would have done so just then, but this affair belonged in the hands of men.

"Now, Theo, really—" began Colin, his face livid and confused. "I had no idea—"

"You, sir, are a sniveling dogsbody!"

"I will not allow you to insult me in my own house!"

"Not yet it isn't, Colin Pemberton, not while I live."

While the shouting continued, my head began to throb. It must have been the wine at dinner, I thought; I had too much of it. And now this quarreling. It was too much.

When I excused myself, the two men seemed not to notice, so engrossed in their heated debate as they were. It distressed me to see them fight so, with Uncle Henry's body not yet even buried, but I had neither the inclination nor the courage to intervene.

The way up to my room seemed eternal. The gaslights were turned down low, and all about was a deepening gloom. As my headache grew, I recalled my poor uncle's face of the night before, his madman's eyes and twisted mouth. I thought of the immense suffering that had preceded his death—the headaches, the nausea and vomiting, the severe abdominal pain, the delirium and convulsions. And I wondered when my time would come.

Inside my room, I sought relief by the fire, sinking into the easy chair and putting up my feet. Rain streamed against my windows; everything was in chaos. My headache was increasing, becoming worse than the previous ones, and to such a degree as to slightly upset my stomach. I took some laudanum, a larger dose this time, thinking my distress to have been caused by the excessive tension in the air.

At the same time, now that I was away from the study where the family sat arguing still, I was nagged again by that little nemesis in the back of my brain: Thomas Willis.

So I decided to retire. The medicine calmed me, freed my mind a little, and was beginning to melt my limbs with a characteristic euphoria. Once in bed and under the covers, I picked up Dr. Cadwallader's book and let it sit in my lap unopened, hoping that, by staring at it, I would suddenly remember what the dream had been.

But instead of the dream, another memory floated back to my opiated mind: the conversation I had had with Dr. Young three nights previous. "You read the book, did you not, by Thomas Willis?" I recalled having asked. And his reply had been, "Thomas Willis? He lived many years ago. I read his works when I was a medical student."

Even in my sleepy state, I was aware of coming close to the answer. Opening now to the page in question, I scanned Dr. Willis's long ago written words: "After having unfolded the Nature of the Plague . . . Feavers, called Pestilent and Malignant . . . more minute appellation a Pestilential Feaver . . ."

What was it that nagged at me? Something about this book had disturbed me, and I had only realized it in a dream.

Dr. Young's words came back to mind: "Of Thomas Willis I recall tedious sentences, baffling anatomical diagrams, and abominable spelling!"

My eyes raced ahead to the important page, which started out: "When this Feaver first began . . ." I read the entire page, came back to the start, and read again. Then I stopped. Near the bottom of the first page was the phrase: "Sir Geoffrey had suffered the same Fate as the son which was now troubled by the Symptoms of the Fever . . ."

I stared at it incredulously. The word "fever" was spelled wrong. Not according to present day, but for Thomas Willis and his century. All throughout the rest of the book, he wrote of "Feavers"; yet here it was "Fever."

I flipped the page and read the last line: ". . . the Brain Sickness (or Pember Town Fever) will not bow to Empirical Remedies."

Again "fever" was spelled wrong.

That was what my dream had been about. Now I remembered it. In my sleep I had realized the incongruity in spelling throughout the Pemberton passage, and it had disturbed me.

Although now, staring at the aberrant words and thinking of the dream, I did not see why it should have nagged me so. After all, people in every age make errors, and no doubt his printers had not caught the mistakes.

I placed the book on my night table and blew out my lamp. As I lay curled under the covers listening to the rain pelt my windows, I opened my eyes and stared at the silhouette of the book in the darkness.

Still, I thought as I drifted off to sleep, it wouldn't do harm to show it to Dr. Young tomorrow.

Although it used to be that women of genteel society did not attend funerals, the custom was changing as bolder and more liberal women chose to attend. To my surprise, Aunt Anna was such a one, although I do not believe she acted so out of a social rebellion but rather a profound grief that drove her to spend the last possible moment with her deceased husband. Martha and I did not go, she mostly to remain out of the wet and knit by the fire, and I because I firmly thought it improper. Edward and Dr. Harrad and a few friends had accompanied my mother to her grave while I had mourned privately at home. There are some things ladies never do, such shocking things as play tennis or smoke cigarettes, yet there are always a few in every society who consider that equalizing themselves with men is positive reform.

So Aunt Anna went with her son and Colin in the coach-and-four, while Martha and I remained solemnly indoors.

After breakfast, the small beginnings of a headache began to manifest themselves, but a dose of laudanum took care of it. Then I tried to read for a while, but my mind would not concentrate, and neither could I sit for long at the pianoforte. It was the Thomas Willis book again. It continued to puzzle me, even though I had decided it very inconsequential. It prickled my mind ever so lightly, causing me to ponder it as I ate a light dinner in my room, as I pored over the book spines for something to read, as I sorted through sheet music for a melody.

The three had not yet returned from the funeral by one o'clock, so I decided to take my usual walk. Remembering where Dr. Young had said he lived, I struck off in that direction with Thomas Willis snugly under my arm.

The Ivy farm, sold six years before by a man who had lost both his wife and two daughters to an epidemic of scarlet fever, was not difficult to find after two hours' brisk walking. I would have preferred to take the dogcart, but that might have roused someone's suspicion, and for some reason I did not want my family to know what I was about. I was also apprehensive about the propriety of my actions, for it certainly was not my habit to go unescorted to gentlemen's homes. I was able to rationalize this away somewhat by the fact that the man was a doctor, of excellent repute, many years older than myself, and no doubt had a housekeeper. Also there was the need for secrecy (although just why, I was not certain), else I would have brought a maid along with me.

A column of gray smoke spiraled out of the chimney and up to the cloudy sky, a sign of life that indicated the resident might be home. And there were lights on in the farmhouse, the front windows that must be a parlor or drawing room. I grew increasingly hesitant as I tromped along the muddy drive. I knew that only women of the *demimonde* visited gentlemen unescorted, but this was a matter of importance. I needed my laudanum—the headache persisted—and there was still that funny little puzzle about Thomas Willis's book.

To my vast and infinite relief, a tubby old woman answered the door, a spotted apron over her belly and a mobcap atop her gray head. She eyed me with unabashed surprise when it was obvious I came alone.

"Are ye ill?" she demanded, leaving me to stand on the threshold.

"No. Is the doctor in?" I asked a third time.

She looked at my abdomen for maternity signs. The woman was also a midwife. "Be he expectin' ye?"

"I don't believe so. I am a friend of his, from Pemberton Hurst and—"

The expression on her face stopped me. Yes, I was from that house of horrors, the subject of so many stories about diabolic goings-on. What had this poor creature heard—that we eat children?

I was saved from another shivering moment on the doorstep by Dr. Young himself, who suddenly appeared behind her. "Hello, Leyla. What a pleasant surprise. Come to visit me, have you?"

The fat woman begrudgingly stepped aside and continued to eye me with suspicion. Wasn't I supposed to be home mourning the death of another of my kind, no great loss to the world?

"Mrs. Finnegan, it's about time for tea. Can we have it in the drawing room, please?"

I was thankful when she waddled away, for the woman had no conscience about a brazen stare, letting all her opinions be displayed on her face. Dr. Young took my cape and bonnet and, hanging them up, proceeded to ask after my health.

"I've a headache again, Dr. Young, and out of laudanum."

"I see." He regarded me with some concern.

"It's what's been happening, sir, Uncle Henry's death, the will last night, now the funeral and such beastly weather . . ."

"Yes, of course." He led me from the tiny entrance hall into a very cozy drawing room that was spotlessly clean and tastefully furnished. "Over there," he said pointing to a door, "is my examining room and surgery. Down the stairs and under the kitchen is my laboratory where, I am certain, Mrs. Finnegan believes I collaborate with the Devil."

I laughed as we sat down. Dr. Young was handsomely dressed in a close-fitting, gray double-breasted frock coat and black trousers. His shirt and tie were immaculately white, and there was the faint smell of a cigar about him.

"I'm glad you came, Leyla. It was such a joy to an old man's ears to hear the name of Oliver Harrad again. After I left the Hurst yesterday, I came home and at once dispatched a letter to him. Old friends, dear friends should not lose one another because of distance."

While he spoke, his eyes sparkled with happiness, and I was glad to have done such a small thing for this kind man.

"I see you brought a book. Ah yes, Dr. Cadwallader of Oxford. Eighteen twenty-two. And here's old Thom himself." We gazed at the face of the long dead anatomist. "Yes, I'm sure I have a copy of this somewhere. Haven't had time to look for it."

"There's only one page I want you to look at, sir. It wouldn't take long." He grinned broadly. "Then I suppose I must read it."

I flipped the pages for him until we arrived at the important one, and I sat on edge, my hands tightly clasped while he read silently.

Presently, for it was only a short passage, Dr. Young looked up at me, and his face congealed into a frown. "I understand now, Leyla, why you thought it important for me to read. Here is proof of the Pemberton tumor and actually documented by one of history's most honored scientists. This is most edifying. I am quite impressed."

"Did you notice anything else, sir?"

"Anything else?"

"Like abominable spelling?"

He threw back his head and laughed. "Oh yes! Physick, no less. Diaphoretick! Pleurisie!"

"And *Fever,* Dr. Young."

"Yes. Feaver of all things."

"No, I mean—" I reached for the book and pointed to the two "fevers." He stopped laughing. "What do you think?" I asked.

"What do I think?" Dr. Young shrugged. "Typographic errors, I imagine. A bit unusual for scientific works. Maybe they're misprints from Thom Willis's time, and these new publishers—ah—Mortimer and Sons just transcribed them as they were. That wouldn't be unusual. Seventeenth-century printing wasn't like what we have today. What's wrong, Leyla, you look worried."

"I don't know, Dr. Young, I can't put my finger on it. Like a premonition or something. I suppose I'm just being silly. Could we look at your copy?"

His silver eyebrows arched. "My copy? Certainly, if you'd like. It'll take me a moment to find—Ah, here's Mrs. Finnegan with tea."

I tried to smile amiably at the suspicious old woman, but her exterior remained stern. Her disapproval of my sitting alone with the doctor might have been tolerable were it not mingled with an ignorant mistrust of anything Pemberton.

Still, sitting before a roaring hearth in the company of this comfortable gentleman, sipping excellent English tea while a light rain began to fall without was relaxing indeed. In the midst of his bachelor clutter and Mrs. Finnegan-cleanliness, I was able to forget a little of my concern about Thomas Willis's book.

"What was it you said, Leyla, about a will? As you came in—"

"Oh, Uncle's will. Or, rather, lack of it. Mr. Horton informed us all last night that Uncle Henry died intestate and that my grandfather Sir John had provided a clause in his own will for just such an occurrence. Otherwise, Mr. Horton said, the matter of the estate would have gone to the courts."

"Sir John provided, did he?"

"And such an uproar, too. It seems Colin's got everything and Theo nothing."

"I beg your pardon?" He placed his cup on the table and gazed at me with dark bewilderment. "Did you say Colin got the whole inheritance? Completely?"

"Why, yes. I suppose the elder grandson, Theo, should have had more consideration, but Sir John seems to have thought Colin the better man. Oh, Theo was frightfully angry . . ." My voice drifted off. "Is something wrong, Dr. Young?"

"I just find it quite surprising is all. Yes, a shock indeed." He picked up his cup and started to sip again. "Considering."

"Considering what, sir?"

"Considering Colin isn't really a Pemberton at all."

CHAPTER 14

The sound of my cup clattering against the saucer brought me to close my mouth at last, for it had been hanging open. Then I said most stupidly, "What?"

"Didn't you know? Your uncle Richard married Colin's mother when he was only a baby. About two years old, I believe. Richard Pemberton adopted the boy, so it's all quite legal, and under the law Colin *is* a Pemberton, but inherently he comes from another family. Oh, what was that name?"

"How do you know all this, Dr. Young?" I heard a roaring in my ears.

"Dr. Smythe, if he was nothing else, was an excellent keeper of records. I have the histories of every family within a 20-mile radius of East Wimsley, including all sorts of details about the Pembertons. If memory serves me, your father's brother Richard brought a widow to that house back in, let me see, 1825 and married her. She had a boy with her. That would be little Colin. Dr. Smythe was called upon soon after the wedding to attend to Madame Jane's vapors, which turned out to be a maternity condition. Martha was born that year . . ."

Dr. Young continued to speak but I did not listen. I heard only the thumping of my heart, resounding—I was certain—off every wall of this cottage.

"Leyla? Miss Pemberton?"

I blinked twice. "Oh, forgive me. I was thinking." Yes . . . I was thinking about many things. For one, why had Colin never told me he was not a Pemberton and therefore not in danger of the Curse? And I could see now why Theo had been enraged about the inheritance. And it also explained why Colin did not look like the rest of us.

"I can see this certainly is news to you. But you've gone positively pale, Leyla. Why does it upset you so?"

Because I am in love with Colin, cried my mind, and his not telling me was the same as having lied to me.

"It—doesn't upset me, Dr. Young. I was just caught off-balance. I had thought Colin was my cousin, a blood relation. Of course, he's free from the Pemberton sickness."

"Yes, he is. And speaking of which"—Dr. Young replaced his empty cup and stood vigorously—"shall we look at my copy of Cadwallader now?" The astute man was attempting a diversion, since the shock had so distressed me, and I was grateful for it I needed time to get used to the idea. Colin not one of us . . .

Dr. Young was gone for only a minute, or what seemed only a minute but might have been longer, considering my lack of attention. I came out of my reverie when I felt him sit again on the sofa and I saw the familiar book in his hands. For the moment, I wanted to forget Colin.

"Now let me see, that was page . . ." He looked in mine and then flipped through his own. "Here we are. Oh no, just a minute. Wrong page." I saw out of the corner of my eyes those white sheets rippling by, and all I could see was Colin's face. His face not like mine, without the Pemberton nose and chin. I suppose I should have been happy, he being free of the Fate . . .

"Wait a minute," I heard Dr. Young's nasal voice murmuring. "What's up here? The page numbers match, yet the writing doesn't."

"I beg your pardon?" I shook away the fog and gave him my attention. "Have you the same errors?"

"Or something. Look at your book, Leyla, read the page preceding the Pemberton passage."

"Very well. That Diaphoretick was only the pouder of Toads, purged thoroughly with Salt—"

"That's enough. We agree there. Now read from the top of the facing page."

I felt myself frown. "Those Feavers differed from both the Pest, and from one another according to the degree, and yet by their Nature they were all of the same vehemency." I stopped and regarded Dr. Young. He wore an expression I had never seen before. "What is wrong?"

Without a word, he extended his own volume to me, opened out to the same pages as my own. I looked down and read the first few lines. They were not the same.

"I don't understand."

"Neither do I. Hand me your book, please, Leyla." On his lap Dr. Young lay both copies open, flat so that two pages faced up. The pages on the left matched exactly, yet the ones on the right—the ones that were about the Pembertons—did not. In fact, only one copy contained that particular passage. Mine.

"Yet the page numbers match," I said, confused. "What happened? I don't understand."

Dr. Young picked up my book and brought it close to his eyes, turning it over in his hands and studying in particular the binding. Suddenly a light dawned on his face. "There it is, Leyla."

"What?"

"This is a bogus page. Do you see? Someone at some time very meticulously removed the original page, which we can read in my copy, and replaced it with a fake. When we turn the Pemberton page, we see that the same text in both books continues on the next leaf. In other words, the original page was taken out and this one put in its place."

"I don't understand." But in a strange way, I did. Now the dream was coming back to me in full. An unconscious part of my mind had intuitively recognized the fraudulence of this page, yet unconsciously I did not see it. Now I was beginning to, and it also explained why Thom Willis's book had nagged at me so.

"Someone tampered with this book to create the Pemberton sickness."

"Create it!" I cried in a most unladylike way. "Do you mean it does not exist? *That there is no tumor?*"

"Certainly Thomas Willis never wrote of one."

"Dr. Young—"

"Now see here, Leyla, how the stitching of the binding appears slightly different. That this is a spurious page is beyond a doubt, although a look under my microscope to compare the two can give us final proof. However, I am not so concerned with the fact that it was done as to *why* it was done."

"Why?" My voice was small, distant Two great shocks within five minutes.

"What would be your guess, Leyla? Are you thinking the same thing as I?"

"I'm not thinking anything, Dr. Young . . ."

"Then let me hazard a guess, if you will permit me. This fake bit of writing must have been manufactured for the purpose of justifying the Pemberton sickness, which, by the same token, must also be false."

"False? Then there is no tumor? But why? Why would anyone create such a thing? I can't accept this, Dr. Young."

"And why not? Have you a better explanation?"

My lower lip came under the assault of my teeth as I stared at the two books. It was obvious, once one knew what to look for, that the page in question was a fake. It was also obvious that it had been placed there with great care and that someone had no doubt undergone great pains to make it appear as genuine as possible. But why?

"I have no explanation, sir. I am only confused."

"Nor am I too clear on the matter. Whoever did this was an artist, or certainly a meticulous person. With the exception of misspelling 'Feaver,' an easily made error, the bogus page is an excellent copy. It follows Willis's literary style, maintains the grammar and spelling of the day; even the printing type and paper are exquisitely matched. Someone, he or she, was determined to give a good, solid foundation to the tumor story and so chose Dr. Willis as his or her agent. In other words, it would seem that an unknown party had invented the Pemberton sickness for one reason or another and then went to great pains to invent evidence that would convince others as well."

"But it is all so preposterous! If what you are theorizing is true, that there might not after all be a tumor, then what did my father die of, and Great-uncle Michael, and Sir John?" I stopped short to gape at Dr. Young. I could see that the same thought was passing through his own mind. *"Then what did Uncle Henry die of?"*

His crystal blue eyes, so patient and intelligent, could only return my questioning gaze. The page in the book was false; then might not the Pemberton legacy also be false? And if that were so, then what *did* Uncle Henry die of?

"My dear," said Dr. Young in a soft, pliant voice. He was close and reassuring. "Permit me to do something right now. In my laboratory. I shall be gone for only a short while."

"Well, yes, of course, but—"

"I shall explain afterward, if what I find is true. If not, then you must go away from here still believing in the tumor. Will you agree to this, Leyla?"

"Yes."

"I won't be long now, and you can ring for Mrs. Finnegan if you want anything."

I sat rigidly on the sofa as I watched him go, his broad back and square shoulders, his stride so youthful for a man his age. We were friends, he and I; I had to trust him. And he was a man who extracted confidence, who commanded the utmost respect and faith. Whatever he was going to do now, down in that mysterious laboratory, and whatever answer he returned with, I would accept it unconditionally.

The rain had gotten harder, and the fire had to be stoked many times by Mrs. Finnegan in the ensuing hour, but I did not notice the passage of time. All I could concentrate on was my dear Colin. Colin with sea-green eyes and hair the color of teak. Colin with his weathercock nature and unpredictable moods. How I had loved him! How I continued to love him yet! Colin had a reason for not telling me about himself, I was sure of it . . .

I don't know how long Dr. Young had stood in the doorway before I noticed him, but when I did, I started, for he had made no sound. Then, seeing him, I became all the more alarmed, for his appearance had changed. Gone was the fashionable frock coat and tie. His sleeves were rolled to the elbows in navvy fashion, and there were unidentifiable stains on his vest. But what startled me even more, more so than his shocking state of dress and abrupt intrusion into the room, was the expression on his face.

White as the linen of his shirt, drawn and taut with age, the doctor's face showed evidence of shock, of worry, of upheaval. It was this that brought me to my feet.

"Leyla—" he began uncertainly, hesitantly. "Please sit down."

"What is it?"

"Please, I—" He came across the room and took my hands. His touch was the coldness of snow. "Leyla, sit down."

We sat together, our hands clasped tightly. He began to speak. "As you know, I came here to retire and at the same time work on a pet project of mine, which is to find a possible cure for diabetes. Doubtless you know nothing about scientific research, but suffice it to say that what is required for thorough investigation and experimentation are a laboratory, good equipment, chemicals, and certain . . . other substances. I do not wish to offend you, and forgive me if I do, but you must be told. In researching the properties of diabetes, I require a certain supply of . . ." he hesitated, ". . . *blood* in order to conduct the necessary experiments. With my chemicals—oh, it's an involved process, Leyla—I experiment with both normal blood and the blood of a diabetic. Again, please forgive my indelicacy in the use of the word, but you will see in a moment why it is necessary. As I said, I test the properties of both healthy and diabetic . . ." again he paused, ". . . blood in hopes of discerning the properties and causes of the disease in the latter, and thereby discovering a way to define the proper medicine for combating diabetes. Now, my difficulty lies in supply. With the new *post mortem* laws in England, I can have blood delivered to me from Guy's and Bart's, but it usually arrives in bad condition. If such is the case, then I try to look for samples locally, say, for example, from mill workers when I treat them in their homes for injuries. Now then, Leyla, when your uncle died, I took the liberty of approaching your aunt on the matter of obtaining a small sample of your uncle's blood, to be saved and used at a later time in my studies of normal blood."

Much as I tried to fight it, I shuddered involuntarily.

"Anna graciously consented. So in my laboratory, in an ether cooler, I have kept a vial of Henry Pemberton's blood." He stopped here.

"Please go on, Dr. Young," I heard myself say from afar. "I am not going to faint."

"Very well. As we were talking a while ago, you posed an excellent question. What did your uncle die of? So a thought occurred to me. If I were to examine a drop of his blood under the microscope or run a few tests on it in my tubes . . ."

I put my hand to my clammy forehead. "Please, Dr. Young, tell me what you found."

"You agreed, did you not, to accept my findings? That if it were nothing, then you would still believe in the tumor and trust me? Well, trust me now, Leyla dear, for your uncle did not die of a brain tumor."

I gawked incredulously at the man who held my hands in his icy own. The room seemed to swim a little, the air to grow stifling. "He did not?" I managed to say. "Uncle Henry did not die of a brain tumor?" The words sounded like the tolling of a great bell. "Then . . . do you know, sir, what he did . . . die of?"

"Yes, I do. And it is beyond a doubt. Do you recall our discussion that evening in your room about Henry's symptoms? I had said they were not typical and not textbook at all. Now I know why. Headaches, nausea, abdominal pains, delirium, and convulsions are all part of a syndrome of an illness quite different from a brain tumor. And had I, in my experience, had more dealings with it, I would have more readily recognized it. But I was too quick to accept a diagnosis of brain tumor and a prognosis of death."

"Tell me, sir, what you found."

"Leyla, your uncle's blood contained massive quantities of digitalis, the foxglove extract."

The room swam even more, tilted this way and that. Where had I heard of foxglove before? Spoken in the same voice as this man's over a supper table.

"Because I rarely ever dealt with patients suffering from heart ailments,

I rarely encountered the symptoms that are so classic with overdoses of digitalis. But now that I look back, the headache and nausea—"

"Dr. Young!" I said sharply. "Why was my uncle taking such medicine?"

He regarded me for a long, weighty moment, then said gravely, "The percentage of digitalis in your uncle's blood was far from medicinal. It had been ingested as a poison, not as a medicine."

Instantly, my mind snapped. The room stopped its motion, and I was suddenly, sharply clearheaded, "Poison!"

"Administered to him bit by bit and then countered with laudanum. Indeed, it is hard to say exactly which killed him in the end—the digitalis or the morphine—there was so much of both in his blood."

"And you say . . . *administered* to him?"

"Certainly, he never took it on his own. Digitalis is a cardiac medicine, and your uncle never suffered with his heart. Besides, upon examining him, he would have told me. It's not in Dr. Smythe's records at all."

"So you think my uncle was murdered . . ."

Dr. Young paused before saying, "Yes, Leyla, I do."

Finally, I sank back with exhaustion. So much had happened, so much to think about. First Colin, then the book, and now Uncle Henry. My head started to ache.

"We must go to the police, Leyla."

"Police . . ."

"I'll help you. We have irrefutable evidence that your uncle was murdered—"

"No," I said quickly, my mind working fast. "What could the police do? Arrest my entire family? They'd only question each one and let them go. And then you and I would be in danger . . ." Something else was beginning to occur to me. "Dr. Young, you said to me the other evening that, according to Dr. Smythe's records, my father and Sir John also followed the same course of symptoms and died exactly the same way."

"Yes, it's true."

"Then they must have been murdered, too!" I sat bolt upright "So I had been right all along! That intuition I had had, that vague doubt about the credibility of my father's death. He *was* murdered after all!"

"I don't know about that, Leyla. I can only testify for your uncle. The others, well, that's in the past. We can't go back to that now."

My eyes narrowed at this. "Oh, can't we!" I said almost gloatingly. There was one way we could go back into the past and see what really happened. We could search the mind of a five-year-old child named Leyla Pemberton.

"I think you are handling this wrong, Leyla. If you suspect someone in your family of murder, then you should go to the police. You must not take it upon yourself. It is too dangerous. Leyla; please, don't make me regret having told you!"

"I would have known eventually anyway, Dr. Young, if not by direct evidence such as the blood, then at least by surmising upon the basis of that false page. There being no brain tumor meant that my uncle died by other means. If the same person who printed that page abetted in my uncle's death, then he is a murderer. But who and why? None of this follows. That bogus page must have been printed long ago, possibly before my father died. I don't understand. Whoever killed him and Sir John must have killed Uncle Henry. It's obvious in the manner of death. Don't the police have a special word for it?"

"Modus operandi," he said with resignation. Dr. Young was shaking his head.

"Oh, I have to think. I'm a jumble of thoughts. My mind is all chaotic. Who on earth would want Uncle Henry dead? And why? For what possible gain? Certainly not Anna and Martha. They gained nothing upon his death. It is said that poison is a woman's weapon. If so, then which of the Pemberton women would have motive to kill Uncle Henry? His own mother, Abigail? For what reason? Maybe one of the servants, a grudge? Or how about Theo and Colin, what had they to gain—"

The word caught in my throat, leaving my mouth agape. Now Dr. Young brought his head up sharply. "Colin! Now *there's* one with everything to gain and nothing to lose."

"Dr. Young!"

"The entire Pemberton fortune? The mills, the mansion?"

"No, no!" I cried. "I won't hear of it! Not Colin!"

He tried to calm me by taking my hands once again in his. "I am beginning to understand, Leyla, that there is more in your heart for Colin than simple cousinly affection. However, whatever it is you feel for the man, you must not let it cloud your judgment. Just because you love him does not mean he is incapable of murder. Do you understand me, Leyla?"

I could not fight Dr. Young's logic, his persuasiveness. "But no one knew about the will being lost," I said in a small voice. "Indeed, Theodore was certain his father had left one. We all thought that. And since Theo was quite definitely expecting something big from the inheritance, then it is just as reasonable that he committed the murder. If you could have seen his rage last night to learn he got nothing! And Colin claims to have known nothing about Sir John's will . . ." I opened my eyes wildly. No, I refused to think it. Colin was innocent. *He had to be.* Last night, he had insisted he knew nothing about Uncle Henry's being intestate or Sir John's codicil to leave everything to him. "And what's more," I heard my voice proclaim more strongly, "I believe the same person committed all three murders: my father, Sir John, and Uncle Henry. If that were so, then Colin would have been 14 years old at the time."

Dr. Young remained still, pensive. Behind those blue eyes was a mind working very quickly, acutely. To my relief, he eventually said, "That is a point in Colin's favor. If he is telling the truth that he did not know Henry died without a will, then it is indeed quite reasonable to assume Theodore is guilty. After all, he would have been 18 years old at your father's death and physically capable of murder."

I felt my body suddenly go weak all over. How absurd it all seemed, sitting as I was in this delightful drawing room with my skirt spread over the sofa, my gloves in my lap, and a tray of tea and biscuits before me, trying to imagine which of my family was a murderer!

Reading my expression, Dr. Young said, "Had I known this afternoon would bring such startling revelations, I would have offered you brandy instead of tea."

I smiled thankfully at him. As usual, this perceptive man had the acumen to understand another's feelings and to offer exactly the right words. Because of that nagging dream and my constant rereading of Thomas Willis's book, I would have eventually made my own discovery of its suspiciousness. And with one observation leading to another, I most likely would have arrived at certain conclusions on my own. But what I was most grateful for now, leaning back on the sofa to hear the rain close to my ear, was the fact that Dr. Young had been with me through it all. Without him, it would have been much harder to bear.

"What do you plan to do now, Leyla?"

"I don't know, Dr. Young. I shall have to move carefully, give great thought to it all. I am convinced one of my family is a murderer, and I intend to find out who."

Suddenly, I was back where I started. All of a sudden, the past week vanished as if it never existed, for I was back at the family supper table on my third evening there, standing like Nike of Samothrace above them and crying, "I think the Pemberton Curse was a fabrication, a spurious tale to lay the blame upon my father and conceal the true murderer!"

It was as though nothing had happened in between; Thom Willis's book now faded as though it had only been a dream. The old determinations came flooding into me once again. The old angers and bitterness began to fill the space that had, only hours before, been taken up with sadness, defeat, and doom.

The metamorphosis must have been apparent on my face, for Dr. Young said, "I can guess what you are thinking, Leyla."

And something else was growing inside me, too, something new that had not been there before. It was a rage, a blind fury that all joy and happiness had been robbed from that house *because of a hoax*. That simple page in Cadwallader's book had done more damage than simply bring sadness; it had robbed my family of hope, of a future. It had caused Colin and Martha and Theo to commit themselves to a life of celibacy, a life without love or children or a future to grow with. That fraudulent piece of paper had robbed my family of the will to fight and had made pawns of them, marionettes that moved without will of their own.

This was my greatest anger of all. And for this reason, as well as the other original ones, I was all the more determined to unravel the mystery at Pemberton Hurst.

"It's dark out, Leyla," I heard a soft voice say.

"I have a lot of thinking to do, Dr. Young. So much to sort out." My mind, as if floodgates had been raised, was being assailed by a myriad of thoughts: Aunt Sylvia's letter, Theodore's ruby ring, my letter to Edward burned . . .

Edward, of whom I had not thought in days.

The dam had burst, and all the old puzzles of the week before drenched me in a swirling confusion. Who had stolen that ring and why? Was it because it was in some way connected with the coppice? And what about the coppice—how could I make myself remember what had happened that day 20 years ago? Who had burned my letter to Edward? Who had sent my mother a letter in Aunt Sylvia's name?

There was a hand on my arm. From somewhere on the other side of a wall, a gentle voice was murmuring, yet I did not listen.

I was furious now beyond speaking. That murderer had not only taken three lives but had also killed the spirit of the Pembertons! Poor stale, faded Martha. My sweet, embittered Colin. Grandmother Abigail entombed before being dead. My own mother, sweating among the stinks of Seven Dials because she had thought her daughter was the victim of a foul and insidious disease.

Such misery, such unhappiness because one criminal had manufactured the Pemberton sickness and had inflicted its imaginary doom upon my family.

That soft voice behind the wail, coaxing, urging. Leyla . . . Leyla . . .

My mind at once grew still, and I gazed finally at Dr. Young. His hand was on my arm. He was murmuring my name.

"Forgive me," I whispered.

"Your expression is so curious. Tell me, Leyla, why do you take all this upon yourself?"

"Because I am in a way responsible. I am an outsider, free from the years of monasticism the others have lived in. I alone can view the entire scene with an objective eye and search for the answers. The others won't."

His eyes scanned my face, which must have been crimson, for it burned. I knew what Dr. Young thought: he saw anger, grim determination, confusion. He was also wondering: And you believe you are being objective?

So I turned away, for I did not like what I saw. My soul was a maelstrom of emotions: love for Colin, grief for those dead, defiance against the unknown enemy, and—above all—anger. Dr. Young knew this. An expert in reading people, he was able to see into the very depths of my soul and understand clearly what it was I felt.

"May I take you home now?"

Although he had reminded me of the lateness of the hour—past tea time—I was astonished to see how long I had been here. Rising quickly I yanked my gloves over my trembling hands. "I accept your generous offer of a carriage. Forgive me if I've taken you from your work. I had only planned to be here a short while."

"It was all my pleasure," said the doctor, truly meaning it. "And my work is helping people. If I have done that much in these past few hours, then I have accomplished a great deal."

Now it was my turn to put a hand on his arm, saying, "I don't know how I would have managed without you."

"I must say one thing, Leyla, before you go. It is my duty, as a physician, to report my findings to the police. No, wait. Let me finish. I have to tell them, you know this. But in deference to you and what you must do, I will wait as long as I ethically can before going to them. In the meantime, you have my trust."

Mrs. Finnegan was still disapproving of me as Dr. Young assisted me with my cape. Her eyes held unreserved condemnation of the hours I had spent alone with him, and I wondered if she had possibly overheard our words. I did not care. I was beyond caring about many things: London and Edward belonged in a past that seemed as distant as a dream. Only Colin mattered to me at that moment as I fumbled at the ribbons of my bonnet. Colin and the Pembertons and the duty I had to them.

I shall never forget the smell of the damp leather as we pulled away from the farmhouse or the sound of the rain pelting the carriage. The horse's hooves made dull thuds on the puddled road, sloshing through the mud and drawing us over the ruts and occasional rocks. As the carriage jerked and jolted along the lane, I stared at the horse's bobbing ears, his mane wet and clinging to his neck. Heavily laden branches brushed us as we sped past. Rain fell into the carriage, sprinkling my face and wetting the blanket over my knees. I did not speak. There was nothing to say. The man who handled the reins so deftly at my side remained silent, for there was no need of communication between us. He knew what I was thinking.

Where the road met the unpretentious junction of the drive that led up to the Hurst, I asked Dr. Young to stop the carriage.

"It's only a short way from here, and I wish my family to believe I was only out walking."

He considered this, reluctant to discharge me at such a lonely spot, and said, "Very well, although I think it unwise. Promise me, Leyla, that when you have come to any decision—if indeed you do—then promise me you will let me know before you act."

I smiled at his concern. "I promise you that. And act I must, for we cannot tolerate a murderer among us. Besides, we don't know if he or she will strike again. Three people are dead. Another might soon be."

Dr. Young appeared surprised. This had not occurred to him. "Leyla," he said, his voice heavy with care, "be careful. Please be careful."

"I will, sir. And thank you again for what you did for me this afternoon."

Dr. Young climbed down from the carriage, stood in the mud, and helped me down. His eyes said: Take care. Then he sat and waited until I had walked around the bend and could no longer be seen. As I tramped along a ridge of high ground, trying to keep my skirt hem out of the puddles, I heard the carriage roll off down the lane.

Now that I was at last alone with myself, alone among the trees and rain and gray sky, I was able to make a start at sorting out my thoughts. Colin had primacy in my mind, as he should, as he always would. Yes, I had to admit that Colin was the only one who had benefited from Uncle Henry's death. But that did not necessarily mean he knew beforehand that he would. Motive lay in premeditation, and it was possible that Colin had believed Uncle Henry had had a will, just as Theodore had believed it. If this were so, then it followed that, rather than who did in fact gain by the death, it would be the person who had expected to gain from the death who would be most likely culpable.

This line of thinking seemed most reasonable to me until, as I neared the house, and its turrets appeared above the treetops, I remembered my father's and Sir John's deaths. These did not fit into my comfortable theory, for, if Theo had thought he would gain from his father's death, then what had he hoped for by killing his uncle Robert and grandfather? Besides, he had been away in Manchester when Sir John died.

None of it made sense. Singularly, I could arrive at a motive for each, yet collectively the murders did not make sense. Although they shared in common the same method of execution, a common denominator for motive could not be arrived at.

And it was this quandary that I worried over as, quite wet and red-cheeked, I approached the steps of the house.

Martha, in a surprising show of energy, flung the door open before I could reach it. Her eyes were bright, glassy, and gaped at me in a most peculiar way. "Leyla!" she said breathlessly. "Where have you been! No one knew you went out! We've been home hours and positively worried for you!"

"I was walking," I said simply, being certain she could not see Willis's book under my cape.

"Grandmother's absolutely livid. I have never seen her so angry! She's been waiting for you—"

"Why? What am I supposed to have done now?"

"Come in, Leyla. No, no, don't go to your room. She's in the parlor. We *all* are."

"But I'm wet through."

"A hazard of walking in the rain," she said with a sharpness I had not thought her capable of. "Now come along or be in even worse graces with her."

Not to be cowed, I let Martha hurry off in her swishing crinoline and bombazine mourning dress while I took care to remove my cape and bonnet and gloves. Pressing my cold fingers against my cheeks, I felt how hot they were, and I knew they must be as bright as apples.

Just as I somehow intuitively knew my father had not been a murderer, so did a vague prescience in the back of my mind assure me Colin was also innocent. With this conviction firmly resolved in my heart and with Willis's book carefully concealed behind my back, I marched stoically into the parlor.

The usual arrangement in Grandmother's presence was again put into practice with her, stiff and unmoving, sitting at the center, Anna and Martha seated before her, and Theo standing between them. Colin was not there.

Unlike my aunt and cousin, I did not sit, preferring to stand defiantly. The mood was there, hanging over all of us as it dominated the entire house. Grandmother's austerity, her lack of warmth, her abstentious aversion to mirth and conviviality. A pragmatic woman, dealing with life as a Spartan, she dominated this house and her family with a severity that touched upon tyranny.

"Where have you been?" she demanded suddenly, crustily. Her tiny black eyes drove right through me,

"I have been out walking, Grandmother."

"On a day of mourning? Where is your respect, child?"

"We all mourn in our own fashion, Grandmother."

"Don't be cheeky with me, mistress. I am in no mood for your cockiness. Indeed, I am quite angry and put out with something that happened today." She pressed her lips together, driving the blood out of them until they were hard and white. "We have a thief in our house!" she nearly shouted. "I will not tolerate criminals."

I almost smiled at this, thinking of the possible murderer in our midst, yet I was self-controlled enough to hold myself in check. I had never before witnessed the full wrath of this formidable woman and was not about to invite it now. "Am I being accused again of something?" I asked coldly.

"I never accuse, young lady. That is a trait of weaklings. I want this to stop, whoever is doing it. For I intend to see that it is not gotten away with. The crime occurred this morning during the funeral service and was discovered upon everyone's return. The theft was again of jewelry, a valuable necklace and brooch, taken from my daughter-in-law's room while she was paying last respects to her husband."

I glanced at Aunt Anna as she sat in the *prie-dieu* like the victim of some horrible crime. Her face white and drawn, her eyes staring dazedly ahead of her; my aunt seemed highly agitated and nervous.

"How do you know they were taken this morning?" I asked.

Grandmother's face adjusted itself into a disagreeable frown. I was doubting her credibility. "Anna said they were there before she left and not there when she returned. What I want to know from you, young lady, is where you walked to this afternoon."

Our eyes locked again as if they were antlers in a clash of wills. I refused to be dominated by this headstrong woman. I also thought of what Dr. Young told me—that Uncle Henry had been murdered—and I decided I was not ready to publicize my discovery. Not yet. Not until I could be sure I would be free from danger, which, at the moment, I was not. In the next decisive minute, I was spared from having to answer her by the interruption of a sixth person.

"A gathering of the clan is it?" came the voice.

I turned as Colin entered the room, and my heart gave a sudden leap. This was a new sensation to me, at once confusing and pleasurable. His eyes passed over the others, alighting only fleetingly upon Martha, Theo, and Aunt Anna—a brief, searching, wandering look—until they finally rested upon me, and then the scantest flicker of a smile jerked up the corners of his mouth. For an instant, for the scarcest moment, our eyes locked, and I thought—prayed with all my heart—that Colin felt the same, fleet exaltation.

Grandmother's expression did not change, but her mood altered subtly and so with it the atmosphere of the room. This I could not understand: Colin was not a Pemberton, yet the entire inheritance had gone to him.

He took a few long strides and was across the room, almost at my side. His manner was flippant, offhanded, as though he hadn't the slightest care in the world.

"Aunt Anna's gone and lost her favorite necklace, has she?"

Grandmother became even grimmer. "Not lost, Colin, but stolen. A person of low character went into her room while she was away this morning. There were only two people here at the time. Martha and Leyla."

"And yourself, Grandmother dear."

Her eyes flashed like balls of black fire. "And myself."

"And the servants as well."

"I have questioned them—"

"You might also search their quarters."

"I will not suffer your belligerence, Colin Pemberton." While her voice did not rise, Grandmother's chest began to labor. "How I conduct this investigation is my affair. In fact, I have already searched Leyla's room."

"How dare you!" I exploded. My body took a step forward; I became rigid and would have let forth a rush of invectives had my hand not suddenly been seized by Colin. Although he did not look at me but continued to smile abstractly at Grandmother, I felt a communication pass between our fingers.

"I warned you days ago, mistress, to leave this house and never come back," continued Grandmother. "Yet you are muleheaded, a stubborn ass, and now pay the consequences. There is no right of privacy in this house where the welfare of the family is concerned. The value of the jewels is inconsequential. It is the principle of the thing."

"Aren't we perhaps being a bit emotional, considering the recent death in the family?" said Colin.

Now Theo, standing not far from us, startled me by suddenly whipping about and shouting, "Damn you, sir! What do you care about my father's death!"

Colin remained unperturbed. "That is irrelevant, Cousin. What matters here is that you've all gathered to sit in judgment upon Leyla." He gave my hand a squeeze. "Judge, jury, and hangman—the lot of you. I for one don't find it sporting or English."

"What you think, sir, means damn little to me—"

"May I remind you there are ladies present?"

"A fact that you, sir, have never before taken into account."

"Really, Theodore—"

Theo threw his shoulders back. "I'm damned if I'm going to take any more from you, sir. I shall have my satisfaction."

Colin's ability to remain undaunted during the row amazed me. I had expected this man of passions to lose control of himself and fly into a rage, yet he did not. It was almost as if he were baiting Theodore, manipulating him and being master of the entire affair.

"I have," came his calm voice, "offered you one-half of the inheritance."

"Hang the inheritance!"

"And complete control of the mills."

"You insult me, Cousin." There was fury in Theodore's eyes, in his clenched fists. "I want no charity. What I come by will be gotten legally. And that, sir, is a promise."

Now I finally looked up at Colin to see his casual profile and lackadaisical manner. Was he serious in his offer to Theo, to give him fully one-half of the inheritance unconditionally?

"I will gladly sign any papers you wish," he went on. "You may have full ownership of the mills if you want."

"I do not happen to trust you, Colin, or any papers your solicitor might draw up. I intend to go to London and fight this myself."

"Really, Theo, it's not necessary—"

"Quiet, both of you!"

We snapped our heads toward Grandmother. Her hands, those long bamboo fingers bespotted with brown, trembled as they clutched the arms of the chair. "I will not have dissension among my family. And I will not have my husband's wishes disobeyed. Sir John was in sound mind when he wrote his testament. He must have had good reason for leaving it all to Colin. I forbid this bickering over the Pemberton estate; it debases our name and dishonors yourselves. And I forbid, gentlemen, any further debate on the subject. Now I wish you all dismissed. You've tired me. I am weary to death of you."

Theodore continued to glower angrily as Colin turned to me and murmured, "May I escort you upstairs?"

"Yes," I barely whispered.

The two of us glided from the room as if exiting a dreary dinner party, and I felt two pairs of eyes piercing our backs.

As we began to mount the stairs, I withdrew my hand finally to lift my skirt as we ascended; behind my back I still held Thom Willis's book. We went up in silence, this enigmatic man and I, and I felt I was not in an ordinary presence. With the gaslight barely illuminating our way, I sensed Colin's nearness, his warmth and relaxed air. So unlike that Edward I had known ages ago, this once-cousin of mine took easy steps, swinging his arms insouciantly.

At the top, he stopped me, taking my arms and turning his delving gaze upon me. They're devils, Leyla, to accuse you of thievery."

I bowed my head, for his tone had moved me. Yet I was unconcerned with Grandmother's accusations, for they were nothing compared with what I had learned during my hours with Dr. Young. Had it only been this afternoon?

I raised my eyes to meet Colin's, marveling at this new electricity within my body that I had never before experienced in the company of a man. His hair was slightly mismanaged, his cravat a little off-center. Yet I loved him for it, for his humanness, for his imperfections and shortcomings. And I wondered how he felt about me.

"We'll all be supping alone tonight, Leyla. I'll have Gertrude send you up something good."

"Thank you."

He stared at me a moment longer, seemed about to say something, but then, changing his mind, suddenly turned on his heel and hurried back down the stairs.

I wasted no time in changing into my nightdress and dressing gown, brushing my hair until it hung straight and long, and curling up before the fire with my thoughts. As promised, Gertrude arrived with a tray. There was something odd about her manner, as if she were being extremely cautious or wary. I asked after her health, but she did not reply, coming and going in a silence that seemed somehow ominous.

The meal was followed by a cup of hot milk brought up by a maid, and I drank it down thankfully, knowing how it would relax me.

Then I began to think. There were so many questions flurrying through my mind. What was this trouble with stolen jewelry, and how did it affect me? Who had wanted to bring my mother and me here by sending a letter in Sylvia's name? Who had destroyed my letter to Edward? And who was the woman I had overheard crying in Grandmother's room the morning of Uncle Henry's death?

These were queries without answers. Puzzles in themselves, or perhaps pieces to a much larger enigma. Somehow, I felt sure, they all fit in . . .

I rested back and stared into the generous fire as it warmed my face and crackled comfortingly. All these tiny mysteries fitted into the larger one, the most important of all, the one mystery I had tried to solve from the very beginning: Who had killed my father and brother in the coppice?

And here the only answer lay in my memory. I had to return again and again, hoping that I might stumble upon the correct ingredients that would restore that day exactly—such factors as weather, sunlight, time of day, or even time of year, which might suddenly draw aside the curtain that hid my past and reveal everything to me.

My head started to throb. Impatient with this sensitivity I had never before exhibited, I began to pace the room. In Cremorne Gardens, I had suffered the loud explosions of pyrotechnic displays. On the narrow street where I lived, I had existed daily with the noise and clatter of the many carriages, horses' hooves, and street criers. When my mother finally expired, I had endured the grief stoically, without the usual fits of faint and malaise other young women oft come down with. So why now? Why, after all these years of being strong and fit, was I suddenly beset with endless headaches? Dr. Young had said they were due to tension. Yet I did not feel tense. And now my stomach was slightly upset, as it had been this morning, as though my attacks were growing worse.

As I stood before my looking glass and was about to decant a large dose of laudanum, I caught sight of the reflection of my hands at work. For some unexplainable reason, seeing them made me stop. Something, somewhere at the back of my mind, was struggling to come through. I looked at my glass. Then at the phial Dr. Young had given me. Then, as in a cloudburst, his words came rushing back into my mind: "The digitalis in your uncle's blood was far from medicinal. It had been ingested as a poison . . . administered to him bit by bit and then countered with laudanum."

I froze in horror.

His voice continued: "Headaches, nausea, abdominal pain . . . are all part of a syndrome of an illness quite different from a brain tumor."

"My God!" I cried aloud, letting both glass and phial thump to the floor, "Dear God! I'm being poisoned!"

Now I ran back to the easy chair, sank into it, and buried my face in my hands. "It can't be," I murmured over and over again. "It can't be. Oh God . . . Think back, Leyla. Try to think back."

But the evidence, as far as I was concerned, was conclusive. My headaches had begun shortly after I had found Edward's letter in the fireplace.

And they had continued every day for six days. Each time, I could easily remember, the headache had begun almost immediately after drinking something. The tea at breakfast, poured before I was there. Wine at dinner, poured by someone else. Hot milk at bedtime brought to my room.

It was beyond a doubt that I, too, was now receiving the same treatment as had been given Uncle Henry, and I was equally certain that, if I were to take some of my morning tea to Dr. Young, he would find it contained the extract of the foxglove plant.

To my previous anger and determination was now added fear, a sick, debilitating fear that made me tremble from head to foot and embrace myself with my arms.

Who was it? cried my terrified mind. Which of my relatives wanted me dead, and why?

CHAPTER 15

I SLEPT VERY BADLY THAT NIGHT, TORMENTED BY GROTESQUE nightmares and gripping fears. Also, having dropped the laudanum to the floor, I had to suffer the full effects of the digitalis all night long—the pounding headache, the stomach upset, and finally abdominal pains. When a maid brought breakfast, I said nothing to her but waited until she was quite gone before pouring some of the tea in the tiny bottle that had contained laudanum. Before this, I had washed and dried it thoroughly to be certain it was clean, and I had emptied the rest of the tea into the fire. Knowing what I suspected, and depressed and angry because of it, I did not eat the toast or ham either.

I waited until noon before leaving the house, knowing that by now everyone was accustomed to my afternoon walks and thought nothing odd of it. Aunt Anna was up in her room with a touch of the vapors, while Theo and Martha were quietly engaged in the parlor: one reading, the other knitting. Colin was nowhere about.

Wondering what he did with all his time, I struck out again along the lane, the phial grasped securely in my gloved hands. I knew that Colin went riding a lot and so guessed that was where he must be.

Eventually, I came upon Dr. Young's house.

His blue eyes lost some of their luster as he re-entered the drawing room, buttoning his double-breasted frock coat. The gravity in his face was familiar; I had seen it the day before when he came up from his laboratory. Therefore, I was not at all surprised when he said, "You're right, Leyla; there's enough digitalis in the tea to make you very ill."

"I see." I twisted my gloves in my hands. "So one of my family—or perhaps all of them—had expected me to be prostrate with sickness today. Perhaps he or she had expected to find me moaning in my bed and crying that the tumor was destroying me."

"It was clever of you to bring me the tea. Now we can go to the police—"

"No!"

"Leyla, we have incontrovertible proof—"

"Please, sir, I want no police. Then my life will be in danger."

"And you think it is not now?"

"Well, at least for the time being, I can pretend that I am ill, to give myself time to remember the past." When I had first arrived with the tea, I had told Dr. Young of my determination to remember what I had seen that day 20 years ago. "When the memory returns, then we will go to the police."

"But it might be too late then."

"That is a chance I must take."

"You're a brave girl, Leyla."

I gave a grim laugh. "Another man would call it recklessness. Thank you for your support, Dr. Young, and thank you for the tea and cakes. I daresay I shall eat less now . . ."

"Then stay and have supper with me, Leyla. It can get lonely in this house sometimes, even with my experiments and books."

But I said softly, "You know I must go, sir. But I shall be by again. And next time, hopefully, to ask you to accompany me to the constable in East Wimsley."

Since the afternoon was still new and I desired to be alone with my thoughts, Dr. Young reluctantly let me go by myself. After giving my promise to come to him at once should any danger be imminent, I struck off down the road with great fear and foreboding.

Someone in that house wanted me dead. Someone in that house was trying right now to murder me. But why? Why had I been lured back here from London with that spurious letter to be a murder victim? Who would do such a thing?

Uncle Henry was now stricken from the list of suspects. Could it be his wife? Although she had tried in her polite and matronly way, Aunt Anna had never really succeeded in making me feel welcome or liked. I had made her nervous at first; then she had seemed to politely withdraw from me as though I no longer existed.

Grandmother Abigail had certainly not been pleased with my arrival and had voiced it more than once. Indeed, she above the others had actively tried to drive me back to London as soon as possible. No, there was no love in her bony breast for me, but then I doubt she spared any on anyone. Theodore was my next possibility, always kind toward me, always going out of his way to be a gentleman and a cousin. If he had murderous designs upon me, they were artfully hidden and concealed behind superlative manners.

Martha? She had genuinely liked me from the start, a naive and innocent woman, still a child in so many ways, and very far from seeming capable of murder.

Since I placed Colin above suspicion and I did not think of Gertrude or the servants, this could leave only the four: Anna, Theodore, Grandmother, and Martha. If one of these wanted to see me dead and had indeed even lured me here from London just for the purpose of killing me, then try though I might, tromping through the trees that gray afternoon, I could not think of a single possible motive for any of them.

The house was still and deathlike when I entered. It seemed to hover about me, holding its breath, almost as if it were waiting . . . I did not hurry up to my room but went slowly in case I should meet one of my family. It could be valuable to read their faces at finding I've been out for a walk after such a large dose of digitalis. The innocent ones would betray nothing, but the guilty party might, hopefully, exhibit surprise.

Unfortunately, I ran into no one and arrived at my room without incident. My hands shook as I undid the bows of my bonnet, for fear was beginning to rule my body. How long could I endure this?

A knock at my door caused me to jump. But when I opened it and found Colin grinning on the other side, I relaxed at once.

"Been out, have you?"

"I find country walks more refreshing than the Serpentine."

"This is such a dreary house, Cousin, I was wondering if you'd join me in a glass of sherry."

"I should love it."

We strolled down the stairs without speaking, straining our eyes in that peculiar light that is caused when it is too dark outside for sufficient light to be shed inside, yet still too light to warrant turning on the gas lamps. He led me to the parlor, the cluttered family room that was rife with the pillows and laces and samplers of Martha's nimble fingers, and drew me before the fire.

"It's a biting winter we've had, and a beast of a spring." Colin decanted the wine with ease and assurance, as though he alone were free from the oppression and tension that hovered above us. I watched his hands, tanned and rough, not milky as Edward's had been.

"This is special wine," he said with a sly grin. "Taken from Grandmother's special shelf. Serves it to no one but herself. She'd invoke the Devil upon us if she knew this. Here."

I took the glass and stared into the sparkling liquid. Colin watched me. "Aren't you going to drink it?"

"Yes, of course." It tasted sweet and smooth, certainly better than I had ever had before.

While we sipped, standing close to the fire and simply enjoying one another's company, Colin continued to stare at me in a way that, if he were someone else, would have unnerved me. But instead, because it was my dear Colin, I returned his gaze, boldly, unabashed.

"Leyla," he said suddenly, putting his glass down. "I've been trying to make a decision. And I've finally reached it. I want to talk with you."

"Very well." The sudden gravity in his voice made my smile fade away.

"But not here. What I have to say is quite private, and I would not wish one of our family members to happen in on us. Will you accompany me to a more suitable place?"

I looked at my glass. I had drained it empty. "Of course, Colin."

I followed him from the parlor and back up the stairs where he picked up a small candle from a papier-mâché table and lit it at one of the oil lamps in the hall. When we proceeded to then go up another flight of stairs, I became mildly surprised, yet did not question him. Being with Colin was all that mattered; his presence was comforting, reassuring.

We entered a darker hallway where the only illumination came from our little candle, and I let my cousin take my hand to lead me along. When the stale air and musty odors assailed my nose, I remembered this place as being the one I had run along the night of Uncle Henry's death, when everyone had followed him to the turret. My breath was shallow, for I was growing apprehensive in the dark amid these unpleasant odors, yet I did not question our actions, for I was certain Colin had good reason for bringing me here.

I was not surprised, therefore, when we eventually stopped before the little curtained arch that opened onto the steps going up to the turret. Memories of that other night caused me to shiver. Colin was watching me closely, not speaking, the flickering flame lighting up his face in a most peculiar way.

"It has to be like this, Leyla," he said in a whisper. "I'm sorry."

I watched his eyes, the color of light lettuce.

"We mustn't be overheard, and Grandmother has spies everywhere. Will you be comfortable here?"

I peered up into the darkness as the narrow steps disappeared around a curve. Colin's hand was tight about my own, squeezing all feeling from it. I licked my dry lips and tasted the special wine he had given me.

"No, not at all. I understand. It must be important, what you have to say."

"It is, believe me. I am glad you trust me, Leyla. I was afraid you wouldn't. Shall we go up?"

He preceded me with the light, taking each step slowly and carefully, while he continued to hold my hand with a grip I could not have escaped from. Curiosity surpassed my apprehension; what was so important Colin had to tell me that no other spot in the house was private enough?

We reached the top, and I shuddered again as, for an instant, Uncle Henry's insane face and wild pleadings flashed before me. Colin placed the candle on the stony floor—far enough away from my skirts for safety, yet close enough to give us a bit of light. The turret was a small, round room, damp and chilly, with one window looking out at the nighttime forest. These funny little ornamental rooms—the house had several—served no other purpose than external decorations, so that they were never used and certainly were not furnished.

"This is where Sir John killed himself," said Colin cryptically as he now took hold of my other hand. I could not see his face, and his tone was unreadable.

"Is this what you brought me here to tell me?"

There was a pause. "No, Leyla, this is not why I brought you here." Colin's voice grew strangely detached. "I want you to know that I have given a great deal of thought to what I am going to do next, so that you know I do not do it easily. Indeed, it is something that has been on my mind, almost as an obsession, since the morning you told us you had read Thomas Willis's book. Do you remember?"

"Yes, I do."

"I was very disturbed by your behavior that morning and have been so ever since. Several times before this, I had thought to confront you with it, only to change my mind for one reason or another. But now . . ." His voice dropped even lower, barely above a whisper, and he took a step closer to me. I gazed up into Colin's eyes with limitless fascination—excited by his nearness, anxious to hear what he had to say.

As if reading my thoughts, he said, "I shan't delay any longer in telling you why I've brought you here." He looked around in the darkness beyond our tiny circle of light. "There can't be anyone around to overhear. No one knows we are up here, Leyla. This turret is far from the nucleus of the house. If you were to make a loud noise, say, a scream, no one would hear."

"Why should I want to scream?"

"It was only an example. I am emphasizing the need for privacy. I don't want anyone to know we are here. We are cut off from the rest of the family. I have done it on purpose, for I don't want anyone to know what happened here tonight."

"You know you have my confidence, Colin."

He seemed to smile at this, twisting his mouth in an eerie fashion as we stood suspended in the night. No sound could be heard, no movement save the dancing shadows from our flickering candle. He and I were completely alone and separated from the rest of the world.

"Leyla." He squeezed my hands even tighter. "I know you haven't cared for me up to now and that you surely have not trusted me. I cannot blame you. But I must ask, no, *beg* for your complete trust now, that you will have faith in me no matter what happens."

I was mesmerized by his voice and by his eyes. "Yes," I barely whispered.

"Then you will also forgive me for what I am about to do next, as I fear it will be painful."

A little confused, I said, "I would forgive you anything, Colin."

"Then I shall go ahead." He released my hands and at once took hold of my shoulders. His grip was tight, hard. "I am asking you, Leyla, to return to the way you were before and try once again to remember what happened 20 years ago in the coppice."

At first I did not react, but as his words sank in, my mouth fell open, and I said a flat, "What?"

"I asked you to forgive me and you said you would. Painful as it might be for you, Leyla, I want you to bring back your memory of the coppice and your father's death."

I was stunned, taken aback. "But I don't understand. Why?"

"For the reason that . . ."

I searched his face. There was something new there. "Please go on!"

"For the reason that I believe your father was murdered and I must know by whom."

"Colin!"

"I know what you're thinking, that it's no use to—"

"No, wait—"

"Let me finish, Leyla." His eyes grew wide and animated. "I never believed your father committed suicide, yet I had no evidence. And I could not speak up because this family hates me. Oh, Leyla, I know what a shock all of this must be to you, after I've played their game and pretended all along with them. When you suddenly showed up one evening after 20 years, you were like an answer to my prayers. And when you announced your determination to remember the past, I was alive again. You gave hope back to me. I was with you all along, from the very beginning, and anxious for you to remember it all. But when you suddenly declared the fight over, that because of that wretched book you had given up, I was devastated. You were my only hope to clear the Pemberton name." His eyes penetrated mine as his voice rose. "I know you no longer desire to remember the events you witnessed as a child, but I'm asking you now to try again, as a favor to me."

"Colin, I'm confused. I don't know what to say."

"You know about the tumor now, and you believe your father committed suicide after killing your brother. Wait, let me finish. I am asking you to go back to the way you were before you found Willis's book and try again to remember. I think your father was innocent."

"And you haven't told the others?"

"I can't. I can't. They don't listen to me, Leyla; they—"

My voice was a coarse whisper. "Why does the family hate you, Colin?"

He stared at me a moment, then suddenly released my shoulders and let his hands drop to his sides. "For a reason that I should have told you long before this."

"What is that?"

"I'm not a Pemberton, Leyla, at least not in blood. My mother was a widow when Richard Pemberton married her and brought us both here. If my true father, a ship's captain, had lived, my name today would be Colin Haverson, and I'd be living in Kent."

"Why should they hate you for that?"

"Because I am free from the Pemberton tumor."

"Oh, Colin . . ." I breathed. "This is all happening so fast."

"Long ago, Sir John took an uncommon liking to me, changing his will so that I would be his sole heir. But I knew nothing about Uncle Henry's lost will, Leyla; I swear it!"

"I believe you."

His eyes roamed my face, my hair, my shoulders as if he were seeing me for the first time. "You do . . ."

"How strange," I whispered, "that you should be telling me these things."

"Then you will do as I ask? I know how confusing it must be for you, thinking that I too had wanted to keep you from remembering, yet in truth hoping you would.

"Oh, there's more than that, Colin, much more." My face broadened into a smile. I suddenly felt like laughing. "You cannot imagine what a relief it is to be able to tell you these things."

"What things?"

"Things I have found out. Important, crucial things that I've had to keep to myself. But now I need not carry the burden alone, for I can share it with you."

"Then you've remembered!"

"No, no. Not yet. Although I want to, and not just because you've asked me to. You have no idea what it's been like for me, Colin, keeping everything inside me."

"What is it? What have you found out?"

I took my time, telling him about my first visit to Dr. Young's house, careful to leave nothing out, and when I reached the part about the page being bogus, he blurted, "Good God!" As I continued on, telling him my own reactions of the time and what had gone through my mind, I also included Dr. Young's reactions and ideas. It was when I came to the part about Uncle Henry's blood containing lethal amounts of foxglove that Colin spun away from me and slammed a fist against the stone wall.

"Hell and damnation!" he cried. "So it's true then, and I was right all along!" Colin stopped suddenly, glaring at me from the darkness. Although I could not see his face, I could hear his heavy, uneven breathing and imagined what his expression must be. "But then—" he began uncertainly. "The tumor . . . Leyla, the tumor . . ." He took a halting step toward me. "Do you mean . . . it's a lie? *That there is no Pemberton tumor?*"

"It's true, Colin"

"My God. No tumor, no Pemberton Curse."

"That is what Dr. Young and I discovered."

"My God," he whispered again, his voice totally incredulous. "I can't believe it. I didn't know . . ." Colin began to pace the small room, coming into the light and then disappearing from it again. "It's unbelievable! After all these years! The tumor . . . a lie! For years and years, decades even, *centuries—*" He slapped the wall again. "Sir John and Uncle Robert and Uncle Henry. So I was right all along, your father *was* murdered. Leyla!" He swung about to regard me. His face half in shadow, half illuminated, Colin suddenly cried, "Then you! You're free from the curse! You have no brain tumor!"

"Yes—"

I do not know exactly what happened next, for all I remember is Colin's arms suddenly around me and my face buried in his neck. The embrace was hard and strong with a passion to match his voice. Although stunned by his move, I felt natural in Colin's arms, not at all awkward—as though I belonged there and always would. I felt his warmth and his strength as he conveyed more to me through his touch than words ever could.

We stood thus for some time, our bodies locked and arms entwined, until he eventually whispered, "My dearest Leyla, you don't know how it's been for me. These past few days . . . seeing you, loving you, and yet knowing all the while that you must eventually succumb to the horror of the Pemberton fate. I would sit and watch you across the dining table or across a room, my love for you increasing with each hour, trying to bear the agony of the future that awaited you. I was so embittered, so angry."

He drew me away from him a little and stroked my hair as he gazed down at me. His eyes were glistening. "I didn't know what to do. I had fallen in love with a woman who could never be mine. The pain of it was unbearable. But now you're free. We are both suddenly free from the wretched curse that has possessed this house for generations. Oh, Leyla, my Leyla."

He looked down in tenderness for a moment longer, then suddenly his face changed, clouded over, and twisted into a frown. Just as quickly as he had seized me, Colin released me and fell back. "Good God!" he exploded for the third time. "Please forgive me, mistress! I wasn't thinking! In my joy at hearing the news, I forgot myself. I must apologize for my behavior, and I wouldn't blame you if you were to slap my face!"

"Why should I do that?" My heart was soaring. I wanted to laugh and cry at the same time.

"I've blundered most terribly and have taken advantage of your weakness. Believe me, mistress, I am not in the habit of assaulting young women. I was momentarily—"

Finally I had to laugh. "Oh, Colin, I don't care what you're in the habit of doing. And if you are a blunderer, then I love you all the more for it."

He stared at me in disbelief.

I had even amazed myself—not by what I had said, but how easily I had said it. "I do love you, Colin," I whispered.

He rushed to embrace me again, and this time we were joined in a kiss—one that was both electrifying and tender at the same time. It seemed *so* natural that we should do this, standing embraced in the turret, kissing in a way I had never been kissed before. Nothing else mattered. Not the false tumor, nor the murderer, nor all the unraveled mysteries at Pemberton Hurst.

When he stepped back to regard me again, I saw a new light shine through Colin's eyes. His whole face had changed; it was softer, smoother, as though even his character had been altered. "I cannot believe this is happening to me. To suddenly have little Leyla in my arms, to be kissing her is like a dream realized. Never did I think I would fall in love. I had thought I would remain a cynical bachelor all my life. And then you were there, a phantom from the past, standing on our doorstep." He gently laid a hand along my cheek. "Do you recall your first words to me? You said, 'Aunt Anna told me to meet you in here and avoid at all costs running into eccentric Colin, which would be a disaster.'"

"I was devastated!"

"And the expression on your face! It will remain forever enshrined in my memory as a classic. I had never thought a person could turn red *and* pale at the same time."

"Oh, Colin . . ."

He drew me to him again and embraced me with a fierceness that stopped my breath short. "I shall not lose you again," he whispered harshly.

"Twenty years ago, you disappeared from me without a trace, but now you are back and you are here to stay! Nothing can tear us asunder, Leyla, for we were brought together by God."

I rested contentedly in his arms, listening to the power of his voice. If this were a dream come true for him, then it was the end of a nightmare for me. With Colin at my side, I needed no longer live in fear for my life or carry the burden of my knowledge alone.

"What good deed had I done in my worthless past," he was saying against my ear, "that caused God to deliver you to me two weeks ago?"

These words brought me sharply back to reality.

The joy, the excitement of Colin's touch had made me forget for the moment that there was more I must tell him.

"Colin, I haven't finished. It was no coincidence that I came to Pemberton Hurst when I did. I came because of a letter."

"Letter?" Colin stood all the way back from me now but still held my hands. I explained briefly about the letter supposedly from Aunt Sylvia requesting my mother and me to come visit her. I explained how it had arrived shortly before Mother's death and how I had discovered the letter had not been written by Sylvia at all.

"But I don't understand. Do you mean someone in this house actually *lured* you here under false pretenses? Why use Aunt Sylvia?"

"My own guess is that it was because she was dying and therefore a convenient instrument. Whoever wrote the letter did not want his or her identity known, for now that I am here, that person is pretending to want me to leave. But who could it be, Colin?"

He pondered this. "You'll have to show me the letter and possibly I can recognize the hand. Still, who would want you here and not identify himself?"

"Well . . ." I hesitated, uncertain of how to impart the next news. "There's something else, Colin, that you must know. It's a matter of the foxglove extract that killed Uncle Henry. I, too, began to suffer from headaches, so, on an intuition, I secretly took some of my morning tea to Dr. Young for analysis."

We both hung suspended in the air—his hands gripping mine till they were numb, his eyes delving deep into mine. "And what did he find?"

"That I, too, am being given the extract."

"Christ!" he exploded, startling me. "Hell and damnation! Leyla, I've got to get you out of this house!"

"Colin—"

"And forgive my language, but I cannot stand on formalities now! This is unbelievable! How little I knew of what was going on before my eyes. I brought you here to ask you to try again to remember your past, as you had once been determined to. I had expected you to argue with me, to think my theory preposterous, and in the end to give in reluctantly. Instead, I find you had already made the decision to remember that day at the coppice, that not only was your father murdered, as I had suspected, but Uncle Henry and Sir John as well, and that you are the next victim of this brutal murderer. Leyla!" He seized my shoulders again. "I want you to go away at once. Let me send you to London."

"No, Colin," I said softly.

"It is not necessary for you to endanger yourself. I'll work on it myself and join you afterward—"

"Colin, please, I must stay."

His eyes were hard, angry. "I cannot let you."

"And I cannot go." I softened my voice yet held my ground. "We have so much information, Colin, yet we remain ignorant. The one vital piece of knowledge is denied us—the identity of the murderer. And we both know that that detail is locked inside my mind, buried along with the rest of my childhood memory, as if behind a heavy curtain. It remains for me to draw that curtain aside. And I can never do it in London."

Colin glowered at me in frustration, his fingers digging deep into my flesh. There was no denying the truth of what I said, yet his emotions—so patent on his face—argued against it.

"I'm not in danger," I said gently, "as long as I do not reveal awareness of being poisoned. I must continue to act the part, pretend headaches and illness until I make the one visit to the coppice that tells us all the answers. It is only if the murderer were to learn I've discovered his plan—"

"Or hers."

"—that I am in danger. Otherwise, we have time."

I heard Colin's heavy breathing in the darkness. Our little candle flame had shrunk so that its light could hardly do battle with the shadows. "How much time?" he asked thickly. "You remembered nothing on your first visit. How many times must you go back?"

I weighed my words before answering. "There was one thing . . . that I did not tell you. At the coppice, when I stood alone among the trees, a very brief image flashed in my mind."

"What was it?"

"It might have nothing at all to do with it—"

"And yet it could be extremely important. What did you remember?"

"Not remember exactly, but a quick image such as one gets during a flash of lightning. In my mind, I saw the ruby ring Theo wears."

Colin stiffened perceptibly. "Ring?" he said distantly. "That's odd."

"I thought so. It must really have nothing to do with my father's death, and yet it did come to mind in the coppice. I might have dismissed it altogether had it not been for the fact that the ring has mysteriously disappeared."

"I am sure that is only a coincidence," he said unconvincingly. Although I could not see his face, I had the distinct impression that Colin was suddenly disturbed.

"May I ask you something?"

With obvious effort, he brought himself out of his thoughts to regard me.

"Why were you so certain my father was innocent? I would think that with Willis's book and the brain-tumor story, you would have accepted the explanation like everyone else. Yet you did not. Did you doubt the veracity of the Pemberton tumor?"

"Not at all. I have accepted—rather, I *had* accepted it—just as everyone else does, and believed Sir John and Uncle Henry died of it and that you and Martha and Theo were just as doomed as they. Yet your father was the one exception, because of a small detail about his death that no one knows. Indeed, were it not for this one small item, I too would have explained away his death as tumor-caused and not been obsessed all these years with the idea he was murdered."

"What detail was that, Colin?"

He seemed to consider his next words. Then he said, "You were not the only person in the coppice that day, Leyla, when your father and brother died. There was someone else, a fourth party."

"Who?"

"Me."

I heard myself make a sound in my throat. Then I stretched my eyes in utter surprise. "You!" I whispered.

"Yes, I was there in the coppice, too, Leyla, and was present when your father and Thomas were killed."

"Then you saw!"

"No, I did not." He spoke quickly, breathlessly. "I had been scavenging in the wood nearby when I heard little Thomas cry out. Thinking him to be hurt, I ran at once toward the direction of the sound but arrived too late. Entering the coppice, I found you standing among the bushes peering out with a peculiar expression. Then I heard a dull sound, as of someone falling to the ground, and when I, too, looked I saw your father lying next to your brother. At the same time, there was a rustling nearby, someone running away through the trees. I went after, but could not glimpse who it was."

"You saw the murderer!"

"In a manner of speaking, yes. But all I really saw was an indefinable form and the movement of branches. Whoever it was made good the escape."

"Didn't you tell someone?"

"Who, Leyla? Who could I have gone to? I was 14 years old and frightened to death. For the first time in my life, I saw a dead person. It shocked me, scared me. Who could I run to? All I knew was that someone at Pemberton Hurst had committed two murders. How did I know that the person I was running to wasn't the murderer himself, who would then turn around and kill me, too? Where, Leyla! Where could I have gone? All these years, 20 long and lonely years, I have lived with this horrible secret locked in my heart, sitting at the dining table with my family and wondering all the while . . . which of them had done it!"

"Colin," I whispered, a single tear trickling down my cheek.

"And then suddenly, out of nowhere, you appeared at our doorstep like an Angel of Retribution. I thought my prayers had been answered!"

"But why didn't you tell me all this from the very first!"

"I couldn't, Leyla. You didn't trust me. How could I have poured all this out to you and have expected you to believe me? It was my word against the family's. And besides, I needed the remembrance to come from you, free from any distortions I might put in your mind. I coaxed you a little, gave you hints to start you on the right path, but could not reveal it all to you lest you be fired with imaginings and mistake them for real memory. Tell me, Leyla, would you have trusted me back then?"

"I . . . I don't know. It's all fantastic. Who would have done it, Colin? Have you no ideas, no suspects?"

"There are many." He turned away and started pacing again. "I've lain awake at night wondering, trying to figure it out. The motives are there, surely. My own father or Uncle Henry could have done it simply as a way to increase their share of the inheritance. Sir John was old, and his three sons would divide up the estate. With your father dead, it left more for the remaining two brothers. Yes, they had motives. But it couldn't have been Henry, for now *he* is dead. And it couldn't have been my father, for he was killed many years ago, and since then two more deaths have occurred."

"Very well, the three sons of Sir John were victims and not suspects. Had you thought of Theo? Could he have a motive?"

Colin stopped suddenly and stared at me. "Did Theo have a motive? Leyla, he above all had the most to gain from your father's death. But then you don't know this."

"Know what?"

"That Theodore was in love with your mother."

I fell back a step. "What!"

Colin's face grew distant, his voice detached. "Theo was 18 at the time and your mother 25. God, but Aunt Jenny was beautiful. Our cousin did nothing to hide his feelings for her, or the fact that he was embittered with your father for being her husband. Theodore loathed your father, Leyla, and everyone knew it."

"How strange . . ." I was thinking of that evening almost a week ago when Theo had come to my room. He had been so odd with me, so curiously gentle and sentimental, speaking of the way my mother had worn her hair. I understood it now, that strange manner.

"And Aunt Anna? She was a possessive, domineering mother and was blind to her son's faults. Maybe she thought Theo should have Jennifer. Or maybe she held a grudge against your father for unknown reasons. It's possible Aunt Anna also wanted the inheritance to be shared by fewer brothers and so killed your father so that her own husband would have more. It's possible."

"And Martha?"

"She was only 12 at the time. Capable, I suppose, but highly improbable."

"There is also Grandmother Abigail."

"Yes, there is. And not beyond murder, I suspect, if driven to it. But why would she kill her only three sons? She loved Uncle Robert very much; that was apparent. And she was fond of Jenny. Grandmother wanted the estate to go equally among the three sons, so I doubt there is a motive for murder to be found in her. Although I suppose we should not discount her entirely."

I gaped expectantly at Colin. It was all coming at me so fast. "Oh, Colin, who could it be?"

He came back to me and took my shoulders again. "Yes, who could it be, Leyla? And even more important, *why* did they do it?"

"How desperately I wish I could remember!"

"Then go back to the coppice, Leyla. Go at once before this insidious murderer claims you, too, as a victim." Colin pulled me into an embrace again so tight that I could barely breathe. With my face buried in his neck, I prayed silently for this nightmare to end. All I wanted now was to love this man and be loved by him. The past and the present were all entities belonging in a dream. Only our future was real. Only my life with Colin from this moment on had any meaning.

And there was only one way to end it all.

CHAPTER 16

THE NIGHT WAS A BAD ONE FOR ME, FILLED WITH LONG waking hours and intermittent shallow sleep. It was a dreamless slumber, and one without rest. I welcomed the dawn with a mingling of excitement and anxiety. I was both impatient for the day to begin and yet reluctant to face it.

Colin was foremost in my thoughts. It had all been something out of a dream—his arms, his kiss, his telling me he loved me. In the metallic-gray light of sunrise, as I gazed from my high window and out over the skeletal trees, I wondered if it had all really happened. Can we truly have met in that dark tower and kissed and embraced as we did? And did we truly exchange those confidences, murmuring secretively as we did about murder and revenge and family greed? Although it had happened just a few hours before, although we had lingered together in the turret long after all words had been spoken, it seemed it must have happened ages ago.

I dressed with great care, donning my best morning gown and twining my hair into perfect plaits, for this was to be an important day and one that warranted all my best care. Today, I was going to go back to the coppice and try anew to remember the event I had witnessed 20 years ago. But this time it was going to be different, for this time I knew with certainty that a murder had been committed there. And this time it was of even more importance that I remember, because now my life was in danger. Each day that my memory remained tenaciously blank was that much more time I lived in fear for my life. The murderer was closing in on me as he had done to Uncle Henry. I had to save myself.

I entered the dining room with great trepidation. Martha and Theo were quietly at breakfast, so I took my usual place and helped myself to some toast and jam. Our conversation was light and full of platitudes—discussing Aunt Anna's vapors, wondering when the tardy spring would arrive, whether or not to replace the old brougham.

When Colin entered, my heart gave a jolt. Would I never get used to him, to being near him, to his sudden entrances? I hoped not, for it was a wonderful feeling, this electricity. He sat opposite me, smiled politely, and poured himself some tea.

So far, I had not touched mine.

The conversation, somewhat stilted now, turned to problems at the mills, to a new Reform Bill at Parliament, to rumors of that French scientist Pasteur dispelling the "spontaneous generation" theory.

"These are rapid times we live in, Cousin. No longer slow and placid as days gone by. This is the era of gaslights, of steam engines, of hot-air balloons." Colin waved his arms dramatically. "Never before has man traveled so fast or so far."

Suddenly, his flying hand accidentally slapped my teacup, spilling it all over. "Oh, do forgive me, Leyla, how boorish of me."

I stared at Colin as he mopped the spilled tea with his napkin. "Here," he said sheepishly, handing me his cup. "Do have mine."

Realizing what he had done, I thanked him with my eyes and my smile and then gratefully accepted the tea.

"It's an age of progress, and we must move with it or else fall to the wayside like things obsolete. You'll have to compete, Theo, with the other mills. They're all going to start buying the new looms, and from what I've heard, they'll speed production by 50 percent."

So the conversation went, with Martha obsequiously mute, Theodore disdainful of Colin's suggestions, Colin talky and mannerless as usual, and myself on the edge of my chair. I thought they would never leave, but when Theo and Martha finally departed, I gave a sigh of relief and relaxed a little.

Then Colin turned his full attention to me. "Will you be going to the coppice today, my love?"

"Yes, as soon as possible. But I wish to go alone. Thank you for offering last night, but it's best I'm alone. I have some thinking to do as well. There are so many questions to be answered,"

"If you're gone long, I shall come after you."

"Thank you . . ." I fell to staring into my empty cup. Yes, there were questions badly in need of answers. Who had written that letter to lure me here? Who had burned my letter to Edward? Who was stealing valuable jewelry, that ring among them?

That ring.

I lifted my eyes to Colin's and saw the kindness, gentleness there. Yet last night, I recalled now, he had seemed somehow . . . agitated on the subject of the ring.

"What can it mean, Colin, that the ruby ring would flash into my mind only in the coppice and nowhere else?"

Yes, there it was again, and this time we sat in a well-lit room with morning light coming through the windows. Rather than merely sense it as I had the night before, this time I *saw* Colin change with the mention of the ring. But he tried to conceal it.

"I can't imagine."

"Theo inherited it from Sir John, did he not? Why didn't it pass on to Uncle Henry first?"

"Actually," Colin cleared his throat, giving me the impression he was trying to decide what to say. "The ring was first handed down to my father. He had received it as a little boy long ago and had worn it many years. After his death in the carriage accident, Sir John took the ring back and wore it until his own death from the turret two years later. Then Theo got it because Uncle Henry had no preference either way."

"So why do you suppose it has been stolen?"

He casually buttered a slice of bread. "Servants, I suppose."

His manner was too idle, too offhanded, yet I did not press it. If Colin did not wish to discuss the ring, then neither did I, for it could not have been all that important.

"I'm going for a walk now, Colin, and will end it with the coppice. If I have recalled anything, I will tell you this evening."

To my great surprise, he rose abruptly and came round the table to meet me. His face was taut, drawn as he said, "Promise me, Leyla, that I will be the first to know when you do remember!"

"Of course—"

"I mean, *no matter what you discover,* you must come to me first. Not Dr. Young or anyone. Do you understand?"

The wildness in his eyes alarmed me. "I promise, Colin."

Then his passion subsided and was replaced by a smile. "I worry about you, Bunny. How I wish I could convince you to go away from here and wait for me to join you. Don't shake your head; your manners are as bad as mine. Very well, my stubborn love, I shall see you later."

It must have been my imagination that the day was unusually cold and gray, for the sky did not seem so foreboding or the wind so fierce. And it must also have been my imagination that, as I trudged away from the house in cape and bonnet, I felt very strongly as if someone were watching me.

Only once did I turn to look back, but all the windows were either dark or shuttered. I saw no one, not the slightest movement; neither could I imagine who would be spying on me. Theo and Martha had not seemed to care that my tea had spilled, although this could have been excellent acting on their part, nor did they seem to care much about my physical condition in general. If one of them were slowly poisoning me, they were being devilishly clever.

My nerves were tight as bowstrings, which was probably why I imagined eyes upon me, and the walk was not at all relaxing. I was anxious for all this to end, and I knew only too well that all it needed was the return of my memory.

As I stood looking down upon the coppice, I felt a strange feeling come over me. It was almost as if I knew something was going to happen there, that I would not, after all, have to return repeated times in order to discover its secret. Gray, heavy clouds rumbled over me. The biting air itself prognosticated a momentous hour.

There was no turning back once going down; I was determined to enter that gathering of acacias and claim my right to the past. They guarded a secret that rightfully belonged to me, and I was going to challenge them for its possession.

I was Bunny again, standing at the edge of the little wood. I was a small, wondering child looking for my father and brother, who had entered here minutes ago. With my cape flapping in the wind and my eyes set against the cluster of trees, I felt a small metamorphosis begin to happen. Slowly, almost imperceptibly, I started to change. Like a statue awaiting the kiss of life, I rooted myself to the ground and stared as if mesmerized by the trees. It was happening. I was beginning to remember.

On tiny feet, I trekked over the crunchy ground, being ever so careful not to snag my frock. Mummy would be furious if I were to spoil it now. But Daddy and Thom are in here, and I want to play with them.

As a grown woman, my body entered the coppice, but as a child did my mind go. My eyes perceived everything in a different way, eyeing the gigantic trees as if they were vanguards from another world. This was a fantasy land for me, full of mythical things and great absurdities. I was five years old and making believe. Ahead of me was a sound.

"Daddy?" I thought.

Daringly, I pushed forward. Distant echoes sounded in my ear—a little girl's laughter, a crying bird overhead. It was another realm I walked in now—the wonderland of a five-year-old child.

I was remembering. I was remembering . . .

I stopped suddenly. There was that rotting log. The smooth boulder. The moss-covered medieval wall. And sounds. Sounds incongruous with nature—scuffling, struggling sounds. Against a backdrop of dense trees and damp earth I saw phantom shapes moving. There were two adults and one small boy. I smiled, recognizing all three. They became more distinct now. Suddenly, my mind was filled with a vision of my father—tall, handsome, and striking. He looked like a younger version of Uncle Henry, with jet-black hair and the poignant Pemberton features. He was showing Thomas a toad. This was a little nature lesson. The other person stood behind, unseen.

I stood rigidly among the trees as if in a trance, my eyes glazed and staring ahead at images only I could see. Time had not only come to a standstill;it had begun to move backward, like the damming of a river, the churning back of its current. Beneath the eddying waters, I saw the distinct faces of these three people; I heard their voices as if they truly spoke at this moment. I saw the Other Person. I knew now who the murderer was, yet I could not move. The drama had to be played out; it had to be enacted once again to its bloody end before I would be released from this frozen moment in time and allowed to return again to the distant future 20 years hence.

As I stood and stared, I saw the Other Person make a sudden move, dash out from behind the bushes, and fly at my little brother. Before my voice could act, a knife flashed in the air and did something curious to Thomas's throat. I was stunned. My father turned, started to scream, but fell back against the impact of the knife into his chest. My eyes bulged from their sockets. Something red, the familiar ruby ring fell to the ground, was *thrown* to the ground where it joined the other redness on the earth.

"Dear God!" I cried suddenly, snapping myself from the past and to the present. My hands flew to my face as the pain shot through my body, the pain of memory and horror and naked fear. I had remembered it all, each minute detail, and felt the same terror I had 20 years ago.

Only this time I could cry.

"Colin!" I sobbed into my hands. "Oh, Colin, Colin!"

And as I wept, I did not hear the approaching footsteps until it was too late. Remarkably strong and violent arms had a hold of my neck, a murderous hand wielding a knife.

"You are damned like the rest of them!" came a coarse, hot whisper against my ear. I struggled, but in vain. I had lost my balance. "You must die as they did to stop the evil from going on."

"No, please—" I managed, but that amazingly strong grip cut off my breath.

The knife rose high, flashed against the treetops, and gray sky, and came slamming down to my breast.

There was a shriek. Another voice made grunting sounds. When the knife should have sliced me, I felt nothing. Then that steel embrace fell away from me, and I spun about, seeing Colin in a mortal struggle.

And then others came. And then it was over.

Grandmother lay upon the bed, breathing laboriously. Her face was a sickly gray, her pupils dilated. Dr. Young, having arrived moments before, stood over her in taciturn study. He, too, had been surprised by her strength.

From somewhere in the room, a voice was saying over and over again, "It's impossible. I don't believe it." This came from the *prie-dieu* where Theo had his face in his hands and was shaking his head. Aunt Anna sat opposite him, her face an alabaster mask, unmoving and unthinking. Martha stood next to Dr. Young and across the bed from Colin and me. Her face was all childish wonder and speechlessness. If she understood the events of the past hour, she did not show it.

Then there was Colin, Colin who had saved my life, his arm solidly about my waist, supporting me. I needed him now more than ever.

A half-dead voice drifted up from the body of my grandmother. "Damned . . ." she whispered. "You're all damned. It's got to end . . ."

Dr. Young, his gaze thoughtful and penetrating, inclined himself just a little to her and said softly, "What has to end, Abigail?"

Although her poor body was spent, Grandmother's eyes still held life and fire. "The bad Pemberton blood. It should have ended long ago. But none of them had the courage to end the line. That tumor is the Devil's curse upon this family, and it will go on for as long as any Pemberton is alive."

Colin, his handsome face twisted in bemusement, leaned close to her and said, "You were trying to end the Pemberton line? Because of the sickness?"

"I had to . . . Too many suffered because of it. Over the ages, the centuries—"

"And Uncle Henry?" He moved away from me and toward the recumbent old woman. "Did you kill him, too?"

"I had to. He was a wretched Pemberton."

My eyes flickered to Dr. Young.

Colin went on, "Did Sir John know this, that you killed Robert and Thomas?"

Her small black eyes searched the ceiling as she lay on her back, her mouth open and gasping for breath. "I suppose . . ." she struggled to say, ". . . that I can tell it all now. Yes . . . Sir John knew. Henry, Thomas, Robert, and . . . Richard, too."

Colin stiffened. "My father? What do you mean?"

Her eyes flickered closed for a moment, her breathing falling into deeper stages.

"Grandmother, what do you mean about Richard?"

Her eyes slowly opened. "The carriage accident was no accident. It was arranged."

"Dear God—"

"Colin," she said pleadingly, her bony hands groping the air. "Colin, listen to me. Sit by me now and listen."

His face suddenly sick and pale, Colin sat on the edge of the bed and stared at Grandmother. She spoke haltingly but lucidly. "This wretched illness, Colin, has caused too much suffering. I want to end it all. I've been trying to end it for years. You're not a Pemberton, so you will carry on the name and inherit the fortune. That's why I destroyed Henry's will. He was going to leave it all to Theo, and I couldn't have that. It all had to go to you, Colin . . . not a Pemberton but still a Pemberton. You would be a fresh start for the family."

"But that's insane!" he cried.

"Insane, am I? I killed three sons so that you would inherit the fortune of the Pembertons. So there would be no future suffering from the tumor. I killed three sons so that future generations would not have to live in the fear and doom that Martha and Theo must now endure. Look at you! Pathetic creatures! Would you wish this sort of life upon your children and grandchildren?"

"But there is no tumor, Grandmother!" he cried again. Colin seized her hands and drew them to his breast "It was all a lie, a hoax!"

"No, no," she said with strength. "Sir John tried to tell me the same tale, but I wouldn't listen. He said that his brother Michael had been deranged and had devised an elaborate scheme to get the Hurst all to himself. Since he was mad, the plan had been outrageously intricate, involving—John said—some counterfeit printing and the fabrication of a family curse. John had the audacity to tell me that Michael . . ." Abigail gulped more air, ". . . that Michael, in his insanity, had invented the tumor story, created false evidence to back it up, and then had proceeded to try to kill John and their mother. According to John, Michael had believed no one would suspect him of murder if he could convince the authorities that the deaths were due to this brain illness. Yet John found out the plan, or so he told me, and turned it against Michael. Two people were killed—Michael and his mother. When John saw what he had done, he perpetrated the brain tumor story in order to clear himself of guilt. He was believed, and the two victims declared dead of a brain tumor. This is what your grandfather told me the night before he died . . ." Grandmother stopped talking to heave for air. Something rattled in her chest as she labored so. We watched her in a mingling of horror and fascination, trying to picture the mad Michael and the great scheme he had invented to free himself from suspicion of murder. Yet it had backfired, killing himself instead, and Sir John, also afraid of the police, had clung to the fabricated tumor story for his own safety.

"I killed Robert and Thomas in the coppice because I wanted the line to end," she went on with great difficulty. "I had to kill Robert before he fathered any more children, and I had to kill little Thomas because he would grow himself someday to father more poisonous blood. And . . . I would have killed . . . little Leyla, if her mother hadn't . . . run off . . . with her."

A sob escaped my throat, but no one heard.

She went on, laboring, "Sir John knew I had done these killings, but he loved me and so kept quiet. But I spoke one day of having to kill . . . Richard . . . and of course Henry and Theo, and this is when . . ." She ran a dry tongue over her cracked lips. Grandmother was now the color of birch bark. "John told me his insane story about Michael, but I knew he had made it up. He said he was going to fight me . . . go to the police . . . I poisoned him and pushed him off the turret. John was a fool; he didn't believe in the tumor. But you see . . . there *is* a tumor—" She suddenly started to cough, delivering up a milky substance at the corner of her mouth.

Now Colin bent low, spoke deeply and firmly, "Grandmother." He placed a hand upon her shoulder. "There is no tumor. John told you the truth. Michael *had* made it up."

But she seemed not to hear. "Then I found out where Leyla and Jenny had gone to and that Leyla was planning to marry. I couldn't have that. She would have children, pass on the bad blood. So I lured her here with that letter . . ."

"You!" I whispered.

The withered old woman, peering through the doorway of Death, said, "And to be assured that Leyla would remain once she arrived, I kept insisting she should go away. How well I know human nature . . ."

I bent my head and fought back the tears.

Abigail gasped even harder, and the area around her eyes and lips began to turn a queer purple.

"But that Leyla . . . obstinate and tenacious. She tried to send off a letter to that man of hers in London, but I got it in time, burned it . . ."

I raised my head and looked at Colin. He appeared to have drifted far away.

"And the ring?" I heard myself say. "The ruby ring?"

Grandmother's head rolled from side to side. Her coherency was fading away. The battle in the coppice just a while before had tapped the last of her strength. "The ring?" she barely whispered. "It used to belong to Richard. Someone might not believe the story of Robert killing Thomas and then himself. Maybe leave some evidence to point to someone else. Richard didn't miss the ring. Throw it to the ground to be found later." Her stricken face coagulated into a frown. "But Colin . . . picked it up. Bad idea, I suppose . . . Everyone believed me about Robert and his delirium. Ring wasn't necessary . . ."

While Grandmother muttered on, I looked again at Colin, his eyes heavy with infinite sadness. "My father wore that ring," he murmured so no one else could hear. "I found it in Thomas's blood and thought my father had done the murders. Oh, Leyla . . ."

My hand found its way to his shoulder, and I wanted to cry. "You were protecting him," I whispered.

"Doomed!" shrieked Abigail all of a sudden from the bed. No longer the tyrant who had once wielded absolute power over this household, my grandmother was now just a shrunken, dying old woman. "I have saved future generations from the bad Pemberton blood. I have done a good thing." Again her frail white skull rolled from side to side. "Now they are all dead. And Leyla will soon be, too. And Martha . . ." Her voice creaked like an old door. "Well, it isn't necessary to poison Martha. She'll never marry. Not now. She's way beyond the marriageable age, too old to find a man. No fear from her. Martha can live out her life here, along with Colin and . . . and . . ."

To my great surprise, Martha suddenly exploded. "How dare you!" she shrieked as if it had been building up in her. "How dare you spoil my life this way! I wanted to marry and to love a man and have children. But you, you selfish old woman, would not allow it of me. I was stupid! I should have run away long ago when I was young and pretty!"

"But the tumor . . ."

"I don't give a hang about the tumor! If I die from it, then I'll die from it. But in the meantime I want to live, *to live!* But you, you witch, you drove me to desperate measures, you forced me to steal—"

Martha stopped before another word spilled out. She gaped at me across the bed. "Yes, steal!" she shouted at me. "Do you think I enjoyed being a nun all these years, Leyla? I'm 32 years old. I'm a spinster! An old maid! And Grandmother would have cut off my money if I had left this house. So I had to find my own way; I had to steal in order to get enough money to run away. What else could I have done? I am a woman alone with no man to protect me. Without money, how far do you think I would get? So I stole. Yes, I stole from my own family!"

With this, she seized that ever-present carpetbag by her feet and threw it upon the bed. It fell open, spilling out the yarns and threads of her hobby and spilling also the false bottom, which hid the countless treasures she had hoarded. "It's all here!" she cried vehemently. "The money, the jewels! Enough to set me up in London as an independent gentlewoman where I might—"

"Martha!" cried the old woman from under the covers. "The sickness—"

"I don't care if there is a tumor or not," wailed Martha with tears running down her cheeks. "Do you think I stayed a prisoner in this house by my own will? I was only biding my time, Grandmother! I have to get out!"

"But, Martha—"

My cousin fled from the room in a storm of tears, leaving behind her pathetic cache of jewels and money that had been her insurance toward a bright and happy future.

I gazed at Colin in patent wonder. His silence was that of Theo and Dr. Young. We were all too shocked, too astounded to speak. The revelations of this past hour had taken their toll on us.

So Grandmother had lured me here to murder me. She had been the one to place Willis's book in my bedroom at the right moment. For the past 20 years, Pemberton Hurst had been governed by a madwoman.

"It was for the Pembertons . . ." we heard a barely discernible voice utter from the pillows. "I did it because I love Pemberton Hurst. I love it more than my own life, and I didn't want to see it destroyed. But I had to cleanse it, free it from the curse, and then give it to Colin for safekeeping and for the perpetuation of the name. I did it all for Colin . . ."

Martha went to London to live, where, with a generous allowance from her brother, she opened a ladies' hat shop in one of the fashionable districts. Theo moved back to Manchester after having settled all business agreements with Colin and went with plans to expand upon and build new cotton mills. Aunt Anna, a woman without identity since the night of her husband's death, continued to live with us in tranquil seclusion and seemed not aware of anything that had gone on.

Dr. Young became our closest and dearest friend and was on hand at the birth of our first son, whom we named Robert for my father.

FROM

THE DIVINING

A NOVEL BY BARBARA WOOD

NOW AVAILABLE

1

SHE CAME SEEKING ANSWERS.

Nineteen-year-old Ulrika had awoken that morning with the feeling that something was wrong. The feeling had grown while she had bathed and dressed, and her slaves had bound up her hair and tied sandals to her feet, and brought her a breakfast of wheat porridge and goat's milk. When the inexplicable uneasiness did not go away, she decided to visit the Street of Fortune-Tellers, where seers and mystics, astrologers and soothsayers promised solutions to life's mysteries.

Now, as she was carried through the noisy streets of Rome in a curtained chair, she wondered what had caused her uneasiness. Yesterday, everything had been fine. She had visited friends, browsed in bookshops, spent time at her loom—the typical day of a young woman of her class and breeding. But then she had had a strange dream . . .

Just past the midnight hour, Ulrika had dreamed that she gotten out of bed, crossed to her window, climbed out, and landed barefoot in snow. In the dream, tall pines grew all around her, instead of the fruit trees behind her villa, a forest instead of an orchard, and clouds whispered across the face of a winter moon. She saw tracks—big paw prints in the snow, leading into the woods. Ulrika followed them, feeling moonlight brush her bare shoulders. She came upon a large, shaggy wolf with golden eyes. She sat down in the snow and he came to lie beside her, putting his head in her lap. The night was pure, as pure as the wolf's eyes gazing up at her, and she could feel the steady beat of his mighty heart beneath his ribs. The golden eyes blinked and seemed to say: Here is trust, here is love, here is home.

Ulrika had awoken disoriented. And then she had wondered: Why did I dream of a wolf? Wulf was my father's name. He died long ago in faraway Persia.

Is the dream a sign? But a sign of what?

Her slaves brought the chair to a halt, and Ulrika stepped down, a tall girl wearing a long gown of pale pink silk, with a matching stole that draped over her head and shoulders in proper maidenly modesty, hiding tawny hair and a graceful neck. She carried herself with a poise and confidence that concealed a growing anxiety.

The Street of Fortune-Tellers was a narrow alley obscured by the shadow of crowded tenement buildings. The tents and stalls of the psychics, augers, seers, and soothsayers looked promising, painted in bright colors, festooned with glittering objects, each one brighter than the next. Business was booming for purveyors of good-luck charms, magic relics, and amulets.

As Ulrika entered the lane, desperate to know the meaning of the wolf dream, hawkers called to her from tents and booths, claiming to be "genuine Chaldeans," to have direct channels to the future, to possess the Third Eye. She went first to the bird-reader, who kept crates of pigeons whose entrails he read for a few pennies. His hands caked with blood, he assured Ulrika that she would find a husband before the year was out. She went next to the stall of the smoke-reader, who declared that the incense predicted five healthy children for Ulrika.

She continued on until, three quarters along the crowded lane, she came upon a person of humble appearance, sitting only on a frayed mat, with no shade or booth or tent. The seer sat cross-legged in a long white robe that had known better days, long bony hands resting on bony knees. The head was bowed, showing a crown of hair that was blacker than jet, parted in the middle and streaming over the shoulders and back. Ulrika did not know why she would choose so impoverished a soothsayer—perhaps on some level she felt this one might be more interested in truth than in money—but she came to a halt before the curious person, and waited.

After a moment, the fortune-teller lifted her head, and Ulrika was startled by the unusual aspect of the face, which was long and narrow, all bone and yellow skin, framed by the streaming black hair. Mournful black eyes beneath highly arched brows looked up at Ulrika. The woman almost did not look human, and she was ageless. Was she twenty or eighty? A brown and black spotted cat lay curled asleep next to the fortune-teller. Ulrika recognized the breed as an Egyptian Mau, said to be the most ancient of cat breeds, possibly even the progenitor from which all cats had sprung.

Ulrika brought her attention back to the fortune-teller's swimming black eyes filled with sadness and wisdom.

"You have a question," the fortune-teller said in perfect Latin, eyes peering steadily from deep sockets.

The sounds of the alley faded. Ulrika was captured by the black Egyptian eyes, while the brown cat snoozed obliviously.

"You want to ask me about a wolf," the Egyptian said in a voice that sounded older than the Nile.

"It was in a dream, Wise One. Was it a sign?"

"A sign of what? Tell me your question."

"I do not know where I belong, Wise One. My mother is Roman, my father German. I was born in Persia and have spent most of my life roaming with my mother, for she followed a quest. Everywhere we went, I felt like an outsider. I am worried, Wise One, that if I do not know where I belong, I will never know who I am. Was the wolf dream a sign that I belong in the Rhineland with my father's people? Is it time for me to leave Rome?"

"There are signs all about you, daughter. The gods guide us everywhere, every moment."

"You speak in riddles, Wise One. Can you at least tell me my future?"

"There will be a man," the fortune-teller said, "who will offer you a key. Take it."

"A key? To what?"

"You will know when the time comes . . ."